The Miracle Tree

Another story from the Adventures of Harry and Paul

Paul John Hausleben

The cover artwork, design, and cover concept by Paul John Hausleben
All photographs by Paul John Hausleben

ISBN: 978-0-9886336-5-0

DEDICATION

To Paul Edmund, because sometimes you just have to have faith and never, ever give up in life.

CONTENTS

"Mankind created religion and all the confusion that goes with it. God sends us faith and miracles to sort out all the mess that mankind makes."

Paul John Hausleben
March 2014

ACKNOWLEDGMENTS

Thank you as always, to Harry M. Rogers Junior. Thank you to Advent Lutheran Church in Wyckoff, New Jersey for the design of their campus and buildings, which provided endless inspiration. Thank you to "Honest" Rafael Innis, my family, The Center for Disability Services in Albany, New York, David Redmond, John Z, and the rest of the upstate New York gang. A very special thank you, to my old friend, Pastor Donald F. DeGroat who taught me that holy water should never just be disposed of; it should return to God. In retrospect, that was wonderful advice, and for that, I thank you once more Pastor DeGroat.

The Miracle Tree

Another story from the Adventures of Harry and Paul

Preface from the Author

This book was born out of a simple practice by a United Methodist minister whom I was good friends with many years ago. He was a wonderful man, and a kind and gentle soul. I am sometimes amazed at how such simple ideas can progress into a Harry and Paul adventure. The strange fact of the matter is that this book was going to be anything but another adventure for those two characters.

As I began to write it, it was a simple, short story. I reviewed the framework of notes that I had created as a prelude to the story, and it made me realize that it was the perfect vehicle for another one of their wild adventures. I felt it was an exciting opportunity to create a project with the two characters having moved on in years, as well as their individual careers, and yet still retain that special bond that they have enjoyed since their boyhood.

The Miracle Tree allowed me to explore the characters of Harry and Paul in an in-depth manner, much more so than I was able to in any of their previous adventures. *The Miracle Tree* also allowed me carefully to expose their individual personalities within a more intricate and complex methodology. First, Pastor Paul John Henson, who despite his success, retains his individual self-doubts and inner conflicts, along with his constant dreaming of number twenty-seven, and a professional hockey career that he left behind. Then, the bombastic, Harry M. Redmond Jr. and his overwhelming personality, and raw emotions, combined with his reliance on his best friend, and his firm belief that Paul John Henson will always know what to do, no matter what the situation. The storyline was wide open for me to delve into their unique and special friendship, in a way that I previously never touched upon before.

Those readers who are religious in their beliefs will interpret *The Miracle Tree* to be a religious book. Those readers, who are not religious, will see it in their own way, as a book about simple faith, strange coincidences, trust, and support between close friends, husband and wife, and families. They will feel it is a book that displays how people who love and support one another will always survive, no matter what happens.

I will leave it to the individual readers to enjoy in their own manner.

I just know that in my life, staying positive and having faith, no matter what the circumstances, has been the key to many things for me, but mostly it has been the key to success, and in some cases; my own at times, debatable sanity! Faith in your own beliefs, and in whatever higher power or inner strength you feel guides your life, is a strong motivation for pushing ahead through adversity in life. I hold that belief close to my heart at all times.

Religion can be many things for many people. Miracles do not need to be fire and brimstone pelting us from Heaven. They are truly all around us every day, in the simple things that we often take for granted. That is sometimes why we tend to overlook them, since they become commonplace, obvious, and in many cases, natural. I often think that in the gentle breeze in the morning, I can find a miracle, as much as I can see it when I experience a skilled piano player at their craft. I see it when I watch a person who can run faster than another runner can, or a surgeon who can perform delicate operations, or when I actually prepare and cook a homemade meal that is edible.

It is the simple things in which we often overlook.

This book depicts that.

Oh my, here they go again! Harry and Paul off once more to face all the challenges and adventures that life can throw their way! This time, we mixed different topics all into one adventure, tossing in a touch of humor, along with raw emotions, fantasy, religion and even a bit of science fiction. Let's see where this adventure takes us!

I hope you enjoy reading this book as much as I have enjoyed putting it all together.

Thank you for reading it.

Paul John Hausleben

April 2014

Prologue

"One goes right here, Charlie. I will dig the hole here if you want to grab a tree over there and tear the burlap from the bottom a little."

"Oh, all right, Hank, but the only tree we have left here is this scrawny, red oak tree. It looks like it is half-dead already. I can walk down to the front and get another one off the truck, but that will take forever, and it is almost quitting time, anyway." Hank looked down at his watch and then back to his partner.

Hank pointed at the scrawny oak tree on the ground next to Charlie and he said, "Nah, just use that one! These trees all have guarantees from the nursery, so I don't really care. If it dies, then it does not matter. We can easily plant a new tree in place of this one. It is just an oak tree, Charlie. They are a dime a dozen around here."

Charlie nodded his head, bent down, and started to work the burlap off the root base with his knife. Hank struck the ground with his shovel and started to dig the hole. Hank was tired, and it had been a long day. He did not exactly dig the proper size hole. The hole was narrow, and certainly not the specified depth and width for an oak tree for this size of nursery stock. It did not matter to Hank, as he said, it was late in the day and the tree had a guarantee.

Across the parking lot, a gust of wind blew a cluster of dried dirt and some old, spent oak leaves. It gathered some speed; it whipped across the parking lot and blew directly into the faces of Charlie and Hank. The two workers covered their eyes and bent their heads down until the wind died down.

"Wow! Where did that come from?" Hank looked up at

Charlie, who had now pulled and tugged the tree over to the hole. Charlie shrugged his shoulders as the two men picked the tree up, and dropped it rather carelessly into the freshly dug hole. Hank began to throw the dirt back over the top of the root ball and fill the planting hole back in with dirt.

"Should I get a pail of water and some starter fertilizer?" Charlie asked.

Hank stopped throwing the dirt and looked at his watch.

"Nah, we don't have enough time. This tree will not make it, anyway. We can get it tomorrow when we come back." Charlie nodded, and he began to clean up for the day.

Down deep under the dirt, inside the root ball, a root popped out, and it clutched the dirt, surrounding it with fury. It grabbed hold and dug deep into the ground.

The Miracle Tree

1

An Unusual Afternoon

Where, oh where, could they be now? I looked down at my watch while I sat on a little bench in the backyard of the parsonage house of Reunion Lutheran Church. Harry had taken my wife Binky, his wife Rose, and our children, down into town to pick up a few things for the trip we were taking together. I still had to pack a little bag of items that I wanted to bring along on the trip, so I had stayed behind to complete the packing of my bag. They all told me that they would be, "right back" in a few minutes.

I knew better.

A "right back" trip with my wife and my best friend, Harry M. Redmond Jr. could mean a side trip to Australia or New Zealand in search of buried treasure. They sure had been gone for a long time, but I knew my wife so well. Binky may have come across something to research on the way, someone in the food store from church to talk with, or a myriad of other potential diversions. Harry could have run into a broken shopping cart or started talking with a random stranger in an effort to once again, "sell ice to an Eskimo." It was obvious by the time they had been gone, either Harry or Binky had found some type of diversion from their initial mission.

Harry and our wives had lured me into a weeklong getaway without actually telling me where we were going. Of course, they always made plans and picked a spot to travel to or visit, without any input from me. They still had not told me where we are all going! Some things never changed.

I leaned back on the bench. I had to admit to the fact that I needed a little break. I had been going great guns for the last few years here at Reunion Lutheran Church, and it had been a whirlwind, it really had. Binky and the children were very excited about getting away. Other than a few short trips here and there, and some holiday gatherings, we really had not had time to take a nice break, so this was long overdue.

I breathed in deeply and enjoyed the air and the freshness of the morning. It was a fantastic June morning, the sun was warm, yet the morning air was still quite cool.

As I sat there, it gave me time once more to think. The past year or so, had been a challenge, well no, that is actually a huge understatement to say that this past year was just a challenge. My best description of this past year or so would be that it was more as if it was a test of fortitude, faith, and courage. It had exhausted me. It really had both mentally and physically. Now, it seemed as though my family and I were about to open a new page in our lives, a new adventure, a new journey.

Knowing my life, it was bound to be weird, unusual, and different. When you throw in a mixture of Harry M. Redmond Jr. influences, then it really becomes interesting!

The sun was warm, and the warmth felt good. I could have drifted off to sleep right here on this bench because it was so relaxing. Yet a few months earlier, it had been anything but relaxing. It tested my faith to the maximum level, and although I could not clearly ever explain, or be sure of what had happened to us all, I knew that I came out of the past year, a better man and a better pastor. I think that many times in your life, when challenges to your faith, or challenges in whatever you choose to believe in occur, then you have to follow your heart, you need to reach inside so deeply that you cast aside all other thoughts. Even though you have doubts, or other people might be telling you that you are wrong, you just need to follow and trust your faith.

You see, the wonder of life is all around us every day; sometimes, you just have to open your eyes to the wonder. I know that now . . . better than I ever did before.

My eyes caught a few scattered acorns sitting upon the ground in front of me. I reached over, picked them up, tossed them up and down in the air, and caught them in my hand. They had tumbled off the oak tree looming above my head, the tree behind me here at the parsonage. Lining the property of Reunion Lutheran Church are many varieties of trees; such as maples, oaks, birches, pines, you name it, we have it here. Carved out of a forest, in an enclave of peace, solitude and wonderment, the campus and buildings of Reunion Lutheran Church, sat almost hidden away in the hills of northwestern, New Jersey.

It really was one of the most fantastic and lovely places on the entire planet Earth.

As I fiddled with the acorns, I thought how simple things that God has created really represent other things in our lives, tying us all together somehow in one big package. Acorns and trees, they represent life, miracles, and creation. How could something so huge, strong, tall, and powerful such as an oak tree, emerge from a little acorn? You see, miracles are all around us all the time, but they tend to hide in the smallest things that we often take for granted.

Once more, as I sat on the bench, my mind traveled back in time to a few short months earlier. I really wished that I did not travel back in my little book of memories so often, but I do think that these memories enrich my life in so many special ways. I remembered the challenges that we had faced together, as well as the tests of our faith that we endured together as families and friends. Tests that we never faced before, and maybe will never face again. To me, as a young Lutheran pastor, I had to stand up to the fact that I had doubts at that point that I could not answer. As I have mentioned before—I still cannot fully explain what had happened to us all, but I knew that in the end, the result was nothing short of a miracle.

Then again, nothing in my life, or the life of my best friend, Mr. Harry M. Redmond Jr. was ever normal or ordinary.

My mind whirled back to what events and adventures the last year or so had brought to all of us, and to a tree.

One extremely large and special oak tree.

It was, as my English grandfather would have said, "A dull, dark, day before Christmas." It was early December in 1994, and I had some free time to poke around my office in Reunion Lutheran Church. Despite starting my tenure here at Reunion about six years and six months earlier, I had never really taken the time to organize my tasks or my timetables. I had been a busy man since my arrival, and while the church family grew, I found that my spare time had grown increasingly short. This was a rare afternoon indeed that I had my schedule under control, and I sat behind my desk realizing that I actually had two free hours this afternoon.

I thumbed through my appointment book and spotted that at four this afternoon, I had a counseling appointment with Mrs. Whipley.

"Oh no, Mrs. Whipley!" I complained loudly to myself. Mrs. Whipley was a long-time parishioner and truly an adventure to deal with these days. I always felt that a meeting with my father-in-law, the now retired, Senator William T. Hobnobber, took me a long time to recover from, but he was a walk in the park compared to Mrs. Whipley. Part of the job, I guess . . . and I turned my attention back to the small window of time that I had available before she arrived.

I bowed my head and spoke a short prayer aloud in the air, "Lord, please guide me to make the best use of this time that has been given to me."

That was all I said as I sat back in my chair. I seldom had the room or time to breathe these days, nonetheless, to have what I perceived to be free time. My eyes scanned the office and for some reason, settled upon the bookcases that lined all the walls of my office. I knew that I had found the answer to my prayer as I had been putting off the task of going through the many books and papers contained within the oak cases. With a loud sigh, I climbed out of my office chair, and I finally took on the task of addressing the mountains of papers and books in the bookcases that lined my office. As I scanned the books and checked each one for either deciding whether to retain it or toss it, I noticed an older, leather-bound book that had no title or name imprinted on the end of the binding. I pulled and tugged at it, and with some effort, I finally managed to free the book from the hiding spot that it had so firmly entrenched itself for many years. While I stood in front of the bookcases, I opened it and thumbed through the pages.

"Hmm . . . this appears to be a journal," I observed aloud. Indeed, this was not a book, but instead, I realized that it was a daily writing journal.

I carried the book over to my desk and opened it up while I sat down to scan the pages. The first entry went back to January 1960, which was a month or two after the construction of the church upon the present site. It was a journal created by the first pastor assigned to Reunion Lutheran Church, whose name was Reverend Charles P. Braun. I had seen his name on a plaque out in the front narthex that also contained the names of the charter members of the church from the original location, which was downtown in the nearby city. The church charter was under the original name of First Lutheran Church. In and around 1959, or thereabouts, when the construction finished on the present complex, the charter carried over to this new site.

Upon completion of the construction, the congregation changed the name of the church to Reunion Lutheran Church. The congregation wanted to emphasize the rejoining of the congregation in the new location, therefore they chose, in my opinion, the very appropriate name of Reunion.

The only remaining, still active charter member, who had been a major supporter of mine since I first came to Reunion Lutheran Church, told me that Pastor Braun was quite a character, and that he had been a dynamic and powerful leader. He had unfortunately passed away at an early age, and the church sorely missed his leadership at a critical time. My charter member friend proudly told me that I was the most dynamic pastor that he had seen since Pastor Braun. I took that as a major compliment. I could tell by his testimony that he felt as though Pastor Braun had been an excellent pastor and minister to Reunion Lutheran Church. My right-hand man and facility manager for Reunion Lutheran, Mr. Dave Sharp also knew Pastor Braun, since Dave has been here forever. He also told me how Pastor Braun had been a great man and leader.

I thumbed through a large collection of general, handwritten notes on the pages, which contained general observations of attendance, maintenance issues with the facility, money collection troubles, some congregational disputes, and other notes. To be honest, it was a bit difficult to read Pastor Braun's handwriting, and I was about to close the book, when my eyes spotted an entry towards the center of the book.

"January 13, 1960. The young acolyte on duty this Sunday, approached me after the service, and questioned me as to the fate of the water in the baptismal font. At first inclination, I went to instruct him to pour it down the sink in the communion kitchen, but for some reason, I stopped hard in my instructions, and thought about it. Rather than pour it down the drain or toss it out, I had the strange feeling that something more sacred should become of the blessed water. I led the young man outside, and I felt that the Holy Spirit was leading me the entire way. I looked around the property, and my eyes fell upon a smaller oak tree growing near the right side of the fellowship hall building, about twenty feet away from the southwest corner of the building. I recalled that this particular tree was part of the original, landscape construction project, and although the poor tree was still alive, it remained very small and feeble in appearance. I instructed the young acolyte to pour the holy water on the base of that tree. For some reason, the small tree seemed as though it was struggling to establish itself, and I felt compelled that the addition of some holy water would assist it in growing into a strong and powerful oak. Therefore, I began the routine of always pouring blessed or holy water upon that same tree."

I closed the journal and thought to myself how strange an entry that was. I quickly got up from my chair and wandered outside into the parking lot of the church. It had snowed a few days earlier, and it was cold now, but the cold weather and snow never bothered me before. I surely was not going to let it bother me now. I did have to admit, as I had grown a bit older, that I could feel the cold in my surgically repaired right knee, the same knee that had ended my hockey career, but I never let that stop me. I walked across the parking lot towards the fellowship hall, and I stopped, while my eyes scanned the many trees that surrounded the building. Sure enough, I spotted a tall, strong, oak tree that loomed ominously above the fellowship hall.

"My goodness that indeed, must be the tree," I said aloud to no one in particular. "There are no other oaks close to the location mentioned in the journal." I knew that the holy water must have worked some type of influence as this was a fantastic tree. It had grown tall, proud, and it was a fine specimen. I decided that Pastor Braun had stumbled upon something, and I felt that I should continue his tradition. As I walked back to my office, I knew what I had to do. I would change the instructions to my own league of acolytes, and we now would pour blessed and holy water in that same location.

I opened the journal and turned back to the page where I had found Pastor Braun's entry. I then jotted a note down on a piece of scratch paper, "Continued the tradition, 11 December 1994, Pastor Paul John Henson." I then folded the note and placed it on the same page, closed the book, and tucked the journal away in the top drawer of my desk. After completing my note, I then returned to the task of cleaning and sorting through what seemed as though it was endless volumes of books and papers in the bookcases.

"You see, that is when the strange noise comes along, Pastor Paul!"

"I see, Mrs. Whipley. No, actually, I am not sure what you mean by the strange noises. What kind of strange noises do you hear?"

"Well, Pastor Paul, you do need to understand that when intruders are on my property, or specifically in my backyard, I am indeed keenly aware of them."

"I imagine so, Mrs. Whipley, I think that this is a matter for the police rather than your pastor. Did you call the police?"

Mrs. Whipley leaned back in the chair in front of my desk and waved her right hand impatiently at me. She seemed to be implying that I was not correct in providing my advice to contact the police.

"Oh, Pastor Paul, you are quite the character! For such a smart man, you are not following me at all."

Mrs. Whipley sat back in her chair and adjusted her

large, horn-rimmed glasses. Mrs. Whipley lived very close to the church, in a large Dutch colonial home that was just behind a row of large trees, near the rear access road to the church parking lot. Before the completion of the new access road from the state highway, Mrs. Whipley's house was one of the first houses that you had to pass in order to gain access to the church. She was short, slightly overweight, and she had a huge bosom, upon which would always lay a long, stringy necklace with some type of large, gold medallion on the end of it. She also had the typical white hair with the blue highlights from some sort of spray that the older gals used to keep their hair all in position. The blue would glimmer and glow in the lights of my office as she moved her head around while she spoke. She was about eighty years old or so, and she had been a widow for many years.

How shall I be gentle in my assessment of Mrs. Whipley? She was a bit on the eccentric side, no . . . in fact, most of the church felt that she was a nutcase. She was a huge supporter of my ministry and a fan of mine since the first moment I had come to Reunion Lutheran Church. She was wealthy, donated quite a large amount of money to the church, and she would always make an appointment at least once every month to come in and chat. She would mostly ask about scripture interpretation, and she actually had quite a high acumen for Bible study. This visit, however, even for Mrs. Whipley, was really quite strange indeed.

"No, I am afraid that I am not really following your story or testimony, Mrs. Whipley. Please, let me revisit your testimony and make sure I have all the facts. You hear strange noises in your backyard every Saturday night, followed by flashing lights. This occurs after dark, and you rush to the window to check it all out. When you look out, you do not see anything. Am I correct, Mrs. Whipley?"

"Yes, you are quite correct indeed, Pastor Paul. You see,

I miss them every time. I am afraid that the part that you do not understand is why it is your expert counsel that I am in need of, and not the police. You see, the noises must come from a spaceship that hovers in my backyard. I think that it contains visitors from Heaven that have come down to check out our church. I am sure they are all angels. When I look out, the craft must have taken off and flown away. I think it then flies over here and it hovers over the church. I am so surprised that you do not see or hear it from the parsonage!"

Mrs. Whipley was becoming a little wild-eyed as she recalled her experience. I sat back in my chair and sighed as soon as I heard spaceships and visitors from Heaven in adjoining sentences.

"I need to be honest, with all of that hair in your face—I am surprised that you can see anything, but that wife of yours, she is as sharp as a tack."

Mrs. Whipley waved her hands in the air in my direction and she smiled broadly.

"Oh my, that Binky Henson, she is such a doll, and what a great cook! Did I tell you she made an afghan for me to keep my feet warm this past winter? She is wonderfully, talented, Pastor Paul. She is also one of the most beautiful ladies that I have ever seen, and those two children of yours, they both have inherited their parent's extraordinary appearances."

"Yes, she is Mrs. Whipley, and the children are extraordinary! I am a lucky man to have such a wonderful wife and family."

"Yes, you are Pastor Paul, but she is very lucky too. You are one hunk of a man. I still get all kinds of shivers up and down my spine when I see you in that pulpit on Sundays. I have not felt that way since my dear Henry passed away so long ago. He was quite a looker as well. I tell Mrs. Crankshammer that you better, never, preach on the Song of Solomon, or I may just jump your bones right then and there!"

"I have been advised to stay away from that part of the Old Testament, Mrs. Whipley. Not to change the subject, but to get back to the noises and visitors. . .."

Mrs. Whipley chuckled loudly and covered her mouth in embarrassment.

"Oh yes, so sorry, Pastor Paul, what meager amount of my hormones that are left in my body, became a bit stirred up. Please forgive me. Yes, the spaceship. I think the spaceship then leaves my backyard, and it hovers right over the top of the fellowship hall there. The reason I feel that way is that, on occasion, I see a light beam come out of the sky, and it shines down upon that large, oak tree there. I cannot understand why the angels or visitors find that one tree so intriguing. It seems so strange."

Mrs. Whipley climbed out of her chair and scurried over to the window in my office. She pointed out the window to the large tree that I had just read about earlier in the journal from Pastor Braun.

I felt a cold shiver go up and down my spine.

What a strange afternoon this has turned out to be!

Mrs. Whipley returned to the chair in front of my desk, adjusted her dress, and sat back down.

"There are, of course, angels in Heaven . . . are there not, angels, Pastor Paul?"

"Yes, Mrs. Whipley. The Bible mentions them many times, even describes them in details, but I am not sure that. . .."

"Yes, of course!" Mrs. Whipley interrupted me. "Legions of angels came on the night of the savior's birth."

"Why yes, the scripture tells us that the sky was full of legions of angels and that was why the shepherds were so frightened. But Mrs. Whipley, I am not really sure that. . .."

"How many angels are there in a legion, Pastor Paul?"

"I do think that there are six thousand angels in one legion, Mrs. Whipley. But once more . . . we need to check on. . .."

"Oh yes! Of course, the scripture, Pastor Paul! You are so smart. You remember everything. What was the scripture that one angel defeated the multitudes of men? I think it was somewhere near two hundred thousand or so!"

Mrs. Whipley was smiling broadly at me now, and I think I now understood where she was going this afternoon. She wanted to hear about the comfort and power of Heaven. Spaceships, aliens, light beams, noises in her backyard or not, she wanted to know that she was not alone. I knew she would never let me voice my advice or opinion, so I just went with the flow.

"That would be Isaiah, chapter thirty-seven, verse thirty-six, Mrs. Whipley. I do think it was one angel that obliterated one hundred and eighty-five thousand, men in a battle in one night."

The old gal sat back in the chair and she sighed. She reached for her Bible from her purse and clutched it tightly to her chest. The smile of joy that she had just displayed faded a bit from her face. She reached into her purse again, pulled out a tissue, and dabbed at some tears that I saw had formed in her eyes.

"Oh, Pastor Paul! You are such a wonderful man. We all have had such joy in our hearts since you came here. I cannot imagine what would have happened to this wonderful place if God had not sent you to save our church. Mind you, Pastor Paul, I am giving all the credit to God, and not to that awful, crabapple, Bishop Von Houten, who shows up here once in a while with his big ego, taking all the credit for your success. That man! Why, last time he was here, I wanted to sock him one, right smack in his big, loud, mouth!"

I sat back in my chair as Mrs. Whipley made a punching motion with her arm and fist. She was a tough old bird for sure. She relaxed back into her chair once more while her display of affection for my famous boss passed over. A calm look came over her face.

"What a wonderful thought that the power of Heaven is so massive and immense. It is such a joy to know that the angels are here watching over us all at our beloved church. One angel has that type of power! Can you imagine the power and the glory of Heaven? You have answered all of my questions as usual, Pastor Paul. Thank you so much."

I smiled at Mrs. Whipley, as she actually had answered her own questions, and she had found the information that she was seeking entirely on her own. I certainly was not going to burst her bubble and pursue it any longer.

"Thank you again. I must be on my way to feed the cats. I have taken up way too much of your time already."

Mrs. Whipley rose slowly from the chair and leaned in close to me over the desk. She lowered her voice to a soft whisper, "Please keep my comment about jumping your bones, just between us pastor. I would not want Mrs. Henson becoming jealous over our relationship, you know. She seems as though she has a wicked, right cross. I do have a reputation to maintain, Pastor Paul. I would not want people here to think of me as some kind of floozy."

"I understand, Mrs. Whipley. I will not say a word." I led Mrs. Whipley out of my office, and watched as she walked down the hallway, and disappeared out the rear door.

"Oh my, that was an interesting meeting, Martha." I turned and spoke with my administrative assistant, Mrs. Martha Wiggins. Martha had been with Reunion Lutheran Church for about four years or so now. We were able to hire her once the church was back on solid ground and our finances were in order. We also brought at the same time, my right-hand man, David Sharp, back to full-time status as the church's facility manager.

Martha was middle-aged, very confident, capable, and she had a wonderful sense of humor. Her husband and two children attended church along with her, and she was an important part of the church family.

I was very lucky to have her as my assistant and I enjoyed working with her. Her husband was also a serious ice hockey fan, and we enjoyed chatting about the sport together from time to time.

"Well, Pastor Paul, on the heels of that engagement and I am sure, most wonderful time with Mrs. Whipley, you will be more than happy to retrieve your messages."

Martha started to hand me slips of paper with the handwritten notes of telephone calls that had apparently come in while I was in the meeting with Mrs. Whipley. She then pulled them back and held them in her hands.

"No, on second thought, let me first read them off to you. Some of them will be happy calls for you to answer and one of them, well, they may not be quite so happy. First, Mrs. Henson called. She would like you to call her before you leave the office. That one is not so bad, but sounds as if Mrs. Henson is sending you on another one of your famous shopping missions after you finish work. Second, we have Mr. Redmond, who I had a wonderful conversation with, as he chatted up a storm. He seemed as though he was in a fantastic mood. He is one of the funniest men I have ever known! He was very excited and asked that you call him back as soon as you could. The last message on the hit parade is the bomb." Martha started to hand me the previous two messages, and then she stopped and held them all in her hand.

"I bet you can guess the last one!"

"Bishop Werner Beck Clodhopper Von Houten, of course!" I said as I reluctantly pulled the papers out of Martha's hand.

"Ah yes, the wise Pastor Paul wins the prize! Everyone's favorite old curmudgeon. Good luck there, pastor! Do you need me to slap you on your backside and encourage you to get back in the game? You know, like your old hockey days. I will be more than happy to do so." Martha playfully said while winking at me.

"No, I do not need any backside slaps. I know the drill. Thank you, dear Martha, for your inspiration and support."

I turned and walked back into my office, as I heard Martha yell back to me, "Anytime!"

I was going to close the door to my office when I remembered something. I dashed out and returned to Martha's desk.

"Martha, when you have a chance, could you please type up a memo for me? I would like to place it in all the church leadership mailboxes in the mail sorter, as well as the heads of all the committee's boxes. It simply should say to see me first, for proper disposal of any holy water or water in the baptismal font. If you could also, please make enough copies for me to distribute to all the acolytes. I will hand them out at communion class. Thank you, Martha."

"I will be glad to work on it for you, pastor. Ahemmm, however, the proper disposal of holy water, Pastor Paul. Where will they dispose of it?"

"It is a little unusual. It is hard to explain. I will need to show folks individually, so that is why I would like to keep the memo very simple."

"Unusual, I see. Hmm . . . you do something or are involved in something unusual. Pastor Paul? Nah, it cannot be!" I smiled at her wit and went back into my office.

Martha knew me all too well.

Inside my office, I knew that my wife would be the first call that I would return, my boss would have to wait. I could have walked across the rear lawn to the parsonage to speak with her in person, but instead, I dialed our home number. Two rings and there she was, on the other side of the telephone line, Mrs. Binky Henson answered the call.

"Hello, twenty-seven. I knew that this call would be you returning my earlier call. You see, I spotted Mrs. Whipley leaving the rear of the church, I then calculated the time it would take dear Martha to give you a rundown of messages. After some additional time that I added for some small talk, including her flirting with you to offer to slap you on the backside. I then added the time for walking from Martha's desk to your desk, which is about fifteen seconds. I also knew that even if you have other calls to return that you would return my call first. Keeping all of that in mind, I knew it would be you! How did I do, my dear Paul?"

"Right on the old research ball, as usual, my dear Binky, right on."

I could picture her on the other side of the telephone line fluffing her hair and smiling as she does when she knows she has hit research pay dirt.

"Good, well, the reason that I called is that I do need you to run out for me to the drugstore and pick up Paul William's allergy medicine. I am working on a special dinner. I do not want you to see what I have prepared for you until it is dinner time. It is a big surprise. With that in mind, I would like you to run directly to the drugstore after you finish working. I cannot bring the children to the pharmacy right now, as they have their afternoon homework and research activities, plus I will ruin my dinner preparation if I leave the meal unattended."

"Sure, sure, Binky no trouble, any hints as to what the dinner will be?"

"No, I am sorry, twenty-seven. Please finish your work and be off to the store. No probing questions and please do not be too long. If one of the calls that you have to return is that crusty, old boss of yours, then do not allow him to bully you, Paul!"

"I love you, Binky."

"I love you too. Now, please do not linger. Goodbye, dear Paul."

"Click" . . . the line went dead.

Oh my, oh my, that wife of mine. She could be quite

overwhelming at times, that was for sure. I wondered what the special meal occasion was for this evening. My curiosity had now been aroused. I shuddered to think that perhaps my in-laws were coming over, but a quick glance out the window of my office over to the driveway of the parsonage, confirmed that the Hobnobber's big, black, Galaxy 3000 automobile was not parked there. Next on my call list would be Harry. Bishop Von Houten did not yet make the cut, and I justified my reasoning by telling myself that I needed to go in the exact order that the calls came into my office . . . yes, that was correct . . . I convinced myself.

"Twenty-seven, what are you doing first thing in the morning?" Harry had answered the telephone on the first ring. I must be very predictable that everyone knows it is Paul John Henson calling even before I say a word.

"Well, I have some church business, and then. . .."

"Good. Meet me at the driving range over on Oldham Road. This will be sort of church business for a parishioner. I need, ah, ah, well . . . emergency pastoral counseling."

"The driving range, Harry, it is December you know."

"I know that! The bozos cleared it out of snow. It is open, I checked, ya know that the owner is a money-grubbing machine, he only closes after Christmas for two weeks unless it is a blizzard."

"You only go to the driving range when you are nervous, upset, or you need to relax because you want to blow up something. Is everything all right, Harry?"

"Everything is great! Fantastic, as a matter of fact! Now stop being such an old lady, Paul! Yes, I am nervous, but that is all I am going to tell you until tomorrow. Meet me at eight in the morning."

"Click." The line went dead. Same old Harry, he never says goodbye, and he never provides me with any details of his latest schemes over the telephone. Some things will never change. This was shaping up to be some afternoon, that was for sure. Next was the man himself. I dialed his number and waited for the onslaught. One ring, and sure enough!

"Henson! What took you so long to call me back? After all, I am only the bishop around here. You know, the big chief, your boss, Henson! Besides, you have more free time than any human being I have ever met, so what was the delay this time, Henson?"

"Good Afternoon, Bishop Von Houten. It is always so nice to hear from you, sir."

"Oh, please, Henson! Save it, for someone else. It is never nice to hear from me. Please, just stick a sock in your big trap for a minute. Where have you been? Goofing off as usual, or poking around the boiler room repairing pipes and wires? Better yet, were you flying around in your superhero cape, rescuing people in distress, and warding off evil spirits with Redmond and his smudge-a–dub-dubber sticks?"

"No sir, I was in a Bible interpretation session with a parishioner. Mrs. Whipley made an appointment with me for some advice this afternoon, sir. We discussed some scripture, and other interesting things."

"Whipley? Whipley? Whipley . . . is that the old bag with the huge chest who always wears that same weird necklace, and who lives in the back near the old, rear access road?"

"Yes sir, you are correct, that is Mrs. Whipley."

"Oh, please, Henson . . . she is a nutcase, a certifiable loon! Why do you fiddle away the afternoon, quoting scripture with old, confused, battleaxes such as Mrs. Whipley? Why not be productive for a change, Henson?"

"Well sir, I feel that all parishioners are important, and our mission is. . .."

The bishop was in rare form this afternoon as he interrupted me, "Henson, you will never change! I know all about the mission, geez you are so annoying, Henson!

You really are!"

"Sir, Mrs. Whipley is quite wealthy, and she donates an extraordinary amount of money to Reunion Lutheran Church every year. In fact, last year, she was our top donor."

There was silence on the other end of the line.

"More dough than Redmond gives?"

"Yes sir, that is correct."

"Well, by all means . . . then you should counsel her, Henson. Good call on your part, after all, I agree that all our parishioners are important. As I was just saying Henson, it is all about the mission. Was I not just saying that, Henson?"

"Yes sir, I do believe I heard you say the word mission."

"Good work, Henson. Say, the reason that I called was that I came across some information about a program that the synod is running in conjunction with some finance company. A bunch of mumbo jumbo, nonsense, Henson. Crooks, thieves, and charlatans, looking to get rich off the Lord, you know the drill. The long and the short of it is that this organization can provide low-cost bonds, finances, and other tangible assets, for construction projects. I know you are under the delusion that you will need some additional space out there, and want to add on to the sanctuary, and the fellowship hall, so I thought this would be of some interest to you, Henson.

"Why yes, thank you, Bishop Von Houten. Please send the information to me, it sure sounds great. We really need the space, and I was going to open the discussion on the potential of adding on here at the next buildings and grounds committee meeting."

"I will send it ahead to you in the mail, since you never come to visit me anymore in my office. Wait! It is not that I want you to come here, Henson."

"I will keep that in mind, sir."

"I also will include a picture of me winning that final

golf tournament in the fall of this year. It is fantastic. You can see Rabbi Goldberg in the background, sulking over the crushing defeat. You can hang it in your office or somewhere in the church, perhaps in the narthex."

"That will be wonderful, I will enjoy seeing that sir, as well as reviewing the loan information. I promise that I will find a nice spot for the picture here somewhere."

As we spoke, I kicked a box under my desk with my boot that contained about two hundred other pictures of the bishop winning some kind of award, trophy, or attending some presentation of honor being bestowed upon him. When he does arrive here and visits Reunion Lutheran Church, Dave, Martha, and I run around the entire complex of church facilities, hanging the pictures up here and there in strategic locations. When he leaves, we then have to gather them all back in and put them back in this box until next time.

"I know you are under the illusion that you have grown the congregation there, Henson. If I can stand to hear the answer, what are you up to now in total membership?"

"We are around two thousand members now, sir."

Once more, there was silence on the telephone. I could hear the bishop rustling some papers and then he spoke.

"Henson, you are amazing. You drive me nuts. Put these dates on your calendar. The fifteen, sixteenth, and seventeenth of July of next year, Henson. I want you to attend a leadership meeting of the synod. It is in upstate New York, in Albany, and if I recall . . . you enjoy that dump. You can relive your glory days, Henson . . . playing hockey, running around acting as if you were a wild barbarian, beating people over the head with your goalie stick, all in the name of sport."

"I have put the dates down, sir. I do enjoy that area. It has been a long time since I have visited there."

"Good, good, it is time you learn about the inner workings of the upper echelon of the church, Henson, ya know, rub elbows with the big boys. You know the drill, make believe that you know what you are doing, Henson. I have some future plans for you. I will be there to guide you, so you cannot mess up too badly. I do not suppose I could convince you to cut your hair and shave for this special event. Goldberg bet me a ten spot that you would not cut it off."

"No sir, I am afraid not. I do think you owe the rabbi the ten dollars. I am sorry, sir."

Bishop Von Houten complained loudly, "I cannot stand it when Goldberg is right! Someday Henson, someday, I will get you to cut that mop off and shave that hairy mug of yours! You will need babysitters for the kids, bring them over to their whacko Grandparents for a few days, Henson, because you can bring your lovely wife. At least, she has common sense. In addition, you can bring along two or three lay leaders or members from your church, Henson. I would bring the Redmonds. Unlike you, at least your buddy Harry has a keen business sense. He may be able to pick up some tips, guide you, and mentor you into paying attention to the business end of things Henson, instead of your incessant focus on praising the Lord, and saving the lost souls of the world, who do not want your pastoral assistance. I also know that Redmond has a lot of dough, and I know he will pick up most of the dinner and drink tabs, and it will keep my expense budget down. Besides, those sure are two pretty ladies to have around us. It may make folks not pay so much attention to how you look as if you are some wayward, wanna be, hippie, who is stuck in the nineteen seventies, Henson."

"That sounds wonderful, Bishop Von Houten, a very enjoyable time for all of us. You say that you have future plans for me sir, I am curious as to what you have planned."

"Forget it for now! Just pay attention, and simply go along for the ride, will you! You are always flapping your jaws, asking questions, and trying to dominate the conversation."

"Click."

The line went dead. My boss operates a telephone in the same manner as my best friend does. They both attended the same school of telephone etiquette.

I looked at my watch and realized that it was getting late. I still had to get to the pharmacy and pick up the prescription. I grabbed my vest and hustled out the door. Martha had already left for the day. She must have known that I was embroiled in a Von Houten conversation, because she did not even stick her head inside the office door to say goodbye. She most likely felt that she would pick up some type of bad karma for the night right through the telephone.

"Hello. Please, I am here to pick up the prescription for Henson."

I stood at the front of the counter of the pharmacy speaking with the young lady working the prescription counter.

"Hello, Pastor Paul. How are you?"

"I am well, thank you. How are you?"

"Fine. It is always nice to see the handsome, Pastor Paul! I have to check in the back because the prescription is not here. I will be right back." She winked at me in a flirtatious manner, and I just made believe that I did not notice. I thanked the young lady as I watched her turn on an extra wiggle as she scurried off behind a wall. Oh brother, I do not have time for this, I thought as I mindlessly stared at the ceiling while I waited for the young lady to return.

"Pastor Paul! My, it is so nice to see you here!" I turned around to see Mrs. Crankshammer, standing next to me, smiling broadly.

Oh no! Mrs. Crankshammer! The constant parade of weirdness of this now, very long afternoon, was not over yet! It had been one character after another lining up to speak with me today.

Edith Crankshammer was a member at Reunion Lutheran Church. She was not only Mrs. Whipley's best friend, but she registered quite high on the weirdness meter herself. She was also a widow, I prayed hard not to think about it, but . . . I could not help but attach a correlation between the two friend's personalities, and the fact that both of their husbands checked out a little on the early side. Mrs. Crankshammer was very tall, lanky, with long white hair, a pointy nose, and deep-set eyes. She might have been a few years younger than Mrs. Whipley might be, but only by a few years. She could talk the ears off an elephant! She would drill down into the most minuscule detail of everything while flapping her jaws for hours on end without even taking a breath. She also was a hopeless hypochondriac.

In my six years or so of knowing her, she had complained of contracting every illness and injury known to mankind, but in actuality, she was as healthy as a horse. She was indeed a bit of a whacko. It was no twist of fate that she was in a drug store, that was for sure. She was most likely picking up a prescription or over-the-counter drug for some unknown or fictitious malady. It was just my luck, as along she had come, just as I was pressed for time too!

"Mrs. Crankshammer, how. . .." I started to ask how she was out of habit, but I caught myself in mid-question. It was too late; her jaws had already been unleashed. My ears twitched in horror and anticipation of the upcoming verbal punishment.

"Oh, Pastor Paul. I am so glad to have run into you! I wanted to call Martha to make an appointment to see you. I have this strange rash and growth, and I fear it is finally the end for me! I need to make some preparations with you and settle things with the Lord before my demise. The rash just popped out here on my midsection, last night, it is so terrible!"

When she finished her statement, she unabashedly lifted her dress up over her waist, displaying her bare midsection, while pointing at her waistline, and exposing her thankfully, covered private parts!

"Here look, Pastor Paul, look at it here!"

A nearby woman, who was innocently shopping, screamed in horror at the sight of Mrs. Crankshammer's efforts to show me her rash. The poor woman dropped her basket and ran off towards the front of the store, while I swooped in to cover up Mrs. Crankshammer.

"It is all right! I am her pastor, she has an illness, she was just showing me her troubles, and I mean . . . that I am her minister!"

I waved my hands and made a very weak attempt to explain to the poor woman, who still screamed and ran away.

"Please, Mrs. Crankshammer! Please, you do not have to show me! This is a public place!"

"Oh phooey, what a bunch of old prunes around here these days! I do not have anything they have not seen before, Pastor Paul!" Mrs. Crankshammer said as she lowered her dress.

"Have you seen your doctor yet, Mrs. Crankshammer?"

"No, not yet! Pastor Paul, I might pass away before I can make an appointment."

I thought for just a moment of how horrible a job it must be to be Mrs. Crankshammer's medical doctor. I would have to find out who he or she is, take them out for a few beers, and compare notes as to which one of us has it worse.

"I am sure that it could be just some dry skin. It might not be quite that serious. It is December now, and we have had no rain or snow these last few days."

She tilted her head and seemed to be pondering my diagnosis. "Oh, Pastor Paul, perhaps, you are right! I was just speaking with Mrs. Whipley before I left to come here, and she suggested that I speak with you. She is sure a strange one, Pastor Paul. I know she is my best friend, but my goodness gracious, seeing spaceships and angels. I do not know how you deal with it all!"

"Well, I do think that it may be a bit better than people pulling their clothing. . .."

"Perhaps, I should look for an ointment or cream, pastor. Do you think I should do that? I wonder in what aisle they are located. Could you ask? What kind should I buy? There are so many creams these days. Should we check into them?"

I sensed a brief interlude of a nanosecond where I might be able to make a break for it and actually say something, so I blurted out quickly, "I will ask for you!"

I prayed that the young woman was back at the counter and I turned quickly towards the counter. I saw that the young woman was carrying my prescription over, but there was another young man standing there smiling. I was about to wipe that smile right off his face. Sorry pal, but sometimes, it is the survival of the fittest. I would pray for forgiveness later.

"Say, young man, if you have the time, could you please assist Mrs. Crankshammer in finding some creams for her dry skin?" I smiled and pulled my coat down so he could see my clerical garb.

"Why sure, Father Paul, I can do that," the young victim smiled enthusiastically, as he came out from behind the counter to meet the talking miracle known as Mrs. Edith Crankshammer. Mrs. Crankshammer walked closer when she spotted the young clerk come out from behind the counter.

"Young man! It is, Pastor Paul John Henson. He is not a

Catholic priest! He is an exceptional Lutheran minister. Please do not allow his hippie appearance to fool you!" Mrs. Crankshammer scolded the young man for his error.

"Oh, I am sorry, Pastor Paul. I could not really tell the difference."

"It is fine, it happens all the time. Please, if you could assist my parishioner with the creams, I assure you that all will be forgiven!"

"Sure thing! Right this way, Mrs. Crankshammer." The young clerk led her towards the aisles.

"I will be right back, Pastor Paul. Please, we will only be a minute. Now, young man, let me teach you the difference, between the Lutherans and the Catholics. It all began with Martin Luther, and he nailed his thesis to a door in. . .."

I felt bad about sending the young man off to being a step closer to deafness, but hey, that is the way the ole mop flops. I would certainly overcome my feelings of guilt rather quickly. Mrs. Crankshammer never takes only a minute for anything, and explaining the origins of the Lutheran Church sure would be a long one.

"Here is your prescription, Pastor Paul. I so want to be in your Bible ministry classes to hear you teach. All the young gals join just to stare at you. No one actually pays any attention at all to the actual material that is being taught." The young gal had returned, and she handed me the prescription while she batted her eyes and tugged at her white clerical coat to pull it down a bit around her neckline and expose her cleavage. I tried not to let the truth hurt that no one paid any attention to my lessons. I was in a hurry now.

"That is fine. Please join us, Saturday at three in the afternoon. Say, can I put this on my tab? Mrs. Henson will be in to settle it up. I am in a bit of a hurry. "

The young lady frowned and said sadly, "Oh yeah, yeah, yeah, I always forget that you are married. That is unfortunate for all of us. Sure, Pastor Paul, not a problem, anything for you."

"Thank you. Can I slip out this rear door?"

The young lady laughed as she knew I was working hard to escape Mrs. Crankshammer. "Sure, Pastor Paul, you are trying to get away from that old chatterbox, I understand, please go right ahead." I smiled, thanked her, and made my escape. I hustled over to my old jeep and looked down at my watch. Oh boy, Binky is going to be upset with me! I climbed in the jeep, started the old wreck up, and made my way back home as quickly as the old jalopy would get me there. I pulled in the driveway, shut off the engine, picked up my briefcase and the bag from the pharmacy out of the back seat of the jeep. I jumped out and made a mad dash for the rear door. It was so good to be home after this long and unusual afternoon. It was a parade of one weirdo after another, that was for sure.

"Sorry, Binky. I am finally home. It was some crazy day! Here is the prescription."

Binky was standing next to the sink in our kitchen, smiling at me. "Oh, no trouble, twenty-seven, I knew it would be quite a long time before we saw you. I had earlier prepared a snack for the children to hold them over for dinner, as I had calculated that it would take you a long time to make it out of the office, and then off to the drug store. The young gal who works the counter there, has a terrible crush on you, so I knew she would purposely make the pickup procedure linger longer than it should, so she could engage in more conversation with you. I was sure she would tug at her neckline to reveal her chest cleavage to you, in hopes of obtaining some type of rise out of you. Then the odds are always good that you will run into a church parishioner there at this time of day. You see, the congregation has grown so large, and since it was the rush hour after work, when many folks would be stopping at the store on their way home, the odds were very good for you to run into someone who knows you. Therefore, I added extra time for you to run into someone from Reunion. Now, whom did you run into that delayed you, and am I correct about the young lady behind the counter?"

I smiled at my wife and her incredible accuracy in every intricate detail. After her long testimony of the situation that caused the lateness of our dinner hour, my wife zoomed in for a really intense, Binky wide-eyed stare as she awaited my response.

"Mrs. Crankshammer, and yes, you are correct about the counter gal."

"Oh, my, my, my . . . Mrs. Crankshammer. You must have created some type of diversion to be home this soon. I am afraid that I did not calculate enough time for you to have run into her. Indeed, most of my research was correct. I just did not anticipate or calculate a Mrs. Crankshammer factor into my research."

Binky smiled, fluffed her hair, and tugged at her dress. I had confirmed her accurate research, and she was quite satisfied with the results of her precision timetable prediction. She was wearing one of her blue, form-fitting dresses, and let me tell you, she was just as gorgeous as the day I had met her. After bearing two children, her figure was still amazing, and she was a one-of-a-kind beauty! Binky came over and gave me a hug and a kiss. She always smelled so good! As she had grown older, she grew more captivating. About the only real change that she had undergone in the last few years, was that she now wore eyeglasses as her eyes had changed a bit. Other than that, she still looked the same as she did on the day when we first met, on that wonderful night so long ago at Lord Crudley's bar.

"Sit down here and take your vest off, dear Paul, we have a surprise for you. You really should wear something heavier than just this vest. You are not twenty years old any longer, Paul. Your muscles need to stay warm. I need to speak with you more about that subject." Binky dug her left foot into the floor as she always does when she wanted to make a point or have her way.

"The children have been working on a surprise for you. They will hear your voice shortly and come running."

"Surprise, surprise, what is all this talk of a surprise? As far as I know. . .."

"Father, you are home! Here! Heather and I made this card for you!" I turned around, and running into the kitchen was our son, Paul William, followed by our daughter, Heather Sarah. They both jumped into my lap and I gave them a hug and each a kiss, as they chatted on and on, to me about this card they had created.

Paul William was now almost five years old and Heather Sarah was just a month or two away from her fourth birthday. Paul William was already tall, he had blonde hair, and blue eyes as his mother does, and I must say he already had an athlete's body. Binky, of course, would not cut his hair, so his hair hung down as long as mine did. Heather picked up some type of British Island blood from way back, as she had the most fantastic head of lovely red, curly hair.

Mum was convinced that it came from a Scottish gene of some long forgotten relative of hers that was Scottish. She said it was the same gene that her Aunt Alma had, as well as her daughter, the famous, Cousin Pat also had. They both had red hair, but Heather Sarah's hair was much curlier than both of their hair was. I took Mum's word for it. Everyone that met our children would tell me how much they looked exactly like their mother and I had to agree. As Paul William grew a bit older, I could see a little more of me in him, but it might have been my imagination. They were great kids and I could not ask for a better family.

Heather smiled as she carried her faithful, stuffed dog companion named, "Fritzie." Paul William was dressed in his ever-present hockey jersey. He wore only sports team tee shirts or hockey jerseys all the time; he loved sports. It was a struggle on Sundays, to force him to wear a buttoned up or a pullover shirt to church. He was wearing a vintage Long Island Roosters jersey with "Henson" emblazoned on the back along with the number twenty-seven. Hockey, football, and basketball seemed to be his favorites, and much to the chagrin of his mother, he wanted to be a goaltender. Binky loved hockey, but I think she much preferred that Paul William plays another position. I secretly could not wait for the day to get him out on the ice and show him how to play the position. We fooled around in the backyard on roller skates, and I was starting him slowly with his hockey training. Very slowly!

"All right gang, now, you have my curiosity. What is this talk of a surprise, and these fantastic cards and a special meal? From what I can smell, it appears to be one of my favorites and that would be your mother's Shepherd's Pie!

"Open your card, dear Father! Open your card!" Heather was jumping up and down in front of me.

"Now, wait just a moment, twenty-seven. I feel we do owe you an explanation. Once you open the card, then you will know the reason that this is a special day and what the subject of our celebration is all about," Binky told me as she zoomed in on me with an intense Binky stare.

I knew better, so I placed the envelope containing the card back down on the table and I patiently listened to my wife.

"I was conducting some recent research for a small project, for a course that I am teaching, when I stumbled across an article from a local newspaper. Does this date of December third not ring any bells, twenty-seven?"

I shook my head and shrugged my shoulders, as I scanned the memory bank in my mind, but I did not come up with anything.

Binky continued, "Well, how about this one, December 11, 1978?"

"We helped Mother with her research, Father! Heather and I are learning how to check into stuff just like dear Mother does!" Paul William jumped in and shook his head, as did his sister in agreement. I had my hopes and dreams to teach the children, and so did my wife. The kids were going to be chips off the old research block.

"Nice work kids, but the date still does not mean anything. It was a long time ago."

Binky reached up on top of the kitchen counter, tilted her eyeglasses down, and she picked up what appeared to be an old newspaper copy.

She then started to read from it, "Eddie Austeri, general manager of the Long Island Roosters, announced today that for tonight's game versus the New York Colonials, Paul John Henson will be starting in goal replacing the injured Mike Stanley. Henson, nineteen years old of Paterson and nearby Haledon, New Jersey, is a local player that was just signed to a short-term contract by Austeri a week or so ago. Henson is a product of local New York and New Jersey ice hockey as well as the roller and street leagues, but this will be his first professional start. 'We feel bad about the loss of Stanley, but we hope he will be back in a week or two or make it back in the goal right before Christmas,' Mr. Austeri told the Paterson Evening News. 'Henson is young, really young, but he has great potential. I signed the kid myself. He is big, tall, tough, and fearless. I think that despite his lack of experience, he is a good one. He will hold us in there until Stanley returns.' Rooster fans will be disappointed if Henson fails, as the Roosters had the chance to sign the veteran goaltender, James Hikibin who was available after a short stint in the Ontario Hockey Association. Time will tell if Austeri made a big mistake, but for now, Henson will get the start. Henson will wear number twenty-seven for the Roosters. Henson was not available for comment and no telephone number was found for a Paul John Henson before press time."

Binky smiled and put the paper down.

"Number twenty-seven, Paul John Henson! Kick save and a beauty by Henson!" Paul William was running around the kitchen screaming, while mimicking a goalie in the net and a radio announcer calling the play-by-play. Heather was jumping up and down in delight as she and Fritzie danced together in the kitchen.

I sat back in my chair and smiled. I motioned for all of them to come over to me and I opened my arms. They rushed in and we gathered together as I hugged my wife and children. They were indeed very special. In a million years, I would not have remembered that today was the anniversary of my first professional game. Only my wonderful wife could have stumbled upon this fact. I was a very lucky man.

"Binky, I do not know what to say. Thank you to you, Heather Sarah, and Paul William. It is very special to me."

"Open the card, Father! Open the card!" The children yelled at me.

I tore open the envelope to see a homemade card out of construction paper. On the cover was a hand-drawn picture of me, number twenty-seven in the net, playing goal. They had written the words, "FIRST GAME" in big block, letters across the front of the card. Upon opening it up, there was the final score of that game so long ago. They wrote, Roosters three, Colonials one. Signed with love, beneath the scrawled final score of the game, were the signatures of Heather Sarah, Paul William, and Binky.

"Not a marble, twenty-seven, not a marble got by you that night, dear Paul," Binky said as he smiled at me and placed her arm around my shoulders.

"I do remember the game now! Not exactly, I did not stop them all, Binky. One puck rolled in behind me when our defenseman . . . a chap named Mulligan, had trouble with it. The puck rolled on edge, I relaxed for a second, and it went in our own net. After that, we shut them down! I even stopped O'Malley dead to rights on a backhand shot right in front of the net. He had the whole top of the goal open, but I just managed to get my catching glove up there in time. I think it was at the eighteen-minute mark of the third period."

"It was at the seventeen-minute mark, twenty-seven. Seventeen minutes and twenty-seven seconds to be exact." Binky, of course, corrected me.

I smiled at my family and simply said, "Thank you, I love you all very much. Thank you for remembering a piece of me that sometimes, I need to remember. It feels really good to be number twenty-seven every once in a while."

"Wash up for dinner, children, wash up! Time to eat." Binky hustled the two children off to the bathroom to wash their hands. There was no better mother in the entire world than Binky Hobnobber Henson.

Binky lectured the children as they ran off to wash up, "The pie should be extra delicious. It has been slow baking for a long time! Hot Shepherd's Pie on a cold winter evening. It is full of peas, carrots, beef, and some wonderful potatoes. It will help you to grow as strong and tall as your father has. I took Grandmum's recipe and tweaked it a bit. You know how I usually do it, Paul. I know how much you enjoy the extra gravy that I tend to add. We have a little cake for you as well. It is vanilla, just as you like it, with a twenty-seven across the top! The children helped me with the preparation. Paul William drew the goalie on the top of it. Heather Sarah drew the number twenty-seven."

I smiled at her as Binky went on and on with her explanation.

I did not say a word, but instead I chose to sit there, smile, and admire her. When there was a short pause in my wife's words, and I was sure the children were out of an earshot, I spoke up. I could tell by my wife's face that she already somehow knew that I wanted to speak with her about something, in which I had on my mind. Binky could always read me so well. . ..

"Thank you again, for all of these special festivities. Say, Binky . . . by chance, have you ever seen any strange lights out over the church at night, or ever heard any strange noises?"

Binky looked at me a little strangely as she went over to the oven to check on our meal.

She stood next to the oven and looked back at me, as she said, "You are very welcome. No, I never have. Why do you ask?"

"Oh . . . just a conversation, which I had with Mrs. Whipley this afternoon. It was quite strange indeed. I suppose it would be easy to dismiss it as the ramblings of an old lady, but she seemed so sincere. She claims that angels visit the church, and they are at times, hovering over the fellowship hall. She said that it happens most every Saturday night."

Binky did not answer me right away, but she continued to stare at me. She then put two oven mitts on her hands, reached into the oven and pulled out the dish of Shepherd's Pie. She carried it over and placed it upon the countertop.

Binky turned towards me with one hand on the lid of the cooking dish and said, "I think you have learned in your life, Paul, to never dismiss anything. Haven't you?"

"I sure have learned to keep an open mind, dear Binky, that is for sure. It was just such a strange afternoon, Binky. Believe me, when I say it was strange . . . then it is a supreme and sincere qualifier. I also found an old journal in and amongst the books in my office today. It was a handwritten logbook with the daily notes of Pastor Charles P. Braun. I think you have seen his name around here and there in the church. He was the first pastor to serve

Reunion after they built the church here on this site. Dave Sharp told me he was a good pastor and a great man. Dave also told me that he had a lot of respect for him, and that he passed away suddenly at a very young age.

Binky nodded at me as she worked to scoop out the individual portions of our dinner onto our plates.

"I recognize the name. If Dave said he was a good man, then I am sure it is true. What did Pastor Braun write in the journal?"

"Oh, a lot of general notes and daily logs of events. As usual, a lot of infighting amongst the old guard of the church and some logistical troubles related to the construction projects of the church. To be honest, it is hard to read his handwriting. He might have written at an extreme angle and with his left hand. I was about to give up on reading it when I noticed an entry that was very peculiar. He explained how he had instituted a strange procedure for draining the holy or blessed water used in worship services or out of the baptismal font after a baptism. He instructed the acolytes to dump the water only upon a specific oak tree that was growing next to the fellowship hall. Apparently, the tree was planted during the construction. He felt the young tree was struggling, and that the water would help it grow."

"Oh my . . . that is very strange, twenty-seven! Is it not? But is that not the tree that has grown so tall and fabulous?" Binky glanced out the window of the parsonage in the kitchen. But it was too dark to see the tree now.

"It is, Binky. I decided that I am going to do the same thing with the blessed or holy water. I am going to pour it out on the same tree. It cannot hurt. Can it?"

Binky gave me a rapid head nod to signal her agreement with my new procedure. I could tell that I had intrigued Binky by telling her of my discovery during this unusual afternoon, but she was also aware that I needed to ponder it alone for a bit of time . . . without her influence.

"Is that why I spotted you walking out the back of the church and traipsing through the snow wearing, as usual, only your little vest? You must have been going to check out that tree."

Oh boy, from her lookout post of the kitchen window, Binky could detect anything. I nodded my head to confirm my guilt. Binky frowned at me as she acknowledged the thought of me wearing my usual, thin, winter attire.

"I can research any information, if you need it, dear Paul, you know that. I think I will study oak trees. That particular tree does seem very large for an oak tree of that age. If I remember correctly, from my other research, oak trees grow rather slowly. I will be available to assist you, dear Paul."

"I know, Binky, thank you. You know the other really strange connection to all of this, is that particular tree is where Mrs. Whipley told me she sees the bright lights shine upon at night. She claims that is what the angels focus upon. It just seemed to be such a weird and unusual coincidence." My wife turned around, and she stared at me when I spoke the two words, "weird and unusual." After all, she occupied a center seat for a few years now to the adventures of Harry and Paul, so weird and unusual was actually the normal mode of operation.

I imagined that I needed to clarify that a bit more.

"Well, even a little more so than usual."

Binky smiled at me as our two children ran into the kitchen to join us at the table. We both did not want to speak in front of the children about the subject, so I decided we could finish the conversation later. Maybe we would, or maybe we would not. I had to pray and think about this one for sure.

My loyal wife said, "You will figure it all out, you always do. Would you like a nice cold, beer, twenty-seven?"

"Sure, Binky thanks."

Binky opened the refrigerator and stared into it.

She turned and looked at me as she asked, "Would you like a Big Boulder or a Dingleberry?"

"A Big Boulder, please dear Binky. It seems as if the popular opinion is that those Dingleberries are way too sweet."

2

Joy in Harry's Heart

I was waiting at the driving range a few minutes before eight in the morning, just as Harry had asked me to do yesterday. I have to admit that I was more than a little curious as to what had the big guy so nervous and fired up. After all these years of being friends with Harry M. Redmond Jr., I had learned not to ask too many questions. The answers with Harry M. Redmond Jr. eventually always come along. Sometimes in my vast and numerous Harry experiences, you were better off not knowing ahead of time of what he may have planned. That way, the tumult of troubles or the hurricanes of adventures did not overwhelm you.

While I sat alone in my jeep, I had to think how it was so unusual to be sitting in front of a golf ball driving range in the beginning of December. Just as Harry had described, the driving range was open. There was snow here and there along the edges of the property, but it was open. There was an older man out there hitting golf balls. The gentleman had so many overcoats on that I was actually amazed that he could even swing his driving club. It was a cold morning, somewhere in the mid-twenties, but Harry knew that the cold did not bother me.

It sure seemed as though it was an unusual request to meet him at a driving range, but then again, I was dealing with Harry M. Redmond Junior.

Driving golf balls was a release for Harry. He did not play golf, nor did he have any interest in playing the actual game. Harry came here when he needed to release energy. Harry, in his older age, received some exercise here, and he found it therapeutic to hit the golf balls with his crushing blows, while I sat and spoke to him. He called it, "his special pastoral counseling sessions," and I went along with it. I usually sat on a pillar, while he purchased a bucket of golf balls, teed them up one after another, and drove them out of sight. While he was blasting golf balls into outer space, I chatted with him on the latest subject that may be on his mind.

Years ago, when we were younger, we had the sacred kitchen table at 20 John Street, now we had the driving range!

Harry was still very successful in his career, and I had to think, in his life too. Since he and Rose were married back in 1988, they lived a whirlwind life. That was, of course, no surprise with Harry. You always had to hold on tight as he jumped from one idea or adventure to another. I do think he and Rose were very special together, and their eventual marriage was part of God's plan. Although it had taken quite a while after he returned to New Jersey for them to reunite, it had been a joyful and wonderful union for both of them. Harry still had his nightclub and restaurant establishment, and other business ventures, although he left most of the operation of the restaurant and nightclub to my brother-in-law, Tinky Hobnobber to run and operate, along with Tinky's wife, Betty Ann.

Rose stayed at home, working with Harry on ideas from their home office for new ventures, and assisting him in some charity work that he was involved in on a daily basis. There were always new ventures either in the works or on the horizon with Harry.

Boredom still set in very quickly in the world of Harry M. Redmond Jr., Harry never remained idle for very long, he always had some type of wild plan that he was working on. If he was not working at his welding shop, or in his little factory producing the latest gizmo or gadget, he was on the local news broadcasts, touting inner city development, or advocating for the downtrodden. We both never forgot where we came from, no matter where we traveled or went to, we never forgot.

From what I could tell, Harry and Rose were very happy together. After he had married Rose, Harry also joined the membership of Reunion Lutheran Church. They both were quite active members. Shortly after they were married, Harry sold his small house in Manchester and they moved out to a large, custom-built mansion in Shadow Lakes.

It was, as Harry proudly proclaimed, "The high-rent district." It seemed very large for the two of them, but Harry deeply desired a family, and he told everyone that someday, he would fill the house with screaming kids, and blast *Dinky the Orange Teddy Bear* cartoons all day long. After all, Harry had made a very good living for an awful lot of years, and he was now going to enjoy it.

Harry, of course, was still Harry. He was still very loud, outrageous, bombastic, and at times very obnoxious and carefree.

One day, about six months ago, he found a lost, mixed-breed puppy. The little doggie, which was part husky and part, some type of other breed, was wandering the streets down by his welding shop. The little pup was a stray dog, and he reminded Harry of Cocoa, the world's smartest dog, who was a constant companion and friend to both of us when we were kids, until we were young men. The little pup did look eerily similar to Cocoa, but his coat was just a little darker than Cocoa's coat was. Harry took him into his home, and in typical Harry fashion, he named him Cocoa Two. Now that particular name has caused all kinds of confusion, as the intention was for the dog to be named the figure two, in numerical order after the world-famous Cocoa. Folks would think that Harry was referring to Cocoa as well as other dogs, items, or persons, and it caused scenes that were quite comical indeed. It all fell in line with Harry, his unusual lifestyle, and remarkable sense of humor. They were a happy family in this big, fancy home, the three of them, Harry, Rose, and Cocoa Two. That being . . . Cocoa figure two . . . not Cocoa as well.

I told you that it was very confusing.

The home in Shadow Lakes was fabulous. The house had grand scale patios in the backyard, fantastic wooden decks, a huge kitchen, large rooms, ten bedrooms, grand foyer entrances, and large, wide hallways. Of course, they held parties all the time! It was the centerpiece for all kinds of typical Redmond activities and some more of those famous shindigs. Not much changed as far as the Redmonds go. Harry even had a large, in-the-ground swimming pool.

It was Harry's Resort all over again, just on a different scale and in a much different setting.

He invited my old man and Mum over to the house one day when he first opened the pool and Harry told us all that he had to put it in the ground for fear that it would blow up one day!

Ah yes, the memories of 20 John Street and exploding swimming pools were never far away.

Our dear friend Rose was, in many ways, the perfect companion for Harry. She was the only woman who finally could tame his spirit and his wild ways. She was his soul mate, his one true love on this Earth. There was, in my opinion, true joy in Heaven over their union.

As far as Harry and I went, it was much of the same. The same as it had been since we were ten years old and playing together in the backyards and streets of the old neighborhood. I still encountered that strange circle of weirdness that followed me around, and Harry seemed to be the center of an awful lot of these strange encounters. Nothing had changed there, that was for sure. In such a roundabout way, I had become his pastor, his friend, and in many ways his brother. There was very little, if in fact, there was anything, of which he and I had not experienced, shared, or discussed over our lives together. It was a bond, a type of brotherhood, which, other than those words to label our relationship, I could not fully describe. I only knew that he and I were bound by an understanding from God, from far beyond what I could comprehend or pretend to know.

An awful lot had changed since the marriage of Harry and Rose. Binky and I, of course, had become proud parents. Paul William was our first born in 1990, and Heather Sarah followed about a year and a half, or so later. We had moved out of the little rental home in Great Falls and into the parsonage on the property of Reunion Lutheran Church. Let me say again that there was no better wife and mother anywhere on Earth than Binky Hobnobber Henson was. She was all that I could dream of in a wife and a mother to our children. Binky stayed home most of the time and worked as a mom and homemaker, but she did now and again teach a course in research studies at a local college. I could see her working a bit more once both of the children were older and in school full time.

Mr. Hobnobber had finally retired from being a state senator and from his law practice, and settled down to a life of ease. Or in fact, a life of driving Binky and me crazy would be more accurate. Now that he had more time on his hands, he was always around. He loved his grandchildren, and they surely loved him, it was just that he was so overwhelming and exhausting! My mother-in-law tried hard to keep him under control, but that was a full-time job in itself. Mr. Hobnobber did stay busy working with Harry on some urban renewal projects, as well as some charities in the city of Paterson. Harry was utilizing Mr. Hobnobber's many contacts, as well as tapping into both of their huge circle of connections. Together, they made quite the team, that was for sure.

My brother-in-law, Tinky Hobnobber, had married his sweetheart, Betty Anne Schmidt, and they rented a small house out in Manchester. They were married at Reunion, and it was with great joy that I performed the ceremony. It was a wonderful day, and the reception afterwards was a one-of-a-kind shindig. Suffice it to say, with Schmidts, Hobnobbers, Redmonds, Hensons, Boatmanns, and other assorted characters, we all rocked the joint. Bishop Von Houten came along with his wife, as well as Rabbi and Mrs. Goldberg, and we all had a time to remember. Harry loved Tinky or as he fondly called him, "Tink-a-roo-ski." The big guy went over the top and gave them a brand new, Rhino 400 automobile for a wedding gift.

Harry was amazing.

Tinky worked part-time at Reunion Lutheran Church as the music director, as well as running, "The Lovely Rose" restaurant and nightclub, for Harry and Rose in Paterson. Betty Anne still worked with her father in the site excavation and construction company, and she pitched in at the restaurant. For sure, they were both very busy people. They had a happy marriage, and although they were the odd couple, they surely were partners in life. Tinky had found his true love. Tinky, Betty Anne, and Harry's oldest sister, Linda, had a little band and some sideline musical aspirations going on for years. They performed around the metro area, cut a few records here and there, and had some great success.

After many years, Linny finally retired from the music business, although occasionally, she would perform a guest solo singing appearance for us at Reunion Lutheran Church. She and Ronzo still lived out in the woods of Pennsylvania. We still would share in the pleasure of a reunion when we could, for special occasions and holidays, but they were getting older now, and did not travel quite as much. Binky still spoke with Linny on the telephone quite often, as well as with Patty, who along with the Big Spike, were still living out on the west coast. So many wonderful times together, such fantastic people, we could never allow space to divide us.

Mr. Redmond was old now, well into his eighties, but he was doing well, getting along in Florida in a small community. We spoke on the phone here and there, and exchanged Christmas cards, but we really only had the pleasure of seeing him at Christmas, as he did not travel much at all.

What a joy to see him when we could. He was a great man!

Mum and the old man were doing well, still living out in the country of Sussex County, New Jersey. The old man had a health scare with a little vein that popped in his abdomen, when he would not listen, and he shoveled too much snow one day. We rushed him to the hospital, and he had to have a procedure to close off the bleeding, but he recovered nicely. He still bought himself a new Rhino 400 automobile every few years, puttered around in the garden, and watched his baseball, hockey, and the football games. Mostly, he just drove poor Mum crazy, so we knew he was feeling very well.

My sister was still living in southern New Jersey, and she and her family were in a whirlwind of activities. I had two nieces and a nephew, and they were one of the busiest families I had ever seen. My sister was always very active in her church, and she decided after many years of flip-flopping between her United Methodist Church, and my brother-in-law's Catholic Church, to convert to the Catholic faith. I thought it was wonderful, and my brother-in-law was very happy to have the family all be worshipping together in one church home.

Sadly, there was one member of our circle of friends who had passed on. In many ways, though, I looked upon it as our loss, but it was certainly Heaven's gain. About a year ago, right after Thanksgiving, I received a call from a bishop's assistant in the Paterson Catholic Diocese, to inform me that Father Mark O'Leary had passed on in his sleep one evening. Father Mark had been in a home for retired priests for many years. He was in his upper nineties in age, and he went away quietly in his sleep one night. I had the pleasure of visiting him just a week or so earlier, and he was very frail, but still alive in spirit. He and I spoke, read, and shared an abundance of memories together for many hours that afternoon. It was now a fond memory in my little book of memories that I keep close to me at all times.

The true shock came when the assistant asked me to hold on the telephone line to speak with the Bishop of the Paterson Diocese himself. The bishop came on the line to explain that Father Mark had left special instructions in a letter for me to participate in his funeral service. Father Mark had wanted me to be there and had also asked for Bishop Von Houten and Rabbi Goldberg to attend along with me. He deeply wished for the three of us to be an active part of the service. Father Mark had met Bishop Von Houten and Rabbi Goldberg at many of our weddings, parties, and various, assorted family and church gatherings. Father Mark always told me how much he enjoyed Bishop Von Houten and his crusty, yet heartwarming ways. The four of us very strange and unusual clergymen, all had wonderful discussions and shared great times together. When Father Mark was up to it, I would pick him up for dinner, and the four of us would gather and spend time together. Father Mark was very ecumenical in his beliefs, and it was something that he had taught me, we shared, and I respected. The man knew no real boundaries between our religions; he only knew faith and belief.

I knew that I owed Father Mark an awful lot.

He had written in his letter for Bishop Von Houten to

read certain scripture, then an Old Testament reading from Rabbi Goldberg. I had a much larger part of the service. He left instructions for me to read certain scriptures, prayers, as well as to read aloud, a hand-scrawled note that he had left.

I knew even before the bishop explained anything about the note or showed me what the words were going to be on the note.

"I know that the note says blue skies all around us, Father Mark, nothing but blue skies."

"Why yes, Pastor Henson, that is indeed what it says," the bishop told me over the telephone. He seemed amazed that I knew beforehand what Father Mark had written upon the note.

I would never expect it to say anything else.

"Hey wake up, twenty-seven! Were you up late last night, chasing Bink-a-roo-ski around the house? I bet you cannot catch her, you are getting slow, ya know!"

I nearly jumped out of my skin as Harry arrived alongside the jeep, opened the side door and jumped in, while he yelled at me.

"No, no, no, I was just daydreaming here, watching that chap hit buckets of golf balls, while I waited for you. Man, oh man, Harry, you scared the collar right off of my pastor's shirt!"

"Oh, stop being such an old lady, will you! Hey, let me go buy a bucket of golf balls and I will meet you back here. I am going in that driving booth right there in front of the jeep. Save it for me, will ya. That is my lucky booth!"

Harry pointed at a driving booth painted in a bright blue color, mounted right in front of where I parked my jeep.

"I want to aim for the fence and see if I can knock a few over the top into the lake. I have to see if I still have it there, twenty-seven! I would love to see that stupid golf cart going back and forth with that guy in there collecting golf balls. I love to pick him off too. Cocoa Two is in the Rhino, I will whistle for him, he will stand right next to you, while I go and get a bucket. Hey, when are you going to buy a new jeep? You have had this old wreck forever. It is a big, rusty, bucket of bolts. You are just the same as your old man was with that old, 1964 Putter Classic car. He drove it until the wheels rolled off, and the floorboards fell out."

"Well, it still runs good, Harry, but I may. . .."

"Man, oh man, you are such an old lady, Paul. You really are! C'mon, let's smash golf balls!"

I had to laugh at that same old criticism of me. It sure was nice to hear at times.

Harry and I climbed out of the jeep, Harry ran over to his Rhino 400, and opened the side door. Cocoa Two jumped out, wagging his tail and panting. It was uncanny how much that Cocoa Two resembled, Cocoa. What a flashback I had in my mind, to all the times that Cocoa, Harry, and I spent together!

"Cocoa Two, go and stand next to twenty-seven, and wait for me there. I have some of our special biscuits in my pocket here. Once I hit the first ball over the fence, you and I can eat one," Harry motioned with his arm, and then he trotted off to the main service counter to purchase his bucket and pick out a driving club. The dog looked at me, then back to Harry. He came running over to me and sure enough, he sat right down next to me.

"Hey, Cocoa Two, how are you doing?" I patted his side, and the dog wagged his tail. He was happy to see me. He knew me well. I had spent quite a bit of time with Cocoa Two when Binky, the kids, and I had cared for him for a few weeks when Rose and Harry took a little holiday. He went everywhere with both Harry and Rose, and he was always over our house. Cocoa Two was part of the Henson family, too.

I mean, he was part of our family as well.

The best we could guess upon the veterinarian's advice and estimate was that Cocoa Two was about a year and a few months old now. He was a gorgeous dog, and very well behaved. He seemed to enjoy my company, just as his namesake did so many years ago. He sat next to me and watched Harry move along the sidewalk. He was intense; he definitely knew who the boss was! While we waited for Harry, I remembered that I had left a hot cup of coffee in the cup holder in my jeep. I moved towards the direction of my jeep where I had left my coffee cup in the holder. As I moved away, Cocoa Two stood up and followed me as I moved closer to the jeep.

"Stay there, Cocoa, I will be right back," I instructed him, but he did not listen. I then realized the mistake I had made, and I almost laughed aloud. Time, old habits, and flashbacks had caught up with me.

"Stay there, Cocoa Two, I will be right back."

The dog immediately sat down, wagged his tail, and smiled at me. Unreal, it really was. Cocoa Two was just as smart as Cocoa, or at least he seemed to be! After all, what did I ever expect out of Harry M. Redmond Jr., something normal?

I returned with my coffee. Cocoa Two and I waited together in the booth that Harry had selected to drive golf balls on this chilly, but sunny morning.

"So, how many times did you slip up and call Cocoa Two, Cocoa? I bet you slipped up and called Cocoa Two Cocoa, didn't you?" Harry returned, smiling broadly. He was carrying a bucket of golf balls and a driver club.

"Well, I have to admit, Harry that. . .."

"I still do it, but he knows his name now, and he ignores me when I make a mistake. Once I explained to him who Cocoa was, he was good to go. He is just about as smart as the world's smartest dog was. I just have to teach him a few more words from the dictionary. I teach him most every night, Rose thinks that I am nuts. You know better though, twenty-seven. After all, she did not know Cocoa as we knew him. I mean, she knew Cocoa too, but not like, we knew him. That is Cocoa, as in Cocoa also, not this Cocoa Two. Oh man, you know what I mean, Paul. Anyway, Cocoa Two will be expanding his vocabulary more and more. He is gaining more words every day."

I shook my head in acknowledgement, but I am not sure I was following all of the conversation. All of these various Cocoas were becoming a bit confusing to sort out.

The Redmonds always had dogs, and they treated them as if they were real humans, so it was no surprise to me that Harry was teaching his dog actual English words from a dictionary.

"Rose wanted to name Cocoa Two, Woofie! Can you imagine that instead of Cocoa Two?"

"Well, in retrospect, it may have been a little less confusing, Harry, but. . .."

Harry cut me off, "So everything is great, twenty-seven! What a great day! I just need to tell you something or I will burst! First, though, I need to bash a ball into the next county. Pent up energy, you see!"

The big guy was all kinds of fired up. He seemed to be very excited, but I could not get a feel yet for what it was that had him on a roll. Cocoa Two and I watched as he set up the tee in the booth, took a ball out of the bucket, and lined it up with his club. A quick twist, a big swing backwards, and his powerful body unleashed a gigantic swing at the helpless ball.

"Whoosshhhhhh!"

The golf ball rocketed out of sight, launching down across the wide-open range. The ball headed for the big fence installed at the end of the driving range that bordered the lake. The three of us watched as it finally lost momentum and fell just short of the fence. Harry could hit a golf ball to the moon and back if he wanted to.

"Not bad for a first whack! I feel better already!" Harry yelled out as he turned back towards the two of us.

"C'mon, Harry, you are driving me nuts now! What is

the cause of all the excitement?"

Harry dropped his driver, came over next to us, and stood there with a smile as wide as his shoulders.

"Okay, okay, all right! Twenty-seven, listen—Rose, and I are going to have a baby! Finally, a baby, Paul! I am going to be a father!"

I felt my heart leap with joy inside of my chest, and Cocoa Two jumped up as I jumped off the edge of the booth that I was leaning on. The dog started to bark, jump in the air, and run around. The excitement of the moment and the news had caught Cocoa Two up in the excitement too . . . I mean as well. It seemed as though he knew and understood the word, "baby" that was for sure.

"Oh, Harry, that is fantastic! Praise the Lord! This is a wonderful day! Now, I know why you are leaping for joy!"

I embraced the big man as we shared in the joy together. I looked at him as tears of joy ran down his cheeks and he wiped them away. I knew that Rose and Harry had been trying to have a baby for years now, and it was just not happening for them. Doctors had checked both Rose and Harry from top to bottom medically, and the doctors could not find anything to be wrong, yet pregnancy for whatever reason just would not occur. Finally, Rose had conceived, and I could see and feel the joy in Harry's heart. It was the long-awaited answer to many of our prayers.

"It is incredible, Paul, just incredible. Rose found out yesterday. I did not know what to do, to run outside and scream up at Heaven, or fall down on my knees and pray. Therefore, I did both! I knew we had to tell you and Binky first out of the whole, entire world, but I am just so nervous. Well, actually Cocoa Two has heard it now, along with you." He looked down at his dog and patted his head. I guess that explained Cocoa Two's reaction.

My goodness, he was just as smart as Cocoa.

"Rose and I worked the deal, we would tell you both at the same time, it was just that I had to come here and bash a few golf balls. Rose is calling Binky right now and telling her. Rose understood—she knows that I am a basket case."

Harry was rambling. He was indeed a basket case. He finished his explanation, ran off to the club, picked it up, set another ball on the tee, and swung at it.

"Whoosshhhhhh!" Another ball rocketed off the tee, out of sight, far out into the driving range field. This one hit the fence way down the range and dropped to the ground. Cocoa Two barked as he saw Harry fist pump in the air at his shot. The big guy was blowing off the nervous energy in any way that he could. He placed the driver back down and hustled over to the two of us.

"Twenty-seven, I cannot even describe the joy that I have buddy. It is unreal. We are finally going to have a baby. It has been such a long time, we were just getting ready to adopt, which was our plan now for quite a while, when all of a sudden, Rose felt as if it had happened. Sure enough, she was right. Now do not get me wrong, it has not been so bad trying the natural way for so long there, twenty-seven. . .."

His voice trailed off. He winked at me, and he burst out into laughter as he punched my arm. I joined him in his laughter and joy, because I am sure he was making a very factual statement!

"It was so strange. It was almost as if we were going off to work every day! Ho hum, punch the time clock, let's go make a baby!" Harry was laughing until his side hurt.

"Now Paul, I am beside myself in nerves, I just do not know what to do next. I have such joy, but such fear too." He ran back over to the golf tee and repeated the scene.

"Whoosshhhhhh!"

This time the ball went out of sight, farther and farther, and, yes! It flew over the big fence and into the lake. Harry could hit a golf ball farther than most professional golfers could.

"Yes!" Harry screamed when he spotted the ball go over

the fence. He came over, reached in his pocket, and took out one of his, "special Harry biscuits." He threw one biscuit to Cocoa Two, who caught it in midair. He reached back in his pocket, and took out another biscuit, which he promptly stuck in his mouth, and took a big bite out of it. While he chomped the special Harry biscuit, he reached down and patted Cocoa Two on top of his head.

"I am really feeling better, Paul. Did you see that one?"

I nodded and smiled.

He told me through bites of his dog . . . I mean . . . Harry biscuit, "Here is where I am at, twenty-seven, and you as my pastor, and also as my best buddy in the entire world, will understand this better than anyone."

Harry leaned on the side of the booth as he spoke to me. Cocoa Two sat down at Harry's feet and listened. It was uncanny how he was so similar to Cocoa in his human-like actions.

"I am a nervous wreck, Paul. I will give Rose, the baby, and Cocoa Two all that I can give them, all the best that money can buy. I have worked hard to provide all of that. I have no doubt that will be the case. Love, fun, warmth, food, clothes, joy, Redmond parties, vacations, Christmas trees upside down in trees, swimming pools which do not explode, all of it!"

I smiled and said, "I would never expect anything else, Harry. So, what is the trouble?"

Harry jumped off the booth and waved his hands in the air nervously while saying, "Twenty-seven, how can I give them what you and I had growing up? How can I ever duplicate 20 John Street, the joy and adventures that we shared, the old kitchen table, the Porters, the Clipclocks, Joe Hinky Doo, the Lens, you know . . . the old neighborhood? The streets where we grew up and learned a million lessons of life that the schools do not teach. How do I teach him or her about hard work, or staying the course when it feels as if your feet will fall off from roller-skating for forty hours? How about teaching them the ins and outs of making your way through snowstorms that you had to get to work in, or all about Geyer Street Gardens? How about believing in the magic of a long-haired kid with a number twenty-seven etched in black marker, on an old sweatshirt to lead your team to victory? Why you should never give up, even though you are heartbroken and crushed, because you ran out of tears five years ago, and there are no more tears left to cry. How do you teach a child to find the strength to go on after pain and hurt? How do I teach our child all of that?"

Harry shifted on his feet uneasily and he stood up straight and tall. He had finished his biscuit, and he bowed his head down for a moment as he collected his thoughts. He was searching in his mind for more words to explain his fears of becoming a father. He then came over closer to me and stood in front of the two of us.

"Where do I find them all, Paul? Where are the Sal Zucchinis, the 20 John Street gang, your old man, Mum, Mr. Porter with his bullet key ring in his pocket, and his cool Sunbeam car that could go in the water, Jeff Porter with his hat on backwards, time bombs hidden in cupboards, the garlic breathing dragons of men who wanted to knock our choppers out, the hockey fights and games we played in? Where are all of the Howard Pailets of this world, and all the rest of them? Where do I find a summer's night like the one when we rode backwards on the Hamburger Turnpike in a 1971 Takajunky model 10 car, which had a blown transmission, as we tried desperately to make it to the dance on time? It was what we are, and what we were, Paul. It was where we came from, twenty-seven. It is what made us who we are today. Who . . . we are, right now. I cannot give our baby that, it is not the same world, Pastor Henson."

Harry turned serious as he looked at me and then down at his dog.

"How do I duplicate the joy of owning the world's smartest dog and then finding another dog just like him? Or, loving a woman so much that your joy extends from here to Heaven, and then losing her to Heaven itself. Then God sends another woman who loves you the same way, and your love is more important to each other than anything on this whole Earth is. Or, having a once in a lifetime friend such as you, and then later on, Binky. I could not even imagine where I would be right now without youse two guys. Do you know what you both have meant to me? People who stick by me no matter what, through God knows what, for all of these years, through all of these adventures, standing with you on hillsides screaming The Lord's Prayer, setting hope and joy upon our dreams and wishes. How do you give that to your child?"

I smiled and placed my hand upon Harry's shoulder. He was rambling in his excitement and his concern. I understood exactly what he was saying, I really did. I too struggled with the same thoughts when my children arrived in this world. I knew exactly how to calm Harry down. The answer was actually very simple.

I told him, "You can never duplicate the experiences that we had, Harry, or where we lived, or the people we met. Your child will have their own magical times, adventures, people, and memories, but they also will have a piece of your life, as well as your wife's life. You just need to speak about all the memories, Harry. Tell them from your heart, my friend, just as you have told me about them. You see, we all have wonderful stories to tell, it is a shame that many of us choose never to share them anymore. You will share them together as the years pass. You will relate to him or her, some of the adventures of Harry and Paul, and all the joy, as well as the sorrow. You and Rose can tell them story after story, tell them every day over dinner, or next to a Christmas tree, or after church, or sharing a beer or a glass of wine with them when they are older. Don't worry, you will do fine. You will share a part of your life and Rose will share all the parts of her life. Combined, the child will sense your joy, they will learn and follow, and through his or her parent's memories, the child will share what you both have been taught and experienced. It will be just as if he or she grew up at 20 John Street too."

Harry smiled. I could tell he was feeling better about himself. He collected his thoughts for a second or two, then he spoke, "You still are a smart guy, Paul. I think you are right. I bet Uncle Paul and Aunt Bink-a-roo-ski can tell a story or two as well."

"Somehow, I think that might be true, thirty-five, it really may be quite true. As well as Ronzo, Linny, your old man, my old man, Mum, Tinky, Patty, and the Big Spike too."

"Say, Paul, I bet we should leave certain parts out until the kid gets a little older!"

"That might be a good idea Harry, in fact some of them, we may have to keep under our hats forever."

Together we laughed, and Cocoa Two barked in glee with us. Harry dashed back over to the booth and his tee. He picked up his club, placed another ball on the tee, and he let it have it.

"Whoosshhhhh!"

Out of sight it went, over the fence once more. Harry smiled, and he set another, and then another. The big guy was letting it all loose. As he bashed one ball after another, he rambled on and on endlessly. Cocoa Two and I both just stood there and listened. He was feeling better!

"Rose will do fine. Binky will help her. Binky is most likely researching it all right now. The rest of the family will be there too. It will all be fine. I just keep telling myself that."

"It will be fine, Harry. Binky will be there. For sure . . . you know that."

"Whoosshhhhhh!"

"Whoosshhhhhh!"

Golf ball, after golf ball, flew into the cold morning air and over the fence; they all went out of sight.

"I so wanted this to be a special Christmas, twenty-seven. I thought that maybe we could all go up to Christmas Tree Mountain and cut trees down. My old man is coming up from Florida, Patty, and the Big Spike will be here too. Rose needs to rest and relax, so now, I am not so sure."

I laughed at Harry's caution and care.

"Rose will follow what the doctors say. The ladies know what to do, and it will be fine. We can still have a big Christmas celebration, Harry."

"Whoosshhhhhh!"

Another ball went out of sight. I suddenly became aware of the fact that now standing around us, watching Harry launch golf balls into the lake, were four or five men, who had previously been driving golf balls themselves. A few of them went and sat down on a bench and observed the display of golf ball driving prowess that Harry was putting on. They were mesmerized at the drives that Harry was hitting. I looked up at them and smiled. One of the men caught my stare, and he smiled back. He was an older gentleman, bundled up to fight the cold and the wind, and even bundled up, you could see that he was equipped with what seemed to be more, "official" golfing gear than Harry had on.

"Pardon us, Father, but all of us come here all the time to drive golf balls. We are getting in our last practices before the snow and cold shut us down for good until spring. We had to take a time out, since none of us guys have ever seen anyone hit a ball as far as your friend there can hit 'em. Do you realize that the fence out there is at about four hundred yards out, and that guy is putting the balls over the top of them? There are professional golfers that only dream of hitting a drive that far."

I looked down and smiled as I spotted that my collar and pastor's black shirt were both clearly visible under the light vest that I was wearing.

"He can sure whack 'em, that is for sure."

I stood up off the edge of the booth, motioned for Cocoa Two to stay where he was, and walked over to the group of men.

"Good morning, men. I am Pastor Paul John Henson. I am the pastor at Reunion Lutheran Church in Hibernian, New Jersey. The big guy, over there, whacking golf balls into the solar system, is my best buddy, Harry M. Redmond Junior. The dog there is his dog, Cocoa Two."

"Oh, I apologize. Got it—Pastor Henson. I just saw your collar and assumed that youse was a priest. Or, a monk. The Lutheran Church allows you to have all that hair, huh?" One of the men answered.

"It is fine, it happens all the time. Yes, God does not have rules on hair length and beards, and neither does the Lutheran Church." I went around the group and individually shook their hands, being careful and mindful of my sometimes-overzealous grip.

"Is your friend a golfing professional?" One of the men asked me.

I turned and looked back at Harry, who was now turning it up a few more notches now that he had an audience. Not much had changed with Harry. He surely loved an audience! He launched the golf balls out of sight, one after another.

"No, he is not. He is an old hockey player. Right now, he is blowing off some steam, because he just found out that his wife is pregnant with their first child. He takes his nervousness or anger out on golf balls. It is sort of an energy release for him. I can tell you from experience though that he surely could also shoot a mean slap shot in hockey. I have a few scars on my face and legs to prove it!"

The group of men seemed puzzled, but they were amazed at Harry and his fantastic golf ball driving ability.

The first man, who had spoken, smiled at us and yelled out to Harry, "Go man, go, and congratulations on the baby!"

All of his friends joined in, and then they suddenly all stood and clapped in loud applause, as Harry belted the last ball out over the screen and into the lake. The big guy's bucket was empty. Harry turned around, and he bowed to all of us while we cheered for him and the unbelievable performance. Cocoa Two barked and jumped around in celebration. The dog was quite amazing in his understanding and awareness.

One of the men from the group took his wool cap off and rubbed his baldhead.

He then shouted out to Harry, "I have five children and I still could never drive a golf ball like you can there, son. I am pretty darn old now, but if it works, I am willing to go home, find my wife, and give it a good whirl with her." The man then looked over at me, looked at my collar, and he turned red-faced in his embarrassment.

"Oh, forgive me, Pastor Henson. I am very sorry about that comment!"

"No offense, sir. I bet many guys would feel the same way! I am a married man myself, sir!"

Harry came over and introduced himself to the group of men, shook their hands, and gave them some quick tips on how he could belt the ball that far.

"Nice to meet youse guys! Harry M. Redmond Jr. is the name. Inventor, businessman, entrepreneur, hit songwriter, welder, womanizer, and general, all around windbag and a loudmouth, but overall, I am not a bad guy! That fantastic dog over there is Cocoa Two. He is the world's second smartest dog. Youse guys have already met the best long-haired, hippie, pastor in all of New Jersey, who also happens to be the famous, now retired, long-haired, hippie, greatest ice hockey goaltender of all time, number twenty-seven. I am sure youse guys heard about his famous career!"

Harry sure was pasting it on thick today! The group of men looked at me, mumbled, and fumbled, as I am sure they never heard of me, and were finding it difficult to imagine that I had at one time, played professional ice hockey. Before you knew it, he had trapped all of them with the famous silken-tongued flim-flam, and spoken magic, of Harry M. Redmond Jr. He handed out business cards, told them about his club and restaurant, his inventions, and his charities. The man was amazing, and his ability to sell ice to an Eskimo was still as sharp as ever. On and on he went, covering every subject, in which you could ever imagine, and then some. He even slipped in some pitching on how they should all come to a worship service at Reunion Lutheran Church! He was extremely excited about the news of the baby, and his newfound fan club seemed to sense that fact. The men were being very good sports by allowing Harry to vent his enthusiasm.

One of the men, in an effort to stop Harry from speaking, piped in and asked, "You said the dog's name was Cocoa too, but I missed who else was named Cocoa."

"No one else . . . he is Cocoa Two." Oh, boy, here we go, this is going to be confusing.

"I understand," the man said, "but I am missing the other Cocoa."

I chuckled and walked away as this was going to be a long one. I walked back over to the driving booth and stood next to where Cocoa Two was sitting. I motioned for him to come and sit next to me as I sat on the edge of the booth and listened with half of an ear to the comical explanation going on in the distance. I rubbed Cocoa Two's thick coat, while he and I stared out at the sun climbing higher in the sky.

"What a glorious day, Lord." I prayed aloud. "Keep

Rose, Harry, and the baby safe, dear Lord. I pray for Harry's joy, Rose's health, the health of the baby, and the safety and comfort of them all. Amen."

Cocoa Two snuggled up under my arm, and he thoughtfully looked at me with his eyes. It was as if he knew the prayer was required, and as if he knew that Heaven listened.

I thought how it was a strange reaction to the prayer. He was a special dog, just as his namesake was.

The sun was warm on us now, and the joy and hope of Harry and Rose filled the air with warmth, and our hearts with cheer.

3

The Quest for Peppermint Ice Cream

"Can we go up the Christmas Tree Mountain next year, Uncle Harry, after you and Auntie Rose have the baby? I want to hang Christmas trees upside down from trees in our backyard!"

"Yeah, yeah, yeah, kid, next year. Now, keep your legs closed and the pads tight, or you will open up the five-hole and I can score all the time. Your old man could never be beat in the five-hole. He would run himself crazy, get all tired out, and that was the only way you could beat him. When he was tired, you would shoot low and on the stick side to score."

"Got it, Uncle Harry. I need to close my leg pads tight, right?"

"Yeah, yeah, yeah, here you go, kid!"

Harry, Paul William, and I were shooting some street hockey balls around in the church parking lot, late on a Saturday afternoon just a few days before Christmas. Harry was bouncing the ball softly off Paul William's pads as he stood in front of a small, street hockey net. The goaltending bug had seriously bitten Paul William. He wore a cage-type mask, (it surely offered a lot better protection, than my old white fiberglass mask did!) some street hockey leg pads, chest protector, shoulder pads, and a full set of gloves.

Oh yes, he also wore a jersey with the number twenty-seven on it.

He looked good in the goal for a five-year-old! Looking back, this sure was a lot better equipment than Harry, Jeff

Porter and I wore when we first started out. In fact, all we had were baseball gloves for catching the puck, and work gloves that we stole from our father's shop for hockey gloves. If it were up to Binky, our son would wear a suit of metal armor when he was in the net. I watched from the sideline with my hockey stick in my hands as Harry tapped the ball gently into Paul William's pads and he made the save.

"Good one, Paul William!" I yelled as I made a fast break and swooped in to gobble up the rebound and passed the ball back out to Harry. Harry faked that he was going to blast a hard slap shot from the point, and Paul William got down into a low crouch. He looked as if he was a seasoned goalie. He had all the right moves. I had been teaching him very slowly here and there. Harry laughed at the little goalie's courage.

"Wow! Just like his old man, never backing down from anyone or any shot! Hey kid, take a close look at your old man's face and you can see . . . he should have ducked a little more!" Harry slowly rolled the ball into Paul William's pads; he gloved it up and made the "save."

"Father, did you and Uncle Harry, really steal some drinks of Ronzo's booze that he hid in the cupboard that made the men all drunk at Christmas time?" Paul William asked as he tossed the ball back out to us.

"Who told you that story?"

"Uncle Harry! Didn't you, Uncle Harry?" I looked at Harry, who shrugged his shoulders and then frowned back at me. "Did you and Uncle Harry get drunk and fall in the snow singing, 'Silver Bells' too?"

"Forget that story until you become a bit older Paul William and don't tell your mother that Uncle Harry has been telling you Harry and Paul stories."

"I guess that is one of the stories that we need to keep under our hats, eh, twenty-seven?"

I shook my head and laughed. "Well, Harry, I would

like to. . .."

"Come on in here, guys! Aunt Rose, Heather Sarah, and I have some just baked Christmas cookies for everyone and it is getting cold and dark. Bring it in, now!" We turned and spotted Binky calling to the three of us from the front porch. Cocoa Two scooted out from behind Binky and he dashed out the front door to see what was going on that he might be missing.

"Ah, dear Mother, we were just getting warmed up! It is not cold! I am warm! Look! Father, only has on a little vest!"

"C'mon, Paul William. You will never win. It is time to go into the house." I recognized our fate, as did, Harry.

"Yeah, yeah, yeah, kid, take some advice from your Uncle Harry, you will learn that you have very little chance of winning any debates with women, besides those cookies sound good."

I could see, even from this distance, Binky shaking her head. She then dug her left foot hard into the ground. I knew that I was going to get a Binky lecture on wearing my vest in the cold air. She watched as we made our way to the house. We were gathering up the net, sticks, and hockey balls while heading back to home port.

"My dear, Paul! You act as if you are all a bunch of little boys playing back on Geyer Street Gardens. You need to start wearing a heavier coat, twenty-seven. You are not twenty years old!"

Sure enough, my wife was scolding me from the porch for getting caught wearing only my favorite vest, despite the low December temperatures. We helped Paul William take off his pads and equipment, and the three of us, followed by Cocoa Two, went back into the house. The aroma of fresh-baked cookies immediately hit us. I had to admit that they sure smelled good! After another short, research-laden lecture from Binky on the merits of actually wearing a heavier coat, I grabbed a cookie off the cooling tray when Binky was not watching, and I wandered into the living room. I sat down on the sofa next to Rose.

Harry, Cocoa Two, Paul William, and Binky were still in the kitchen working on a few more Christmas cookies. Heather Sarah, clutching the ever-present Fritzie the stuffed dog, climbed upon my lap. Heather Sarah smiled at me and made me pretend that I was feeding cookies to Fritzie.

"How are you feeling, dear Rose?"

"Great, twenty-seven, never better, I could have gone for a Christmas tree with everyone you know. Harry is driving me crazy with his over protectiveness. I cannot even take a step without him guarding my every move!"

I smiled and laughed. "Well, it is going to be a special eight or so months, dear Rose, that is for sure. We will all hang in there, but I may have to sedate my old buddy, number thirty-five. Harry is beside himself with excitement. You are all he talks about these days. It is going to be a great Christmas. Will we see you on Boxing Day? I think Binky is going all out for a full-blown feast this year. Mum, the old man, and the gang will be here. We are having Roast Beef, Yorkshire pudding, and I have an extra special Christmas pudding for serving this year. My Aunt Lois sent it to us."

"Sure, Paul. I know you will be busy on Christmas Day with church and the children, we will be in church Christmas Eve, and then see you on Boxing Day." Rose paused and then looked at me for a brief moment. She then looked away and then back again. Her mind seemed to be wandering a bit. "Paul, it is all going to be all right, isn't it?"

I reached over, grabbed Rose's hand, and clutched it tightly. "Of course, it will be, Rose. Why would you think it would be any other way?"

Rose smiled at me. "I don't know, but I know you will be there for us, to guide Harry and me, no matter what the situation."

I thought it a bit strange that some type of self-doubt had set into Rose, perhaps Harry and his excessive over protectiveness, had planted some type of apprehension into Rose's mind. I did need to speak with Harry about loosening his grip on Rose. Positive thoughts produce positive results!

"Rose, it will be fine."

Heather Sarah piped in, "My father is, Pastor Paul John Henson! He can do anything, Auntie Rose. Do you need anything right now?" My little daughter stared into Rose's eyes deeply and intently. She had picked up the famous Binky stare from her mother's side.

Rose looked at Heather Sarah, stared deeply back and she held her little hands.

"Peppermint ice cream, Heather Sarah. Auntie Rose needs peppermint ice cream."

Oh no! Oh no!

Cravings! I can remember these adventures with Binky, running out at all hours of the night to pick up various food items and fast-food tidbits, as Binky's taste buds ebbed and flowed with the pregnancy.

Heather Sarah jumped off my lap and ran into the kitchen yelling at the top of her little lungs the entire way, "Auntie Rose needs ice cream! Auntie Rose wants peppermint ice cream!"

Immediately, Harry appeared as if someone shot him out of a cannon. He came into the living room, and ran over to his wife's side, followed by Binky, Cocoa Two, and Paul William. I watched a trail of cookie crumbs tumble out of Harry's mouth as we had caught him in mid-cookie consumption mode.

"You want peppermint ice cream, honey?" Harry drooled over Rose's request.

Rose nodded her head firmly in a nod that would have rivaled Binky's greatest head nods of all time to acknowledge the craving.

"I never knew that you actually even ate peppermint ice cream."

"I never have had it yet, Harry. I just want it. I saw it advertised on television today and now, for some reason, I just have to have it!"

Binky looked at me and smiled. I smiled back at her. She undoubtedly had remembered a late-night craving for peach gelatin that sent me on a thirty-mile quest at two in the morning, when she was pregnant with Paul William.

Harry was on fire. He turned and looked at Binky and me.

"What were we going to have for dinner? I thought we were going to order some pizza!"

"Yes, Harry, some beer, some wine, and some pizza."

"Rose, cannot have any beer or wine! She is pregnant there, Bink-a-roo-ski!"

"Oh, Harry, stop. Binky and I have it all under control. I know what I can and cannot have. Please, I will be fine." Rose waved her hand at Harry.

Binky walked over to Harry and put her arm around him to calm the big guy down.

"Go and pick up the ice cream, we have had cookies, and we have plenty of food here to hold the children and us over until you return. Twenty-seven, stole one cookie prematurely off the cooling tray, so he also has eaten a snack. We are all good for a while until you can go to the store and pick up the ice cream for Rose.

Obviously, the Binky cookie radar had nabbed me.

"C'mon, twenty-seven, let's go to the store!" Harry was like a man possessed! His eyes darted back and forth in his head like a set of windshield wipers in a thunderstorm.

Cocoa Two jumped into action; he too was ready to join us in the exciting quest for peppermint ice cream! Harry was on a mission. You would think that he was in search of the Holy Grail! Harry ran, grabbed his hat and coat, and started to put it on.

Harry turned to Cocoa Two and shouted, "Cocoa Two, you stay here and guard the house, women, and children!" The dog immediately sat down, barked twice, and wagged his tail three times at Harry as if to signal he was on duty!

My goodness, how dramatic! I thought that this was just like a scene out of an Ian Leadfoot secret agent movie. All we were going for was peppermint ice cream.

To be honest, I was not really sure that I had ever even heard of peppermint ice cream until just a few minutes ago.

I reached for my vest when Binky stopped me dead in my tracks. She dug her left foot into the floor and frowned at me.

"Twenty-seven! Now, what did I just tell you about going out without a heavy coat? I also recommend that you put your collar and black suit on. You never know when your pastoral duties will be required when you are in public. My research just last week, informed me that at least ten to fifteen priests, rabbis, and pastors were called into official, emergency duty for God's work when they were out on routine supermarket errands."

Paul William looked up at me and told me in his most forceful little voice, "If dear Mother researched it, then you better believe it is true, dear Father."

Heather Sarah nodded at her brother's statement. Heather Sarah had also inherited her mother's famous head nods.

I looked down at my usual canvas sneakers and my rock-and-roll band "No Way" tee shirt and then back at my wife. Binky was standing with her arms folded, looking at me. Her left foot dug convincingly down hard into the floor. She always was lecturing me on wearing my "uniform" just in case that I was pressed into action, for some type of pastoral duties, when I was out and about.

Just to add to the pressure, Heather Sarah ran over and stood next to her mother, dug her left foot into the floor, folded her arms across her chest and continued to nod. She looked like a red-haired miniature version of Binky.

I had to admit that I would rather fly under the radar when I was out. It seemed as though; I always attracted a strange collection of assorted whackos that would spot my clergyman attire. Almost without fail, whenever I wore my collar and black out in public, it always led to some type of bizarre adventure.

Oh well, I do not know why I would think that anything would change at this point!

However, I knew there was no winning this argument. Alas, there was no way out of this Binky motivated, sticky wicket. I mumbled a few words in Welsh under my breath, but I had to be very careful as Binky had tilted her ears toward me . . . she knew the language fairly well herself these days.

Harry blew his cork with his patience running out, "For the love of Pete! Just change, will ya twenty-seven! It is a tag team match of nods and research between ya wife and daughter. You can't win! Rose is desperately waiting for her peppermint ice cream! I will be outside in the Rhino 400. I will drive, cuz, ya drive like an old lady, and it would take forever to get us to the store!"

I folded like a cheap tourist camera. After a quick change to my black suit and my collar, I pulled a winter coat out of the closet that was longer than my other coats and had a zipper along with some buttons on top. My intent was to zip and button it all the way up to hide my attire. I also stuck a wool hat in the coat pocket. Under the watchful eye of Binky, I put the coat on. I immediately felt like an inferno.

I disliked bulky winter coats!

After I gave a kiss to Binky, (after which she fluffed up her hair and winked at me) a kiss on the cheek of Rose, as well as our children, I gave a pat on the head to Cocoa Two, and finally, I was off into the Rhino 400 to meet the waiting, Harry. The frenzy of the quest for peppermint ice cream had captured me too. I climbed into the Rhino 400, and Harry slammed the big vehicle into gear and tore off as if he was in the driver's seat of his famous Trans Whizzer once again.

"Easy Harry, the ice cream will not melt."

"I know, twenty-seven, but this is serious stuff. These cravings are serious! At least . . . I think they are serious." Harry glanced over at me. "Are they serious?"

I shook my head and told him, "No, Harry, it is all fine. Rose's body is changing with the pregnancy. That is all. It is normal. You are just starting out, my friend. The best is yet to come."

I wished that the driving range had not closed for the season. Harry needed to blow off some steam for sure. He fired the Rhino's big engine up as he pulled onto the highway. Soon, Harry was roaring along.

The afternoon had waned now, and it was starting to grow darker. A little remnant of a sunset remained on the horizon in front of us. Harry was still the same expert driver that he always was, weaving in and out of traffic, slipping into and then out of lanes easily, as if he were on a racetrack. After all, the peppermint ice cream waited!

"Are you headed for the Foodworld in the center of town?" I asked.

Harry nodded his head. I said a little prayer that they actually sold peppermint ice cream. We pulled into the supermarket lot and jumped out of the vehicle. Harry was just about sprinting into the store, so I jogged behind him. A few folks stared at us, I am sure they wondered why two grown men, (and one who happened to be dressed in clerical attire) were running across the supermarket parking lot.

Harry burst through the doors and grabbed a shopping cart. I wondered why he needed a shopping cart for a gallon of ice cream, but I did not say a word.

Then it hit me!

Harry and his famous habit of always picking out a defective shopping cart. He never failed to pick out the one cart in the entire store that had a defective wheel, broken handle, or holes in the metal basket. Sure enough, I stood there and watched as he hustled up the main aisle, pushing the cart with greater effort than should have been required. The cart had one broken wheel stuck sideways in the mount. The wheel was not spinning, but instead was making an ugly, black mark on the polished floors of the supermarket. I could not help but laugh as I watched Harry stop and look down at the wheel. He then looked at the black mark that the wheel had made on the floor.

A young store clerk, with long hair, and wearing big, thick eyeglasses, was working in the produce department. He had noticed the situation. He now came over to offer us his expert, in-depth analysis of the situation.

He pointed at the cart, the mark on the floor, and the wheel, as he proudly told us, "Youse guys picked out a bomb of a cart. The wheel is not spinning, and it is making a big mark on the floor!"

The young man was very helpful.

Harry looked at him. I could tell by the look on his face that he did not appreciate the helpfulness of the young store worker quite as much as I did.

"What do I look like . . . you, hockey puck, some kind of doofus? I can see that the cart is broken. If your managers would concentrate more on maintenance than selling stuff at outrageous prices, then we would not have these problems!"

"I was just helping, sorry sir. No, you do not look like a doofus. In fact, I do not know what a doofus is. But you are sure unlucky, as I have never seen a broken cart here before, that must be the only one in the entire store."

Oh, oh!

Time to diffuse the situation before the eye of the tiger

appeared in Harry's eyes. I walked over to the cart and pulled it out of Harry's hands. I thanked the young man for his observation, asked him to place the cart out of service, and pushed the cart to the side.

"C'mon, thirty-five, we do not need a cart just for some ice cream."

I pushed Harry away, and we walked down the aisle. Harry glared over his shoulder at the young man, but he walked away as I pushed him along. He was mumbling loud enough that I could hear him, "Stupid, thick eyeglass wearing, half-blind, hippie, dope. I should poke him one right in his @#$^&* face!"

"Young man! You should be ashamed of yourself! My word! To use that type of language right in front of a priest!"

Harry and I looked ahead of us, and there stood a short, elderly woman with silver and blue hair. She had crossed herself as a defense against Harry's colorful vocabulary and then folded her arms in protest in front of her. She had overheard Harry, and she was upset at his use of highly descriptive language in a public place. She screwed her mouth up in horror, and now she had a stern look upon her face.

Next to her was a tall, lanky man with thick, white hair, who we had to assume to be her husband. He pointed his finger at Harry and joined in the berating of the big guy, "My wife is right, and there are ladies and children around here too!" I looked down to see that I must have unzipped my coat, to prevent my body from melting, and I had not realized it until now. I had revealed my attire and profession to the world now, and unknowingly, had unleashed the whacko parade! This was unreal. We had only been in the store for about one minute, traveled a hundred feet or so from the Rhino, and already it was turning into a mega-adventure.

"I am sorry, I apologize, I did not mean for anyone to

hear me." Harry offered up his apology.

It reminded me of a very similar incident many years ago, when Harry cussed in a store, while we were shopping for hockey sticks, and another elderly woman overheard Harry and his use of colorful language. That was, indeed, a whole other story.

The couple both shook their heads in agreement. The woman spoke up, "Apology accepted, but you need to speak with the priest here and apologize to him."

I stepped in now and put my arm on Harry's shoulders.

"It is fine, ma'am, I am not offended. You see, this is my best friend. He is a little nervous, because he just found out that his wife is pregnant, and we are here to pick up some peppermint ice cream. You see, she is having food cravings tonight. So please excuse him, he is just a little on edge. By the way, I am not a priest. I am a Lutheran pastor. I am Pastor Paul John Henson, of Reunion Lutheran Church."

I reached out to shake both of their hands and I smiled at them.

"Oh, I apologize, but I saw the collar, and we just assumed you were a Catholic priest or a monk," the silver and blue-haired gal smiled at me.

"It is fine, it happens all the time, it is fine. Well, have a nice evening." I started to move Harry away when the tall gentleman placed his hand on my shoulder.

"Say, if you do not mind me asking, the Lutheran Church allows you to wear your hair that long? You are some kind of hippie minister, I guess, with a beard and long hair like that. You look the same as he does. Just ain't got them big glasses on ya eyeballs." The man turned and pointed at the same long-haired young man working in the produce aisle, who was so kind to observe our malfunctioning shopping cart. I smiled . . . same old critics, same old human race! I could spot Harry out of the corner of my eye, winding up once more.

"James! What a terrible thing to say. I think that Pastor

Paul looks very handsome. He is a striking man. Tall, strong, very handsome, and powerful. You have seen pictures of Jesus and Moses, have you not! Now you need to apologize!" Her husband frowned and sulked away, pretending he was now interested in some grocery products on a shelf.

"It is fine, it happens all the time. It is really okay, and we are in a bit of a hurry. Have a nice night now. . .."

The woman crept in closer, and she looked up at me. She motioned for me to bend over so she could speak very quietly in my ear. I towered over her; she could not have been more than five feet or so tall.

"Pastor Paul, could I please have your business card, or your contact information? James and I are in need of some Christian marriage counseling services and you seem as though you are such a kind man. I can tell by your eyes. We are not Lutherans, but I just know that you can help us. You see, he is such a crab, and our sex life has stalled." I stood up, and looked over at Harry, who had been listening, and now was rolling his eyes. I looked over at her husband, who had returned from the shelf observation, and he now was watching us with his arms folded in front of him, while he was tapping his right foot on the floor.

I reached into my pocket, found one of my business cards, handed it to her, and said, "Sure, right after Christmas, please make an appointment with my assistant. Her name is Martha. She will be sure to get you in right after the holidays. Merry Christmas now, peace be with you, and have a great night."

The woman winked at me and said, "I sure hope it is. I am going to chase James around the house when we get home. I bought some of these fresh lemons." She showed me a pile of lemons in her little basket under her arm. "I read in my Ladies House, Home, and Happy magazine that it improves your sex life. I am going to squeeze a bunch of them into his Dingleberry beer after he has had a few, and he is half in the bag. Those Dingleberries are so sweet that he will never notice the taste."

She winked at me once more and I smiled at her.

"Well, that sounds as if it will work, we will see you now."

Harry grabbed me by the arm and yanked me away, before she could begin to speak to me anymore, and we hustled off.

"I see now, why you did not want to wear the collar and black in public twenty-seven, it is a magnet for lunatics. Those old bags must be ninety years old and she is worried about their sex life!"

I shrugged my shoulders. I actually saw nothing wrong with it. In fact, more power to them both.

Harry was gaining speed now, and he looked over his shoulder and shouted to me, "Let's go find the freezer section, poor Rose must be drooling by now!"

Harry stepped up the pace even more, and we wandered over a few aisles. I reached down to zip up my coat to conceal my attire when Harry stopped and turned up an aisle.

I was fiddling with my coat and mindlessly following him when we bumped into a young couple in the middle of the aisle. The two of them faced each other and their shopping cart was blocking the aisle. Harry checked out the young woman first, smiled at her, and then he glanced at the young man she was shopping with tonight. The young gal was tall, lean, and very pretty. Her hair was a bleached blonde color; the dyed color was so pale that it was almost white. She reminded me a little of Harry's now deceased, first wife, Sky Blu, with her fancy-colored hair.

I had a quick flashback.

The young man she was with was short, lean, and he had flaming red hair and a little faint trickle of a red beard on his face. His hair was almost as red as my brother-in-law Tinky's hair was. In fact, he could have been Tinky's double! They made a handsome couple and Harry's eyes certainly wasted very little time in checking out the attractive young woman. I was still fiddling with my coat, when I noticed that we were in the toilet paper, paper roll towel, and the paper plate aisle.

"Harry, a wrong turn buddy! Why are we in the paper products aisle?"

"Oh . . . yoo hoo . . . Father! I am so glad you came along!" I looked up as the young lady had spoken to me and she now was smiling at me. The young man half-heartedly smiled back, and then he frowned. I had not zipped my coat up quickly enough.

"Oh geez, for the love of Pete," I heard Harry whine. Harry went to leave the aisle, but I guess the lure of what was going to happen now, as well as the appeal of the young lady, was a bit too much for him, so he stuck around.

"Oh, hello, but I am not a priest, I am a Lutheran pastor. I am Pastor Paul John Henson of Reunion Lutheran Church."

I reached out my hand and shook each of their hands in a greeting. This was wearing a bit thin, repeating this every aisle or so in the supermarket.

"This is my best buddy, Mr. Harry M. Redmond Junior." I introduced Harry, who got over his grumpiness when he spotted the shapely figure on the young lady. He was now more than happy to greet the young lady. He virtually ignored the poor young man.

"Hey guys, it is very nice to meet you both. We are in a hurry, but. . .."

"I am so sorry, Pastor Paul. I mistook you to be a priest, or maybe, a monk."

"It is fine, it happens all the time."

"I am, Maria, and this is my husband, Salvatore."

I heard Harry mumble that he had never seen a red haired or red-faced Italian guy before, but I do not think they heard him.

The young lady was fired up as she explained, "You see Pastor Paul, we are shopping here for toilet tissue, but I am so mad at Salvatore that I could wring his neck!"

"Oh my, why?"

"My mother-in-law is coming for a visit, and for years, I have had no toilet tissue holder in my bathroom. We have been married for six years and we have been in our house for three years. Three, long, long years, Pastor Paul. I have had to put up with endless construction projects and Salvatore tearing our house apart. We did not even have a toilet bowl for a few days, and I had to pee in our kitchen sink."

I heard Harry choking; he almost spit out his false choppers when he heard that comment.

Maria continued with her rant, "On top of that, this entire time, I have had to make do without a toilet tissue holder! I have had to place the tissue on the edge of the toilet, on the edge of the tub, and until now, it has all been fine. Oh sure, it escapes sometimes and rolls around on the floor a little, and you have to lift your @$$ off the bowl and chase it down, but it is not so bad. Now all of a sudden, as a supposed gift to me, Salvatore brings home a toilet tissue holder. A fancy one nonetheless! It cost a fortune. It is one of those chrome ones that stand on the floor, and you put the roll, right on top of them."

"Well, that does sound as if it is a practical gift. Don't you think so, Harry?"

I was working to defuse the situation. After all, she did seem a bit upset at poor Salvatore.

I turned to look at Harry, who waved his hands back and forth in the air, while he said, "I do not think it is that bad, not really romantic, but not so bad there, Salvatore. I have heard of worse, like when my old man gave my mother a rolling pin for Christmas. All Mom did was chase the old man around with it, trying to belt him in the head."

Salvatore nodded and smiled at Harry, "Thanks buddy! I thought it was a cool gift."

Maria crossed her arms and looked at her husband. She continued scolding, "You know very well that the gift was not for me . . . it was for your mother, so she could wipe herself in an organized and fancy fashion. For years, I made do with rolls running all over the floor, now all of a sudden . . . we have to have a fancy tissue holder! To top it off, we can no longer use the former brand of toilet tissue that we used for years. Noooo . . . your mom's backside is too special, so we have to run out here to Foodworld and buy the extra pleated, special Big Bob's scented brand, to use with our new fancy holder."

I am not quite sure how all of this happens to Harry and me, but it does. Since we were ten years old, the same routine. It does not seem to matter where, how, or what we do; it always turns into some strange, peculiar, and unusual incident. There is something about food stores and my karma. I think that I will have Binky research the connection for me. First, we have broken wheels on carts, then; the next aisle has ninety-year-old, sex-crazed senior citizens. Now we have run into a young couple fighting about a toilet tissue holder, peeing in sinks, and shopping for special, scented toilet tissue.

"Well, I am not quite sure this is a matter for the middle of the Foodworld aisle, Maria. . .."

"That is not the half of it! Pastor Paul, now he announces that we have to go out and buy a rug, and a new chair for our living room! For years . . . nothing! I have to sit on old milk crates and use a towel for a throw rug. Now, that Mom is visiting, all of a sudden, we have to dash out and buy fancy stuff!" Salvatore looked down at the floor to escape our eyes. I seemed to sense that there might have been a bit of truth to Maria's testimony.

Harry leaned in and whispered to me, "Shake your doodle, the ice cream is melting! Please give them your card, twenty-seven, and have them make an appointment. She sure is pretty, and nice to look at, but I am afraid we have to ditch poor Sal-a-roo-ski and let him fend for himself. He is toast, anyway. The cute chick is shredding him into bits. We have other fish to fry."

I nodded my head and began to think quickly. I took out my cards, a pen from my coat pocket, and wrote a scripture address on the back of it.

"Here, Maria and Salvatore, please look up this scripture and when you return home . . . read it together. I think it will be of great comfort to you. If you still need to talk some more, then my contact information is on the card. Please give my assistant Martha a call, make an appointment and we can talk some more after the holidays."

I handed the card to Maria.

She smiled at me, came over, and gave me a big hug. "Oh, you are such a wonderful man, Pastor Paul! You are very handsome too. I can tell by the look in your eyes that you care about people. We are so happy to have run into you here in the toilet tissue aisle. Aren't we happy, Salvatore?"

Poor Salvatore weakly shook his head in agreement.

"Say Maria, I could use a hug too. After all, I did offer up some good advice as well." Maria came over and gave Harry a big hug. She seemed to thrive on hugs.

"Come along, now Salvatore, you heard what Pastor Paul said about you being wrong!"

"I don't really remember that he actually said that, dear." Salvatore said as he pushed his cart weakly along. Harry and I made our escape and scooted out the aisle in the direction of the frozen foods.

When we were safely clear of the young couple, Harry stopped and abruptly turned towards me.

"Zip and button up that stupid coat, will you, Paul? If one more nutcase stops us, the baby will have been born by the time we get the ice cream!"

I stopped and buttoned the coat up so high that only the top of my eyes poked out from the top of the coat. I pulled the wool cap out of my coat pocket and pulled it down over my head.

I looked like a bank robber hiding my face.

I peered over at Harry with just my eyes exposed, and spoke a muffled question, "How's this? Can you see anything?"

He nodded his head in agreement and we hastily took off towards the frozen food section of the store. Finally, we reached the ice cream aisle. I felt as if we had reached the peak of Mount Everest for the first time. We bent over to check out the two hundred and fifty-six thousand different flavors of ice cream. Our heads went back and forth, scanning the case as if we were watching a tennis match.

"Ya see it, twenty-seven?"

"No? You, thirty-five?"

"You mean that after all of this, they don't have it! Whoever heard of a store that does not have peppermint ice cream?" I stood up for a second, thinking that I had never even heard of peppermint ice cream until about one hour ago, but I stopped short of saying anything.

"Can I help youse two guys?" An older chap who was working the frozen food aisle must have heard us say we were looking for something. He had come over to rescue us. He was almost bald, with a little white beard and very thick glasses on.

Harry looked over at me and pointed. He shouted, "Don't you say a word! Keep your coat and hat just like that! Peppermint ice cream pal, we need ten gallons of peppermint ice cream! Quick!"

The old chap looked at me and shook his head, "Are you cold or something there, chief?" I nodded my head up and down to indicate that I was. He rolled his eyes at me, then bent down and placed his nose and eyes right up against the glass case. It was obvious that even with his eyeglasses on, this guy had a poor set of peepers.

"Ten gallons, oh my, you must be having a party. Let's see here, wintergreen mint, chocolate chip mint, butter mint, spearmint, peanut mint, whiz bang Substantial Industries mint, banana mint, summer mint, spring mint, autumn mint, pumpkin mint, Christmas cookie mint. . .."

"Oh, for the love of Pete! How many mints are there, pal?" Harry was flipping his lid.

"Hey, I only stock 'em. I do not make 'em. Mr. Bluebird chirping in my ear mint, Christmas Tree Mountain mint, Big Boulder beer mint, happy mint, sad mint, Boryeungous flavored mint, Sal Zucchini's famous, garlic-flavored mint, Dingleberry beer flavored mint," on and on, he went down the line.

Harry leaned over to me and whispered in my ear, "What is it, a requirement, to be half-blind to work here? This guy is blind in one eye and can't see out of the other. This is unreal, twenty-seven."

Not willing to risk any slip-ups, I only repeated my head nod, while making sure that I concealed my true identity.

"Nope, sorry pal, we are all out of peppermint." The old chap stood up and blinked his eyes five times at Harry and me as he announced the current status of peppermint ice cream.

That was the final straw. The big guy exploded.

"WHAT! ARE YOU KIDDING ME, PAL? THIS STORE IS OUT OF PEPPERMINT ICE CREAM AT CHRISTMAS TIME! WHAT KIND OF DUMP IS THIS? YOU HAVE EVERY FLAVOR OF ICE CREAM MADE ON THE FACE OF THE EARTH, BUT YOU RAN OUT OF PEPPERMINT!"

Harry calmed down a little, but not much. "I demand to see a manager, call my congressman! What is this, a conspiracy to make young fathers flip their lids, and go nuts?"

Not much seemed to rattle the old store clerk. I am sure

he had run into quite a few irate customers over the years. He wandered over to a phone on the wall, picked it up, and pushed a button. He blew into the phone and we heard his voice come over the public-address system in the store, "Please, the store manager to the frozen food aisle. We have another nutcase looking for peppermint ice cream."

He hung up the telephone and walked over to us. "You're the tenth guy in here today looking for peppermint ice cream. That television commercial has folks all snookered. While you scream at the manager, I will go and double-check the stockroom in the back."

He wandered off as I spoke a low, muffled, "Thank you," through my coat. We stood there for a minute or two, listening to the canned Christmas music loudly broadcasted over the store's public-address system. Just as another verse of, "Silver Bells" was coming on, a nervous looking fellow, wearing thick glasses, and having short, close-cropped, black hair, made an appearance at the top of the aisle and he nervously approached us.

"I am Mike Orsini Junior. I am the manager of Foodworld store number x two-dash y three. What seems to be the trouble here, gentlemen?" He glanced at me and asked, "Are you cold?" I nodded once more. I seemed to recall another Foodworld store manager named Orsini from years ago, but I was not sure that I was correct.

"Look, Orsini Junior. My buddy and I have suffered through broken shopping carts, been accosted by sink peeing lunatics arguing over toilet tissue, been yelled at by old sex-crazed battleaxes, assisted by half-blind, long-haired nitwits, and when we finally make it to the frozen food section, old soda bottle eyeballs, tells us that you are out of peppermint ice cream. What is the deal here? I never run out of my famous Harry Burgers at my restaurant and nightclub! You do know that I am Harry M. Redmond Jr., inventor of the famous Harry Burgers!"

"Harry Burgers, yes sir, we have them, right here in the

frozen section in aisle nine."

Harry was shaking his head. He turned towards me and said, "This boob is a half-blind, half-deaf, clueless, dreamer too, twenty-seven." He was just about to send Orsini Junior to the moon without a rocket ship, when the older chap appeared wheeling a two-wheel hand truck, loaded with peppermint ice cream. Orsini Junior had gone off to show us where the Harry Burgers were, so we just let the poor confused chap go on his own.

"Twenty-seven, quick, we need a cart! You pick it out will ya!" I quickly headed off to obtain a working cart. I had better odds than Harry did of picking out a cart that actually rolled.

"Good work there, soda bottle eyeballs. I knew you would save the day!"

He looked at Harry, blinked and explained, "You were lucky. This transfer shipment just came in from Foodworld store x three dash two. They cannot sell even one gallon of the stuff. The television commercial must not be showing in that area yet."

I was back in a flash with the cart and we loaded up the ice cream. Harry whipped out fifty dollars and stuffed it in the older chap's pocket. "Here put this towards a new pair of eyeglasses, pal. Merry Christmas, you're on the payroll."

"Thanks buddy, hey don't tell, Orsini Junior!" We gave him a wave and headed for the checkout lanes. We were almost clear, one more obstacle, and we were free!

"You stand over there, twenty-seven. I don't want any slip-ups now that we are finally home free." Harry pointed to a spot on the other side of the checkout counters. I nodded and stood there watching as Harry walked up to one of the checkout counters. The cashier was a short, middle-aged woman, who was chewing gum, and loudly snapping it in her mouth.

She, of course, also had on big, thick eyeglasses.

She had her hair all pinned back tightly behind her head

in a little bun. Her head was very thin, straight, and narrow. All I was able to focus upon were her enormous eyeglasses.

"Whatcha got in the cart there, big boy?" She stared over the counter's belt, and leaned over to peer at Harry's cart, loaded with ice cream.

"Ten gallons of Big Bob's, Special Holiday Peppermint Ice Cream!" Harry almost blew her over as he screamed the contents at her.

"Whoa, easy there, my eyes ain't so good big boy, but my ears are just fine! Ten gallons, oh my, you must be having a party."

She continued to lean in and you could see her squint her eyes at the ice cream in a vain effort to see what the label said. Harry moaned and groaned, and I could hear him mumbling something about big, thick glasses as he reached in the cart, pulled one of the gallons out and handed it to the cashier.

"Here! Now, you can focus your eyeballs real close there, honey."

"Thanks, big boy. Now let's see. . .. I need to find a price tag here. She began to squint once more, and she spun the gallon of ice cream around and around, while she peered in at the carton to try to detect the price tag. She moved it in and out, up and down, as her eyeballs tried to focus on the price tag. All the while, Harry stood there ready to blow his cork.

Harry turned to me and shouted, "Remind me to open an eyeglass store in this town next week, will ya twenty-seven! I could make a fortune!" I nodded at him, not moving a muscle, or saying a word, while making sure my disguise was still intact. Other shoppers passed by me and stared nervously at me, while I was standing there like some kind of weird hoodlum, but I did not move an inch in fear of risking that it would expose my secret identity. It was amazing how a simple trip to the Foodworld could turn into some kind of extraordinary adventure.

"Oh yes, here it is, no . . . no, no . . . that is the stock number. Oh, I do not see a price on this one. . .. "

"Give me that!" Harry tore the gallon out of the cashier's hands and pointed at the price tag. "Here it is here, in big, giant, bright, orange letters, one dollar and ninety-nine cents!"

"Oh, thank you, big boy. Now, how many did you say you had?"

The line behind Harry now stretched all the way back to the long-haired guy in the produce aisle.

"TEN GALLONS! GEEZ, MY ICE CREAM IS MELTING, LADY!"

"Oh, hold your horses there, big boy! What is the big deal? I have to look at them and count each of them. Our manager, Orsini Junior, watches everything you know. His father was even worse, but thank goodness, he finally retired."

"Oh, for the love of Pete! Orsini Junior is blind as a bat! He could not see a freight train right in front of his eyes before it ran him over! I am telling you there are ten gallons in there. Please, lady . . . just check them out!"

"Oh, all right! You seem as if you are an honest guy. Impatient, but honest." She focused in and out on the buttons for the cash register, pushed a few of them and presto! A ding-dong here and there and a total popped up in the window of the cash register. She then peered in at the total. Her nose was right up on the numbers when Harry ran around the end of the counter and looked at the total for her.

"It says, twenty dollars and eighty-nine cents with the sales tax. Here is thirty-five bucks. Merry Christmas! Keep the change lady and put it towards a new pair of eyeglasses!" Harry threw the money at her, ran back around the counter, grabbed his cart, and sped off.

"Thanks, big boy, please do not tell, Orsini Junior!"

We made a beeline for the front door. We were just about home free and heading for the Rhino 400 with our precious cargo when out of the corner of my eye . . . I spotted Mrs. Edith Crankshammer! She was walking right in front of us, heading for the front door to the store.

"Run, Harry, run! It is, old lady, Crankshammer!"

"Oh geez, no! This is unreal! Not blabbermouth Crankshammer, the baby will be in college by the time she shuts up! She loves you, Paul! Go, twenty-seven, turn those old jets on, I will block her vision! I hope she does not recognize me!"

I took off with the cart full of ice cream and flew as fast as my legs could take me, still bundled up in my disguise, as I made my way across the lot, while Harry quickly ducked behind a soda machine in the front of the store. I saw Mrs. Crankshammer stop, and look our way, but she did not seem to make the connection, and she hurried into the doors to Foodworld. Harry slunk and lurked his way to the Rhino, darting from car-to-car, while looking over his shoulder. Just in case, Mrs. Crankshammer pulled a swift maneuver and pulled a surprise attack on us by doubling back. He made it to the Rhino 400; we tossed the ice cream in the back, jumped in the vehicle and took off.

"Man! That was close, twenty-seven! That was all we needed, to run into that old bird." I pulled off my wool hat. I could not stand it anymore. I was sweating to death.

"Yeah, yeah, yeah, Harry. That was some adventure! Do you realize how long we have been gone? The girls are going to kill us."

"Nah, stop being such an old lady, Paul, we are fine, I will step on it here, and we will be back in a flash. I sure wish I could have grabbed one of those super rare, ultra-limited-edition Substantial Industries Rhino 500S, with the nine-hundred-cubic-inch, jet pack, super whiz-bang, dual turbo infused, nitro-burner engine. They sold out before I could get one. I always have my eye on the used market for one, though."

"What on earth would you do with that, Harry? As it is, this vehicle rocks."

"Yeah, yeah, yeah, but you know me. It sure would remind me of the old days in the Trans Whizzer running secret agent type guys off of the road!"

We pulled out onto the entrance ramp to the highway when suddenly we noticed red lights flashing behind us. A police officer was pulling us over!

This adventure was not over yet!

"Oh geez, twenty-seven, this is unreal, it is really unreal," Harry complained. "I was not even speeding yet. I cannot even imagine what I am getting pulled over for! Hey, pull your coat off and show him that you are a clergyman!"

I gladly pulled my coat off and tossed it into the back. Harry pulled the Rhino to a stop along the ramp and took out his paperwork. He rolled down the window just as the police officer made his way to the side of the Rhino.

The policeman moved slowly and carefully as he crept up to the side of the vehicle with his right arm held down alongside of his body. He obviously had his hand poised on his gun holster. He was being very cautious, as if we were serious criminals!

"License, registration and insurance card there, sir!" He shouted to Harry. I looked over in the dark as Harry went to hand him the credentials. I recognized the police officer as Charlie Shay, who was one of our parishioners at Reunion Lutheran Church.

"Charlie?" I asked.

Harry looked up and smiled as he said, "Shay-a-roo-ski, it is me, Harry M. Redmond Jr. and Pastor Paul!"

Charlie peered in, took his flashlight, and turned it on me, and then he looked at Harry.

"Oh man, sorry, pastor, sorry, Harry! Man, youse guys had me shook up for a minute. I thought I had a real mess on my hands! I did not recognize the Rhino 400 in the dark, Harry. I am sorry, youse guys! We got a call over the radio that came in from the Foodworld. They reported two suspicious guys running across the lot and jumping into a black Rhino 400. One of the guys had a hood pulled over his head and the other guy was running like a madman. I spotted your vehicle getting on the highway and I thought I had nabbed them."

Harry and I burst out laughing, and Charlie looked a little puzzled.

"Charlie, you have nabbed them. It was us."

"What . . . Pastor Paul?"

"Yes, it is a bit of a long story, but you see, Rose had a craving for peppermint ice cream. . .."

"Oh, yeah, Harry, congrats on the baby coming, man that is great. My wife told me. Thank you also for the donation of all of those bulletproof vests and special winter boots you made to the force. We all appreciated that." Charlie shook Harry's hand through the window. "Sorry to interrupt ya, Pastor Paul."

"No sweat. Anyway, we came over to the Foodworld, and it took forever to get the ice cream. When we came out, who did we almost run right into, but Mrs. Edith Crankshammer!"

Charlie leaned back and whistled as he handed Harry back his paperwork.

"Yes, sir, that is who the store manager, Mr. Orsini Junior, said, made the complaint. Old, flap jaws Crankshammer. Wow, that would have made for a long night, Pastor Paul! Therefore, you pulled your hat over your head and then youse guys made a dash for the Rhino. Wow, that was a close one. She caught me last week when I was walking the beat downtown and it took me two hours to lose her. She even walked with me when I responded to an official call! The only way that I ditched her was to tell her that I had to go to the restroom. I thought she was going to follow me there too."

"Just don't ask her about her rash Charlie, believe me it is a bad scene."

"Hey, Charlie, our ice cream is melting and Rose is waiting. Is there any way that you can kinda break all the rules because I am a big shot, give us an official escort here, and plow the road back to church? We are all hanging out over at the parsonage for dinner tonight, and my poor wife is most likely jumping out of her skin for this ice cream."

"Sure, Harry, I know the drill. Mrs. Shay drove me nuts with cravings for apple strawberry pie. I will call it in on the radio and get clearance. Once they hear that it is an official church business for Pastor Paul and Harry M. Redmond Jr. we can roll. Youse guys are celebrities around here, you know."

"Thank you, Charlie. Hey, will we see you for Christmas Day services?"

"No, I have duty, Pastor Paul, but I will be in church for Christmas Eve."

"Please, come on over to the parsonage with Mrs. Shay and the children for Boxing Day, if you are off. Binky is going all out this year."

"Oh man, Binky is cooking Mum's Roast Beef and Yorkshire Pudding recipes! Yeah, man, we will stop by! Hey follow me guys, I will turn the lights on and we can roll." We did roll up the highway, with the red lights blazing ahead of us. Harry was eating it all up. There was nothing that he enjoyed more than the spotlight.

Finally, we made it back to the parsonage.

We pulled into the driveway, thanked Charlie, and once more reminded him of the invitation for Boxing Day. I grabbed my winter coat and hat from the back of the Rhino and put it all back on as not to face the wrath of Binky. We both made our way up the driveway and headed into the house with our load of precious peppermint ice cream.

We burst into the door and Cocoa Two met us as he

jumped and barked at our joyous return.

"Good boy, you took care of things while we were out!" Harry patted his head as we walked into the kitchen.

"Sorry, that it took us so long, gang, but. . .."

Harry, Cocoa Two, and I stopped in our tracks as we almost bumped into one another. Our mouths dropped at the scene in front of us. We stood there staring, holding our gallons upon gallons of peppermint ice cream in our hands. We stared at Binky, Rose, Paul William, and Heather Sarah, while they happily sat around the kitchen table with half-eaten, ice cream laden bowls set in front of all of them. They were laughing and smiling as they shoveled the last scoops of what appeared to be plain, old, vanilla ice cream into their mouths.

"Oh, hello, dear Paul! Hello, Harry." Binky smiled as she stood up and took the ice cream from our hands. She tugged at my coat and hat and took them off of me while I stood there unable to move. Harry also did not say a word. We were both in shock.

"Hello, darling Harry! I missed you, thank you for running out for me," Rose shouted to Harry.

"Hello, Father! Hello, Uncle Harry!" The children shouted in unison between ice cream scoops.

"It is nice to see that you are listening to me for a change twenty-seven and wearing your winter coat." Binky gave me a quick kiss, and I tried to smile. Binky stood back, fluffed her hair, and explained, "Rose changed her mind. She just wanted good, old, vanilla ice cream, so we went down to the corner store and picked up a gallon or two. I knew from my research that the odds were very high that you would run into a number of delays due to my husband's attire, therefore, we were not worried at your late hour. Did you pick up some potential new parishioners, twenty-seven?"

We both stood there while frozen in time, but we both finally managed to nod our heads.

"Good, I knew it." Binky took my hat and coat as she fluffed her hair at her research accuracies.

"Please, put all the extra ice cream in the freezer downstairs. We can use it for the Christmas social at church tomorrow. I knew that Harry would go overboard and buy ten gallons or more of the ice cream. It will not go to waste. Besides, Cocoa Two is the only one of us that actually enjoys peppermint ice cream. Thank you, so much dear Harry, for the donation of the ice cream to the church. Go and wash up now, I ordered the pizza pies. Paul, please grab a Big Boulder or Dingleberry beer, mix me a Martini, shaken not stirred, and please mix Harry a double Wallcrawler. He does need to relax a bit. Rose will have no alcohol, Purple Pirate beer. They are on the bottom shelf of the refrigerator. Please join us in the living room, dear Paul and Harry. The pizza will be here shortly."

Paul William jumped out of his chair and ran up to me. He looked up and asked me, "Father, can I play you in Warship, after we have pizza? Uncle Harry taught me how to move my ships around on the board so that you will lose. He says that you never cheat, so I will be sure to win."

"Sure, Paul William, sure," I managed to mumble, while Harry was shaking his head at our son, in an effort to stop him from talking and revealing their clandestine plots.

The ladies and the children moved happily into the living room. I took a bowl from the cupboard, opened a gallon of the peppermint ice cream, scooped some out, and dumped it into the bowl. I looked at Harry, who was still standing there numb and staring straight ahead.

"You want some, Harry?"

"Nah, do you, twenty-seven?"

"Nope. Here you go, Cocoa Two." I set the bowl on the floor and Cocoa Two happily jumped into it. As we watched him eat the fruits of our mission, I turned to Harry and asked him, "Do you think Ronzo knows that they now make Boryeungous flavored mint ice cream?"

"Doubt it, twenty-seven. I should have invented it though."

"I have to wonder how the Dingleberry beer mint ice cream tastes."

"I would guess that it is really, really, sweet, Paul. Those Dingleberries are always way too sweet. Say, make sure that Wallcrawler is really strong. Maybe a triple there, twenty-seven. Will ya do that?"

I nodded, walked over to the counter, and grabbed some booze bottles out of the cupboard. I had to mix the drinks for Binky and Harry. As I worked there, I could not help but move the curtain and stare out into the parking lot in front of the parsonage. I looked out, scanned the sky, as well as looked towards the fellowship hall, and the location of the large oak tree. I did not see a thing, except for the twinkling of some Christmas lights that we had strung out on the front porch.

I wondered if angels enjoyed peppermint ice cream.

4

A Difficult Decision

"Mark Davis told me that his older brother Jimmy says you are a long-haired, hippie, who is a little crazy from being hit in the head too many times with hockey pucks," Paul William proudly told me in a loud voice as I walked in the back door of the parsonage after work.

"Well, he may or may not be correct there, Paul William. What did you tell, Mark?"

"I told him that no matter how big he is that I would punch his brother in the nose."

"Oh boy, don't do that, and please, do not let your mother hear you talk like that. You know that she will blame your love of hockey. You cannot go around punching people in the nose, Paul William. Why do you think that Jimmy Davis thinks I am a nutcase? He is in my confirmation class, he serves as an acolyte, and he seems as if he is a calm, young man."

I sat down in a chair in the kitchen and grabbed Paul William. I pulled him up on my knee and looked at him.

"So, what is the inside scoop, Paul William? Why is your old man a little crazy?"

Paul William pushed all of his long, blonde hair up out of his face and looked at me, as he explained, "Because you make the acolytes pour the holy water on the bottom of that big tree out there!" Paul William pointed out in the direction of the fellowship hall.

"Oh, I see! Well, I have done a few things in my day that would make folks think I am a little crazy, but that is not one of them. Trees need water, and holy water used for a blessing, or the baptism of a baby or person, is special water. It can only be good for a tree. Correct?"

Paul William nodded his head in agreement and smiled.

"Don't ever worry about what people say about you, Paul William. When you get a little older, I will teach you what your great grandfather taught me about that. For now, go get ready for dinner. Where is your mother?"

"I ate already. She is doing research upstairs." He jumped off my lap and tore across the house screaming, "Mother, dear Father is home!" I went over to the sink and washed my hands. Something smelled very good. Binky was cooking something, but I could not place the smell.

It was now a few weeks into January and the winter was cold and dark. It had been an inspirational Advent season. The church was packed; it had been a very successful season for Reunion Lutheran Church. After Christmas Day, we had a wonderful Boxing Day celebration with the entire crew of Redmonds, Hobnobbers, Hensons, Wiggins, Boatmanns, Shays, Sharps, and the rest of the gang. It had been a fantastic gathering, and it was extra special with a big feast and celebration.

Now that I had to work every Christmas Eve and Christmas Day, Boxing Day became our special holiday that we could all relax and enjoy together with our friends and family.

Ronzo even saved a special glass or two of his latest, "time bomb in the cupboard" for us all to enjoy. It was indeed a less-fortified version than some of the more legendary past concoctions were. Therefore, everyone stayed in line!

It had been another memorable time in our lives together.

Rose was doing well, Harry had settled down a little with regard to her health and watching her every move, and she looked great. It was now time to get back to work as I had been working on the expansion plans for the church that we had shelved for the Advent season. Now that Advent season had passed, I was working hard on the management and the planning of the construction project. I was meeting with and in discussions with the church buildings and grounds committee, outside banking agencies, and other church groups. We were carefully planning and investigating the construction, funding, and other logistics for the expansion of the church facilities and campus.

The materials and information that Bishop Von Houten had sent to me proved to be very helpful, and I was now knee deep in applying for funding, loans, bonds, and all the other madness that goes along with construction projects. My former life as a contractor sure was helpful now. Contractors, engineers, and architects were no trouble for this long-haired pastor to work with and relate to during the project. Besides, we had a multitude of professional help within our own congregation; therefore, we did not have to look very far for assistance in the construction fields.

The church was full of tradesmen!

Harry's company could do all the steel structural construction as well as some miscellaneous work, Betty Ann Hobnobber and her father's excavation company had already been lined up for the site work. Even Ronzo told me that he would come out of retirement, to supervise and assist on the electrical work, and I was planning to head up the heating and cooling trades. I felt we were in good shape as far as the trades would go.

The main trouble was deciding with the assistance of the "old guard" of the church, where the addition would be, how big, how much, and what it would look like.

The "old guard" of the church could be difficult and exasperating. They were a small group within our congregation that consisted of about ten or fifteen, longtime members, who enjoyed nothing more than to argue, fight, and disagree with every new idea that came along. If it were not for the last remaining, very powerful, charter member who always had my back, as well as the power and support of Dave Sharp and Mrs. Sharp, Harry and Rose, Binky, Mrs. Whipley, Mrs. Crankshammer, Tinky, and Betty Ann, and some others, I am afraid I would wither into a powerless leader.

It was exhausting, because this project forced many of the members to come out of the woodwork, to fight, argue, and offer their own opinions. It was difficult to sort it all out. At times, you would think it was more of a hockey match than a group of Christians. The fighting that went on amongst the old members was brutal. Sometimes, I felt as if the best way for them to settle their disputes was to give them some hockey sticks and let them go a few rounds on each other. I could always ring up my old buddy and retired hockey goon, Pastor Jim O'Malley to help me!

Bishop Von Houten knew the obstacles I faced, and while he could offer very little help, he did make a very good suggestion. Rabbi Goldberg, a few years ago, had experienced a large construction project at a synagogue that he was serving. Bishop Von Houten felt that Rabbi Goldberg could help me with his experiences. I met Rabbi Goldberg and Bishop Von Houten for dinner and a few beers one night, and he offered up some helpful advice on how to manage all the opinions and politics of the membership. Rabbi Goldberg was a great guy, and despite the friendly jabs at one another, he was Bishop Von Houten's best friend. I now felt that I had the information I required for sorting this all out, and it was now just a matter of time, in order to bring it all together. We were creeping closer now to a final game plan.

Binky walked into the kitchen. I stood up and gave her a warm hug and a kiss. She looked great, and she smelled so good. My wife always smelled so good. I held her for a long time. It was so nice just to hold her.

"Beef stew tonight, dear twenty-seven. Paul William has already eaten, as have I. You are late. I gave him some research assignments to finish, so he is off on them now."

"I have already seen him. He told me all about how some boys at school think that I am a nutcase. Stew sounds great Binky. It sure smells great! Nothing like a stew on a cold winter day. How is Heather Sarah feeling? Can I go see her or is she still sleeping?"

"No, please let her sleep, twenty-seven, she is better since I spoke with you an hour or so ago. Paul, you do realize that you called about her at least ten times today. She just has a little head cold. She is fine. I gave her some soup and a little dish of stew, and she is sleeping now. If she sees you, she will jump all around and it will pick her fever back up."

"Got it Binky, I understand. I will be a good little goalie and stay back in my net."

"Good, now let me dish you out some stew. No beer for you tonight, you need a clear head for the big project meeting tonight. What time does it start?"

"Seven o'clock. I tried to arrive home earlier, but it was one of those days." I looked up at the clock and made a note of the time. I had a bit of extra time to enjoy my dinner before the meeting.

"Tonight, is the final vote of the construction steering committee, is it not?"

"It is. I am curious to review the final plans that the architect has come up with, and to see if it will all fly with the membership. On the steering committee, tonight, I only have allies in Mrs. Whipley, our one charter member, Dave, Harry, and Mrs. Crankshammer. I am afraid that it is going to be a long meeting. Mrs. Crankshammer alone will take up to an hour just to state her case. My main concern with the early plans, conceptual drawings, and proposals was with the addition to the fellowship hall. The sanctuary location and plans looked great. I loved those ideas. It was just the new classrooms off the hall, which bugged me."

My wife seemed very unconcerned. She always had the utmost confidence in me, and my efforts. She displayed the confidence by telling me, "It will go fine, dear husband, you will know what to do, you always do, Paul."

Binky set a dish of stew in front of me and I eagerly shoveled it in. I was hungry. She sat down at the table next to me and smiled.

"This is great, Binky. Thank you. I will need to work out on the weekend. You know that I gained a few pounds over the holidays."

"Nonsense! Good, I am glad that you gained some weight. You need it. You still are way too skinny, and you work way too much. Harry is correct in his statement that you are always running yourself around ragged."

I smiled at my wife and her concern about me.

"I could still play. You know that I could, Binky. I could still stop the puck."

She shook her head and did not answer me. I think she thought I was crazy too. I finished my stew, cleaned up, changed into some fresh clothes and I was ready to go. It sure was nice to open your front door, walk across a parking lot, and go to work. I looked in on the children, who now were both sleeping, kissed Binky goodbye, and made my way to the door.

Binky was sitting in her chair watching some television, doing some handwork on her latest throw blanket. With my hand on the doorknob, I looked back at Binky while she said, "It will go fine, twenty-seven. You will not allow a marble past you! Be sure to wear your winter coat!" I smiled at her and made my way out the door. As I walked over to the church offices, I glanced over towards the fellowship hall and I could see the large oak tree looming over the top of the building. Even in the dark, I could make it out, towering above all of us.

The room for the steering committee meeting was overflowing with people and with "stuff." The architect had brought easels, boards, charts, and graphs with him to make his final presentation on the design of the additions as well as providing some supporting information. The information and equipment took up an awful lot of space in the room. In retrospect, we should have moved the meeting to a larger room; it was going to be close enough quarters. After greeting everyone in the room, I settled in a seat between Harry and Dave.

I leaned over and spoke with Harry, "How is Rose?"

Harry nodded, "Good, all is well. Linny and Ronzo are down for the week, and they are hanging out together tonight. She sends her best. Ronzo told me he has his tools with him in the truck if you need him. Ya know, I am not worried about this meeting. It will go the way you want it, Paul. We have enough folks on our side."

Dave Sharp poked me in the side and whispered to me, "Johnson is here, Pastor Paul."

I looked up and spotted Mr. Chris Johnson entering the room. He was our chief nemesis on the "old guard" group of Reunion Lutheran Church. No matter what the majority or I desired, you could always count on Johnson to vote the other way. He was a chronic whiner and a major crybaby. He weaseled his way onto the steering committee because he, in a very roundabout way, worked in the construction business. Therefore, the perception was that he was an expert on all the subjects. He actually knew very little, but he was very convincing, dynamic, and was a master of weaving flim-flam. He could go on and on and convince folks that he actually knew what he was talking about on virtually any subject. In reality, as Dave and Mrs. Whipley would say, he just enjoyed hearing himself speak.

Mr. Johnson settled into a chair directly opposite us on the other side of the table. He nodded his head to me, "Evening, Pastor Paul. Evening, Dave and Harry. How are youse guys?"

I answered for all of us, "We are fine, Chris. How is it going?"

"Good, good, I am looking forward to getting this project going now. Way too much talk and no action now. The membership is becoming anxious. We need some forceful action from leadership now."

Shot number one across my bow! Mrs. Whipley rushed into the room. She was removing her coat while her eyes were scanning the room. I was sure she heard Johnson's comments. Mrs. Whipley was old, but she could hear a pin drop from one hundred yards away.

Mrs. Whipley, who was now sitting down in her chair next to Harry, leaned over and whispered to us, "I am going to sock that clown right in his smug puss before the night is over. He does realize that he is that obnoxious. I am quite sure of it." Harry patted Mrs. Whipley on the back and told her to relax. Mrs. Crankshammer came into the room with her jaws flapping already, as she spoke to some poor soul who had walked in with her. Mrs. Crankshammer sat down next to Mrs. Whipley. Mrs. Whipley immediately went into a vain and futile attempt to stop Mrs. Crankshammer from talking. But until the meeting actually started, it would be hopeless.

I scanned the room and counted the votes. I did not really know why I was ready to have a face-off on this plan. I just had a gut feeling that there was going to be something that was not going to pass muster with me. I had learned from playing goal to go with my first instincts. We had Johnson and five others on the "old guard" side and five on our side. I was missing my old buddy from the charter member group. He had told me after worship services the other day that his legs were bothering him, and he had been having a difficult time dealing with the fact that his wife had passed away just a few months earlier. Perhaps he could not make it out this evening for this meeting.

That was not good, as he alone yielded more power and influence than anyone in the entire room had. I knew that without his support, we were out-gunned.

The architect set up his easel and conceptual drawings and pictures, and he was now ready to begin his presentation, when the door opened, and the charter member slipped into a seat. He was an elderly man, and he limped a little but made his way rather quickly to a seat on the other side of Mrs. Crankshammer, greeted everyone, smiled, waved to us, gave Harry and me the thumbs up signal, and sat down. He had made it.

Harry nudged me in the side and smiled. He knew we were now good to go.

"We have the advantage now on the teams, twenty-seven. Power play is over. Get in the net and stop the biscuit, will ya," Harry whispered to me. Harry could sense my apprehension about something, and he wanted me to know he would rally the troops to support my ideas. He knew me so very well.

The chairperson asked me to open the meeting with a prayer and a few words. I performed both, and the chairperson called the meeting to order. The presentation began, and the architect began his outline of the vision, and plans he had come up with for the church. He droned on for a very long time, showing us plans, drawings, budgets, and other endless information on boards that he had set up on an easel. The architect was a relative of a church member, and he had reduced his fee for the church as a favor. He was doing an outstanding job; he appeared as if he was very detail oriented, and to be on top of his game. I appreciated his efforts.

He had asked us to hold questions or comments until he had finished with his presentation. That request was causing Mrs. Crankshammer, intense pain and suffering. For her to sit this long without speaking was a difficult experience for her.

As we listened to the details of the presentation, I made a note that the plan for the sanctuary had some minor changes implemented over the original plans. The architect did utilize our initial feedback, and he made changes that were definite enhancements. I was feeling good about the plans that I had seen so far, and I became a little more comfortable. The presentation moved from the sanctuary, over to his proposals to add on more classrooms for education on the rear wing of the fellowship hall. The existing classroom space was woefully inadequate, and the Sunday school as well as the adult education groups had been pleading for more rooms. I actually had a class of adult Bible study that utilized my office for meetings when I was busy with other duties on Sundays.

My feeling of comfort was short-lived. When I spotted where the proposed location for the addition of the new education wing to join into the existing structure for fellowship hall was, I immediately sat forward in my chair and clenched my hands with tension.

I felt a cold shiver run up and down my spine when I heard the architect explain, "There is an existing, rather large, oak tree right about here, which will need to be cut down and the root structure dug out."

The architect was showing us the location of the tree on one of the diagrams presented to us on the easel in front of the room.

He continued with the explanation, "It will add a few thousand dollars to the budget to remove it correctly, but it is a better location for the structure than we had previously proposed. There is a utility easement in the original location that would propose a much greater obstacle than removing this large tree would."

I shifted uneasily in my chair and sat back, but in adherence to the architect's request, I did not ask any questions, nor did I comment.

I was not very pleased with the original location of the education addition, but this location was far worse, the tree needed to stay. It was, in my opinion, historic to the church property, and there was something special about the tree. The strange thing was that—I was not exactly sure what it was about the tree, which was so special. All I really knew was what Mrs. Whipley had told me, and of course, after my recent discovery of Pastor Braun's notes, my continued tradition of pouring the water upon the trunk. Until just a few months ago, I had not really paid much mind to the tree, but now, for some reason, I focused upon it quite frequently.

I had followed the eyes of everyone at the table, and they all seemed pleased. Only Mrs. Whipley seemed to react at all, when she heard the news of the potential removal of the tree mentioned. I spotted her look quickly over in my direction. She studied my face, then she looked back down at some papers, which she held in her hands. Harry also sensed that something had stirred my emotions. He sat next to me without moving, but he was glancing at me out of the corner of his eye. He had picked up my body language that I had some concerns as to the tree removal.

"The tree is a fine, red oak specimen, very tall, and straight, and the wood will be very valuable for lumber. I would think that we could arrange for the church to recover most of the costs of removal of the tree in lumber value. In fact, I feel the church will even make a few dollars on the tree! The correct connections will pay a great deal of money for some oak of this exceptional quality. I did find it very unusual for a red oak such as this one to have grown so large in the almost forty years since its planting. Red oaks do grow faster than other oak species, but this one is huge. It must have enjoyed the location!"

The architect chuckled a bit at his comment and thoughts and then he continued, "My assumption is that the tree was part of the original landscape construction project, regardless, it is very large for its age."

The presentation concluded, the architect sat down and awaited the onslaught of opinions, questions, and concerns. Mrs. Crankshammer raised her hand right away, and when the chairperson of the committee recognized her, she was off to the races. I guess the chairperson thought that we might as well let Mrs. Crankshammer loose and allow her to get it all out of the way. Our only hope was that somehow, someway, Mrs. Whipley could control her friend's loose jaws and manage to reel her in within an hour or so. After we politely listened to Mrs. Crankshammer beat to death, some kind of moot point of something that made very little sense, I spotted Harry sending me one of our famous hand signals. He wanted to meet in order to see what was bugging me. I excused myself to use the restroom, of which I knew Harry would be right behind me.

As I got up and passed the charter member at the end of the table, he leaned into me and caught my ear.

"I will follow your lead, Pastor Paul. If you are pleased, then I will vote with you." I placed my hand on his shoulder and nodded. It was wonderful to have such profound trust and support from such a key person.

I went to the restroom, and sure enough, Harry met me in the hallway. Dave Sharp also appeared right behind him.

"What's bugging you, twenty-seven? I spotted the look on your face." Harry knew me so well.

Dave joined us. He smiled, and looked at the both of us as he said, "Hey, I had to get out of there. Crankshammer is tearing the joint up. I knew youse guys had some kind of pow-wow planned. I know your hand signals now, too. The duck quacking thingy in the air, means to head for the restroom."

"Well, men, it is the oak tree, I would rather not see it go."

"The tree? It is just a big, old, tree, twenty-seven. You have about a million of them around here. The property is full of trees. Did you suck down a bunch of Big Boulders before you came here tonight?" Harry seemed surprised at the source of my apprehension. Dave looked at me as he knew more of the history of the tree than what Harry did.

"No boss, it is a special tree, I know that Pastor Paul has recently gone back to sprinkling the tree with holy and baptismal water, just like Pastor Braun did."

"You have? Really Paul, you dump holy water on a tree?" I nodded my head in response to Harry's words. The big guy seemed taken back at my sudden wandering into the unknown world of strange ritual practices.

I was usually so conservative.

"It is a long story, Harry, but the long and short of the story is that I found some notes a month or so ago that Pastor Braun began the practice of pouring the water on the tree, way back when the property was first built. Pastor Braun was the first pastor assigned here when the church relocated to this property. He presided over the construction of the facilities. Dave knew him very well."

Harry looked at Dave and asked in typical Harry fashion, "Was he a whacko or a loon, Sharpie?"

Dave shook his head and answered, "No way boss, he was a good man, passed away way too young. He was a good guy. He was really smart like, Pastor Paul is."

Harry nodded and then looked back at me.

I continued, "He sensed the tree was not going to survive from when it was first planted. He began the practice of dumping the water from a baptism, or any other blessed water, upon the roots and trunk. I read it in a journal that he kept from back in 1960. I found the journal in my office. It sure seemed to work as you can see it is quite a tree. I know it is just a big, giant, tree. I assure you, guys, I am not getting overly soft or sentimental, but besides the water connection, I just dislike killing trees like that. They are part of God's creation plan too you know."

Harry leaned on the hallway wall and pushed his hair back from his forehead.

"Yeah, yeah, yeah, I get that Paul, but it is the correct spot to go with the addition. It will save us a lot of dough. To deal with the utility easement and all that mumbo jumbo, will be a little rougher. What do you think, Sharpie?"

Dave looked at me, then at Harry, and then back at me, "It is a nice tree . . . but, it is just a tree, Pastor Paul."

I smiled, as I knew my friends were doing their best to see my side, but they were not following my reasoning.

"I understand. I have to warn you that, in order for us to defend the tree, it is going to get a lot worse in this meeting. Once she successfully manages to shut up, Mrs. Crankshammer, Mrs. Whipley, eventually is going to have her turn to speak. She will protest the tree removal because she believes that angels from Heaven circle around it on Saturday nights."

Dave and Harry both sighed at exactly the same time.

Harry spoke up while shaking his head, "You have got to be kidding me! Now, we are going to join her in the defense of a tree with angels floating around it. C'mon, Pastor Paul! Whipley is a nice old bird, but she is a loon. No one is going to take us seriously if she is spouting off all that pie in the sky, loony stuff. Look, Paul, you know that Sky taught me to believe in many things that I cannot explain and neither can you. If you think this is some kind of plan from God, well, then I am with you. I am not the kind of guy who goes around doubting anything. I have seen too much. We just need to have a strategy that makes sense. The old guard and Johnson will run you out on a rail, if you go back in there and agree with Whipley on some kind of, Old Testament angelic fantasies."

Dave nodded in agreement and I knew Harry was right.

"Guys, honestly, I do not know what I think. I just think

that there is a reason that Pastor Braun saved that tree, that is all I am saying."

"Twenty-seven, you are the smartest guy in the world. You had better come up with something . . . maybe, to stall them, until we can cover some more of the angles. I am thinking that old man Hobnobber and I can work some connections with big shots at the utility companies to work some kind of deal on the easement. Go in there and stall them for some extra time. Ya never know what we may come up with in the next day or so. If you feel that strongly about it, we are with you. I may not understand it, but we are with you."

"I will come up with something. We better get back in there and see if Mrs. Crankshammer has finished yet."

Dave looked down at his watch and shook his head. "I doubt it, Pastor Paul."

The three of us walked in the room and we heard Mrs. Whipley saying, "Edith, Edith, that's enough now, Edith, we all get it now. EDITH! EDITH! Will you please shut up now?"

Mrs. Crankshammer finally stopped speaking as her friend had somehow managed to shut her up. The committee members who were sitting around the table were all now holding their heads in pain from the long chatter of Mrs. Crankshammer. The three of us sat back down at the table.

Mrs. Crankshammer looked at us, then smoothed her hair out, tugged at her dress a bit, and smiled. Of course, she had to say just one more thing, "Well, I can add a little more information and some of my additional opinions later. I would like to see what Pastor Paul thinks of all of this."

Everyone in the room looked at me. I looked up from my notepad and simply said the truth, "I have only one item that I would like to discuss, so please go around the rest of the room. I would enjoy hearing what everyone else is thinking."

The chairperson acknowledged my comments and around the room, we went. On and on, the discussion continued for well over an hour and a half. The hour was growing very late. I half-heartedly listened to the comments, questions, and some concerns, while in my mind, I was running around and around what I was going to do about the tree.

I kept telling myself that it was just a tree. It was nothing special. It was just a tree. For some reason, the thought that it was so much more than just a tree would not go away.

Harry had some comments, Dave added a few here and there, but for the most part, it seemed as though everyone was very satisfied with the plan. Johnson and his old guard side of the table seemed very pleased. The architect implemented most of the suggestions that they had requested from previous meetings, therefore, they felt as though he adopted and addressed their agenda and concerns.

I knew the decisive moment was arriving, and sure enough, here we were about to go. The chairperson asked Mrs. Whipley what she thought, and we were off to the weirdo races!

"Well, I think this is all great and wonderful. My dear husband would be so pleased to see such wonderful things happening here at Reunion Lutheran Church. I do have a great concern with the removal of the oak tree, though. I know for a fact that particular tree is a holy tree. It is indeed, very special. Just after this past Thanksgiving, I met with Pastor Paul at great length, to explain how that tree is the center of attraction for angels that arrive here every Saturday night and visit the church. They project a beam of light from Heaven on that tree, and for some reason, it is of great interest to them. I have seen it many times with my own eyes. To remove it, would, in my opinion, be a grave and serious error."

Chris Johnson leaned forward in his chair and placed his hands upon the table. I watched the architect's eyes roll back in his head and he sighed. I knew that he felt that this was going way too easily up until this point.

"Angels, Mrs. Whipley. You now, see angels in trees?" Johnson was stunned at the level of weirdness of this one. I heard Harry sigh a little. I knew that he was hoping that I had a plan, and that I planned to move in quickly on the heels of Mrs. Whipley's statement.

Mrs. Whipley dug in hard for this one.

The dear woman believed what she believed.

She stuck to her guns, "I do! I have had extensive discussions with Pastor Paul about this. He assures me that there are indeed angels in Heaven. I firmly believe that they watch over us here at Reunion Lutheran Church."

Johnson smiled, since there was nothing that fit more perfectly in his mind than to see me locked into a sticky wicket. He was not a fan of the long-haired number, twenty-seven. He knew that Mrs. Whipley was one of my biggest supporters as well as a large donor to Reunion Lutheran Church. He wanted to see how I would handle this one. The old guard was never very thrilled with having a long-haired hippie pastor as their leader anyway, even if I did assist in some way of bringing Reunion Lutheran Church back from the brink of extinction.

In their minds, I was now expendable.

Behind the scenes, the work of the church could be as ruthless as any hockey game. Thankfully, this group was certainly a minority within our ranks.

"So, Pastor Paul, since you are our spiritual leader, and our *perceived* overall leader of sorts, how do you think we should handle this situation of angels and the tree that seems to be in the way of progress?" Johnson's tone was so condescending that it seemed as if it even embarrassed his fellow old guard supporters.

I felt Harry give me a kick under the table. I did not dare

look at Harry for fear that he was turning towards the eye of the tiger in his eyes. I knew he was close to leaping across the table and putting an "O'Malley type beating" on poor Mr. Johnson.

I felt a little flow come over me, it was not too strong, but I was feeling good. I flipped all of my hair up over my shoulders and pushed it back from my face, to exaggerate the length of my hair, and burn Johnson's backside just a little more.

I knew that would fire them all up.

"Certainly, there are angels. There is little doubt—the scripture is quite clear." I pulled my Bible out from under my notepad and tapped it with my hand.

"In the interest of time, I will not read the exact verses, but I would hope that all of us share in Mrs. Whipley's faith and belief that they watch over all of us! I see no reason at all to dispute what Mrs. Whipley has said. Be it angels, saints, or whoever, in the trees, or in our hallways, or in our communion service, we just have all witnessed a profound and stunning display of faith, in which Mrs. Whipley has testified to all of us. She has displayed her insightful beliefs and had the courage to declare it in front of this committee, and after all—that is why we are all here. We are all here to justify our faith. I admire her forthright and honest witness to her love of the Lord, as well as her scripture testimony. We are all justified by our faith alone. It is our heritage and our universal belief as Lutherans!"

I smiled at Mrs. Whipley, who smiled back. I decided to call in Johnson's cards and lean in hard on him.

The old hockey goalie was now back. I was defending my net.

"Chris, I am sure that you also have that type of faith too. Don't you? Would you also care to witness your faith in front of the committee? Please, share with us, just as Mrs. Whipley has tonight, in unabashedly sharing her own beliefs and strong faith."

Caught in his own smug trap, he had little choice but to agree with the old woman's testimony of both scripture and faith. Johnson slowly sighed, and then nodded his head, as did his old guard sidekicks.

Johnson finally spoke up, "Yeah, yeah, yeah, sure, I share in the faith of which is the basis of being a Lutheran. In the interest of time, perhaps we can skip my own testimony as to the level of my own faith."

I smiled at his reluctance. Harry kicked me under the table again, as if he was tapping my pads as he did years ago, on the ice.

Mrs. Crankshammer jumped into the fray. She now was thrilled that Johnson himself conceded and confirmed Mrs. Whipley's faith and accuracy.

"As usual, Pastor Paul is correct! It is all of our beliefs and the basis for us to be Lutherans!" She echoed my words and spouted off proudly.

I started speaking right away to discourage Mrs. Crankshammer from going on any longer. Now that I had neutralized the old guard by utilizing the basis for our Lutheran faith, (thank you, Martin Luther) I also had another ace in my deck that I was going to use right now.

"I think that now lost in the conversation of faith, angels, and their exact whereabouts is another fact." Turning towards the architect, I spoke to him, "Sir, my wife Binky Henson does spend quite a bit of time checking into things. She is a bit of a researcher of various things, and I think she happens to be very good at it! You do know, Mrs. Henson, do you not?"

"Oh yes, Pastor Paul! Mrs. Henson is wonderful. She is very detailed in her research, to say the least. I attended one of her classes at the community college just last year. She is quite remarkable."

"Oh good, very nice. Yes, well, just the other day, Mrs. Henson and I were discussing the project, and she reminded me that the local laws of both the township, and the county, have a tree coverage ordinance. Were you aware of that?"

The architect turned his mouth up into a little frown, so I knew he had not checked into that. "No, Pastor Paul. I missed that one. Please thank Mrs. Henson for backing me up on that one. It would be premature to speak of pulling out trees right now and calculating our budget until I check into that. It may very well be that we are still all right, we just may have to replace trees that we remove, and that will, of course . . . adjust our numbers."

"Yes indeed, I agree. We need to be a bit more accurate on our numbers to have a final vote. I will also convey your appreciation to Mrs. Henson."

The architect smiled a weak smile. He had missed that item, but thank goodness, Binky was always on top of her game!

Our charter member raised his hand, and he finally spoke up, "In light of the lateness of the hour, I move that we table a vote. Please have the minutes record a preliminary agreement of all of these plans, until we can check into the local ordinances, and then determine how much money this will cost us. It may very well be okay, but I think we need to be sure before we go knocking down huge trees that will cost a fortune to replace."

Harry seconded the motion, and the chairperson put it to a vote. The old guard was not happy, but there was very little they could do to dispute the facts. We conducted a polling of the committee, and everyone agreed to gather the missing information and then meet in a few days for a final vote. Thanks to Binky, and an innocent conversation that we had based upon some of her facts, I had stalled just enough time to pray and think about this one, a little more.

I kept telling myself that it was just a tree, just a big, old oak tree. For some unknown reason, I just needed to be sure.

The meeting broke up, and we all ducked out quickly,

making sure that we avoided Mrs. Crankshammer. She had captured the architect in a corner, so we all left him to fend for himself and ducked out. After all, the architect had quoted an upfront price; therefore, we did not pay his fee on a per hour basis.

It was late, so we were happy to make an escape. I did meet Mrs. Whipley in the hallway and assured her that I would call her in the next day or so to discuss the tree a bit more. She was thrilled. That was going to be an interesting meeting for sure. I thanked our charter member, bid him goodnight, and off we went. Soon, it was just Harry, Dave, and I standing in the cold, January air in the middle of the parking lot.

"Nice work in there whipping up that razz-a-ma-tazz to push back on Johnson. I swear that guy is such a doofus. It was great. You held the line just long enough. Now what are you going to do?"

"Thanks, Harry. I just need a little time to think about it."

Harry put his hand upon my shoulder, and told me, "Paul, it is just a tree. It is just a tree, but you do what you need to do and let us know. You know we all believe in you and will follow your lead. I have to get home to Rose. It is really late now."

I bid them both goodnight and watched as Dave and Harry climbed into their vehicles. They both drove off into the night. I stood there for quite a long time, staring into the blackness over in the direction of the tree. The stars made a silent backdrop over the landscape. It was a clear, spectacular winter evening. The oak tree stood there, tall, strong, and silent. If it could speak for itself, I wondered what it would say. I simply could not explain the connection. I knew that I had found that journal for a reason, but for what reason, I was not sure. Sometimes, the answers are always right there behind your closed eyelids, and all you need is faith to make you open your eyes.

I needed to pray for faith to open my eyes.

A strong winter wind picked up, and I walked closer to the fellowship hall. I could hear the wind whipping through the tree's mighty oak branches. A handful of stubborn, dried up, old leaves still clung desperately to the branches in random packs here and there. Somehow, as I stood there listening, and watching in awe as the wind moved the mighty branches with such ease, I could not help but think that perhaps in all of its power, the wind was trying to tell me the tree's purpose.

Perhaps.

I walked through the back door of the parsonage and wandered into the living room. Binky was still in the same chair working on her latest handwork creation. I was sure that it was a baby blanket for Rose and Harry. She looked up at me and smiled.

"Please turn off the television, Paul. Oh my, you look so tired. Sit down in your chair here and tell me how it went."

I switched the television off, gave Binky a kiss, and sat down in my chair next to her.

"Would you like a cup of tea? It is very late."

"No, thanks, I am fine." I let out with a deep sigh and pushed back in the chair to extend the footrest. "How is Heather Sarah?"

"Fine. She is sleeping. She is fine. Paul William is fine too. They are both sound asleep. Everything is okay here, twenty-seven."

"I am happy to hear that Heather Sarah is feeling better. Well, the meeting was good, in fact, very good. Johnson was his usual self, but it all went very well, actually, except for one item. The huge oak tree is in the way of the construction of the education wing and it will need to come down."

Binky frowned.

"Oh my, I know that is causing you some conflict. I was afraid that side of the building would present a troublesome situation. There is a utility easement on that side. I remember researching the layout and seeing it on a site plan at the library."

"You are correct, dear Binky, and the logical solutions are for us to move the addition up a bit and bypass the easement. That is, of course, right where the tree is located."

"I see, but easements can be expensive, time consuming, and tricky, Paul. I know you feel that Pastor Braun saved the tree, but it is just a tree. You could plant a new one in another location, somewhat near to the original tree's location. Why do you feel the need to preserve this specific tree?" Binky leaned in for a long, intense, Binky stare. She was probing a bit, I did not have anything concrete to hang my hat on, and my wife sensed that. She was, after all, very factual.

"I do not know, just that I should. It is faith. I only have a gut faith that I should. I stalled them tonight for a vote, so that I could think, pray, and come to a decision. I remembered what you had said about making sure we had checked into the local tree coverage ordinances and adhering to their requirements. The architect missed that, so he needs to recheck his numbers. Your research bought me a few extra days to think. Thank you, Binky."

She fluffed her hair and smiled at me.

"He was not very detail oriented in class either, Paul. I passed him with a seventy-percentile grade or thereabouts. Please let me double check all of his work before you proceed."

"I will. Sure thing, Binky." I smiled and thought how I would not want to have to be on the receiving end of a grading exercise in a class conducted by Binky. She was one tough cookie. I leaned back in the chair as my wife stood up.

Binky walked over by me and stood over me as she said, "Please come and get washed up for bed. You need to rest now. The answer will come to you." Binky reached out her hands to me to invite me to come along with her.

"I have the answer. The tree needs to stay. I need to find a workaround. Perhaps, between Harry and your father, we can find a connection to work on the utility situation."

Binky nodded, but she did not answer me. Instead, she led me by my hand up to our bedroom. I felt that she was guiding me to sleep on the decision before making a final choice. I could tell that Binky did not agree with me that the tree should stay, but I think deep down, she did not want to state that fact right at this moment.

I washed up and changed for bed. By the time that I climbed into our bed, Binky was already sound asleep. As I laid there in the bed, staring at the ceiling, I could hear my wife breathing softly as she does when she is in a deep sleep. Binky was tired too. It had been a long day for the both of us.

I prayed softly to myself, "Lord, guide me, I need to make the right choice, guide me to which direction that I should take."

The next thing I knew, I awoke to what I thought was a lightning flash in our bedroom. I shot upright as though I was frightened out of my wits. I rubbed my eyes and my forehead while I glanced at the clock.

It was shortly after two in the morning.

I looked over at Binky and she was still fast asleep. She had not moved. I then realized that sweat covered my body from the top of my head to my toes. My long mop of hair was wet and stringy, and my pillow was soaked. I shook and trembled from cold chills while I pulled the covers off me. There had been no flash of light. It must have been a dream or my imagination. There was nothing here in our room. How could we have had an electrical storm in the middle of the winter? The power was still on, so it could not be an electrical problem.

I then recalled that the flash had come in a dream. On

the other hand, was it a dream? I swear that I had dreamt that a storm had come, and a bolt of lightning had taken down the big tree.

The tree was gone. Vaporized to ashes right before my eyes. In addition, all I had right now in my head was a Bible verse reference. I could not shake the book of Job verse fourteen, something, something.

What was the missing number? It was embedded somewhere deep in my mind. I could not remember the words, but I saw some numbers clearly.

Why was I so confused?

I jumped up out of bed and hurriedly moved down the hallway to look in on the children. I checked on Heather Sarah, then Paul William. They were sound asleep in their beds and all was well.

I felt as if I was full of fever. Oh great, I have caught some kind of bug, maybe what Heather Sarah had for the last few days.

I felt the strong need to check the entire house. I crept slowly downstairs, shaking and trembling the entire way. There I was, a former professional athlete, and I barely had the strength to make it down a flight of stairs!

What had happened to me?

I checked every inch of our home. Everything was quiet and secure. I pulled the curtain aside in the kitchen and stared out into the darkness. There it was, the tree was still there, and all was calm and quiet. No wind, no lights, no angels, or spaceships. No sign of Mrs. Whipley screaming, or running across the parking lot.

Nothing . . . but an eerie silence.

I felt awful. I climbed back upstairs, and headed for the bathroom, when Binky walked out of our bedroom and met me in the hallway. She had heard me get up, and I had awoken her.

"Oh, Paul, are you ill? You look terrible. You are flush with fever!"

"Sorry, Binky, I didn't mean to wake you, I will be fine, please go rest, I just need to wash up."

I ran a washcloth under the cold water and placed it on my forehead while Binky grabbed a blanket and she covered me.

I was shaking like a leaf in a windstorm.

"I think I have come down with the same bug which Heather Sarah had."

"She did not have this type of bug, Paul. You are suffering from something more than a head cold. You are full of pain and fever. I have never seen anyone tremble as badly as you are trembling right now. Please take some aspirin. I will get you a cup of water." Binky was now holding my forehead, feeling for my body temperature.

I took a bottle of aspirin from the medicine cabinet and shook two of them out into my hand. As I waited for the cup of water, I sat down on the lid of the toilet and held my head in my hands. I felt as if my old hockey nemesis, Jim O'Malley had stopped by to bash me in the head with his stick about one hundred times and annihilate me. Every muscle in my body was screaming. Yet as badly as I felt, I still could not shake these thoughts deep in the recesses of my mind.

"Please, dear Binky, I need a Bible, grab the Bible from the side of our bed." Binky had returned, and she handed me the cup of water. I swallowed down the two pills.

"Oh, please Paul, please stop! You need to rest."

"I will, Binky. Please, could you get it for me? I promise it will be just a minute. I need you to look up a verse. The Book of Job, please look . . . somewhere around chapter fourteen or so."

My wife shook her head at me as she stood in the doorway. I shivered, shook, and I started the words in my mind, and then I spoke them aloud.

"For there is hope for a tree, if it were to be removed. . .. The Book of Job, Fourteen. . .."

I lost the rest of it. I just could not find the words. My mind was spinning, and I had no control of my thoughts. The verse tore and nagged at me with such force that it was hard to think straight. What was happening?

I looked at her from under the blanket with the sweat running off me. I was sweating worse than the third period of a hockey game when the sweat would run like a river off the end of my fiberglass mask. My eyes must have been pleading. Binky looked at me for a moment, and then she turned and disappeared.

I then recalled some more of what I was searching for, and I paraphrased the verse as close as I could from my memory, "If the tree is removed or taken down, something, something, about growing once more. . .."

Binky returned wearing her reading glasses, holding the Bible in her hands—she had heard me stumbling over the words. She had the Bible opened up to a page already.

Binky finished my memory, "I think this is it, Paul. You are correct, as I have found it in the book of Job. Chapter fourteen, verses seven to around nine or so. In the interest of your health, I am going to paraphrase it and not read all the scripture, Paul. You need to stop this and get some rest! Basically, the verse says, that even if the tree is cut down, the tree will once more sprout again somewhere, and the branches of it will never, ever cease."

That was it!

I suddenly stopped shaking and trembling.

I looked up at my wife from under the blanket draped over me, with sweat dripping off my long locks of hair, and the edge of my beard.

I managed to smile widely at her, "I was wrong, my dear Binky. I was dead wrong, and for whatever reason, I now know that I was wrong. The tree needs to be cut down."

5

Recharge!

I, remarkably, felt a lot better after Binky had read the remainder of the Bible verse to me and the aspirins set in. I am not exactly sure what had happened to me, if it was some sickness, or my emotions that had overtaken me. I insisted on sleeping the rest of the night in my easy chair in the living room. I did not want to put Binky to any more of a risk of catching whatever bug I had contracted. Odds were good that I already had subjected my poor wife to the bug during the night and early morning. Binky prepared me a hot cup of tea, with some natural honey mixed in. I sipped the tea and assured her to go back to sleep.

I sat alone in the dark in my chair with two blankets covering me. I no longer felt feverish, nor was I shaking or shivering.

I felt peaceful, calm, and relaxed.

I had come to a decision, and I was one hundred percent confident that I was correct in my decision. I could not tell anyone why, or what exactly had brought me to this conclusion, I could only tell you that after the evening's very strange events, I was certain, beyond a shadow of a doubt that it was the correct way to proceed. It was very strange, and I had no explanation for the entire situation.

I put my favorite record, "Close to the Crevice," on the record player that I kept next to my easy chair, placed my headphones on, and sat back down in the chair. I think I listened to about five minutes of the recording and I was off into a dream world.

I woke up to daylight filtering through the living room window. I had a terrible thought that I had no idea what time it was, and it was obvious that I had overslept and that I had missed work. Oh boy, I had some important appointments this morning! It was morning, or at least it seemed as if it was morning. I rubbed my eyes, peered over at the record player. Binky must have shut it off during the night, and the headphones were sitting on the table next to the record player. Binky must have pulled the headphones off my head when she shut the player off, and I never even woke up or remembered a thing.

This was a déjà vu moment, as I remembered a similar scene that occurred many years ago, at our little house in Great Falls. It was during the week when Rose had left her first husband and came to stay with us. That was how long ago it had been since I sacked out in my easy chair for an entire night.

Life is a circle, we sometimes go around, and around, and it all comes back somehow. It was remarkable how things often evolve.

I pulled the blankets away and stared out to see Heather Sarah staring intently at me. She was holding Fritzie, the stuffed dog in her hand. She was standing right in front of my chair, looking at me with a big, wide smile on her face.

"Are you feeling better, dear Father?"

I smiled at her and nodded my head to indicate that I was.

"Dear Mother, told me to be very quiet, so that I did not wake you. Fritzie and I sat here on the floor watching you to make sure you were safe! Did we wake you?"

I shook my head no, to indicate that she and Fritzie were off the hook. She smiled at me and tore off towards the kitchen. As she ran, she screamed at the top of her lungs, "Dear Mother! Father is awake, and he nodded his head that he is feeling better!" She disappeared around the corner as I stood up from the chair.

I felt like a pretzel. My back was stiff, and I was creaking and cracking, but I felt normal as far as a fever or potential illness would be concerned. Those old hockey injuries were now catching up with me here and there. I stood up and wandered in the direction of the first-floor bathroom. I felt as if once I got moving around that I would be feeling good. In fact, emotionally, I could tell that I was feeling wonderful. I washed up in the bathroom and tried very hard to collect myself. I wandered into the kitchen and found Binky already preparing me a cup of hot tea. Heather Sarah was running all around the kitchen playing with Fritzie. Since I was awake, I guess she was free now to unload all of her excess energy.

My wife smiled at me and asked, "How do you feel, twenty-seven?"

"I feel great, Binky. I see that Heather Sarah is better too. There sure is nothing wrong with her throat anymore! What time is it? I am supposed to be at work."

I looked up at the clock and saw that it was almost ten thirty in the morning. Oh boy, I had missed my early appointments! I sat down at the kitchen table, rubbed my eyes, and tried to shake the dazed feeling that I had.

It was as if I was in a fog.

The evening's activities broke up my normal routine—it was very unusual for me to experience any changes, and it disturbed me to some extent.

Binky poured a cup of tea and brought it over to me, while she explained, "Please do not worry. I called Martha and told her that you were not feeling well. She cleared your schedule for today. You did not have any hospital calls today, so all is well, twenty-seven. In light of last night's events and you not feeling well, I really think you need to stay at home and just relax. You push yourself beyond the boundaries of ordinary folks, Paul. You have been burning the candle at both ends for way too long now. In fact, for years and years, Paul." Binky stared in at me with a famous Binky stare, looking for a reaction to her statement. I nodded my head very weakly, as I was not quite ready to agree in entirety with her assessment of my work habits, yet I was not willing to test the waters either.

Binky continued as she told me, "Dave came over and stayed with Heather Sarah and watched you while I brought Paul William to school. Drink that tea now. I put some more of that natural honey in there for you. You will be feeling better very soon."

Binky went back to the counter to pour herself some tea, and she continued to speak, "I did not want to bring Heather Sarah out in the cold so soon after her not feeling well, so that was nice of Dave to come over. He told me to tell you to relax, to tell you that everything is under control, and that he hopes you feel better. Did you see that it snowed a little early this morning? It was just a little, but I took the jeep to school to be on the safe side. Dave plowed the lots and roads clear."

"Dave is the best. It snowed, eh?" I peeked out the window and saw that there were a few inches of snow on the ground. I thought how that had moved in quickly as I remembered how it was clear last night when I looked out. There was certainly something special about a layer of snow on a church and the churchyard. It was an example of God's greatest work of art. I stared at a peaceful layer of snow, sitting silently upon the land, the trees, the glistening crystals dancing in time with the wind. It was pure magic. Silent, calm, and peaceful.

"It is time now, for Dinky the Orange Teddy Bear, Heather Sarah. Do you want to watch it?" Heather Sarah instantly jumped to her feet and gave her mother a rapid head nod that would rival the best Binky nod of all time. "I will turn it on, bring Fritzie, and come to the living room."

Heather Sarah tore off, screaming in the air, "Father feels better! He is not sick anymore!" She then began to sing the Dinky the Orange Teddy Bear theme song as loud as she could.

I was glad that I did not have a headache.

That stupid Dinky cartoon was still around. It had been on television for what seemed to be ten lifetimes.

Binky left the kitchen, turned the television on for our daughter, and she returned to the kitchen once Heather Sarah settled in to watch the cartoon.

My wife grabbed her tea and joined me at the table.

"She will be asleep in ten minutes. She was up early, and when she heard that you were sick, she just sat on the floor watching you sleep. She was terribly worried. I do not think that she ever saw you sick before . . . ever."

Binky stopped in mid-thought. She looked down at her teacup and then back over at me. She smiled and said, "In fact, I do not think that I have ever seen you sick before either! In reviewing last night's events, though, Paul, I am not quite sure that you were sick. Whatever it was, you recovered from it very quickly. I will research what may have been the cause of the entire situation, but I did find it very strange indeed. It seemed as if whatever ailed you, drained you of both your thoughts and your energy, Paul. Do you not agree?" She leaned in for a very intense Binky stare, looking for an answer.

"My mind is a bit foggy on the details of the situation. I guess, I need to think a bit more about it, Binky."

Binky agreed with a rapid head nod.

"I also found it very strange, Paul, how you changed your mind on the fate of the tree. However, I know when you are firmly convinced about a subject, and I do not detect even the slightest element of doubt at all in your mind. You are convinced, are you not, Paul?"

"I am convinced without a shadow of any doubt. I am not sure exactly why or how I changed my mind, but I know it is the correct decision to make."

I looked at my teacup and then back to my wife.

"It is just an old, oak tree."

She looked at me, smiled, and she seemed as though she was going to say a little more, but then she changed her mind. It had been a strange night, and Binky knew just enough about these types of events in my life, and our life together, to trust me completely.

I smiled back at her and changed the subject, "It is nice to see Heather Sarah so happy about my recovery." I took a long sip of the tea. It tasted good, and I was feeling much better. "I did not know that I was such a hero to her."

Binky stared back at me. She had a different look on her face. It was not a stern look from Binky, but I would classify it as very forceful in nature.

"I think sometimes, Paul—that is what you do not realize. You are not only a father to our children and my wonderful soulmate, husband, and amazing lover, but you are also a friend, pastor, and guide, to an awful lot of folks. You are also a hero, and I do not mean just from your hockey days either. Oh, I know that there are still hockey fans who wear your hockey jersey with your name, and the number twenty-seven sewn on the back, but I am not speaking of the game right now. I am speaking of your life, and your influence on other people's lives. You walk around blind to the fact that you mean a great deal to, many people. It is long past the time that you should have realized what your role has become. You need to play that role up more and stop downplaying it my, dear Paul. People need you, and count on you, they really do. You never give yourself enough credit."

I pondered what Binky had just lectured me on, and deep down, I knew that she was correct. At times, I did not want to be a leader, or a role model for anyone. In fact, sometimes I wished that I could revert to being number twenty-seven, and just hide behind my trusty and faithful, old goalie mask. Nevertheless, those days were long since gone, and I did need to acknowledge my role and responsibilities in a more forceful manner.

"You are correct. Going forward, I will try to do a better job on that. Thank you. I think I needed that advice, and coming from you, it means an awful lot."

Binky finished her tea, fluffed her hair, and stood up. She walked over to me, wrapped her arms around my neck, and kissed my cheek.

"That is because I love you, Paul John Henson, and you are my hero too. I did not mean that as a criticism of you, just an observation, as an eye opener for you. Do you want another cup of tea?"

I gently clasped her arm and hand. "I understand, I did not take it as a criticism. You are right on with your advice. Yes, please, another cup of tea would be great. I really have to write my sermon for Sunday, and I had planned on meeting with Mrs. Whipley as soon as I could, to explain my thoughts on the fate of the oak tree."

Binky dug her left foot into the floor and spun around quickly while she put her hands on her hips.

Oh, oh! I had really fired her up now!

"Pastor Paul John Henson! Please not today, take the day and relax! You have twenty sermons written for backups for emergencies, just like today. I can call Martha for you and set up a meeting for Mrs. Whipley for tomorrow. It can wait for tomorrow. There is no need to meet with her today. You need to listen to me, Paul John!"

Oh, oh, I was treading on thin ice! When Binky addressed me as Pastor Paul John Henson and Paul John, then I had reached the point of no return.

I held my hand up to signal defeat and Binky relaxed.

"You win. I will relax, read a little, and I think I will listen to some music in my chair. I would like to listen to some older, No Way records out of my collection that I have almost forgotten about. That is, it. I will drink tea, listen to music, and relax."

Binky relaxed, and she waved her hands and arms in a motion towards the living room. She then proudly proclaimed, "Excellent, off to your chair then dear Paul. I will bring you some more tea. I will call dear Martha and set up the appointment for Mrs. Whipley. Sleep and rest will recharge you. Even world famous, retired, ice hockey goalies need to recharge once in a while!"

I was not going to argue and off I went. Heather Sarah was sound asleep on the floor in front of the television with her faithful Fritzie tucked under her arm. I shut off the tube, took a blanket, and covered her up. She did not move a muscle. I picked out an old, No Way record, put it on the turntable, and climbed into my chair. I put the headphones on my head just as Binky arrived with my tea. She handed it to me, kissed me on the forehead, and smiled at me. I sipped the tea as I watched her return to the kitchen, and I had to admit, it was quite a view to watch her while she walked away—she was a stunning beauty!

What a woman!

Seldom did I have peaceful times such as this anymore. Our daughter was asleep and peaceful in front of me, my wife waiting on me, looking after my health and needs. It was a different kind of day, but it felt good. I was still not quite sure what had happened last night, but at this point, I resigned myself to just go with it, and see where it all will end up.

I woke up, dazed and confused. I looked around the room, not exactly knowing where I was, or what the exact time of day or night was. Heather Sarah had squeezed in next to me in the chair. She was sound asleep under the blankets with Fritzie in her arms. It was late, but how late was it now? I moved slowly as I did not want to disturb her. Peering around, I stared at the clock on the wall. My goodness, it was seven o'clock at night! I had slept the entire day away. I must have been exhausted. I have not slept like this in twenty years!

What could have drained my energy so much?

I climbed out of the chair as Heather Sarah stirred a bit. I picked our daughter up and pulled her up into my arms. She was dressed in her pajamas and ready for bed.

Binky must have been watching us, or she had been within an earshot, as she came into the living room and walked over by us.

She leaned in and whispered, "She refused to go to bed with you down here."

I nodded and motioned that I was going to bring her up to her room. Binky followed me and we climbed the stairs together. Binky went ahead of us at the top of the stairs and went ahead of me into Heather Sarah's bedroom. My wife pulled down the covers on her bed and I slipped our precious little girl into the bed. She still had not moved. We tucked her in and each gave her a kiss goodnight.

"How do you feel, Paul? Are you hungry? I can prepare you a meal rather quickly."

I shook my head to indicate that I was not hungry. I then said, "Good, I feel good. Thank you, but I am not hungry. But you know what? I still need to recharge. Where is Paul William?"

Binky smiled, and said, "So, who was right? I hope you realize that whatever drained you of emotions and energy, twenty-seven, it was a few years of sleep that you needed to catch up on."

I did not answer, Binky, I slowly and sleepily nodded, but she was quite correct.

"Paul William is fine. He is watching the hockey game on the television in his room. I allowed him to watch the game in his room since you two were sacked out downstairs."

I climbed into our bed, pulled the covers down, and under them, I went.

I didn't even ask if the New York Rovers were winning the game or not.

"Goodnight, Binky."

Binky leaned in and kissed me, "Goodnight, twenty-seven."

That was all that I remembered.

I was off into sleepy land once more, dreaming of making kick saves, riding the Flipper with Binky, ducking while O'Malley zipped slap shots around my head, and he tried to butt end me in the gut with the end of his stick. Then my mind whirled and twirled deeper into dreamland, while I was laughing along with Harry, as we were off together on some type of other wild Harry and Paul adventure.

"I feel a lot better, Martha. In fact, I feel wonderful! I feel fully recharged. It is quite remarkable. I really have no idea what knocked me for such a loop. I cannot ever recall being quite that exhausted. I feel so good right now that I could jump in the net and face one hundred shots on goal. I appreciate you holding the fort down while I goofed off and snoozed the day away. I am sorry that I left you alone yesterday, but maybe, it was a welcome change for you to not have to deal with me."

Martha looked up from her desk, "No need to apologize. I have to ask you, pastor, is this the first day that you have taken off in the last twenty or so years? Since, the horrible time that you told me about, when you broke your toes, playing goal that one night. By the way, we need a pastor. We are not in need of any goaltenders right now here at Reunion Lutheran Church, so please forget the idea of going into the net."

I loved Martha's sense of humor.

"Well, not to deflate your happy balloon, but Mrs. Henson did call, and ask me to set up Mrs. Whipley for ten o'clock this morning, which being the efficient machine that I am, I promptly followed through on that request for you!"

"Oh great, thank you so much. That is very good. That will leave me some extra time to chat with Dave first and check on some things." I looked at my watch and noted that it was eight forty-five in the morning.

Martha began shaking her head and pointing towards the closed door of my office, "Thank me later, if you still feel as if you should. Sorry, Pastor Paul, but Mrs. Whipley is already in your office waiting for you. She told me she could not wait to speak with you."

"She is? She is over an hour early! Oh, boy."

"To think Pastor Paul, they told you in seminary that all you have to do is smile a lot, write a sermon once a week, shake hands, bury some dead folks here and there, and kiss babies. Then you can play golf every day, just as Bishop Von Houten does. You might have been better off dodging hockey pucks, then where you are heading right now." Martha stood up from her desk and gave me an excited high five hand slap, which I participated in with her.

"Go get 'em, twenty-seven! Let me know if you will reconsider the inspirational backside slap!"

I weakly shook my head, turned, and entered my office.

"Oh, good morning, Pastor Paul! I am so glad to see you and hear that you are feeling better. When Martha told me that you were ill, I was so worried. I called Mrs. Henson and spoke with her, and then I told Mrs. Crankshammer. I know that Edith also called your dear wife and spoke with her for an hour or two. That Binky Henson, oh my, oh my, she is quite the woman! And what a figure! Did I ever tell you that I had a figure just like that when I was her age?"

Binky did not mention phone calls to me this morning over breakfast. I wondered how she had survived with intact eardrums.

"Good Morning. Bore da, Mrs. Whipley, and thank you for the concern. I am fine, just a little bug running around here and there. I shook it off rather quickly. Yes, my wife is wonderful, and she took good care of me. I feel great now, in fact, I feel quite recharged. I have been running hard for a bit of time. I think I just needed to catch up on my sleep."

"You look as handsome as ever, Pastor Paul. I must say that you have an extra twinkle in your eyes. It is, although you have an added spirit to your soul of some sort. You know my Henry was quite the looker as well. He used to swirl his hair to the side of his head in a big wave, and my legs would grow weak. He, of course, did not have all those golden locks of hair as you have Pastor Paul, but he was so handsome."

"Yes, yes, yes, well, Mrs. Whipley, I wanted to speak with you about. . .."

"The tree, yes, indeed, I know, pastor. The tree is of great concern to me too. I have not been able to sleep since the meeting the other night. I could see the concern in your face and in your eyes as well. I know that you have re-instituted Pastor Braun's practice of pouring the holy water, or water from the baptismal on the base of the tree. The word on the street is that you are a little weird, and off the wall, but we of course, know differently."

"Well, that is true, Mrs. Whipley. You see, I came to a decision."

"Yes, I understand, Pastor Paul, and I want to say, I was very upset when I heard you were so ill. I was afraid that the turmoil of the other evening had upset your health. I do think that the angel's intended focus is not exactly upon the tree now, it could be the church itself, I am not really sure."

"Turmoil, Mrs. Whipley?"

"Yes, yes, the night of the meeting, it was the only night other than a Saturday night, in which I have seen the lights from the spaceships and heard the entire ruckus. I was listening to my Harvey Crooner records in the living room, sitting in my old, faithful chair, when I heard it all and spotted the lights. Do you know, Harvey Crooner? He had such a wonderful voice. It is so smooth and magical. Have you ever heard him sing that wonderful song, 'The Winds

Beneath Your Backside?"'

"Well, I cannot say that I have."

"It was early morning, around two or so. I could not sleep, since I was so very upset about the future of the tree, so I decided to listen to my music. I jumped up to look out, but it was all gone by the time I arrived at the window, except for the lights over near the tree. Nevertheless, it was different this time, as the beam of light focused downward and over in the woods. It was over more to the left this time, about one hundred feet or so away to the left of the base of the tree. I cannot believe that you and Mrs. Henson have never heard or seen it!"

Mrs. Whipley leaned back, took a few short gasps of air, in order to recover from her long speech, and then she rolled her eyes a little. She seemed to imply that she was being silly to some extent.

"But then again, of course, I know that young people have better things to do at night, than stare out windows looking for visitors from Heaven. I was young once too." Mrs. Whipley winked at me and laughed.

I faked a smile while I felt another one of those cold shivers along my spine.

I was astounded.

Two in the morning was when I had woken up and felt so ill! I had not seen a thing out there in the churchyard! I remembered looking out there and making sure it was all-quiet.

I also remembered my dream.

Ever since I met Sky Blu Redmond all those years ago, my life had changed a bit, and I had learned never to dismiss anything. I knew that Harry felt the same way. He had seen and heard Sky speak of many things that we could never explain. I truly felt that it was all just God's plan or simple fate, but I always kept an open mind, and that is what I decided to do here.

Mrs. Whipley went on and on, rambling all kinds of

opinions and commentary on scripture, Heaven, angels, and prophets. I sat behind my desk, nodding my head as if I was a bobble-head doll and doing my best imitation of my wife's famous head nods. I could never get a word in edge wise anyway, so I might as well sit here, smile, nod, and listen.

Mrs. Crankshammer would defeat Mrs. Whipley in a blabbing contest, but only by just a little. It would be neck-to-neck, down to the wire, that was for sure. At a slight break in the action, I reached down into my desk drawer and took out two Bibles. I placed one on my desk and then slid one over to Mrs. Whipley. When her eyes spotted the Bible, she stopped cold in her blabbing dissertation. Mrs. Whipley loved whenever we conducted a Bible study session together. I knew the sight of the Bible would divert her from whatever it was that she had been telling me.

"I have my Bible here with me, Pastor Paul," she said while reaching down inside of her purse. Mrs. Whipley pulled out her tattered and worn Bible while continually she smiled at me. She then handed back to me the Bible I had given her, and I returned it to my desk drawer.

"Mrs. Whipley, please if we could read together from the Book of Job, chapter fourteen, verse seven."

She eagerly flipped open the pages. Mrs. Whipley was an elite scholar when it came to scripture. Together, we read the lines aloud.

When we had finished, her face lit up, the old gal beamed, and tears formed in the corners of her eyes.

While the tears ran down her face, she said to me, "Pastor Paul, I do think you are the smartest person I have ever met. I think I know why the lights are now in the woods and not focused upon the tree any longer. I am confident that you are correct. There is so much more to this now. The tree is only a physical part of this. The two of us now know it is really about something quite different. I think that it is all about our faith. We can only pray and hope that God will allow us to understand someday, the gifts and the plan that the Holy Spirit gave to us. We can proceed with the new addition. I will vote in favor of it all. Thank you, Pastor Paul, for leading us all here at Reunion Lutheran Church and providing such divine guidance. Thank you for being, well, for lack of any other description, Pastor Paul John Henson."

The building and grounds committee met for another meeting the next week after I had met with Mrs. Whipley. We learned during the meeting that Binky was correct about a tree coverage ordinance and requirement. I knew that no one on the committee doubted that her research would not have been right on target anyway, but the architect thanked Binky for bringing this fact to his attention. The new requirement added some budget adjustments to the initial figures, but we were able to move some money around to make it all add up, and still stay within our total projected budgets. We sailed right through on a unanimous vote, after suffering through an hour and half filibuster by Mrs. Crankshammer that Harry, very strategically cut short by slipping out, and cutting off the main electrical switch to simulate a power failure. The committee would now pass the initiative on to the full membership for a final approval.

A Sunday or two later, the church membership voted in favor of the construction. With our funding in place, our bid list for contractors fulfilled, and our township permits and approvals in place, there were no remaining obstacles left in our way to begin the long-awaited additions to the buildings of Reunion Lutheran Church.

We had journeyed, a full circle, in just about six years or thereabouts, from a church slated for closure, to a bursting membership, in dire need for larger facilities. Not bad work for a long-haired hippie, pastor from poor old Paterson, New Jersey, and his band of what Bishop Von Houten playfully labeled, "merry followers."

Harry and Dave, both questioned me as to what had changed my mind about the fate of the large oak tree. I kept my response purposely vague and simply answered that it was just an old oak tree. I told them once I sat and thought about it, I decided that it was just a tree. Harry seemed as though he did not completely accept my vague answer, but he did not dwell upon it, or ask me any more questions. He knew me well enough at this point to trust that I had made a decision that I was comfortable having made.

All that I needed to do was to keep telling myself that, yes indeed, it was nothing more than just an extremely large oak tree. There remained nothing special about the tree.

Indeed.

6

The Tree Comes Down

Spring arrived and with the weather breaking, construction started on the church renovations. Betty Ann Hobnobber and her father's excavation and site work company had now fully mobilized for the site work. Once the frost had let out of the ground, they began to break ground on the construction. We had a huge, groundbreaking ceremony, with picture sessions of all the key members of the committees in charge of the planning and oversight, as well as the leadership of the church participating in the ceremony. Of course, Bishop Von Houten was front and center of all the pictures. He spoke right after I spoke at the groundbreaking ceremony, rather boldly taking most of the credit for the success of Reunion Lutheran Church, as well as being the, "Key person in securing the required funding" to guarantee the construction loans. Luckily, he escaped without Mrs. Whipley taking a poke at him! Harry leaned over to me while the bishop was speaking and told me in a tongue-in-cheek manner, how thankful he was that Bishop Von Houten had secured all the funding by licking a stamp and mailing the information to us here at the church. Regardless, it was a joyous day! I never let my boss take the wind out of my sails. I would simply wait until he was finished with his usual horn blowing and put a positive spin on the entire situation.

April 18, 1995, broke clear, a little chilly, but it was a fabulous spring day. The site work had moved over to the fellowship hall now, as most of the site work for the addition of the sanctuary was now complete, and the concrete work had started. I stood off to the side of the fellowship hall, watching as the heavy equipment made the way through the woods, to begin to groom the earth and prepare the site. Betty Ann was operating one piece of equipment while her father was working his machine close by her.

I was always amazed at how talented Betty Ann Hobnobber was, from singing so beautifully, to painting, and now I was watching her expertly work an earthmoving machine across the landscape. She sure was a talented woman.

I stood on the edge of the woods watching the work progress, when first, Dave Sharp, and then Harry, came along to join me.

"Looking good, Paul!" Harry was excited to see the work beginning now on the other side of the project.

"Sure is, guys, it is amazing actually, how quickly it all comes along."

Dave Sharp walked over and stood next to me. He began to tell me, "Pastor Paul, I worked a deal with a lumber mill over in Hillsdale for the big, oak tree. I have known the owner for years and years. As you may remember, I dabble a little in woodworking in my workshop at home, and I have some connections with mills, which are always looking for a higher end, quality lumber."

Harry and I both nodded our heads as Dave told us more details.

"Last year, I helped a buddy of mine sell some walnut trees that he had on his property up in Sussex County. I mentioned to the owner about the oak tree here, and what a great specimen it was for long, straight, quality lumber. He looked at it right away. He offered a terrific amount of money for it, so much that it would actually net us a profit, and not cost us a dime to remove it. His crew will be out to take it down in a little while. He works with a local arborist who knows how he wants it taken down to preserve as much of the lumber as possible for producing quality wood. I even worked a little deal for a stash of the oak myself for my projects."

"Great work, Dave. That is great news. Anytime that we can save the church money, then we are ahead of the game."

"Yeah, yeah, yeah, Sharpie, way to work a deal there." Harry slapped Dave on the back.

"I learned from one of the best," Dave Sharp proudly stated. It was obvious that Dave was proud of the deal, in which he had worked and he was glowing in his ability to save the church money.

Harry turned around and frowned as he loudly asked Dave, "One of the best?"

Dave realized his error and came right back, "Oh, sorry, boss. I meant that I learned from the best."

Harry smiled and waved his hands in the air for Dave to continue.

"They will use the entire tree, Pastor Paul, so you will be happy to know that none of it will go to waste. Quality lumber, wonderful solid oak for some project somewhere. They will even grind up the oak bark and turn it into quality mulch. He works with the garden center here in town to supply them bark for the mulch. All of God's creation here will go to good use."

"I am very happy to hear that, Dave. Plants, trees, people, animals, all of it, we are all the same. Part of all the grand creation. It is amazing stuff for sure." I smiled at Dave and patted him on the back. I appreciated him being such a good steward of the Earth's resources.

"Say, I could use a hot cup of coffee. How about youse guys?" Harry said as he led the way into the kitchen at the fellowship hall to grab us all some nice, hot coffee. I sensed my two friends were trying to ease the pressure of the demise of the tree; they wanted to keep me comfortable and judge my mood. We gathered together and enjoyed some hot coffee while sitting together at a table in the fellowship hall.

"How is Rose feeling today, thirty-five?"

"Great, Paul, she is doing great. She is getting pretty large now, and I am having some fun with that, but as far as her health and the baby, all is well."

Harry stopped drinking his coffee, turned, and looked at Dave and me.

"The truth is that I have never seen her look more beautiful, youse guys. God instills beauty and miracles in our world, and we sometimes take it for granted. Rose is gorgeous, simply gorgeous." Dave and I smiled at Harry's joy and praise. I had to agree, we always take glory for granted.

"That is nice to hear, Harry. I know that she had some wicked morning sickness early on, so I am glad that has passed off." I now sensed that Dave and Harry were both comfortable with my mood, they felt my confidence in the decision that I had made.

We made some more small talk until Harry excused himself to go checkout some work on the sanctuary end of the construction. Harry had his crews here for the steelwork, so he was busy these days supervising some welding and steel work going on. Dave and I wandered out to the side of the fellowship hall to watch some work going on there. The tree crew was now on site, and we watched as a tree climber made his way into the majestic oak tree to start the process of topping off the tree and working it down to the ground. I studied the work beginning, and I noticed Dave watching me out of the corner of his eyes. I could tell he was still looking for a reaction from me on the imminent demise of the tree.

"You still good, Pastor Paul, with the tree being cut down?" Dave put his arm around my shoulders.

"I am good. It is fine. I am one hundred percent sure that it is the right thing to do."

Dave nodded his head. The two of us watched and stood together mostly in silence for hours as the big tree was cut down.

"Nice tree, wonderful wood here!" A large, round-faced chap shouted to us. He had red cheeks, and big hands, and he came over to us as he praised the quality of the wood. He lumbered through the woods, mud, and dirt of the site work, and stopped in front of us, while he kicked some mud off his heavy work boots. He took his work gloves off and held them in his left hand.

"James Peterson. I am the foreman here on the tree crew." He reached out his hand, and I shook it.

"Hello, James. I am, Pastor Paul Henson."

"Wow! Strong handshake there for a pastor! What, do you work out or something? You are a big, strong, man, Pastor Paul!"

"I do try to keep myself in good shape. Yes, I do work out here and there. I think that you may already know our facility manager, Dave Sharp. It was his idea to work the deal for the tree."

Mr. Peterson shook Dave's hand. "Yes, it is sure nice to see you, again Dave. We worked together on some walnut trees last year or so."

"That's right, I do remember you. Those were some nice trees, James."

"They sure were, Dave, but this one is a fantastic red oak. It is so unusual to see a tree this young, at only forty years old or so, that is so big. I do not think I have ever seen such a thing. Very special, and strange. The wood is awesome. It tore our chains up! I have to sharpen them all back up when we get to the shop. Heavy, straight, not even touched by a fungus, wilt, lightning, or any insects. Nice tree, it will fetch a good buck." I nodded and then stared off at the large hook and crane truck pulling off large, straight sections of the trunk and branches and loading them all on the back of a huge truck.

"Thank you, James. I appreciate all the hard work by you and your crew. I am very happy to hear that you are able to utilize the tree for a good cause. It is nice to know the wood will be put to good use, and we were able to save the church a lot of money too."

"Sure pastor, sure thing. We will just be a little while longer here to load up the last of the wood and we will take off. Thank youse guys for the opportunity. Nice to see the church is expanding. It looks as if you have a nice place of worship here. You have done quite a job here. A few years back, I thought this church was abandoned."

"Come on by on a Sunday and visit us."

"I will do that, Pastor Paul." We shook hands once more, bid goodbye to Mr. Peterson, and watched a little longer, while James and his crew loaded up the last remains of the fallen tree. The truck was almost fully loaded with oak now; it must have weighed an enormous amount! I thought to myself, what a powerful truck, to be able to pull that kind of tremendous weight. Dave and I both had other work to do, so I went off to my office and Dave was off on his chores.

I was working at my desk in my office when I heard the roar of a big engine and the driver going through the gears of a truck. I looked out of my office window to see the big truck loaded with the wood, with James Peterson at the wheel. I watched for a bit until the truck went out of sight and I then went back to work at my latest sermon.

As I put my pen to the paper, I knew the subject of this week's message would be about a certain verse out of the Book of Job. I then thought about the journal in the top drawer of my desk. I opened the drawer, reached in, and took it out. I thumbed through it until I reached the page with the entries from Pastor Braun. I found the little slip of paper, in which I had written my note on, took it out, and studied it for a second. I wrote on the paper, "Watering practice now discontinued, due to construction of the new addition of the classrooms onto the fellowship hall. Original tree removed, 18 April 1995." I signed it, "Pastor Paul John Henson." I replaced the slip of paper into the journal in the same location within the pages, closed the book, and placed it back in the top drawer of my desk.

The truck loaded with the wood from the remains of the oak tree rolled out onto the highway, then turned down an exit ramp, and onto a long, winding road.

"Boy, man, oh man . . . this is one heavy tree, the truck can barely move here, it is good to be going downhill," James Peterson said to his helper in the cab of the big rig, as he down-shifted a gear or two to assist the brakes in holding the weight back. His helper nodded, just as a loud alarm sounded inside the cab of the truck. Both men glanced up to see that the alarm signaled that the air compressor for the air brake system had failed.

"Oh no, this is not good! All this weight on this hill! Hold on!"

The truck rapidly gained speed as James frantically shifted into another lower gear in an effort to slow the big truck down. James stood up on the brakes since the system shifted over to the backup spring brakes when the air had failed. The truck's brakes screamed, and the wheels smoked, as the friction of the brakes desperately tried to hold back the weight and stop the truck careening down the hill. The brakes were slowing the truck now, but an intersection loomed ahead, and it did not look good for James to be able to stop the truck from plowing through a red light and causing a serious situation ahead.

"James! The light is red! We are going to blow the intersection!" His helper screamed as he pointed at the red light and spotted the situation ahead.

"Hang on! I see it! We are in trouble here! We are going to need a miracle to not kill us or someone else here!"

Out of habit, James Peterson reached up and desperately pulled the cord for the air horn, in order to alert the other drivers in the intersection of the impending serious danger.

His first pull brought no horn response.

"Man, what am I thinking, we have no air!" James then pressed down on the backup horn button on his steering wheel, when suddenly, the air compressor alarm stopped and the air gauge needle bounced back up to one hundred and twenty-five pounds. James hit the brakes and the air brakes kicked in, as he pulled the horn cord once again, and sounded the big air horn. Drivers slammed on their brakes and everyone skidded to a stop in the intersection, just as the big rig ground to a screeching halt amidst smoke and dust from the smoking brakes and skidding tires.

Amazingly, no one collided, as the truck limped across the intersection and came to a stop on the other side of the traffic light. The incident had visibly shaken the two men, and they reached over to one another, and shook each other's hands.

This had been a near miss, and a horrible, heart-racing, experience! After jumping out of the truck and checking it over, the two men surprisingly did not find any troubles with the big rig. All systems seemed normal, and the truck was back in action.

"Got me. I have no idea what happened here," James shook his head while scratching his head. "It is only a mile back to the yard. We can make it. I will have Walt, the head of the mechanics, check out the truck once we get back. Something happened! At least we have no more hills to deal with, so even if the air fails again, the spring brakes will stop us just fine."

James's helper agreed. The two men climbed back into the truck, and they limped back into the yard. James's field crew, that assisted with the cutting down of the oak tree, had gone ahead of James and the big truck, and they were waiting for him in the yard to help with unloading all the cut timbers. James parked the big truck; the two men jumped out of it and met the rest of the cutting crew.

"What took you so long?" One of the tree climbers asked.

"Lost the air brakes on the long hill. It was wild for a few seconds there, but they kicked back in, and we just stopped in time. We were ready to blow the intersection there at Forest Ave, but we somehow avoided a major disaster. With this huge load, we would have knocked cars into the next county."

The other man whistled low and shook his head. He realized how lucky they were.

James looked down at his watch and said, "What a mess. It is late now. Youse guys, please start to unload, while I get Walt out here to check out this truck."

The crew started working to unload the timbers, while James went into the garage, and he found the head shop mechanic, Mr. Walter Dailey working on repairing some chipper equipment in the shop.

"Hey, Walt, do you have a minute?" Walter Dailey looked up from his work and took a little cigar out of the corner of his mouth.

"Yeah, whatcha got, James? I was hoping that someone would not come along and bug me today, but it is not looking good now is it!" Walter was an older man of about sixty years of age, and he bent over at the waist slightly, from many years of working on trucks and equipment. He was tough, and at times, a little on the grouchy side, but overall, he was a good man. He also was a topnotch mechanic. James was not Walt's direct boss, but Walt understood that he was the supervisor of the field crew, so he needed to tread carefully here.

"I lost the air brakes on the long hill there, while we

were rolling back from the church with that heavy load. No air, alarms yelling and hollering in the cab. It was crazy. Let me tell you, it was frightening for a few seconds! We were screaming and standing on the brakes, but the air came back, and we managed to stop. Let me tell you that I am going home today to have a few shots of whiskey to steady my nerves."

Walt nodded and said, "I bet. Wow, we just serviced that truck. Let's go take a look. Are ya all right there, James? Ya look like you are still all shaken up. You say that the air came and went?"

James acknowledged Walt's question with a nod of the head. "Say, I am going to grab a cup of water, let me know what you find with it, Walt. The air brakes worked fine, from Forest Avenue back to here. It was really strange." James waved as he walked away to indicate he was going in another direction. "I will meet you out by the truck, Walt."

James grabbed some water from a water cooler in the front office, and he sat down on a chair in the shop for a few minutes to steady his nerves. He knew that many people could have been hurt or killed if that truck had not stopped. It had shaken him up a lot more now that he had time to think about it. James got up from the chair in the shop and wandered out to the yard towards where the crew was unloading the truck. Halfway there, he ran into Walt walking towards him with a drive belt in his hand.

"No way! James, I am telling you, there can be no way that the air brakes could have worked on that truck! Your nerves must have taken over, and you are mistaken. The belt on the air compressor broke. The belt had a large nick on the edge of it and it was shot. We missed it on our inspection, so shame on us. Ain't gonna have any air without a belt pumping the tank up! Ya stopped it with the backup spring brakes, James."

James stood there shocked as Walt held up the broken

belt. "No way! I had air in the truck! You can ask, Ricky. He was right there with me. The air came back. I even used the air horn when I was blowing through Forest Ave. The gauge on the dash showed normal air, and the alarm stopped!"

"I can only tell ya what I see, and the belt is broken. Ya better go home for some of that whiskey sooner rather than later, James."

I looked at my watch and sighed. It was five thirty, and I had lost track of the time once more. I was surprised that Binky had not called my office phone, in order to coax me over to our home for dinner. I finished the last words on the sermon and closed my notepad. I shut off the light over my desk, grabbed my vest, and dashed out the door. As I walked out the back of the church and headed for the parsonage, out of habit, I looked over towards the fellowship hall. I stopped in my tracks, because it seemed so strange, not to see the big tree towering over the top of the building. I started to walk towards the house, but then I turned and walked over into the wooded area behind the fellowship hall. It was so quiet now that all the construction and heavy equipment had stopped for the day. Betty Ann and her father had pulled the massive stump of the oak tree out of the ground with their giant machines. I walked over to it, and even in the growing dusk of the pending evening, I could see the upturned stump and remains of the tree, projecting out of the ground. I stared for a long time at the stump and the massive roots turned upside down on the ground. I wandered through the dirt and stood about fifty feet or so from the base of the uprooted stump.

I reached down into the dirt and picked up five acorns that had dropped off the oak tree when it had cut loose from the tree's roots. The aroma of newly disturbed dirt and oak wood filled the air. I studied the acorns for a long time, turning them around and around in my hands, while my mind drifted and wandered, lost in random thoughts. I then carefully wiped the dirt off each of them and dropped the acorns in my vest pocket. For some unknown reason, I stood there staring for a few minutes, not focusing upon anything, just staring blankly at where the tree once stood. I then turned away and headed back to the house.

"I am home, Binky! Sorry, I got caught up on a sermon."

"Oh, no trouble, twenty-seven. I knew you would have a drama-filled, emotional day, with the removal of the tree. No doubt, you had to write your sermon on that verse in the Book of Job. I anticipated that you would be late."

She stopped in front of me, gave me a kiss, and fluffed her hair. She did not even ask if she was correct in her prediction, she already knew that she was right on target.

"I have made a special dinner. Actually, to be honest, it is not special at all. I have to admit that I was a bit lazy today, so I whipped up this huge pot of pasta, some meatballs, and a special sauce."

"That is not lazy. It is very special."

My wife stopped and pondered it for a bit before answering, "I think you are correct, Paul. I guess it is a dinner that I could easily classify as easy to prepare rather than being lazy. Regardless, I have to warn you that the reason this is special, is not due to my choice of a cuisine. It is because my parents are on the way over to join us for dinner tonight. You may want an extra beer or two to soften the blow. My dear father's spirits sounded extra enhanced when I spoke to him on the telephone. I think he wants to play a game or two of Warship with you."

Binky turned towards me with the refrigerator door open.

"Have you ever won a game with him, twenty-seven?"

"No. Actually, dear Binky, it is virtually impossible to

win. He cheats and moves his ships all over the board for the first ten minutes or so."

Binky nodded; it was obvious she was not surprised at her father's behavior. She asked me, "Big Boulder or a Dingleberry?"

"You know something, Binky? I will just stick with the Big Boulders. Those Dingleberries are way too sweet. I often wonder why we buy those Dingleberries, except for a surprise visit from Ronzo. He is the only person I know of who drinks them."

Binky stood up and looked at me as she held the Big Boulder bottle in her hand. She seemed to be pondering the reason.

"I do think you are correct, twenty-seven. That would be the only reason. You never know though, one of these days you may surprise me and try one. On occasion, you do have some tricks up and down your sleeve there, number twenty-seven, and try something different."

Binky fluffed her hair, winked, and smiled coyly at me.

I had a feeling that her statement had a dual meaning.

7

Honest Ralph Dennis

It had been a long Friday. It was now early June; the construction was going along very well and was right on schedule. Unlike many pastors, I worked full days on Fridays and did not take a day off during the week. Saturday was the only day of the week, in which I actually took off from work. Binky was always haunting me to take more time off, and I knew that she was correct. I told her and vowed to myself that once this project was completed, I would take Fridays off. We had finished dinner; I played a few games with the kids, and now they were washed up and off to bed. Binky and I had just settled down in the living room to watch a little television when the telephone next to my chair rang. Oh, oh, this type of call was usually an emergency sick call from church!

I picked the telephone up on the second ring.

"Paul! You there?" It was Harry.

"Yes, Harry. I am here. What is going on?"

"Hey, I need your help tomorrow. I have the new baby nursery almost done. I just need some electrical wiring help with the lights and some outlets. I always get the black and green wires all mixed up. Why don't you and the gang come on over? We can knock it out quickly, and then have some pizza, beers, wine, and stuff. I could also cook some chickens on my new Substantial Industries, Super Deluxe, Sonic-Spinner Cooker. It is unbelievable, Paul. You have to see it cook these chickens in about fifteen seconds! The kids can play on the new jungle gym set that I put up in the backyard. It is unreal."

"Well, I will need to check with Binky."

"Great! See youse guys at ten!"

"Click," the line went dead.

Binky looked over at me and asked, "Harry?"

"Yes, he needs some help with some wires in the new nursery and he wants us to come over. I didn't even have a chance. . .."

"Oh, that is fine, Paul. Rose and I had already made plans to go over there. That silly Harry has put up a giant play set in the backyard. He is under the impression that the baby will be able to run, walk, climb, shoot hockey pucks, and talk, right out of the womb! He is a nervous wreck. The children will have a blast playing in the yard on the play set and running around with Cocoa Two. They will sleep for a week!"

"I thought you wanted me to plant those rose bushes you bought downtown at the nursery yard for your garden?"

"Oh, that can wait until Sunday afternoon after church. It is supposed to rain on Monday, so planting them on Sunday, would be perfect to water them in."

"All righty, now. But I had. . .."

"I have to admit, Paul. I am now, becoming very excited for Harry and Rose too! In addition, you know how the children love to go over to Auntie Rose and Uncle Harry's house. Did Harry say whether Linny and Ronzo are coming over? I think I will call Linny and find out. Please hand me the telephone, would you please?"

Not much had actually changed over the years between the four of us. Harry never spoke with me on the telephone for much more than ten or twenty seconds. The gang always made plans for all of us without my input, and it seemed, as though, as of late—I could never actually finish a sentence!

We pulled into the long, winding driveway of the home

of Mr. and Mrs. Harry M. Redmond Jr. in Shadow Lakes, New Jersey. Ironically, the house was not very far from the famous, "ghost hill" on the Ewing Ave exit of Route 208, that we had so much fun together on that night so long ago. Linny and Ronzo's pickup truck sat neatly ahead of us in the driveway, indicating that they had beaten us here from Pennsylvania.

The kids jumped out of the jeep and ran as fast as they could up to the front door. They each took turns, frantically ringing the doorbell. I could hear Cocoa Two barking inside.

I yelled to them, "Once is enough, guys, you only need to ring it once!"

Harry flung open the door and bellowed to the kids, "Come on in! What took youse guys so long? Probably, because your old man drives like an old lady!"

Harry playfully chased the kids all around the main entrance of the home. Cocoa Two ran around in circles, barking and chasing his tail, as the kids ran into the wide-open, grand entrance of the Redmond home. Cocoa Two had some kind of rubber squeaky toy that he held in his mouth, and he was squeezing the life out of it as he ran around. I looked closely to see if it was a rubber Piggy; the legendary rubber toy that his famous namesake Cocoa played with, but it seemed as if it was a rubber goldfish, or some other kind of fish toy. The similarities between him and Cocoa were even more remarkable now. The kids were hugging Rose, Harry, and Cocoa Two. After the greetings, they tore around the house like little race cars, chasing and playing with the dog.

I met Rose and told her, "Dear Rose, you are even more gorgeous than you were last week! You look radiant, more beautiful than I have ever seen you."

Binky followed my lead, "I agree, Paul. She has the look of motherhood on her face."

"Oh, you two are just being nice. I look like a whale!"

"You do not, Rose. You look great," Binky protested.

"I feel like a whale, Paul. Look what your best buddy has done to me! He made me into a whale! I just had my figure perfect too!"

We all had a good laugh and made our way into the house and headed, of course, for the kitchen.

Where else? It was where we always went!

Harry grabbed me by the arm and stopped me.

"Paul, before you go into the kitchen. I have to tell you there is a special surprise in there for you. I am not going to tell you what it is. I want to see if you pick it up on your own."

I was a bit puzzled, but I could go along with this one. I was up for a challenge and now I was intrigued too.

"Okay Harry, I will see how sharp I am."

Off we went through the huge dining room and we made our way into the kitchen.

The Redmond house was unreal. It was a fantastic, sprawling, mansion. The kitchen was bigger than the Hobnobber's kitchen was at their estate, and Harry had equipped it with all the latest gizmos and gadgets. We for sure were a long way from 20 John Street! Walking through the door, we were immediately ambushed by my old buddy Ronzo hanging around in the kitchen. He had a big mug of coffee in his hand.

"Twenty-seven!" Ronzo set his mug down on the countertop. He then jumped up, ran over to me and gave me a big hug, followed by Linny, who was also in the kitchen enjoying some coffee.

"Hey, Ronzo! Hey, Linny! It is so good to see the both of you! How are you guys?"

"Great, Paul! Enjoying life!" Ronzo and I embraced for a few seconds. It had been a long time since I had seen the big guy and Linda. In fact, the last time that we visited together was Boxing Day at our house last Christmas season. They were both such special friends, and we remained as close as ever, even after all of these years. I then greeted Linny in the same manner. Linny and Ronzo then hugged and greeted Binky and our children.

This was turning into a special day.

"So, Paul, do you see the special surprise?" Rose stood in the center of the kitchen and invited me to look around.

Binky must have been in on the surprise, as she walked over to me and put her arm around me, as she said, "Look closely now, Paul."

My eyes scanned around the room and then all the gang as they stood there watching me. At first, I could not pick up a thing. I studied everyone's faces, clothes, hair, and then I started to scan the room itself. It all looked the same as the last time I was here, which was just about a month or so ago.

Then I spotted it! There it sat!

The old kitchen table from the kitchen at 20 John Street! The worn top, the distinctive legs, the curled-up edges. It was the old, sacred kitchen table from 20 John Street! Everyone knew that it had hit me as I nearly jumped in the air as I ran to sit in a chair at the side of the table.

"The old kitchen table, Harry! Where did you ever find it?"

"I had it up in Pennsylvania," Ronzo piped in, "when we sold 20 John Street, and moved all the junk out, I put it in the basement of our house in the Poconos. One day a few weeks ago, Linny, in general conversation, mentioned it to Rose on the telephone. Rose brought it up to Harry, and Harry expressed how much he would like to have it. So, I stuck it in the truck and brought it on down here."

Ronzo slowly walked over to me and put his arm around my shoulders.

"It is just an old table, Paul, but we sure shared an awful lot around it. Didn't we?"

"We sure did, we sure did," I said as I sat there, running my hands over the top of the table. It was torn and tattered along the edges, and the top had some scratches and deep nicks in it. It did not matter though; it still was the old, sacred, table.

I was smiling ear-to-ear, remembering all of those times. How could you not remember? It was around this old table that I first learned about time bombs hidden in cupboards, where we drank our first glasses of beer together, where Harry told me that he was going to marry, Sky, and where Harry's mom, told me terrible news and then shared her inner hope and joy with me. It also was where I had read that fateful letter from Binky, on that day so long ago, when my world collapsed around me. It was around this table that we shared Christmas and holiday joy, where tears fell, where laughter rained down, and where we solved all of life's troubles. I could see all of us gathered around it, Father Mark, the Big Spike, my old man, Mr. Redmond, Harry, Ronzo, and me, as we all made a toast to Harry, with some whiskey right before his wedding to Sky Blu. It was the centerpiece for birthday cakes, Thanksgiving turkeys, and sorting out pledges and envelopes into categories for Harry to enter that famous charity roller skating marathon.

It was a part of our lives. Yes, it may have been just an old kitchen table to most people, but to us, it was a piece of history.

Harry came over and put his hand on top of mine as I rubbed it along the top. I looked up at him and smiled.

"I had to bring it back here, Paul. I knew you would enjoy it too. You really are such an old lady there, twenty-seven! Only you could make us all sentimental about a kitchen table!" Harry's humor had broken the moment for us all, but regardless, it sure was nice to be sitting on the side of the old table once more. The kids came tearing into the kitchen with Cocoa Two following behind them. They were begging and pleading to go outside and play on the new play set in the backyard. Binky relented, and Linny,

Rose, Binky, and the kids headed out there to play.

Cocoa Two turned to Harry for his marching orders.

Harry looked at him and said, "Cocoa Two, go outside, guard the house, the ladies, and the kids. We may be going out for supplies shortly. I will call you when we are leaving." Cocoa Two sat down, barked twice, wagged his tail three times, and ran out after the gang that was heading out the door. The dog was as if he was a well-trained soldier. I could safely say that he was smarter than most humans were.

Ronzo, Harry, and I went into the nursery and checked out what Harry needed for wiring up the new room. Harry was building the nursery room in a corner of the upstairs on the second floor of their home. It had originally been extra bedrooms, Harry had knocked down the walls, and he had made it into one larger room for the baby. The room was fantastic; Harry had gone all out for the baby. The nursery was larger than the entire first floor of the parsonage!

Ronzo and I took out our tools, checked out what Harry required, and we collectively began to get the electrical system in order. Harry needed some lights, some outlets, switches, and some general wiring. We had it all under control in a short amount of time. After some checking and planning, we decided that we needed some more materials from the Rickel Home Improvement Store. Ronzo had written down an assortment of wire, wire connectors, some electrical boxes, and other materials that we needed to obtain in order to complete what Harry wanted. It sure was nice to have all of us working together again on a project. It had been a very long time.

"I will go get Cocoa Two and tell the gals we are heading out, youse guys." We followed Harry out to the backyard. We found the kids and Cocoa Two having a blast on the giant play set, and the gals sitting in the yard drinking coffee and chatting while they watched them all play.

The play set was remarkable. It had towers, slides, bars to climb on, and tunnels to crawl in that led up and down and all around. It took up a huge corner of the backyard as it sprawled over the landscape.

It was a self-contained arena for kids to get lost in for hours.

On the very top of the highest tower was a huge American flag mounted on a long pole. The flag was flapping in the gentle breeze. Below the American flag, mounted on a small staff, was a *Dinky the Orange Teddy Bear* flag with the image of Dinky and his pals emblazoned upon it. Next to that was a television antenna on an automatic rotor mount. On a platform below the main tower, was a telescope to peer out of, a searchlight on a swivel mount, and an air gun on a swivel that shot out these big, fuzzy, balls. There also was a loudspeaker mounted on the face of the platform connected to an amplified microphone. Fuzzy balls, which the kids must have shot the ladies way, littered the area around their lawn chairs.

Paul William was operating the gun while Heather Sarah screamed into the microphone.

"Dear Father, is dead ahead!" She bellowed.

Harry was explaining to everyone that we all were heading for the store while I leaned over to kiss Binky goodbye.

"PLUNK!" A giant fuzzy ball shot through the air and landed on my head.

I turned around and yelled, "Good shot!" Cocoa Two came running over, picked up a ball in his mouth, and brought it back to the kids. Harry leaned over to kiss Rose goodbye and "PLUNK" a fuzzy ball landed on top of his head in mid-kiss.

He looked at me and asked, "What is this kid, Deadeye Mike or something? He never misses. He should be a center iceman, not a goalie. The kid can shoot the eyes out of a fly from four hundred yards."

"PLUNK!" A fuzzy ball nailed Ronzo in the backside as he walked over to Linny.

"All right, children that will be enough now," Binky yelled as the kids moaned and groaned at the loss of their targets. Cocoa Two was busy fetching back the ammo for their stockpile.

"Cool play set, Harry. Maybe the gun and the microphone thingy are a little annoying, but it sure is something," I said; as I stared at the monstrous play set sitting there in the yard. "Where did you get it?"

"Substantial Industries, of course there, twenty-seven! Top of the line! Cost us a fortune. The baby is going to love it!"

Rose rolled her eyes as she said, "Yes, Harry, maybe in five or six years, the baby will love it."

"Most of the thing is made of solid stainless steel and the top deck is made of titanium in case of an enemy attack."

I was hesitant to ask Harry who the "enemy" was, but you never knew with the big guy.

"There is a television up there in the top tower where the kids are now. There is also a water fountain, and it has radar that picks up bullies and jerks in the neighborhood, and the location of your parents. It even has two cots to sleep on when the kids need a nap."

"Geez, Harry. I sure could have used that over in Vietnam," Ronzo reminisced as he shrugged his shoulders.

"Well, we are off. We will be back soon!"

Rose turned to Harry, "Please do not forget to pick up a large package of whole roasting chickens at the Foodworld, Harry. You wanted to show everyone the new, Substantial Industries cooker."

"Yeah, yeah, yeah, thanks Rose, for reminding me. Youse guys have to see this thing work. It cooks a chicken in seconds!"

Harry turned and looked at me and scanned me up and down.

"Okay, Paul, good, you have your usual rock-and-roll tee shirt on and your canvas sneakers. I do not want a repeat of our last Foodworld episode. Hey guys, I have to wait a minute or two here for Cocoa Two to finish. Wait by the Rhino 400. I will be out in a minute. I am going to bring Cocoa Two once he is done fetching the balls for the kiddies."

Harry seldom traveled without Cocoa Two, but I found it strange that he did not leave him here, to, as he would always say, "To guard the ladies, house, and the kids." Perhaps Harry felt safer knowing that, "Deadeye Mike" was on duty!

Harry arrived with Cocoa Two, and we took off in the Rhino 400 for the Rickel Home Improvement Store. We always went to Rickel, even though it was quite a long distance away from our homes. When I was a kid, the store was my old man's home away from home. He loved the store, and I spent a good part of my childhood wandering the aisles with the old man. My dad still always asked me about the store, now that he moved out in the country, and he could no longer shop there. We had to wind our way out of Shadow Lakes and then hit a main drag for a few miles. The store was about four or five towns over, right on the outer edges of Paterson, so we had a little ride in front of us before we arrived there.

It was a warm, early June day, with clear skies and bright sunlight. It was pleasant and relaxing, cruising along in the Rhino. Cocoa Two leaned out the window in the backseat with Ronzo next to him. The dog was sticking his head out the window while enjoying the ride. We were making small talk along the way and sharing the latest things going on in our lives.

We pulled onto the main drag and we were rolling along in the direction of the Rickel Home Improvement Store, when Harry suddenly yelled out, "Did youse guys see that!"

Oh, oh! There goes any hope of pleasant and relaxing right out the window.

He slammed the Rhino down into gear, slowed the big car, and pulled off to the side of the road. He turned to me frantically and asked once more, "Did you see that, twenty-seven?" When I shrugged my shoulders, Harry frantically turned around and asked Ronzo and Cocoa Two, "Did you two see what I saw?"

We all were puzzled. Cocoa Two sat down on the seat, tilted his head, and stared at Harry as he whimpered. I took that to mean that he was as puzzled as Ronzo and I were.

"See what? What were we supposed to see?" Ronzo asked.

I swung my head around and around, as did Ronzo and Cocoa Two. The three of us had our heads on a swivel while we frantically searched the area for what we had missed. In the typical, dramatic Harry fashion, he would not reveal the secret of what we had missed. He slammed the Rhino 400 back into gear; he tore off to a traffic light where he could turn around and come back up the same side of the main road.

"I will show youse guys! Ya must be blind! I thought you were a goaltender, Paul, and you had eyes that could see a puck from four hundred yards!"

Harry tore down the street; he spun the Rhino 400 around at the first available turnaround and came tearing back up the side of the road. Cocoa Two was up in the seat, barking now as he sensed the excitement of a chase of some sort.

I had learned a long time ago, as had Ronzo, not to become caught up in the melodrama of one of Harry's spontaneous moments. He could have become excited over a hockey jersey sale in the window of a store, a bird sitting on a high wire, or a bug walking across the sidewalk. Harry always overly emphasized everything within the wild world of Harry M. Redmond Junior.

Harry roared into a large, used car lot and pulled the Rhino 400 to a screeching halt.

"C'mon, youse guys! I cannot believe that I was the only one who spotted this! This is unreal, just unreal! Now, this is what I am talking about! I love this!"

Harry jumped out of the Rhino and he just about sprinted full speed across the used car lot.

"Well, Paul, so much for going to the Rickel Home Improvement Store. Wonder what has, Harry all fired up now?" Ronzo shook his head as we both climbed out of the Rhino.

Cocoa Two ran ahead, he was barking the entire way, trying hard to catch up with Harry, who was already all the way across the lot, and running in between rows of shiny, used cars that were decorated with banners, brightly colored and spinning pinwheels rotating in the breeze, and sales signs hanging on them.

This was a typical used car lot in New Jersey. We were now on the outskirts of the city of Paterson, and these types of used car lots were commonplace throughout this area of northern New Jersey. The only establishments that outnumbered used car lots in this area were gin mills. These used car lots were all pretty much the same. They all had white, stone pebble gravel thrown around for driveways, with the cars lined up in neat rows upon the gravel. There were wooden poles sunk in the ground along the street frontage, with little white or clear light bulbs hanging from wires strung from pole-to-pole. The bulbs swung on the wires in the gentle breeze. There was a long, white trailer parked in the corner of the lot, with a large sign mounted upon it. The sign proudly proclaimed, "Honest Ralph Dennis' Used Car Sales," in bright, large, block letters. Underneath the company name was the usual mandatory slogan, with the sales pitch, "Where you come for a good deal, and a good deal more!"

Ronzo and I caught up with Harry and Cocoa Two, to find Harry standing with his hands on his hips, as he studied a large vehicle that resembled, for lack of a better description; a civilian version of an armored military personnel carrier.

"Can you believe this? Do you know what this vehicle is?" Harry was beside himself with excitement as he walked around the huge vehicle. Cocoa Two followed his every move.

The car, or whatever it was; had four doors, a giant hood scoop, sidewall scoop vents, and two giant, exhaust pipes exiting the rear of the vehicle. On the rooftop were two antennas, one of which looked as if it was a small radar dish. The paint finish on the car was a deep, highly polished, black color, and I could see my reflection in the finish of the vehicle. It was a gorgeous machine, with a huge chrome grille that resembled a Rhinoceros' open mouth. On the edge of the hood were two horns such as you would see on a Rhinoceros' snout. The vehicle had red and yellow flames painted around the sidewall air intakes to simulate flames and fire. The tires were huge, about eighteen inches around, with big chrome wheels with the center of the wheel covers covered in the famous Substantial Industries logos. I peered into the windows and checked out the interior which resembled a spaceship. The dashboard had all kinds of gauges, knobs, dials, and instruments. It was so complex; I could not even tell you how you would start the engine up. It had a large steering wheel and, on the floor, there was a fancy stick shift with a big, chrome knob mounted on the end. The logo on the center of the steering wheel was the famous Substantial Industries company logo, but it appeared as if it was gold cast! I then spotted the famous Rhino logo on the dashboard.

Before I could open my mouth to take a guess at what kind of vehicle it was, Harry jumped in.

"Youse guys don't know nuthin'! This is an ultra-limited edition, Substantial Industries Rhino 500S with the nine-hundred-cubic-inch, jet pack, super whiz-bang, dual turbo infused, nitro-burner engine! This one even has the coveted on-board radar option! I have been after one of these puppies for a year, ever since they sold out before I could order one! They only made about five thousand of these babies! It is super rare!" I vaguely recalled during our infamous quest for the peppermint ice cream, Harry mentioning wanting this type of vehicle.

Harry was very excited, and he was drooling at the sight of the vehicle. Harry went around and around the vehicle, scanning every inch of it.

"It looks like a tank, Harry. What would you do with it? It does not exactly look like some kind of family car," Ronzo commented, as he was staring inside of the vehicle shaking his head.

"How are you boys doing there today?" I nearly jumped out of my skin as I turned around to see a large, muscular man making his way towards us. He was a light-skinned, black man with short hair, a thin trace of a beard and moustache, and a huge, wide smile with a slight gap in his front teeth. He seemed very happy and friendly. He was waving his hands over his head in a greeting. This was a big man, his arms were the size of my legs, and he was as tall as I was.

This man was also very loud.

"Hey there, men! I see that fantastic vehicle has caught your eyes! One of a kind there, men, one of a kind! A super rare Rhino 500S! I just picked it up, only a few thousand miles on it now, it is just about brandy, dandy, new!" The four of us gathered together as Harry moved close to meet the salesman. Harry extended his hand out to greet him.

The big man was still bellowing out his sales pitch,

"Honest Ralph Dennis here! Where you can get a good deal, and a good deal more! I stand behind everything we sell or do!"

Ronzo leaned over to me and whispered, "Yeah, he does Paul, but he is not saying how far he stands behind them."

"Hello there, Ralph! Harry M. Redmond Jr. is the name here. Inventor, businessman, entrepreneur, welder, hit songwriter, womanizer, and general, all around windbag and a loudmouth, but overall, I am not a bad guy! That fantastic dog over there is Cocoa Two. He is the world's second smartest dog. The guy there in the, No Way tee shirt is Pastor Paul John Henson, the best long-haired, hippie, pastor in all of New Jersey, who also happens to be the famous now retired, long-haired, hippie, greatest, ice hockey goaltender of all time, number twenty-seven. I am sure you heard about his famous career there, Ralph!"

Honest Ralph did not say a word as he stared at us. I am sure he did not expect to meet a loudmouth, horn blower quite on the same level as himself. This was going to be interesting, Honest Ralph Dennis versus Harry M. Redmond Junior. I could tell by the look in Harry's eyes that he wanted this vehicle, and that he was prepared to wheel and deal.

"The big guy over there is Ronzo. He is my brother-in-law, and let me tell you, that he is the best electrician in the entire world. If you have any light bulbs shorted out in these wires here above our heads, then Ronzo is the man for you."

Typical Harry, as he went on and on with a long-winded, overblown introduction that went on forever. The two men shook hands.

"Nice to meet you there, Harry! Nice to meet you, Pastor Paul, Ronzo, and this nice doggie here. By the way, the name is Honest Ralph. I had it legally changed a year or so ago. You mentioned that your dog's name is Cocoa too, but I did not follow who else has the name Cocoa. You said

Cocoa too, so who else is named Cocoa?" Honest Ralph looked around as if he missed someone from our group. Oh no, here we go again.

Ronzo stepped in to try to intercept the usual banter and confusion before it spiraled out of control. "No, Honest Ralph, it is Cocoa number two, there was a Cocoa before him."

"So, was the first Cocoa, Cocoa One, or just Cocoa?"

"Just, Cocoa."

"I got it, wow. That was a little confusing, but I got it now. So, Harry, old boy, you like this fine automobile. I bet you can picture yourself behind the wheel right now, riding down the street, with the wind blowing in your face, people snapping pictures of you, whilst you roll along like some Hollywood movie star! Let me tell you that today is your lucky day because Honest Ralph is here to make you a deal that will light your socks on fire!" Honest Ralph stood and he put his left leg and foot out in front of his right leg. He bent down slightly, tugged at his pants legs, and pointed at Harry with his right hand, while extending his pointer finger out.

It seemed to be some type of pre-negotiation ritual.

I hoped that poor Honest Ralph knew whom he was dealing with. Harry's eyeballs were darting back and forth in his head like windshield wipers in a thunderstorm, and he was about to turn on his super blabber switch.

"Say Honest, let's cut to the chase. You see, I have been searching for one of these puppies for a long time. I am a star already so that sales angle will not work on me. You do know that I am on the television with my commercials right after yours, at around two o'clock in the morning on channel eleven! You know, the world famous, Annoy-O-Meter, Harry Burgers, The Lovely Rose Club and Restaurant. I am that, Harry! Your commercials are pretty good there, Honest Ralph, almost as obnoxious as mine are! I like the one with you lifting up the end of one of your cars and flipping it around. You are one big, strong, guy there, Honest."

Honest Ralph's eyes grew wide as he displayed some type of recognition of Harry.

"Why sure, sure, I knew that I recognized you! I love those little meter things. I owe my career and all of my success in life to that invention! You see, I hung one on the wall of my office where I used to work and put my boss's name on it. He was this super annoying, baldheaded, imbecile. The guy was a maniac, worked all the time, spoke in a bunch of gibberish. I think he was from Paterson. When he spotted it on my wall with his name on it, he canned me. Right then and there, I decided to follow my lifelong dream and open up my own used car lot. So here, we are now! Strange world there, Harry, but I love those Annoy-O-Meters. I have my wife up on it right now."

"Nice story there, Honest. A little risky on the old career move and with the wife-a-roo-ski there, but I am glad it all worked out for you because of my meters. I think you should already provide me with a discount since my meters started you on this lucrative career."

"Don't work that way, Harry," Honest Ralph was shaking his head and shooting down Harry's suggestion of a discount. "I don't owe ya that much. It is a hunk of plastic that hangs on a wall."

"Yeah, yeah, yeah, but people love 'em, cuz there are too many jerks in the world. So, can we start this Rhino 500S up and check it out?"

"Sure, it purrs like a kitten and roars like a rhino. Climb on in there, Harry, you and the rest of your gang."

Honest Ralph unlocked the doors, and we all climbed into the vehicle. Cocoa Two jumped in the backseat with Ronzo and Honest Ralph. I sat in the passenger's seat next to Harry, who was eagerly climbing into the driver's seat. I had to admit that it was some kind of fantastic experience sitting in the Rhino 500S. It was like the inside of a cockpit for a spaceship. Harry turned the ignition on and the giant engine roared to life. Needles, gauges, lights, and buzzers all moved, buzzed, and glowed. The quiet hum of the instruments gave a high-tech glow to the inside of the vehicle. Joy and vehicle exuberance overcame the famous Harry M. Redmond Junior. It was like the first ride so long ago in the famous Trans Whizzer! Blue lights flashed on the dashboard, red lights on the headliner flashed and glowed. A radio came to life, and the speakers thumped with the latest hit song on the radio. As I sat in the seat, all of a sudden, the seat automatically moved and glided forward, then backwards, as did Harry's seat.

"Look at that, Paul, the electronic sensors, they are automatically adjusting our seats for us! This thing is super unreal!" Harry spouted as he sat back and allowed his seat to adjust automatically.

A voice came over the speakers and some kind of weird and strange electronic voice spoke to us, "Hello. Welcome to the Rhino 500S. I am your personal assistant and guide, Howard. Would you like to take a ride today?"

Harry seemed to be well versed in the unique features of the Rhino 500S. He jumped right in there and answered the synthesized voice.

"Yes, Howie!"

This was really bizarre.

"My systems have detected a driver, a passenger, and two passengers in the rear seat along with a dog. Their names, please?"

"I am, Harry, the driver. The front passenger is Pastor Paul. In the back are Ronzo, Honest Ralph, and Cocoa Two."

"I understand, but somehow, I missed who else is named Cocoa."

Oh no!

"No, no, no, Howie, the dog's name is Cocoa Two, as in figure two."

"I do not understand, Harry, in addition to Cocoa."

"No, Cocoa number two."

Honest Ralph leaned forward and pushed a button on the dashboard as he wisely told us, "Hey, guys, let's just override the onboard, personal assistant for now. Harry, we are going around the block, not to the moon." The voice faded away, and a light went out on the dashboard.

"Good idea, we can figure it out later there, Honest Ralph."

Harry put the Rhino 500S in gear and we took off. I had to admit the vehicle was awesome. It was quite the experience just riding in the passenger seat.

"Yahoooooooo!" Harry yelled out. Up and down main roads and side roads he rolled. He was thrilled as he roared through the gears and revved the big engine up.

"Paul, this rig-a-roo-ski has more than twenty times the horsepower than the Trans Whizzer had! What a machine! Where is one of them secret agent guys to race now?"

Honest Ralph was smiling broadly. He smelled that a sale was close, "So what do you say Harry, do we have a deal or what? Let's go back to the car lot and see what we can do to put this fabulous machine in your name!"

Harry was so beside himself with exhilaration over the Rhino 500S that I thought for just a moment or two that he would forget his wheeling and dealing legacy, and fold like a cheap camera.

I was wrong.

"Well, not so fast there, Honest Ralph, hold on a minute or two here. I have not even heard what the price is for this vehicle. After all, a man of my stature, importance, and connections, I could find one of these over on the other side of town, or maybe the other side of the world, over in the big city there."

Honest Ralph was not buying that as he shook his head adamantly, "No way there, Harry, this is a one-of-a-kind vehicle. There are no others in the entire metro area. I am afraid it is a pricey vehicle, but let's see what we can do." Harry pulled into the lot and we all climbed out of the Rhino 500S. It was time to talk turkey and Harry was on it now.

The world's greatest dealmaker versus Honest Ralph.

Retail combat!

Harry rubbed his hands together in glee as the deal making started, "Let's go here, Honest! I got cash-a-roo-ski on the barrelhead, Honest. I can pay cash, no loans, no finance, and no hassle! Give me the cash price there, Honest-a-roo-ski Ralphie."

Honest Ralph leaned in, put his giant leg and foot on the bumper of the Rhino 500S. He looked at us and then at Harry. Cocoa Two sat down and studied Honest Ralph.

Honest Ralph rubbed his face and his neck with his hands, "Well, let's see. Do you want the extended, super-deluxe, Honest Ralph's special warranty, or just the regular deal?"

"Regular deal, Honest, it is a Rhino, they never have any troubles or breakdown!"

The warranty details intrigued me, so I spoke up, "Harry, maybe we could find out the details of the special warranty. . .."

Harry waved his hands at me "Nah, nah, nah, stop being such an old lady, Paul. It is a Rhino! I tell you that I do not need any special warranties. These vehicles never break down. Here we go, Honest, I am the best there is at negotiation, ya know! The keywords are cash, cash, and cash!"

Harry scratched at the stones under his boots with his left foot as he dug in.

Honest Ralph stood back, "Thirty thousand, two hundred for you there, Redmond! Do you want the extra, driveway starter clicker option?"

"No way! I don't need no clickers or clackers! C'mon Honest! Twenty-seven thousand, and five hundred! Or we walk!"

Honest Ralph put his hands in his pockets and paced back and forth a little.

This was getting dramatic.

He suddenly stopped, turned, tugged at his pants, and pointed his finger again while he shouted, "Do you want the special, auto tire inflator option? I will throw it in free for twenty-eight-thousand-two hundred."

"Nope, I am walking, Honest Ralph. All these razz–a-ma-tazz options, let's go men and Cocoa Two!"

"Harry, maybe, we could ask Honest Ralph what the options do for. . .."

"Forget it, Paul! He is stalling! Let's go!"

Cocoa Two jumped up, along with Ronzo, and we all headed for the Rhino 400.

"Hold on, hold on, if you think you do not want or need the options or the special warranty, we can do the deal, Harry! I can see you are the best in the wheeler-dealer business! You say you can give me cash. How soon?"

Harry stopped in his tracks and smiled, "I am a kijillionaire there, Honest. I can get my accountants, bankers, and all kinds of other folks who work for me on the telephone, twenty-four seven. Even though it is a Saturday, all I need is a telephone, and I can have the money wired in a minute. Twenty-seven thousand even, and I transfer the dough to you as soon as we sign the title."

Honest Ralph smiled and extended his hand out, "No options, and no special warranty? I will be honest with you . . . you will need them someday."

"Yeah, yeah, yeah, forget it. Save the extra, up-sells for someone else there, Honest Ralph. I am way too sharp for that angle! That is my final offer, Honest Ralph, take it now or we walk."

I leaned into Harry along with Ronzo. Cocoa Two jumped up on the hood of the Rhino 400 to listen in.

"Thirty-five, I do think that perhaps, we should find out more about the options and the details of the warranty."

Harry put up his finger and hand, and we huddled up a few steps away from the negotiation circle, as Harry excused himself from Honest Ralph.

Ronzo told Harry, "I agree with twenty-seven, Harry, it cannot hurt to ask before you make the deal."

Cocoa Two barked twice. We looked at him and he wagged his tail back and forth three times. Harry seemed to understand that this was the equivalent of Cocoa Two saying that he agreed with Ronzo and me.

"Look youse guys, who is Mr. Deal Maker here? No one has ever out-foxed Harry M. Redmond Jr. on a deal. He is trying to add on to the price with worthless, useless stuff, under the pretense that I am gonna need them someday. Ha! I know that old trick! Someday never comes. No offense, but look, Paul, you are a hippie, Lutheran pastor, who used to be a goalie, and let's be honest here. Ya took a lot of blows to the head. Ronzo, you are a retired electrician, who has sucked down an awfully large amount of Boryeungous mixtures and Dingleberry beers over the years, and Cocoa Two, you are my dog." Cocoa Two's tail sagged down since it appeared to be some kind of revelation to him that he was actually a dog, and not a human.

We all shook our heads and conceded defeat. Harry smiled and walked over to Honest Ralph.

"Can you put one of those paper, whoosie thingies, for a temporary plate and registration on the Rhino, so I can drive it this weekend, Honest Ralph?"

"Sure, sure, sure, we got 'em right in the office."

"Done deal, let's go make the call and sign the papers! Paul, I will be here for a little while finishing this deal. Why don't you and Ronzo head for the Rickel Home Improvement Store and pick up the supplies while I finish the deal here?"

"Cocoa Two and I will work the deal, pick up the chickens, and meet youse guys back at the house. You drive like an old lady, so we will end up beating you back to the house, anyway."

Cocoa Two barked twice, and he wagged his tail back and forth three times. Even a dog knew that I drove slowly. Harry clapped his hands together and pushed all of his hair away from his forehead as he told us, "Rose is going to be thrilled when she sees the new car!"

Harry threw me the keys to the Rhino 400.

I caught them and said, "Sure, Harry, we will meet you back home."

Ronzo and I climbed into the Rhino 400. I started the car up and slipped it into gear.

"You know something, Paul? Harry is the only guy in the entire world, who can go out for electrical supplies and some whole roasting chickens and come back home with a thirty-thousand-dollar vehicle. Rose is going to kill him."

I could only add a very weak, "She sure is, Ronzo, she sure is." Then again, nothing, I do mean nothing, about Harry M. Redmond Jr. surprised me anymore.

Ronzo and I pulled into the driveway of the Redmond home to see Harry showing off the new Rhino 500S while Rose stood there with her arms folded in front of her and a stern look on her face. Binky, Linny, Cocoa Two, Paul William, and Heather Sarah stood there watching.

"Oh, boy, Paul. It looks like some fireworks there," Ronzo elbowed me in the side, as we grabbed our bags of supplies and jumped out of the Rhino. Heather Sarah, and Paul William spotted me, came running over, and jumped around me.

"Pick me up, Father, pick me up! I missed you!" Heather Sarah was tugging at me, so I reached down and picked her up in my arms. She looked as though she could use a nap.

Paul William signaled for me to lean over so he could

speak to me quietly, "Auntie Rose is very mad at Uncle Harry for buying that fancy truck, but we think it is neat!"

"I see that, Paul William, oh well, it will be fine." Paul William then ran over to tell Ronzo the same, "inside scoop." Ronzo made believe that he had not guessed that would be the case.

I walked over to Binky's side as she smiled at me. "Harry is in a little hot water here. It is some kind of amazing vehicle though, Paul. I see that Heather Sarah could use a nap."

Heather Sarah was leaning on my shoulder, holding Fritzie tightly in her little hands.

"Once Rose has finished berating Harry, then we can ask Rose if we could put her down in the extra bedroom upstairs." I nodded and turned to watch the battle going on.

"Honestly, Harry, you are the only man on this entire planet who could go for whole roasting chickens and electrical supplies and come back with a thirty-thousand-dollar automobile!" Ronzo looked at me and winked.

"Oh, please forgive me darling, these are the safest vehicles on the road, you know. It is perfect for the baby!" Rose turned to Binky for statistic and fact confirmation. You could never fudge anything and get away with it with my wife around.

Binky fluffed her hair, tugged at her neckline, dug her left foot in the ground, and answered, "Dear Rose, Harry is quite correct. My research shows that the Rhino 500S is the safest vehicle ever produced. The Rhino 500S chassis is the identical framework and structure as a very similar, military vehicle in use today. It could survive unscathed with a direct hit from a rocket-propelled grenade."

Ronzo looked at the Rhino 500S, rubbed his chin, and said, "I sure could have used one of them over in Vietnam."

As usual, Rose could never stay mad at the big guy for

very long. She smiled and gave him a big hug.

"Oh well, if it is a safe vehicle, and it is best for the baby, then I guess it is fine. You still drive me nuts, Harry, you really do! What will you do with the Rhino 400?"

"Keep it! I would give it to twenty-seven and Binky, except that I know that Paul would not take it—even for free, until that old jeep falls apart, and the wheels roll off of it."

Everything was well in the world of Harry and Rose once more. Binky put Heather Sarah down for a nap. We had a quick lunch, and we finally began to work on the electrical system in the nursery. Between Ronzo, Harry, and me, it did not take us long at all to finish the work. We wired the room in one afternoon, and the room was now ready for drywall and finishing. It was going to be an elaborate and magnificent baby nursery that was for sure. Before we all knew it, the work was completed, we cleaned up, and it was time for dinner. It had been a long, but productive day.

"I have to show you this cooker, youse guys! It is the most complex appliance in the history of the world! Look! Here it is! My brand-new Substantial Industries, Whiz-Bang, Super Deluxe, Sonic-Spinner Cooker," Harry told us as he stood proudly in front of his latest piece of equipment.

Harry, Ronzo, and I stood in front of the counter in the kitchen staring at a large, stainless steel machine sitting upon the counter. It had a thick, glass lid, with a big motor on the side of it. The front of the cooker had the famous Substantial Industries logo emblazoned upon the nameplate. The cord and electrical plug coming out of the side of the cooker looked as if it would power the entire town of Shadow Lakes. Vehicles, play sets, appliances, tools, you name it, and Harry had it. He was a Substantial Industries man!

"You want a beer, Paul? Big Boulder or a Dingleberry?"

"Sure Ronzo, please let me have a Big Boulder, those Dingleberries are just a little too sweet."

I had made a Martini (shaken, not stirred) for Binky. Rose and Linny both were enjoying virgin Purple Pirates in the living room while the children sat in front of the television watching *Dinky the Orange Teddy Bear.* The ladies had asked if we needed help in preparing dinner, but we all puffed our chests out and told them to relax, that we had this all under control. Cocoa Two joined us now as we gathered in the kitchen to watch Harry demonstrate his latest contraption.

"Now, watch this carefully, youse guys, all I have to do is load the chickens on this big rod, dial up the setting on the dial, and in seconds, the chickens are cooked. It is just as the commercials tell you. You will be enjoying a fully cooked chicken within seconds! This thing is beyond belief!"

I picked up the instruction book, and I was thumbing through it, while we watched Harry pull out this long, steel skewer and push it through the center of the chickens. He then placed it inside the cooker.

I read the instructions aloud, "Warning. For three, two pounds or fewer, whole roasting chickens—set the dial to twenty-two. For each chicken after that, use the chart on page ninety-seven. How many chickens do you have in there, Harry?"

"Oh, please, Paul, stop being such an old lady. Everybody knows that instructions are just a bunch of hooey. Ya just guess at the time, what can go wrong?" I had a rather vivid flashback to about a million other times when I had heard Harry utter those same words, and all the things that went wrong after he spoke them.

Harry slammed the lid shut, he randomly spun the knob, and the cooker lit up with a bright glow. The appliance made a loud, whirring noise that grew louder and louder. Harry, Ronzo, and I leaned over and peered into the glass front. Cocoa Two rolled over on his back on the floor, put his paws over his eyes, and whimpered a little.

Louder and louder, the noise from the cooker became. The chickens were spinning around like rocket ships and a bright glow was surrounding them. Faster and faster, they went around and around, spinning and glowing! The glow became brighter and brighter until they suddenly exploded into flames!

"Shut it off, twenty-seven! Pull the plug! My chickens are blasting off to the moon!"

I ran for the plug and yanked it out of the wall, but it was too late. The Substantial Industries, Super Deluxe, Whiz-Bang, Sonic-Spinner Cooker, was smoking like a bonfire. Smoke billowed out of it as Ronzo ran for the patio door in the back of the kitchen and opened it up. Harry grabbed some potholders, picked up the Substantial Industries, Super Deluxe, Whiz Bang, Sonic-Spinner Cooker and sprinted outside with it. He tossed it out on the patio and we watched as it bounced and tumbled across the rear patio. The chickens burst free of the cooker and tumbled here and there, completely burned to a crisp. The chickens were still on fire and smoking as they lit some grass on fire in the back of the patio.

"Well, maybe it is not exactly as the television commercial shows you," Ronzo said as he stood there shaking his head, while watching Harry run around on the patio.

Cocoa Two was running around barking and hollering, the fire alarms had gone off in the house, and the ladies and the kids came running from the living room, to see what had happened. Harry ran, grabbed a nearby garden hose, and hit the entire mess with water to put the fire out. Off in the distance . . . we heard the sound of fire sirens.

"Oh no, the fire department is coming, twenty-seven," was all I heard Harry mumble. He then turned to me and pointed his finger up to me, "Don't say a word about the instructions! Not a blankity-blank-blank-blank word!"

I held my hands up and shrugged my shoulders.

Binky met the firemen at the front door and let them in. The firemen dashed in the front door and the gals led them to the scene of the chicken disaster. The children thought it was an exciting adventure, as they loved every minute of it. Some firemen, when they saw that it was all clear, took the kids, and showed them the fire truck and all the equipment.

"Say, Mr. Redmond, did you read the instructions? This is the fourth call we had this week for one of these Substantial Industries, Super Deluxe, Whiz Bang, Sonic-Spinner, Cookers that burst into flames," the lieutenant of the fire company asked.

"Yeah, yeah, yeah, well thank you, men for coming out. I am sorry about this. I will make a big donation in September to help out you, boys." Harry led them out the front door and thanked them all individually for coming out.

"That was so cool, Uncle Harry! Can you burn up something else now by not following the instructions, so we can see the big fire truck again?" Paul William was up next to Harry, smiling and pleading.

Harry frowned, "Sure, sure, sure kid, go watch the rest of Dinky will ya."

One of the firemen came back, stood at the front door, and told Harry, "Nice rig there in the driveway, Mr. Redmond! One of those fancy Rhino 500S rigs, I think. Fantastic rig, but I wanted to tell you that all of your tires are flat. You must have run over a buncha' nails at a construction site or something like that. I thought that you would like to know."

We thanked the firefighter as we all rushed out into the driveway. Sure enough, every single one of the Rhino 500S tires had gone flat!

Harry was spitting bullets now. The steam was coming off his head, and he was turning redder and redder. I motioned to Binky. She hustled the children inside, and the ladies fled back in the house, in anticipation of the imminent explosions.

"Is Uncle Harry going to use bad words, dear Mother? Can I listen? Are the firemen coming back?" I heard Heather Sarah ask as Binky led them away.

Ronzo offered up a logical solution, "Maybe you have to pump them up with an air compressor or something, Harry. You know this thing has all kinds of gizmos and accessories."

After the Sonic Cooker incident, neither Ronzo nor I were brave enough to suggest, at this point, for Harry to read the operating manual for the vehicle.

Harry nodded while he opened the driver's door and climbed in the front seat. He turned the key as Ronzo, Cocoa Two, and I watched.

Nothing.

He looked at us, then tried it once more.

Nothing. Dead as a doornail!

Oh, oh! The Rhino 500S was nothing more than a giant hunk of fancy, polished metal sitting in Harry's driveway. The door swung open and Harry emerged from the cockpit, looking as if he was a wild man from the island of Borneo.

The eye of the tiger was upon him.

Both eyes!

Cocoa Two took one look at his master, and he sprinted off for the backyard like a rocket ship.

"#$#%^&* Honest my, @$$ Ralph Dennis! @#$%&#@ giant, loud-mouthed, no good, chiseling charlatan, used car salesman, hockey puck!" Harry was yelling and hollering as he walked back to the house. Ronzo and I did not say a word as we followed him into the kitchen. Cocoa two circled back around and crept in line behind us. I guess his curiosity outweighed his fear.

Harry picked up the phone, took out a business card, and dialed a number.

"Dennis! This is Redmond! Don't give me that Honest Ralph mumbo jumbo! My tires are all flat and the Rhino will not start! WHAT? WHAT? WHAT? WELL, YOU HAD BETTER GET OUT HERE! Yes, that is right. One hundred and sixty-five Big Blowhard Road. No, they did not name the road after me! It is the white mansion on the left. You better bring your lawyer!"

Paul William came running into the kitchen and asked, "Do you want me to shoot Honest Ralph in the butt with the fuzzy ball gun when he shows up, Uncle Harry?"

"I will let you know, kid, now go find your mother."

Ronzo and I tried not to burst into laughter, as I signaled to Binky to grab our son, and pull him out of the fray.

Harry slammed down the telephone and looked at the two of us. He folded his arms across his giant chest and frowned before speaking.

"Well, now, isn't this a whole lot of fun? Let's get another beer or two, and I am going to mix a strong, Wallcrawler for me to either drink or pour over Honest Ralph's head. We all will then wait for him in the driveway. He said that he would be right out."

Harry walked to the cupboards, and turned to Ronzo, Cocoa Two, and me and asked, "Does it smell a little like smoke in here or what?"

We did not say too much as we waited in the driveway. The ladies and the children hid in the house. Sure enough, a tow truck came rolling down the street and turned into the long driveway. Painted on the side of the truck was a sign with bright, blue letters stating, "Honest Ralph's Towing Service."

The tow truck parked behind the Rhino 500S and out of the driver's seat popped Honest Ralph Dennis.

"Hey, Harry! Hey, Pastor Paul! Hey, Ronzo and Cocoa

Two!"

Ronzo and I waved very carefully from a safe distance and Cocoa Two barked once. But he kept it very soft, and he did not wag his tail. The dog was too smart to risk stepping on his master's toes.

"Enough with the happy greetings there, Dennis, my car is a glorified paperweight right now!"

"Now, now, Harry, calm down. I can get this back in shape in a few minutes, calm down now, it will all be good very shortly."

We sat on the porch while we watched the scene unfold. Honest Ralph was whistling a happy tune as he went into the truck, took out a toolbox, some boxes that seemed to have some parts in them, and he went over to the hood of the Rhino 500S. He lifted the hood and began to work.

After a few minutes, he asked for the key from Harry, Honest Ralph jumped in the truck and turned the key. The Rhino 500S started right up as the big engine roared to life. Honest Ralph jumped out of the Rhino 500S and stood next to the vehicle. He took a large hand unit out of his pocket, aimed it at the Rhino 500S, and pushed a button. We could hear a loud pumping noise, as suddenly, all four of the tires on the vehicle started to inflate. We stood there in amazement as Honest Ralph walked around the vehicle, picked up his tools, and went back to his tow truck.

Harry stood there with his hands on his hips and his mouth wide open. Honest Ralph stood at the door to his truck for a little while, writing on a bunch of papers on a clipboard. He then glided over to where we were all standing dumbfounded as we suddenly all realized what had transpired.

Honest Ralph smiled widely, as he handed Harry a long invoice and explained, "There you go there, Harry. Back in shape. That will be three thousand, two hundred dollars. The special, auto inflator option is one thousand, the extra driveway starter option is two thousand, and the service charge and tow call is two hundred dollars. I tried to tell you that you would need this all someday, but you would not listen. If you had only taken the extended, super deluxe, Honest Ralph's warranty, then, I have to tell you that the warranty would have covered all of these repairs. After all, I am Honest Ralph Dennis and I was, well, just being honest."

Harry sighed as he took the pen from Honest Ralph's hand and signed the ticket. "I will send you the dough on Monday and sign me up for the extended warranty will ya, there, Honest. I will have my accountant call you on Monday to take care of all of this."

"Thank you, Harry! Youse guys have a wonderful evening. It looks as if youse are having a party! You must be having a barbeque, cuz it smells like smoke around here. Enjoy, and remember come to Honest Ralph Dennis' Used Car Sales for a good deal, and a good deal more!"

Harry weakly shook Honest Ralph's hand, while we watched him back out of the driveway. Cocoa Two squeezed past us as he also watched Honest Ralph back out of the driveway. He beeped the horn on his truck as he waved goodbye. We all waved goodbye as he disappeared down the road. Cocoa Two barked four times as he watched Honest Ralph riding away.

Harry turned to Ronzo, Cocoa Two, and me, as he said, "Not a word out of any of youse about how we tried to tell you, Harry!" We both held up our hands, and Cocoa Two stuck his tail down between his legs and sulked away.

"Rose, I guess we better order pizza, honey!" Harry bellowed as he walked in the house and conceded defeat from what we now had labeled "the great, sonic cooker, chicken disaster."

"I also need the hotline number for Substantial Industries to order me another Sonic-Spinner Cooker!"

"All right, Harry darling. The number is on the pad next to the telephone in the kitchen, my love. I am going to call that new place that just opened up right next to the Foodworld in the center of town. It has a funny name, but I heard from a neighbor that it is really good. It is Honest Ralph's Famous Pizza. They deliver too."

Harry stopped in his tracks, smiled, and shook his head, "That will be fine, Rose. We will be in the kitchen working to get the smoke out!"

Forever in perpetuity, there was a picture of Honest Ralph Dennis on the wall in Harry's office. He was in his famous pose, with his finger extended out pointing at the camera, with his famous, wide, gap-tooth smile, while he tugged at the side of his pants with his left leg and left foot stepping forward.

Harry admired him more than even he would admit.

He was the only man in history that had ever successfully outmaneuvered and snookered, the world famous, Harry M. Redmond Jr. on a deal, and came close to establishing an empire equivalent to Harry's world of gizmos, gadgets, restaurants, factories, and general huff and puff.

Honest Ralph Dennis deserved his place of honor forever more.

8

Blue Cloud on Our Horizon

"Well, indeed, I am counting my lucky stars that Redmond is driving us all up to Albany, New York. You drive like an old lady, Henson, and by the time we would make it to upstate New York, the conference would be over. I could walk faster on one leg than it takes you to drive there, Henson. An old bag on roller skates can move faster than you do, Henson. Especially in that old, relic of a jeep that you drive! You would think with the exorbitant salary that you pull down for doing nothing all day, and being a sluggard, you would cough up a few coins and buy something newer!"

Bishop Werner Beck Clodhopper Von Houten was in rare form today. He stood in the driveway of the parsonage of Reunion Lutheran Church with his suitcases and golf club bags sitting on the ground next to him. The two of us stood together in the driveway, near the base of the walkway that led from the front door of the parsonage. We were waiting for Binky to come out of the parsonage, and for Harry and Rose to arrive and pick us up. It was right after the Fourth of July holiday, and we were all heading up to Albany, New York, for the Lutheran Northeastern District conference that we had planned to attend back at the end of last year.

It was a warm, typical July morning in northern New Jersey. The sun was coming up hard and it was going to be a little hot and sticky later on. It was early yet, a few minutes before eight o'clock in the morning, and we were planning to get an early start for the three-hour or so ride up to Albany, New York.

"Well, Bishop Von Houten, my old jeep is very reliable, but we would all not have been able to fit in there. Harry has this huge Rhino 500S, and with Rose nearing the end of her pregnancy, Harry wanted her to be comfortable. The Rhino 500S is like a floating hotel. You could play baseball in the backseat. It is quite a vehicle."

"I guess, Henson. Nice spin on it, but Redmond knows that you drive like an old lady too."

"I simply try to obey the laws and rules of the road, sir."

"Sure, whatever there, Henson. Someday, you will get a ticket for driving too slow and impeding traffic. Say, you better not let your wife see that you have all of that hair tied up behind your head. It will fire up Mrs. Henson before we can even leave the driveway. So, Henson . . . will you, please tell me once more, when is the Redmond baby due?"

"The last week of July, to the first week of August, sir," I said as I pulled the hair tie out of my hair and put it in my pocket.

"Rose just had a checkup last week, and the doctor thought it would be around the third day or so of August."

The bishop looked at me and asked, "And she is up for this trip and walking around?"

"Yes sir, Harry said that the doctor thought it would be good for her to move around a bit. The exercise is beneficial."

"Things have gone well for Mrs. Redmond, since some of that early trouble she had with the pregnancy? She is around her mid-thirties in age or so now, I would guess."

"She had some difficult morning sickness early on sir, but ever since then, it has been smooth sailing. Yes, I think Rose is around thirty-five or thirty-six. She is around the same age as Harry, Binky, and me. We are all within a few years of one another."

"Good, nice to hear. God bless her and the child. She is quite a wonderful woman, and she sure is beautiful, as is Mrs. Henson. I could never understand what two gorgeous women, such as both of your wives are—ever saw, in two ugly mugs like you and Redmond. You're getting older now Henson, you would think you would wake up and shave that hairball face of yours and cut off that mop of hair!" I did not answer him, but I did crack a smile.

The bishop nodded and put his hands on his hips. He turned and looked around at the church and the buildings.

"It pains me to admit that it is looking good around here, Henson! The construction is really coming along now. I am sure that you had very little to do with the success, yup, without a doubt, it must have been Redmond's business guidance, and his keen sense steering you along. Of course, all of my efforts, leadership, and guidance, have also, unquestionably and rather obviously, contributed to the outstanding accomplishment of this project, Henson."

"Without a doubt, Bishop Von Houten."

"The rededication ceremony and grand opening is still on schedule?"

"Yes sir, it looks good. We are still on course for the big day, to be that first Sunday in September. We can kick off the school year, the new worship schedule, and the new confirmation classes in September. The timing will be perfect. It is very exciting."

The bishop smiled and said to me, "That will work out fine, Henson. I will be sure to be nice and tan from a few rounds of golf over the rest of the summer, so I will look good in all the pictures!"

"Good idea, sir."

"If you would stop bugging me all the time, then perhaps, I could actually get out there and enjoy a day or so of golf, Henson!"

"I understand, sir. I will try to limit my demands on your time."

Bishop Von Houten looked back at me, and he increased his usually loud and overpowering voice, a few notches above even the normal Von Houten level, "I hope you have worked on one of those weepy-eyed sermons that you usually whip up there, Henson! I am counting on you not to blow it since I must have been under the influence of a few stronger beverages the day that I filled out that official form and selected you to make the keynote sermon for our district. I remember that day, I was drowning my sorrows at a rare loss at the hand of Goldberg by a mere few strokes, and I lost my mind for a few minutes. I think I spoke to you on the telephone earlier in the day. It must have upset me, and I lost my concentration on the course. Rabbi Goldberg swooped in and preyed upon me at a weak moment."

"I do apologize for that, sir. I think I have a good one, Bishop Von Houten. Would you like to proofread the draft? The main topic is the power of unity."

"No, no, no, Henson! That is why I have people such as you. I have heard and read enough of your mindless drivel over the last few years. There you go pushing all the work off on me as usual!"

"Hello, twenty-seven! I have our bags packed here. They are in the doorway. You can come and get them for me while I grab a few more things! Make sure you keep the tie out of your hair, I saw that you had it in there a few minutes ago!" I turned around when I heard Binky call to me and waved back to her. She was standing in the front doorway of the parsonage.

"Yoo-hoo! Bore da! Good morning, Bishop Von Houten!" Binky waved from the front door.

Bishop Von Houten sucked in his big gut, smoothed his hair down, smiled, and spun around as he waved back, "Why, good morning. Mrs. Henson! You are looking wonderful as usual today!"

Binky smiled and fluffed her hair as she yelled back,

"Why, thank you, dear Bishop Von Houten!"

I made my way up to the doorway and sighed when I spotted the huge, giant suitcases that Binky always packed. Two enormous black cases loomed in front of me. Binky always packed enough stuff to last us as if we were going away for at least twenty-two years. I knew that the combined weight of the cases would be around thirty or forty tons. Binky, of course, had no trouble moving them from our bedroom to here, with her superhuman strength. Harry and I would just about blow our guts out trying to get them in the Rhino 500S. It was even worse when we traveled with the children. I had to lug about four of these same size cases, and bags of toys, general supplies, stuffed animals of every known species in the world, strollers, snacks, and what seemed as though it was an entire drugstore worth of first aid supplies for a potential, "boo-boo" that one of the kids may suffer.

I picked up the first suitcase, heaved, and hauled it down the front walkway towards the driveway.

Bishop Von Houten watched me from the corner of the walkway and commented, "I remember a time when you would be able to pick that up with one hand there, Henson! Getting a little long in the tooth now and it is not so easy to run around putting your head through walls."

"Well, sir, I am still in very good shape, I still run almost every day. It is just that Mrs. Henson packs a mean suitcase. Excuse me, there is one more."

I stood the first suitcase upright at the end of the walkway and turned to pick up the next one. I grabbed it, heaved, and shoved it as best that I could towards the end of the walkway. Out of the corner of my eye, I spotted Bishop Von Houten walk over to the first one, and give it a little tug on the handle to test the weight. When he did not move it an inch, he turned and walked away from it, hoping that I did not notice that he could not budge it.

Binky was making her way down the front walkway as

she said, "Oh, good, Paul. I see that you brought the suitcases out to the end of the walkway. They were a little heavy. I noticed that I may have over-packed them just a bit, when I carried them down from our bedroom."

Bishop Von Houten stared at Binky, shook his head a little, but he did not say anything.

"I checked the house and we are all good, Dave said he would check the house while we were away. It is so nice to see you, Bishop Von Houten. That golf tan is looking good this summer!"

Bishop Von Houten sucked his gut in once more, smiled, and laughed a little as Binky gave him a hug and a kiss on the cheek. She knew how to work the bishop to turn him into a cupcake with vanilla frosting.

"Well, thank you, Mrs. Henson. Yes, yes, my, goodness. I have been barely able to get in a game here and there, between my busy schedules at work. It is not easy being the big boss, you know! Thank you, for the compliment, and as I mentioned before, you too, are looking wonderful today. Are you looking forward to the conference? It is very important for a pastor's wife to be seen supporting her husband's ideas and career."

"Oh, yes! I do agree, Bishop Von Houten. I am so excited about this trip. I have researched every detail and aspect of the agenda. Of course, it will be such a thrill to hear Paul give the keynote sermon, what a fabulous honor for him. I am so proud of him. I do not even have the words to convey how special that will be for both of us. I imagine you feel the same way. Do you not?"

Binky leaned in for a super-intense, Binky stare, waiting for his answer. The intensity of the stare overcame the bishop, and he stepped back a little to avoid Binky. He recovered quickly when he realized that he was on the ropes.

"Ahhemmm. Yes, of course, I was just saying that very thing to your husband. How I made a keen, well thought out, decision to nominate him for the keynote speaker role, and how we went over his sermon together, double-checking and choosing every word for accuracy and details. It will be a wonderful moment."

Oh, brother! My father-in-law may have been the career politician, but the bishop missed his true calling. He would have given Mr. Hobnobber a good run for his money for sure. Binky, of course, did not buy the act for a minute, but she took great satisfaction in having a little fun with Bishop Von Houten.

"How are those lovely children, Mrs. Henson? I am guessing that you dropped them off at your wonderful parent's home for a few days. Grandma and Grandpa are enjoying that, I am sure!"

"Oh yes, they are all thrilled. My father will spoil them rotten for the entire time. It will take Paul and me weeks to restore order to the rules that he will allow them to break. The children are very excited because Harry and Rose brought their dog Cocoa Two over to stay with them too. They just love Cocoa Two. My parents had agreed to dog sit, Cocoa Two."

Bishop Von Houten screwed his face up like a corkscrew; I just knew the confusion was coming.

"Your children are not being dog sat—they are people, Mrs. Henson. I understand they love their grandparents and Cocoa the dog, but they are not being dog sat."

"Oh no, bishop, it is Cocoa Two, not Cocoa."

"Who else is named Cocoa, Mrs. Henson?"

I stepped in waving my hands. Sometimes I did not have the patience for wading through this Cocoa infused, mixed up, madness.

"No sir, the dog is named Cocoa Two, as in figure or the number two. He is the second dog that Harry has named Cocoa."

"Oh, I see. On the other hand. I think I see there, Henson. Typical Henson and Redmond madness and weirdness, I am afraid. I know I will regret the answer and I should not ask, but was the first Cocoa, named Cocoa One?"

"No sir, just Cocoa."

This was all so exhausting. Only in my life could a simple thing such as waiting in the driveway for my best friends to pick us up for a holiday, become such an adventure.

"Hmmm. I wonder why? I need to ask Redmond the logic behind that name."

"Well sir, you will have about three hours of driving with him to question him on it, because here they come."

We all turned around and looked at the entrance to the church parking lot as the roar of the giant, Rhino 500S engine rolled into the parking lot. Harry blasted the horn to signal his arrival. The horn on the Rhino 500S perfectly duplicated the roar of an actual, wild Rhinoceros. It nearly blew our ears off.

"My, goodness! What in the name of Heaven is that?" Bishop Von Houten almost fell over when Harry blasted the horn and gunned the giant engine.

Harry pulled the Rhino 500S to a grinding halt in the driveway right in front of us. He reached for a microphone which he had mounted on the dashboard, pushed a button, and his voice came booming over a public-address speaker mounted inside the front grille of the vehicle.

"Good morning, fellow Lutherans! What a fine morning it is too! Binky, you are looking wonderful in that nice, tight, dress! Oh my, oh my, ya got a fantastic figure there, girl! Great display of chest attributes, there, honey!"

Binky posed, smiled, and fluffed her hair.

"Twenty-seven, you look like a bum as usual. You need a haircut and a shave, and bishop old boy, you look as if you just kicked Rabbi Goldberg's @$$ all over the golf course!" We could see Rose punch Harry in the arm with one of her famous Rose punches, while she frowned at his outlandish behavior, and Harry roared with laughter at his usual bombastic, grand entrance.

"Atta boy, Redmond! Fine assessment of the situation at hand!" Bishop Von Houten was fist pumping in the air, at the thought of sending poor Rabbi Goldberg down to another defeat on the golf course. "Old Goldberg did not know what hit him this weekend. I was on fire out there on the course! I love this vehicle, I have no idea what it is, but it is fantastic!"

Bishop Von Houten was thrilled at the sight of the Rhino 500S, and he moved in closer to check it out. It had been another grand entrance for the grandiloquent and slightly obnoxious Harry M. Redmond Junior.

Rose and Harry got out of the Rhino 500S and Binky, Bishop Von Houten, and I greeted them both. Harry showed his excitement as he back slapped the bishop.

"I love this, bishop old boy! Now, this is what I am talking about!"

Rose was moving slowly, but she was looking wonderful. Her cheeks were red and rosy and she was full of life. In my opinion, I had to agree with Harry; she never looked more beautiful. She could not help but chuckle at Harry's sense of humor, and even though she apologized for his behavior, we knew that she secretly loved when the big guy acted up.

"Are you doing all right, Rose? My goodness, you look as if the baby is coming any day now!"

"No, Paul, the doctor assured me we are still a good three weeks or so away yet."

Binky studied Rose for a minute, smiled, and proclaimed, "Dear Rose, you have dropped a bit since last Friday when I last saw you. I do not know. You sure have the look! I think the doctor might be incorrect, dear Rose."

Rose shrugged her shoulders and laughed. We were not the doctors, so time would tell, but I knew my wife; and she was always spot on in her assessment of situations. I gave Rose a hug, and I had to agree, she sure looked ready to me!

Bishop Von Houten stood in the front of the Rhino 500S with his hands on his hips as he studied the awesome vehicle. He stared at the custom license plate mounted on the front and he read it aloud to all of us, 'LUVROSE' Much better than that stupid, goal twenty-seven, Henson has on that old relic he drives around! This vehicle looks just the same as an armored personnel carrier that Goldberg and I drove around in during the big war when we were chaplains together! What is it, Redmond? I dare say I have never seen such a vehicle outside of my days in the military during the war"

Harry came over and put his big arm around Bishop Von Houten.

"Bishop old boy, this is an ultra-limited edition, Substantial Industries Rhino 500S, with the nine-hundred-cubic-inch, jet pack, super whiz-bang, dual turbo infused, nitro-burner engine. It produces more horsepower than any vehicle ever made. It has onboard radar to tell you how close another car is to you, a full citizen's band radio communications system, a newfangled, talking, computer thingy that acts as a personal assistant, an easy chair recliner for one of the rear seats, and it is the safest vehicle ever made. Our baby will travel in style and in safety!"

Bishop Von Houten immediately turned around to Binky for a fact check, "Is that true, Mrs. Henson, is this the safest vehicle ever made?"

Binky produced a rapid head nod to confirm the facts, as she told him, "Indeed, it is. Furthermore, the second-place vehicle in the ratings is not even remotely close. The skid plates mounted underneath the vehicle could roll over hand grenades and not even be touched. It is the perfect vehicle for riding up and down State Highway Route 23, here in New Jersey."

The bishop was thrilled and as he walked around

discussing and admiring the Rhino 500S, I started to pack our bags and luggage in the rear cargo area. I opened the rear lid and looked in. It was huge; a person could live in the back of the Rhino 500S. I had managed to lug our two suitcases over to the vehicle, and when Harry came around, I enlisted his aid.

"Say, thirty-five, please give me a hand putting these in the back here."

"Sure, Paul," Harry said as he came over. "Oh no, Binky suitcases," the big guy cried out as he spotted the two black cases sitting there on the ground. We each grabbed an end, lifted, and heaved as we dropped them in the back. We had all we could do to get them in there, and the back of the Rhino 500S dropped about four inches when they landed in place.

"My goodness, what is in these, a ton of bricks? Harry stood up and rubbed his lower back. He smiled at me as he remembered the first Binky suitcase so long ago.

"The Trans Whizzer did not have this feature, Paul! Watch this, youse guys. Howie, are you out there?" We all gathered around as we watched the demonstration.

The dashboard of the Rhino 500S jumped to life, lights came on, and dials spun around and around in front of us. The radar antenna on the roof of the vehicle spun around and around as it searched for signals.

The voice of the onboard computer answered, "Why yes, Mr. Redmond. How can I be of assistance?"

"Howie, activate the anti-rear end droop, overzealous wife, suitcase packing option, would you please!"

Rose and Binky both turned around and looked at their backsides, with their mouths open and fierce looks on their faces, until they realized that Harry was speaking about the rear end of the Rhino 500S.

"Surely, Mr. Redmond. Please stand by."

The engine of the Rhino 500S started up, and we heard a pumping noise as the back end of the Rhino 500S lifted up and leveled out.

"Leave it running, Howie. Please turn the air conditioning on because we are all getting in!"

"Yes, Mr. Redmond."

"Amazing, Redmond! I love this. It is absolutely amazing!" Bishop Von Houten was thrilled. We loaded the bishop's suitcase and golf bags in the back, and we were set to go.

"Yeah, yeah, yeah. That was an option that I just had to go back and pick up from Honest Ralph. He installed a new interactive, voice activated, onboard personal assistant, Howie module. It originally came with the non-interactive Howie module. Howie recognizes my voice now."

Rose leaned over to us as we walked back to the doors of the Rhino and whispered, "Another five-grand worth of hooey that he just had to have installed."

I found it very interesting that Harry's new onboard computer system, with interactive personal assistance, had the tagged name of Howard. It reminded me of another very efficient chap named Howard that we all ran into years ago, at the famous Black Bear Club!

"Bishop, please sit in the front with Harry, I am going to recline in the easy recliner in the back seat with Paul and Binky."

"Are you sure, Mrs. Redmond?"

"Yes, please do. I will be very comfortable. I did not sleep much last night, so I think that I will be able to nap while we ride. The motion of the car always makes me sleepy."

"She will be comfy back there, bishop old boy, climb on up here in the cockpit with me! I can show you all the bells and whistles and we can talk about how many trophies you have won this summer so far on the course," Harry waved the bishop into the front seat. Bishop Von Houten was thrilled as he climbed in and studied all the dials, knobs, and flashing lights on the dashboard of the Rhino 500S.

"Sounds good to me there, Redmond! I never drift asleep while I ride! I am always on my toes, you know!"

We were off while Harry moved the big rig into gear and backed out of the driveway.

"Hello, Mr. Redmond. My sensors have detected three additional bodies in the seats, in addition to Mrs. Redmond and you."

"Correct, Howie, we have twenty-seven and Binky, along with Rose in the back, and bishop old boy in the front."

"Good morning, Pastor Paul and Mrs. Henson, and Mrs. Redmond. Hello, bishop, old boy. No, Cocoa Two?"

"No, Cocoa Two, Howie."

"That is in, Cocoa also?"

"How about we just say no dogs today there, Howie?"

"That will work, Mr. Redmond. Destination?"

"Albany, New York, Howie."

"Yes, Albany, New York. The location, where the famous number twenty-seven won a championship playing in goal for the Albany Flying Dutchman, and a league MVP award. A homecoming for Pastor Paul. Very nice, three hours, fifty-eight minutes to downtown Albany. We shall hope for no traffic."

This computer thingy was creepy, but it was really smart! I have a feeling; Harry programmed it with an awful lot of facts. Binky seemed completely unfazed by the weird voice technology that was coming out of the dashboard of Harry's latest gizmo. She smiled, fluffed her hair, and leaned back into the luxury of the rear seat.

I tilted over a bit towards Binky and whispered in her ear, "It sure is weird that this computer voice thingy sounds and acts, just the same as Howard Pailet did all those years ago, at the Black Bear Club. It kind of gives me the creeps, Binky."

"Oh, twenty-seven, it does remind me a little of Howard, but you are so lost in the old days sometimes. I have researched all of this, and computers will be everywhere in a few years. Very shortly, you will type all your sermons and your other writings on a small computer that you can sit in your lap. I think you need to embrace the technology and become used to it, my dear Paul. It should not give you the creeps. It is the new way, a wave of the future."

Binky kissed my cheek and put her arm through mine as she settled in. She then reached over, grabbed Rose's arm, and did the same. Oh well, I guess Binky was right, the 1970s were far behind me in the rear-view mirror. I was stuck in the past, but in a roundabout way, I was very happy to be there. I had a feeling that all these new gadgets did not necessarily mean they were better.

I think that I would be fine with a foldout road map.

There was no going back now, except in my memories.

Binky and Rose made some small talk, chatted, laughed, and discussed babies and pregnancy related items. Bishop Von Houten and Harry intensely spoke about his recent success on the golf course beating poor Rabbi Goldberg, the features of the Rhino 500S, as well as Harry telling the bishop about the charitable work that he was currently involved in. I listened with a half of an ear, jumped into the conversation when I needed to, and smiled quite a bit.

"Hey Paul, here is a guy who drives slower than you do," Harry laughed as he pointed out an old chap, his hands glued on the steering wheel, barely moving in the middle lane of the highway. He was driving an old wreck of a Zippy model 50 vehicle, and he had big, wide sunglasses on as he moved along. We all stared out the windows and watched him while Harry passed him by.

"I don't know there, Redmond. He may inch out Henson right at the finish line, but it would be close," Bishop Von Houten added, while he and Harry shook hands in the front seat. They were having fun and enjoying a few laughs at my expense.

Harry also pointed out a car, with a bumper sticker that read, "I survived The Flipper at Seashore Heights, N.J." For sure, that one brought back some memories. I thought about how I had to find out where I could get one of those stickers for the jeep.

Mostly, I found myself staring out the window and returning in time. Back to a time in my life that had such dark memories, yet by the same token, such fond ones. We had turned onto the New York State Thruway and we were heading north.

I had very often traveled this road during my days with the Albany Flying Dutchman hockey club, as I went back and forth between my apartment in Latham, New York, and back to my parent's home, and the old neighborhood in Paterson. I knew every exit sign, every mountain, and every roadside view. In fact, the New York State Thruway also brought back some very bad memories of when I hurtled southbound in my old jeep, to make it to the hospital in time, on the night when Sky Blu Redmond had passed away. It also had a ton of great memories that I associated with the area. I could see the faces of teammates, fans, coaches, and newspaper reporters. I could see myself still dressed in my goaltending equipment, and along with my teammates, we were hoisting the league championship trophy high above our heads, as we skated around the ice in victory.

I could see every corner of my little apartment in Latham, New York, and in my mind's eye; I could see myself in my chair by the front window, listening to my No Way records, dreaming of the beauty of a young lady named Binky Hobnobber, who somehow had become lost along the way.

I loved the capital district of New York, with its cool summers that were not too hot, fantastic fall foliage, and long, cold, harsh winters. Wonderful, down-to-earth people lived there, who were honest, hardworking, and sincere.

It was hockey country too!

I had such fond memories of playing hockey there as well as living there too.

I often wondered what led me back to Paterson, New Jersey, after I had finished my hockey-playing career. I had fully intended on returning to the Capital District of Upstate New York to live and wait for whatever my life after hockey would be. For some reason, it just did not happen that way, as I wandered right back to where I had grown up.

Looking around this vehicle, I think I now knew the reason.

Father Mark always told me that the hand of God was upon me. He felt that God led me around to where God intended for me to be, either in my life, or in the lives of others. Only God knows what was ahead for all of us, and I think that in our lives, we all need to trust that fact. You see, the hand of God or whatever higher power you choose to believe in, or fate, or whatever your individual dreams or wishes are, are upon all of us. We just have to open our eyes, hearts, and minds to accept the guidance.

As the mile markers zipped by, I became conscious of the fact that Binky and Rose had drifted off to sleep, as had Bishop Von Houten. I tapped Harry on the shoulder as he sat in the driver's seat and kidded him a bit.

I spoke softly because I did not want to wake up our sleeping passengers, "Looks as if not much has changed, Harry. Our sterling and dynamic personalities still have the same effect, eh?"

Harry chuckled from the front seat, "Paul, I wish I had just a nickel for all the miles you and I have rolled up some road together. To top it all off, I wish I had a dime for every pretty gal that we put to sleep with, as you say, our sterling, and dynamic personalities!"

We shook hands and settled back for the rest of the ride. After just about the estimated time given to us by Harry's new interactive gizmo, we arrived in Albany. We pulled into a hotel parking lot on Wolf Road in Albany, New York. The hotel was conveniently located on the outskirts of the downtown areas. We parked the big rig in the check-in lane, in front of the hotel. I had suggested that we stay at this hotel location since it would allow us quick access to the convention center downtown where they were conducting the conference activities. The three sleepy travelers awoke, and after some light-hearted kidding about their long naps; we stopped and climbed out of the vehicle. Harry picked Rose up out of the backseat and made sure she was steady on her legs after the long ride.

"Henson, I can see why your big ego and brutish past ways as a hockey player led you to this area. It is quite nice, I enjoyed viewing the landscape as we rolled up the road," Bishop Von Houten said, as he stood in the parking lot while looking around and taking in the sights of the outskirts of the city of Albany.

"Must have been a nice view, of the inside of your eyelids, bishop old boy. You were sawing wood pretty good in the front seat!" Harry teased Bishop Von Houten.

Bishop Von Houten smiled, and he turned a little red-faced, "Well, what I saw of it until now, that is. The seats are so comfortable in this vehicle. I am afraid that it forced me to drift off for a few minutes."

The bishop stood in the parking lot and waved his hands around as he pointed in the air. He started a long speech describing his plans, "I have heard they have wonderful golf courses here! One is right down the road from here over by the airport. I hope we can hustle into the hotel, change, and get over to the convention center. After taking it all in, I will offer up my usual key advice, and then begin contributing greatly to the sessions. My plan includes introducing you two bananas, to the key people to pay attention to and rub elbows with here. I can then leave you there and take the shuttle back to the hotel. It is a fabulous day here, a little warm, but not half as humid as it was in Jersey. I can then scoot over to the course down the road here and slip in a round or two of golf. After all, I am the big boss, you know. That is why I have Henson here to gather in all the required data for furthering our cause."

Binky sensed something in the bishop's delivery because she answered right back with encouragement, "That sounds as if it will be a wonderful day for you, bishop! Paul is quite capable of representing all of us as well as your office with pride. You deserve to relax and enjoy yourself."

"Why, thank you, Mrs. Henson, I agree! I have been doing this for an awful long time, you know. I just wish Henson could tie all that hair back, so my higher ups do not think he is some kind of hippie freak, whacko, but I suppose that would be out of the question."

Binky instantly produced a Binky rapid disagreement head nod, to discount any possibility whatsoever of any hair ties appearing behind my head.

After completing her dizzying head nod, Binky led us all towards the front of the hotel, "Well, let us get underway, gang, I want to call my parents and see what dear Father has bought at the toy store for the children. I am sure he is also allowing them to eat junk food when Mother is not watching, despite my specific orders to the contrary. I know that he is also planning on teaching Paul William how to cheat at Warship so that our son is assured of beating his father when he plays the game."

Bishop Von Houten nodded his head in approval, "I like the way that old man Hobnobber thinks, Mrs. Henson! I picked up a few tips from him last week when he stopped by the office in Newark to convince me to sign some charity petition. I plan on taking the game up with

Goldberg next week."

"Hey, check on Cocoa Two, too, would you?"

"Sure, Harry. That is as in, Cocoa Two also?"

"Yeah, yeah, yeah, whatever there, Bink-a-roo-ski. Hey, twenty-seven, buckle your gut up and let's get these bags out of the Rhino 500S. Maybe the bellhops have a crane they can send out here to help us haul these bags into your room."

Harry and I heaved and hauled the two Binky suitcases out of the back of the Rhino 500S while Rose, Binky, and the bishop went to check in.

A young, red-faced hotel bellhop saw Harry and me struggling, and he dashed out the front of the hotel, with a four-wheel buggy to help us load our gear on and bring them into the hotel.

"Good morning! Welcome to the Flying Dutchman Inn on Wolf Road! Please allow me to help you, Father, with your suitcases."

"Thank you. That is very kind of you. I am not a priest. I am a Lutheran pastor. We are in town for the Lutheran Conference downtown. Pastor Paul John Henson is the name. The big guy over there is Harry M. Redmond Junior."

The young man looked up while I carefully shook his hand, being careful not to cause any injuries, as he spoke, "Oh, sorry, pastor. I saw the collar, beard and hair. Thought ya were a priest or a monk. I am Jimmie Jack. They call me the jack-of-all-trades here, the man with two first names. Bellhop, maintenance man, security, and all around know it all!"

I looked over to Harry, who was shaking his head and screwing his mouth up like a corkscrew when he heard the bellhop's sales pitch.

"It is fine, Jimmie. It happens all the time."

"Hey man, this is one fantastic vehicle! Until now, I only have ever seen one of these vehicles in a magazine! It is one of those Rhino 500S vehicles. It is awesome! This vehicle is almost as nice as those two hot chicks a few minutes ago. Did you check out those two beautiful ladies walking in a few minutes ago, with that old, crab-faced priest? Man, they were hot! One of the gals was pregnant. I guess those priests have it made after all!"

Jimmie Jack elbowed me in the side, as he said slyly, "Maybe, you should have gone the priest route there, Pastor Paul."

Jimmie Jack seemed like a harmless guy, but he certainly was not going to win any contests for the brightest bulb in the string. His attempt at humor was not going over very well. I could tell by the look on Harry's face that Jimmie Jack was about to be awarded, in just a mere second or two, the "Not Too Swift Award" for today.

Harry moved in for the kill shot, "Man, you are right there, Jimster! They were hot, the blonde one in that tight dress with the amazing chest and the pregnant gal with the fantastic black hair!"

Jimmie was smiling and nodding his head in agreement.

In order to deflate Jimster's balloon, Harry quickly added, "Bad news, ya ding-dong. They also happen to be our wives. The old guy is Bishop Von Houten as in a Lutheran bishop."

Poor Jimmie's mouth dropped and his eyeballs nearly burst out of his head. He moved quickly, because he must have felt his best defense was to help us as quickly as possible, to prevent Harry from wiping the ground with his face.

"Oops. I am sorry. Really, really sorry, let me load this up for you."

"Good idea there, Jimster! Self-preservation, with more working and less gawking!" I had to chuckle at the advice on less gawking that was coming from Harry. Before he settled down and married, he was, of course, one of the greatest gawkers ever known to mankind.

"You're gonna need a heavier tow truck than that wimpy cart there, loose lips, my brain is not engaged, not too swift award winner, Jimster. I decided you needed more titles, so I made a few more up for you. Those suitcases of Pastor Paul's weigh more than the hot air coming out of your mouth," Harry instructed him as he was beating the young man like a drum for his poorly chosen comments.

With all of our combined strength, the three of us picked the two suitcases up and loaded them onto the cart. Sure enough, the front wheels collapsed, then they bent out to the side, and the cart hit the ground.

"Wow! I never have seen heavier suitcases than these are. Let me go to the maintenance shop, pick up the buggy that we use there to haul out air conditioning units, and I will bring some help. I promise that I will get them up to your room, Pastor Paul."

Harry softened his pressure on the young man and he walked over to him, whipped out some money from his pocket and handed it to the bellhop, "Here you go, Jimster, now, put your brain in gear from now on before your mouth. You are on my payroll now, if we need something, then I will count on you."

"Hey, thanks, Mr. Redmond. I am your man, and I will close my eyes, and seal my lips when your ladies walk by next time!"

After they obtained the replacement cart for the first one, Jimmie and a team of four other men delivered our luggage. We all checked into our rooms, washed up, changed into fresh clothes and we were ready to go. I guided Harry downtown to the convention center since I still remembered the roads as if I had just been here yesterday. The convention center was not far away from the hockey arena where the Albany Flying Dutchman played their home games, so I was well acquainted with the area.

Before we knew it, we had checked into the meetings. We all had received those goofy name tags that say, "Hello, my name is such-and-such," and had our titles or home churches on them for our identification.

Soon, we were as Bishop Von Houten said, "Rubbing elbows with the big boys." Bishop Von Houten had warned me, "To ease up on the power of my handshakes as not to injure anyone, Henson." He was in his glory while he proudly showed us all off as though we were celebrities. He did not want to admit it, but he really did enjoy our company, he just did not want anyone, especially me, to be aware of that fact.

Meeting person after person, Bishop Von Houten, introduced us to an endless array of people, as we wandered through the crowds. It seemed as though the bishop knew everyone. He always introduced our wives first, and then Harry, and Pastor Paul John Henson, of course, well, he always introduced me last. He even slipped up once, showing his hand that deep down, he was actually very proud of me. He introduced me to one of the executive board members of some hierarchy that I did not recognize, "As the young pastor, whom I handpicked to deliver the keynote speech. When all others had pushed him aside as a hippie weirdo, I placed him in a stroke of pure genius, in a leadership position. Now, he is responsible for the remarkable and amazing turnaround of Reunion Lutheran Church in Hibernian, New Jersey."

The bishop was beaming proudly, as the executive stared over the top of his glasses, cleared his throat, and said to me as he shook my hand, "Yes, Pastor Paul John Henson, we have been carefully watching you. Very impressive performance, Pastor Henson. We had given up on Reunion Lutheran Church and we were ready to write it off, sell the facilities, the land, and move on. It is a pleasure, finally . . . to meet you. I am looking forward to your message. The word is that you are quite a dynamic speaker.

I have to ask, do you ever cut your hair off, shave, or perhaps, at least tie your hair back, or is this how you always look?"

I laughed off the implication of the questions and explained to the executive gentleman that this was my normal look. I caught out of the corner of my eye, my wife glaring at the executive, and I prayed under my breath that she did not dig her left foot in the ground, as a prelude to her facing off with the man because of his comments. Once Binky recovered, and she was over his opinion of my hair, she was thrilled at the executive gentleman's comments.

My wife leaned in and whispered, "How proud of me she was." Bishop Von Houten frowned at me, but he moved on rather quickly.

The other person enjoying the meet and greet session, of course, was Harry M. Redmond Junior. He moved and mowed through the crowd with ease, talking up a storm, interacting with everyone, showing off Rose and Binky, while proclaiming my success to the world. He was in his glory with an endless audience to spout off his magical gift of gab to. I went the full course from hockey goalie, "par excellence," to the world's greatest hippie preacher! Harry was on a roll, and he was working the crowd like a master salesman.

I am sure he was searching for a few Eskimos to sell some ice to them.

After the meet and greet session, we had a pleasant lunch, then it was time to work. I was about to find out that these conferences were more about socializing than they were about work, but that was all part of the plan. It really was about mingling and sharing ideas. Binky had studied the agenda for months ahead of time, and she and Rose had their sights set upon two sessions about event planning and church social gatherings. The two ladies were off in that direction rather quickly.

I had wanted to attend a workshop on some Bible study

ideas, but Harry quickly overruled my plans, and he of course, labeled that, "As boring stuff that only a bunch of old bags would be interested in." He added that is exactly the reason why I wanted to sit in on that session. After Bishop Von Houten and Harry had a huge laugh at my expense, Harry then pointed us in the direction of a workshop about construction projects for your church facilities, as well as another one about maintenance and operation of your church facilities.

"Are you kidding me, twenty-seven? We are in the middle of a huge construction project and you want to learn about Bible study? We need to tell these clueless dreamers, about what we are doing, and lend them our real-life experience."

Harry had a good point. Therefore, off the three of us went. Well, correction, the two of us went to the session workshop. Bishop Von Houten ducked out a side door, grabbing the shuttle back to the hotel to head out to the golf course. He had already run into an old friend that he knew at the meet and greet, and the bishop had laid down a few dollars as to who would win in a quick afternoon game. He explained that we would meet back at the hotel around seven in the evening to go to dinner, "So that Redmond could pick up the tab!" Off, he happily went.

The workshops were very enjoyable, Harry jumped up a number of times to offer his expert advice on steel work and welding. At one point, much to the dismay of the person running the actual workshop, Harry took over writing on his drawing easel, while he was providing an in-depth explanation of the various grades of stainless steel. Harry handed out business cards as if they were candy, and he would most likely have drummed up a lot of business from this, just as he always does. The afternoon passed, soon it was time to quit for the day, and head back to the hotel. We met up with our wives and we drove back to the hotel.

Rose and Binky were excited about the information that they had gathered. The two of them went on and on about social events and planning for Reunion when we returned. Binky was already intensely planning committees and groups for our church based upon the information that they received in the classes. I could imagine that within a few weeks or so, she would have half the congregation of Reunion Lutheran Church running for the hills to run away from her organizing and research on church events. Harry kept working hard to change the subject, as event planning and church socials were not high on his "interested in" list, but it was not going to work. I was very glad that the ladies had found something they were so interested in at the conference. Binky and Rose now had mountains of brochures, pens, pencils, papers, and more information handed out at the workshops, stuffed and crammed into tote bags, and boxes. We helped them gather it all in and carry it into the hotel.

After relaxing for a bit in our rooms, washing up and changing into dinner clothes, we all met in the hotel lobby to go to dinner. We met Bishop Von Houten, who glowed red after he picked up a little sunburn from the golf course, but he was in great spirits, since he had soundly defeated his old friend, and won a few extra dollars. We had a round of drinks at the bar inside of the hotel, and then off we were to dinner. I had suggested a steakhouse located out on Route 9 in Latham that I knew well from my days here. It actually was not far from where my old apartment was.

We had a great meal and a big surprise when the owner of the establishment recognized me from my Flying Dutchman days. Once he got over the shock of the fact that I was now a Lutheran pastor, he bought us all a round of drinks. A fairly large group of patrons in attendance had also remembered me, and they joined us in a toast at our table, to the, as Harry said, "World famous, long-haired, hippie goalie, twenty-seven!" Even Rose had just a little taste of red wine in a glass after Binky assured her it would be fine.

Bishop Von Houten was thrilled, and even he had to admit that he had no idea up to this point that I had been quite as famous as this. It shocked him that the owner and patrons recognized me after all of these years. He conversed with the owner of the restaurant who showed him pictures of local sports heroes that decorated his restaurant walls. Sure enough, he had a picture mounted above the bar of number twenty-seven crouched in the net.

That certainly seemed as if it was a lifetime or two ago.

The steaks were perfect and the meal and atmosphere were just what we all needed. I even escaped with only one or two hard-hitting insults from Bishop Von Houten during the entire evening. After he had a few drinks in him, he had his arm around me telling jokes and stories of our relationship. Bishop Von Houten was actually a wonderful man, he was a blast to hang around with, and he and Harry competed for "the life of the party" award for tonight. It had been a great nightcap, to a special, but very long day.

We were all feeling it now, but Rose was especially tired, and she was even dozing off on the short ride back to our hotel. We had a big day planned for tomorrow. The plan was for the conference to move into the large hall for discussion and voting on special items that the councils had presented for leadership votes. After opening prayers, I was on for the keynote address at around one in the afternoon, so we needed to all have a good night's sleep to be ready. We all said our goodnights, planned our meeting time for early in the morning, and we were off.

Around two in the morning or thereabouts, Binky and I were sound asleep in our hotel room, when the phone rang. I picked it up on the second ring. It was Rose calling.

"Twenty-seven, I am so sorry for waking you, but I

would like to speak with Binky. I am having labor pains, and I just want to make sure that it is false labor and not the actual event. I am not due for more than three weeks yet, but I still want to make sure."

"Sure, sure, Rose, hang on. Binky is staring at me now. I will put her on the line." I handed the phone to Binky, who carefully listened for a few minutes to Rose's testimony. I propped my back up on some pillows pushed up on the back of the bed.

"Uh huh, uh huh, and are the pains in your back now dear Rose, or along the front only? How often have they come apart? I see, and no pain in your back, just along the front. Is that correct?"

Binky was nodding her head while she sat on the end of the bed. She motioned for me to grab her bag that was on the desk in the hotel room. I climbed out of bed, grabbed it, and brought it over to Binky. While she was listening to Rose, Binky pulled out some papers and began to study them. I grabbed her purse because I knew she wanted to have her reading glasses on. Binky nodded and mouthed, "thank you" to me. Binky glanced at a large amount of, as she would label it, "portable research," which she had traveled with, and nodded her head. Based upon Binky's intuitive nature, I was sure that this research was pregnancy-related. I could tell by the look on her face, when she studied Rose back home in our driveway, at the parsonage that she was not convinced Rose was still weeks away from delivery.

"I think you are fine for now, Rose. The pains seem to be in the front, and true labor tends to be more intense, and along the back. The pains are too far apart for it to be true labor. I do think, however, we need to be keenly aware of these pains, and monitor the situation very carefully. This could be fooling us into thinking it is only false labor. Try to have a snack and then go back to sleep. Is Harry awake? Oh yes, why would I ask? He is probably handing out cigars in the hotel lobby already. It is fine, Rose. Please call back if you need anything. We are here. I agree, it is still too far away and your water is intact, so you are fine for now. Goodnight, Rose,"

Binky hung up the telephone, stood up, and put her information away.

"Just false labor, twenty-seven. She is fine for now. I am not so sure about the near future, though. She wanted to be sure, because the doctor told her that he could tell by her physical makeup, the labor would be very short and the pains intense. I do think she dropped a bit since last week. I really do. I noticed that right away when I saw her this morning, but I guess, she is still a few weeks away. I am not a doctor, but she seems more than ready to me."

I nodded my head, waited until Binky climbed back into bed, shut off the light, kissed her goodnight, and back to sleep we went.

The alarm woke both Binky and me up. I sat up in bed, as I usually did not sleep past the alarm time, so I was startled. I glanced at the clock and jumped out of bed. Binky was slower to rise; she had apparently tossed and turned a bit more than I did after Rose had called.

"Bore da, dear Binky. I will jump in the shower first if that is good with you."

Binky just nodded; she was out of it. She sat on the edge of the bed and rubbed her eyes, "I will make coffee, twenty-seven. I need coffee. Rwy'n dy garu di wastad ac am byth."

I smiled at her. She looked so cute sitting there sleepy eyed, with her long, flowing hair sticking up at all angles from her head. She was still so tired, but for Binky being half out of it, her sleepiness had not affected her Welsh.

"I will love you forever too, Binky."

She slumped backwards into the bed and laughed. She was really having a hard time getting into gear. We managed to become motivated, showered, and dressed for the day. Binky soon recovered, and she looked gorgeous, as usual, for our big day. I gathered my case with my sermon notes and the rest of my gear. I dressed in my black suit and collar, Binky checked me over carefully, and then pronounced me good to go.

"How do you feel, Rose?" I greeted her with a kiss on the cheek as I patted Harry on the back. We had all met in the hotel lobby, and we were now waiting for Bishop von Houten, before we went into the restaurant to eat our breakfast.

"Oh, fine. I guess. I am just so tired. If twenty-seven was not on the stage today, I think I would stay here at the hotel and sleep."

"Rose, it is nothing special. I appreciate the support, but you surely have heard the same kind of sermons from me before."

"Yes Rose, please if you are tired, then you should stay here," Binky was nodding her head up and down like a bobble-head, Binky doll.

Harry stared at her for a moment, "Easy there, Bink-a-roo-ski, you are on nodding overload. You may shake a screw loose. I told Rose the same thing, but she insists on going with us."

"Any more of the false labor pains, Rose?" Binky ignored Harry; her focus was on the labor, or rather, the false labor pains.

"A few, but I just had a stronger one when we came down the elevator. They had stopped and died out after we had spoken on the telephone. This pain was different. It was along here," Rose pointed down in the front of her belly, when we all noticed Bishop Von Houten appeared next to us.

"Pain? What is this about pain?" Bishop Von Houten stood next to us. He was dressed in his black suit and collar, and he put his hands on his hips.

"Henson! My expectations are that you have this baby

situation under control. Baby stuff is not my area of expertise, but I always remain cool, calm, and collected at all times. Staying calm is always the best course of action."

"Yes sir, it is all right, it is all under control, Bishop Von Houten. Rose had some false labor pains last night, and Binky has checked her research on the subject. We are good. It is all right, sir."

Binky was discussing the pain location with Rose, and I spotted her pull out her papers from her research bag. Binky was studying them intently.

"Good, good, well, if Mrs. Henson is on it, then all is well. I know for certain that she will have the situation under control no matter what comes along. If you or Redmond were involved, then I would be concerned. Say, borry draw, or whatever it is that all of you birds say to one another in the morning! I am starving. Let's go have a big breakfast and some coffee! I need to have a big breakfast as well as strong caffeine to withstand another long, boring, sermon from Henson!"

Harry put his big arm around Bishop Von Houten's shoulders, "You are correct there, bishop old boy! Not about the boredom, but I meant the baby stuff. Actually, you may have a point with the boredom angle too. I agree with you . . . when the baby does arrive, staying calm and relaxed is the way to go. I stood in front of hockey pucks, had my teeth knocked clean out of my skull, walked across steel ledges up hundreds of feet in the air, and I tell you, bishop old boy, the key is to always remain calm, cool, and collected."

"I agree, Redmond. I was not there when my little girls were born. Years ago, they did not allow the husband to become involved in that sort of thing. However, you are correct, Redmond! I would have been calm and relaxed, just as you are. You are my kind of guy! You do not flip your lid like Henson does!"

We all walked into the hotel restaurant and took a seat at

a table near the window. We studied the menus and made our selections. Harry and Bishop Von Houten were chatting up a storm. They were oblivious to Binky studying Rose and her every move. A young waitress came over to our table, and she took our orders. Rose was sitting next to Binky, and Rose winced a little while she moved in her chair. I saw her hold her belly as Binky checked the area. Binky looked at her watch and then studied her papers.

I leaned over and whispered into Binky's ear, "How many minutes apart?"

I suddenly knew by my wife's increased research intensity, and that look on her face, that she was thinking of something.

"Five or six, twenty-seven. If my research is correct, then the doctor was wrong. All we need now is for her water to break, and then I would say it is time for an addition to the Redmond family. In fact, I think another contraction is coming right now by the look on her face. I would also predict that her water could go any minute now," Binky said as she looked at Rose intently.

I sat back in my chair and my eyes widened. Binky was seldom ever wrong; we were in some serious trouble now! Rose grabbed her belly and winced some more. Binky was all over the location and put her hand on Rose's belly.

Harry was in mid-laugh with a huge piece of toast in his hand, when Rose jumped up from the table and pulled her dress all around her.

"MY WATER JUST BROKE! OH, MY! I AM SO SORRY, BUT MY WATER JUST BROKE!"

Binky was doing her best with her napkin to address the situation. I handed her my napkin and poor Rose sat back down. The entire restaurant was looking at us now. Harry dropped his toast and his eyes popped out of his head.

Bishop Von Houten spun his head around and shouted, "Huh, water? What water? Where did the water come from? What is going on?"

Harry jumped up from his chair, ran over to Rose, and held her shoulders. The waitress and manager came over and Binky assured them she had it under control, "I do apologize for just a little mess here, but you cannot argue with a baby's arrival."

Harry was growing a little frantic as Rose bent over with another contraction. He looked at Rose, then at Binky, "Binky what does this mean? What do you mean, a baby's arrival? It is just some more false labor . . . right? She has three weeks yet. Right?"

Bishop Von Houten jumped up from his chair and stood next to Harry. The bishop stood there in shock with toast crumbs lining his mouth and his napkin stuck in his collar.

He blurted out, "I thought this baby stuff was under control, Henson!"

I stood up and put my hand on Harry's shoulders, "Harry, now, listen very carefully to me. I need you to remain calm, just as you said you would. Please go up to your room, pack Rose some of her personal items, get the keys to the Rhino, and meet us as quickly as you can in the lobby. The baby has decided to prove Binky correct . . . and the doctor wrong."

Binky fluffed her hair at her accurate prediction, and she posed when she heard me mention the fact that her research was correct. She piped in, "I knew the baby had dropped into position, when I saw Rose yesterday."

Harry stood there frozen in time. He did not move a muscle, but his eyes were as wide as saucers.

"Harry, hurry! Harry, just don't stand there like a doofus, you, big dope, go get the stupid car keys," Rose screamed as she doubled over with another contraction.

Binky looked at her watch, "Oh my, they are getting closer, awfully quick. The doctor may have been correct that the baby would arrive very quickly. I should have performed more research on the actual delivering of a baby." Binky picked up her papers and began to study them again.

Harry and Bishop Von Houten looked at one another and took off like cannonballs while running towards the elevators. They were screaming the entire way, "Look out! The baby is coming! Get out of the way! The baby is coming! The baby is coming!"

So much for those two ding-dongs remaining calm, cool, and collected. I laid some money on the table, waved to the restaurant management, and we hustled Rose off to the lobby where we waited for Harry and the bishop to return. Rose was in some severe pain and the contractions were coming much quicker than we had ever expected. Binky and I had been through childbirth twice, so we knew the drill. And of course, Binky had all the research at her fingertips. We heard shouting and hollering in the lobby, and sure enough, along came the two calm, cool, and collected individuals, hurtling through the hotel lobby.

"Clear the way! Look out! We have to get to the hospital! Baby on the way!" Harry bellowed.

"I am a Lutheran bishop! I have it all under control, folks! I am in charge here! Look out!" Harry's partner within this wild calamity shouted.

Jimmie Jack was standing in the lobby dumbfounded as Harry grabbed him by the shoulders, "Jimmie, where did I park the Rhino 500S? Where is my car? Help me, Jimster! Wake up you boob! I will give you a hundred bucks. I cannot remember where the Rhino 500S is!"

Harry was panicking.

Bishop Von Houten looked at Jimmie and yelled, "Think, kid, think. Time is of the essence!"

Jimmie exclaimed, "Mr. Redmond! Bishop Von Houten! Calm down! It is right there in the front spot! You cannot miss it! It is ten feet away from you. It is the only Rhino 500S in the lot, sir."

"Great work kid, I will give you the dough later!"

Harry and Bishop Von Houten rushed out the front door

as we followed behind, helping Rose along the way. Jimmie just shook his head. I think that was the easiest dough that he had ever earned.

We arrived over by the Rhino 500S, as Harry and the bishop ran around the vehicle in circles, opening doors and tossing luggage in the rear of the vehicle. Harry flipped me the keys, "Here, twenty-seven, I will get in the backseat with Rose."

Rose looked up at Harry, and then she looked at Binky and doubled over with another contraction, "Please, Harry, you drive. No offense, Paul, but you drive like an old lady, and I really need to get to the hospital."

Binky confirmed the fact with a rapid head nod.

Harry tore the keys out of my hand as he said, "You're right. I will drive!"

Oh well, the truth hurts sometimes.

Harry jumped in the front with Bishop Von Houten. Binky, Rose, and I got in the backseat as Harry fired up the big engine.

"Hello, Mr. Redmond. My sensors have detected that you, and bishop old boy, are in the front, Mrs. Redmond and in the. . .."

"SHUT THE @#$$ UP, HOWIE! WE NEED DIRECTIONS TO A HOSPITAL!"

"Is Cocoa Two here?"

"OH, GET LOST, HOWIE!" Harry pushed the Howie power button and turned around to me.

"Forget that technology nonsense, thirty-five. We are heading for Saint Peter's Hospital on South Manning Boulevard. I could drive there blindfolded. I was a frequent visitor to the emergency room for stitches almost every other night. Harry, right turn onto Wolf Road, then left at the end here. Follow the signs for south on the New York State Thruway. I will get you there in ten minutes." Harry nodded his head as Rose screamed out with another contraction.

"Henson, I knew that previous, barbaric, lifestyle of yours would come in handy someday! Step on it, Redmond," Bishop Von Houten leaned into the dashboard and held onto the grip handles on the glove box.

Harry jammed the Rhino 500S into gear and we took off like a rocket into outer space. If Harry ever needed his expert race car driving skills, it was now. He revved the big engine up and tore around traffic like the expert driver that he was. In, out, and around he wove, beeping his big Rhino horn, flashing his lights, and screaming out on his public-address system, "Look out, a baby is being born in the backseat here! Look out! We are heading for a hospital!"

I had to admit at this point, God bless the Rhino 500S!

Cars were pulling over right and left, allowing us to pass, and in no time, we were flying down the New York State Thruway. I was shouting out directions without even looking as I was assisting Binky in administering aid to Rose in the backseat. The baby was getting closer and closer by the minute! Rose was screaming and sitting on her side because she could no longer sit flat in the seat. I knew that was a bad sign. The doctor had told Rose the baby would come quickly, but this was a little too much to handle.

Binky looked at me, "The baby is coming fast, twenty-seven. We are running out of time, this is remarkable, but we may have to deliver the baby right here, Paul. The baby's head must be right there. Rose cannot sit straight. I have made a miscalculation, and I should have researched the delivery of babies a little more. I think I know the basics, though. Did they, by chance, teach you to deliver babies in seminary?"

I sat back in the seat and for some reason, blinked my eyes rapidly. I think that I was trying to search my memory banks; however, my mind was a blur. How could this adventure happen to us?

I recovered and said, "No Binky, they missed that one,

but we have faith with us. I was there for both of our babies, and between God, you, and me, we can do it."

I was not sure that I was correct in saying all of that, but after all, it was all that I had left in my tank! I made the sign of the cross on Binky's forehead and then did the same on Rose's forehead.

Binky smiled and nodded. She pulled Rose's undergarments off and prepared Rose for the delivery. I stared in and oh boy, sure enough, the baby's head was right there! Binky was correct, of course.

This was unreal.

"Please try to hold back, Rose. Do not push, dear Rose!" Binky held her hands as poor Rose screamed.

Bishop Von Houten glanced at the scene in the backseat, pulled his cross out from his pocket, placed it over his head and neck, and crossed himself multiple times. He then yelled at me, "Henson! It is my expectation that you and your dear wife have this under control. All I can do is offer prayers. I did not prepare properly for this type of emotional stress, Henson. You have done it to me again and pulled me into your wild and wacky world!"

"Sir, praying will mean a lot. We are witnesses to not only another wild Henson and Redmond adventure, but we are witnesses to the greatest of all of God's miracles." Bishop Von Houten smiled and nodded, and then he closed his eyes and started to pray. It was not often that he agreed with me, but on this go around, he surely did.

I looked up, and I could see the rooftop of the Center for the Disabled, and then the top of Saint Peter's Hospital looming in the distance.

"Right turn, quick Harry! The hospital is right at the end here. Make a right turn at the light!"

Suddenly, there were red lights behind us and we heard a siren wailing! A police car! Oh no, we were being pulled over by the police!

"HARRY! NOOOOOO!" Poor Rose screamed.

As Harry ground the Rhino 500S to a stop on the side of the road, he picked up his microphone and yelled into it, "Please, we have a baby being born in the backseat!"

Bishop Von Houten crossed himself and yelled out, "I will handle this!" He jumped out of the passenger's door and he ran towards the police car, frantically waving his arms over his head.

We heard the police officer yelling, "Get back in the vehicle, Father. Please, get back in the vehicle!"

"I am not a priest! I am a Lutheran bishop, and there is a baby being born in the backseat of that big, giant, elephant car, or whatever the @#$# it is!"

Harry rolled down the window, and I looked up to see a police officer stick his head in the window.

The officer took one look at us, saw the scene in the backseat, and yelled out, "Follow me! Quick! I will turn the lights and siren on!"

The officer ran back to his patrol car, Bishop Von Houten jumped back in, and we roared down the street following the police car.

We must have been going one hundred miles an hour!

We pulled into the emergency room entrance of Saint Peter's Hospital behind the police car, and Harry slammed the Rhino 500S into the parking gear. Bishop Von Houten, Harry, and the police officer, ran into the emergency room waving their hands over their heads, while screaming, "Baby! We are having a baby!"

I was wiping the sweat from Rose's head as she held Binky's hand and mine, while she screamed at the top of her lungs. Rose sure could always scream! This was a lot worse than sitting next to her on amusement park rides.

Well, just by a little.

I jumped out of the vehicle, picked Rose up in my arms, and plopped her in a wheelchair that a nurse had rolled out to the side of the Rhino 500S. We pushed her into the emergency room as fast as my legs could roll us. The nurse ran alongside us as Binky gave her the rundown. Binky explained that the baby's head was right there!

The nurse instructed Binky as we ran along, "Let's put her in the first room there, we can deliver the baby if we have too. We have an O-B-G-Y-N doctor on call. He is on the way. I know you are correct. I can tell by the way she is sitting that the baby is right there. You two have done an amazing job!"

The nurse put her hand on Rose's shoulder and told her, "Try not to push, honey, it will be all right!"

The nurse then turned towards me as I wheeled the wheelchair into the first room past Harry, Bishop Von Houten, and the police officer, and she calmly provided an introduction and welcome to the hospital, "Hello, Father. Welcome to Saint Peter's Hospital. I am Nurse Watkins. I do not think I have ever seen a priest with such long hair!"

"I am not a priest, Nurse Watkins. I am a Lutheran pastor. Pastor Paul John Henson is my name. I am the pastor as well as a close friend to the gal giving birth here. This is my wife, Binky Henson, running alongside us. The old guy wearing a collar that ran in there as if his pants were on fire, along with this gal's husband, and the police officer, is the bishop of our district. It is a bit of a long story, actually."

"Oh my, a bishop too. You Lutherans bring out the big guns for a baby being born. Sorry, I saw the collar and thought you were a priest or a monk."

"No trouble, it is fine, it happens all the time."

I picked Rose up out of the chair and placed her on the table in the room as she screamed with another contraction while the nurses and Binky scrambled to get her fully undressed.

I ran out into the hallway and grabbed Harry by the hand. "Get in here thirty-five, you, big doofus, your child is being born!" I pulled the big lug into the room, just as a doctor ran in with his gown on, and his hands covered in gloves.

"Well, well, we have a baby here," the doctor said as he stared in at the scene under the cloth covering Rose.

I could have told him that, and I only went to seminary.

Rose screamed at the top of her lungs as Harry held her hand. I signaled to Binky for us to leave, and Rose, even in her pain, spotted my sign to my wife, grabbed my arm tightly, and said forcibly, "NO! Please, stay Paul. Binky and you both need to stay. I will not allow you to leave. For some reason, I sense that the baby will need you someday, Paul. Our baby will need you, Paul, more than our baby will need any other person on the face of the Earth. You both need to be here when our baby comes into the world. It is very important to me as well as to our baby. Stay!" Rose pleaded with me, and then she screamed once more.

Binky looked my way, as did all the others within the room when they heard her strange request. Binky took my hand and squeezed it hard. I thought how this was all very strange, but mothers know signs that are Heaven-sent straight from God. These are signs that we would never understand, and despite that knowledge and belief, I was very uncomfortable with the situation. However, I knew that we had run out of time to debate, and that I needed to heed her wish. I nodded and made the sign of the cross on her forehead again.

"As you wish, dear Rose," was all I said. Binky and I held hands and stood off to the rear corner of the room.

"Now, let's give one big push there, honey, would you?"

The doctor stared in as Rose yelled out, "WILL YOU @#$%&** PEOPLE MAKE UP YOUR @#@$%&* MINDS! DON'T PUSH, ROSE! THEN TWO SECONDS LATER, NOW WE HAVE TO PUSH, ROSE! WILL YOU PLEASE MAKE UP YOUR MINDS?"

Rose looked over to me and said in a calm voice, "Sorry, twenty-seven, it has been a @#@#*."

I nodded my head and crossed myself.

As Rose gave one big push, she screamed bloody murder, and I heard a baby crying.

9

Sometimes, You Just Have to Have Faith

One strong push and it was over. A fantastic, seven pounds, four ounces, little baby girl, entered the world. She cried and screamed as the doctor held the miracle of life above his head. She was beautiful! I held Binky as she sobbed her eyes out in joy. Harry and Rose held one another in joy, exhaustion, and gratefulness.

It had been quite a ride, the longest fifteen minutes of our lives! As it was so often in our lives, the four of us had ridden it together. Even in the many adventures of Harry and Paul, this one was something special.

"It's a girl! It's a girl!" I heard Harry scream and holler as the tears rolled down his face. "Rose, it is a girl. I love you, Rose! I love you, Rose!" Now that the baby was born and Rose had her attention elsewhere, Binky, and I stepped out of the room to allow Rose and Harry to enjoy their special moment in private. Bishop Von Houten and the police officer rushed over to us, when we appeared from inside the room, and stepped outside into the hallway.

"It is a girl, sir, a fantastic little girl."

Bishop Von Houten smiled, stopped in his tracks, and held out his hands. He bowed his head as he motioned for us all to gather around in a circle.

The police officer looked up at Bishop Von Houten and said, "But, Bishop Von Houten, I am Jewish."

Bishop Von Houten smiled and told him, "Yeah, yeah, yeah, so what! My best friend in the entire world is a rabbi, and sometimes, I think that I am half-Jewish. Now, come on in here, officer. This is about God, not religion. Mankind created religion and all the confusion that goes with it. God sends us faith and miracles to sort out all the mess that mankind makes."

The officer smiled, and he joined Binky, three nurses, a maintenance man who had been changing a light bulb in the hallway, a nun who had been walking down the hallway, and me, as we all joined in the prayer.

"All mighty powers in Heaven, please, bless the little baby just born. Bless all of us who witnessed this miracle of life and join in the joy that we all feel as Heaven rejoices in our prayers of hope and blessing. Amen."

"Amen," we all repeated.

"Hello, pastor. I am Officer Robert Steinman. Nice work there," the policeman was extending his hand to me.

I shook his hand, and said, "Nice to meet you, officer. I am Pastor Paul John Henson and this is my wife, Binky Henson. Thank you for pulling us over. I do not think we would have made it without your escort!"

"Wow, a strong handshake, Pastor Paul. You should have been a policeman! No trouble, what an exciting moment. You two did an amazing job there. I do not think I could have delivered the baby, and they trained me on how to do it too."

Harry rushed out into the hallway and we gathered around him as the big guy sobbed his eyes out.

"I love this! Now, this is what I am talking about," the big guy choked out the words of his famous war cry.

We all took turns hugging him and congratulating him. He and I embraced for a long time, while he trembled in joy, and we held onto one another. I could feel his tears of joy rain down on my shoulders. I gathered my wife in and Binky joined us. We had a group hug going on right there in the hallway.

"Thank you, twenty-seven, thank you dear, lovely, Binky. Youse guys, thank you for being there once more.

You and Binky, you are our rocks. You are our solid guides forever. I need you, and bishop old boy, to come in and bless our daughter, please all of you, put on gowns and come on in."

Harry spotted the Albany police officer and rushed over to him, "Thank you! Thank you, so much! Our daughter would have been born in the back of a fancy, Rhino 500S, if not for you pulling me over. I am Harry M. Redmond Junior."

"Congratulations, Mr. Redmond, I am Officer Robert Steinman."

"Nice to meet you, Steinman. This is your lucky day! Once the dust clears, I will make sure you receive a ribbon for this, and let me tell you, whatever your precinct needs, bulletproof vests, hats, flags, new police cars, radios, coffee makers, donuts, uniforms, whatever! I will buy it for what you have done for my family."

"Wow! Thank you, Mr. Redmond!"

"Come in and see our little girl."

We all dressed up in robes, gowns and booties, and walked into the room. There was Rose, holding their precious little girl in her arms. They both took your breath away. No doubt, they were so beautiful.

"Folks, I present to you, Blue Cloud Rosalina Redmond and the most perfect, beautiful, mother on the entire planet, Mrs. Rose Redmond."

I stopped in my steps and looked at Harry. I knew where the name had come from and he smiled at me. It was a memory of a special night so long ago. Harry knew from the shocked look on my face that I had remembered.

"Yes, Paul, it is from a misstep of my words that her name was born." I smiled at him as we all gathered around Rose and Blue Cloud. We took turns once again congratulating Rose and Harry. Binky could not stop crying as she hugged Rose and kissed Blue Cloud's head. Officer Steinman introduced himself to Rose and Blue

Cloud and extended his best wishes.

I joined hands with Bishop Von Houten as he signaled for me to take the lead. I made the sign of the cross on Rose's head and then did the same on Blue Cloud's forehead as the little baby slept in her mother's arms. Bishop Von Houten then did the same.

I held his hands as we extended our arms together over the bed and I spoke, "May the Lord bless you and keep you. May his face shine down upon you both and be gracious upon you both. May the Lord lift up his countenance upon you both and give you peace. Amen."

I then leaned over and kissed both Mother and child.

"I love you, dear Rose Redmond and Blue Cloud Rosalina Redmond."

Rose looked up at me with tear-filled eyes and answered, "We love you too, Pastor Paul."

What a moment, a magical, unbelievable moment in all of our lives. The raw emotion even overcame the world famous, old curmudgeon, the great Bishop Werner Beck Clodhopper Von Houten.

It was just that kind of day for all of us.

I looked down at my watch and saw that it was just a few minutes past noon! We had only a few minutes left to arrive downtown to the convention center and for me to deliver the keynote sermon for the conference.

"I do not want to bring this up, and break up this joyous moment, but I have about forty minutes to be down at the convention center to give my sermon. It is going to be a very bad scene for all of us if we do not show up."

"Henson! We cannot blow it now," Bishop Von Houten was spewing fire. Baby or no baby, Von Houten was back on the warpath after a brief, emotional interlude.

"I will get you there, Pastor Paul. No sweat, I will turn the lights on and we can roll," Officer Steinman said as he waved to us. The Albany, New York Police Department came to the rescue once more!

Rose, Harry, and Blue Cloud, with a little cry, wished us luck. Before we knew it, we were off in the Albany police car, with the lights flashing and a siren wailing, rolling to the convention center. As we pulled into the convention center lot, and we all ran into the building, I realized that I had left my case with my sermon notes in the Rhino 500S!

Oh well, I will wing it. After the morning we had, I knew that I had plenty of material, that was for sure. I kissed Binky goodbye, patted Bishop Von Houten and Officer Steinman on the back, and ran to the front of the hall.

I dashed up a small set of stairs on the side of the stage, and ran into a man, who looked as if he might know what was going on here. He held a clipboard in one hand and he had on a headset with a boom microphone in front of his mouth.

He looked at me and then at the clipboard and asked, "Are you, Henson? Reverend Paul John Henson."

"Yes sir, I am, sorry for the last second appearance."

The stage man looked at his watch and then back to me. "It is not the last second. Last two minutes, but not the last second. Ya really a Lutheran minister with all that hair, beard, and stuff going on there?"

He waved his hands around as he looked at me.

"Ya look a little . . . how should I say without being too insulting? Unconventional."

"Sir, yes that is a good description, I guess above all, I am slightly unconventional," I shook his hand while nodding my head.

"Wow! Big strong dude here! I guess no demons or devils come along and scare you, Reverend Henson. I think it is time. Don't you need some kind of notes, Reverend Henson?"

I heard the host emcee introduce me as I tapped my forehead to indicate that I had my notes in my head. I turned back to the stage man and yelled, "No, not much to be afraid of in this world, only God and the dentist. By the way, just call me Pastor Paul."

I reached in my pocket, took out my old wooden cross on the cloth lanyard, put it over my head, pulled all my hair out from under my suit jacket, and strode out there. No robes, no fluff, no glamour. I shook hands with the emcee, walked up to the podium, and adjusted the microphone for my height. I looked out at the massive audience that had packed the hall for this event. Scanning the crowd, I spotted Binky, Bishop Von Houten, and Officer Steinman sitting in a row together. I guess Officer Steinman had decided to stay! I heard a few of the usual murmurs echo and filter through the crowd as to my hair, beard, he was almost late, rushed in here, and the usual, "hippie" talk. After all these years, it did not faze me in the least.

I took a deep breath, and began, as I held my arms up over my head, and pointed them towards the crowd, "Let us bow our heads and pray. May the words of my mouth and the meditations of my heart, glorify and justify us all in your eyes, Lord. In Jesus' name, we pray. Amen. Good day! Bore da in my second language of Welsh and welcome. I am Pastor Paul John Henson of Reunion Lutheran Church in Hibernian, New Jersey. I would like to thank everyone for inviting me to deliver the keynote sermon here today. I would especially like to thank Bishop Werner Beck Clodhopper Von Houten, Bishop of the Northeastern District, for nominating me to be here today. Bishop Von Houten is not only my boss but also in his own special way, he is my mentor, guide, and my friend. I also need to thank my loyal wife, Mrs. Binky Henson, for her love and dedication. Rwy'n dy garu di wastad ac am byth, dear Binky. I also need to thank Officer Robert Steinman of the Albany Police Department, who without his aid, we would not have made it here on time today."

I could tell by the reactions that the crowd was

interested to find out the reason the Albany Police Department would be involved, but overall, they seemed relaxed, even slightly jovial. I had their attention with the last comment, as I imagined they had suddenly sensed that in some way, it had been an unusual day for me as well as my companions. Glancing around the huge crowd, I am also sure none of them spoke any Welsh. No one replied to my greeting, however, the audience was now poised to hear the rest of the story.

"I have to be honest. I had prepared a sermon with a theme based upon unity. Unity in Christ, unity in what we do to promote the Lutheran Church behind the scenes, and all the business that goes with it. I worked on it for three weeks, and I do know a lot of the text in my mind by memory, but not enough to preach the entire sermon without errors and stumbling over it here and there. You see, my notes are sitting in the backseat of an ultra-limited edition, Substantial Industries Rhino 500S, vehicle with the nine-hundred-cubic-inch, jet pack, super whiz-bang, dual turbo infused, nitro-burner engine that as far as I know, may be still parked in the emergency room entrance of Saint Peter's Hospital on South Manning Boulevard."

I threw my arms up over my head and waved in the air.

"So instead, I will just wing it! Sometimes, you just have to have faith. Faith that God's plan for you is something that you cannot escape. Sometimes that plan does not coincide with your hopes, dreams, and wishes. Therefore, you just need to go with it. This morning, God's plan was to promote one of his more common miracles. The miracle of life . . . it happens all the time, every, single, day, it is so commonplace that I feel we overlook it sometimes. God decided to overrule a doctor who said that a baby was three weeks away from entering this world. Instead, God agreed with my wife, who just yesterday looked at our best friend's pregnant wife and said that she thought her baby was coming sooner than that! Well, everyone, Mrs. Rose

Redmond is no longer pregnant. Blue Cloud Rosalina Redmond at seven pounds and four ounces was just born an hour or so ago, at Saint Peter's Hospital."

I looked up and spotted Binky fluff her hair at the confirmation of her analysis as the audience broke into a round of applause in honor of Blue Cloud's arrival.

"And all of God's people say!" I usually did not preach with such zeal, but the energy of the morning's events took me in a different direction. A loud, "AMEN" shouted out in unison from the crowd.

"Let me explain the relationship. We are attending the conference with two lay leaders from Reunion Lutheran Church, who also just so happen to be our best friends. In fact, the new father and I have been best friends since we were ten years old. We were all having breakfast together at the hotel this morning, when the labor began, and her water broke. One thing that the doctor was correct on was that Momma would have a short, labor period. That was, by all accounts, a gross underestimation of the situation, because as fast as we could handle it, the baby was just about born in the backseat of that same Rhino 500S that has gobbled up my original sermon!"

I now had the crowd's attention and a few laughs broke out amongst the audience. It was not going too badly so far. Some critics of my last-minute arrival now may have felt a bit bad, since I explained the reason that I was a bit behind my time.

"At one point, while we rushed to make it to the hospital, it looked as though the baby was just going to arrive right in the backseat of that big Rhino 500S. My wife and I were in the backseat of the vehicle with the mother screaming her lungs out, while Bishop Von Houten and the soon to be father, were in the front seat. Both the father and the bishop were praying! When it looked as though we would not make it to the hospital in time, and we would have to deliver the baby, my wife asked me if I had been taught to deliver babies in seminary."

The audience of attending clergy all looked as though they agreed with me. Perhaps a few of my fellow clergy had been in the same position that I had been in today.

"No, I told my wife, that was the one and perhaps only subject that we did not cover. I told her that I had seen our two children born, I knew how smart she is, and that along with God's guidance was all we needed. My wife did not falter. She was ready. Those simple words and her faith had made her ready and willing. Once again, sometimes, you just have to have faith. Then another miracle happened, as Officer Robert Steinman arrived, and he escorted us to the hospital just in time. I am sure today, will be a day that all of us will always remember, and for Officer Steinman of Albany's finest, he will have this as a fond memory of how he was part of God's great plan too."

I stood back from the podium, clapped my hands together in honor of Albany's Police Department, and the audience followed. I pointed to Officer Steinman as Binky and Bishop Von Houten coaxed him into standing up and acknowledging the cheers at his efforts.

When the clapping had died down, I continued, "As for the little baby, she is so lucky, so beautiful, and so loved. It took the Redmonds a long time to have a baby. It was one of their great wishes to have a family, and now the plan is complete. Right in front of our eyes today, it was the joy in fulfillment of God's greatest miracle. That little baby has been born into the greatest, most fun-loving family I have ever known. My best buddy, Mr. Harry M. Redmond Jr. is loud, at times obnoxious, bombastic, overwhelming, and proud. On the other hand, he is generous, loving, fun, and kind. Despite a life that, at times, has had more than a great deal of tragedy and complications, he still laughs and smiles. He is also the one person that I know, who loves life more than any other person that I have ever met. His dear wife, Rose, is his perfect mate. As overwhelming as Harry is, she is calm, relaxed, and the one person in this whole, wide world, who is able to control him. My wife and I love them both as much as we love our own brothers and sisters. That little baby is about to join the Redmond family on a joyous ride. She will enjoy the adventure of life, which will include joy, sorrow, fun, laughter, tears, and hope. I know, I have been there with them, and someday I will write all these adventures down, and a half of the people who read them—will never believe them. That is all right because the other half will have faith that people such as Harry M. Redmond Jr. really do exist. They are part of God's plan too."

I reached behind my head and pulled part of my hair back over my shoulders, as I was now pretty much into a serious flow, and I realized that I had been pounding the podium a little and jumping around a bit.

"I spent a lot of time here in Albany, New York. I love this city and I have fond memories of it. About two city blocks from here, is an arena for sporting events. I know I do not look the part, but I spent a year or two here playing professional ice hockey for the Albany Flying Dutchman. We won a league championship, and I was the goaltender for that championship team. Let me tell you, playing the position of goaltender gives you faith. I had faith in the company that designed the old, fiberglass mask that I wore every game, that was for sure. Without it, I would have spent even more time in Saint Peter's Hospital than I did! However, if not for the time that I spent here in Albany and my knowledge of the roads and shortcuts to the hospital, we also would not have made it to the hospital in time. You see, it was also part of the plan, the plan that evolves every day, right before your eyes, you just cannot see it forming. I believe that miracles are all around us every day. They are not always the kinds of miracles that the Bible tells of, with dramatic events, or some kind of cataclysmic moment that forces people to bow down on their knees and pray in fear or awe. The miracles of God in our lives are much subtler. You have to probe a bit to see them, but they are always there. Sometimes, you just have to have faith to see them."

I was relaxed now, and I actually leaned onto the podium and smiled, while I gathered my thoughts to finish this message.

"So, what can we all take away from this day and my babbling here? This conference, all of these wonderful people working together to promote the church, and the work of the Lord that we feel we should perform to fulfill our calling. In the quest for business success, or our own individual success, or religious success, we sometimes lose sight of the true calling, the true meaning. The business of the church can do that to you. Please, you can take away the assurance that God's miracles are here and now, they are all around us all the time. They certainly are in the emergency room of Saint Peter's Hospital. Miracles are also in the blue skies above us, the rainy days, the snowy days, the puffy white clouds in a clear sky. I see them in the cold beer in our glass that began life as barley in a golden field, the flower buds, which had rested all winter in the cold, which suddenly burst open on a warm, spring day. They are in the cry of a baby, the words of a scholar, the voice coming over our radios, and the smile of our loved ones. They are in the wind in the trees on a crisp, fall day, the glow of the moon on a clear, winter night, and in the first kiss of lovers, when they meet for the first time. I think if we lose sight of that and say, oh well, ho hum, another baby was born today, then we lose sight of the plan, we lose sight of the miracles, we lose sight of our purpose. Who of us here, knows what is waiting for all of us in the grand plan and the passages of time? Only God really knows. The key is to leave good things on the Earth that will glorify God and remain long after you are gone to your reward. I myself, feel that nothing achieves that more than a baby does. What is a better symbol of God's creation and his love than a little child is? Nothing. It is a true blessing, and a miracle of a magnitude that we cannot ever measure. A mother's love of her child, and God's blessing, it is something that we can only all hope someday to understand. God's plan is here for us all, we may like it, or we may not, but it is God's will. Fear, worries, and doubts destroy your soul. However, faith and miracles will restore it! Sometimes, you just have to have faith to accept it, withstand it, and never doubt that another miracle could come along, in a flash and a fleeting moment. That moment, well, it could change the course of your life forever."

I smiled and said softly into the microphone, "Amen."

Lifting my arms above my head, I said, "Grace, joy, and hope to you and your families. May the Lord bless you and keep you and give you peace."

I left the stage as some applause started and the stage man with his clipboard met me, "Forgive me, Pastor Paul, for that rude comment about your hair. That sermon stirred my soul, and I am glad you made it here today. I am not a church going man, but I think I may change that now. By the way, I am afraid of the dentist too."

"Good, no, what am I saying? That is great! I mean about the church part. Remember, church is anywhere, in which you wish, or that you ask it to be. I am very sorry, but I cannot help you with the dentist. Thank you and please no apology is needed," I patted him on the back and walked down the steps, when I spotted the crowd now all standing and clapping. Binky, Officer Steinman, and Bishop Von Houten had rushed down to greet me as I came down the steps.

Binky gave me a hug and kiss as the men gathered around me, "Oh, twenty-seven, that was wonderful. It may be the best that I have ever heard you preach!"

"Great job, Henson! I really enjoyed the part about me the best! You could have gone on a little more about my influence, but it was great!" Bishop Von Houten looked at his watch and smiled as he said, "It was well-timed too. I think I can squeeze in a round or two this afternoon!"

Officer Steinman walked over and he shook my hand, "Pastor Paul, thank you. Thank you for such a stirring message. This has been quite the day. Let me tell you, I know one or two of the guys in our precinct are huge hockey fans, and you are not going to believe this, but one of them still wears your hockey jersey. I made the connection when Mrs. Henson called you, number twenty-seven. Man, you are a hero around these parts, even after all of these years. I cannot wait to tell the guys, I bet they will be over at the hotel to meet you tonight!"

"Well, come on over, Robert, and bring your pals, I am sure that Harry will be celebrating at the bar. In fact, he may buy the entire hotel by the end of the day. You never know with Harry."

I had a long line of greeters who wanted to chat with me for a bit. Bishop Von Houten put his arm around Officer Steinman and asked him, "Say, Steinman, how about a lift back to the hotel in that patrol car? Do you play golf? What time do you get off duty? I am sure we could get out on the course and enjoy the sun, the green grass, and we could make a little side wager on the game."

Bishop Von Houten went along with Officer Steinman in the patrol car back to the hotel while Binky and I worked the crowd and met so many folks that it made our heads spin.

It had been quite the exhausting day for sure.

Afterwards, Binky and I took a cab from the convention center to Saint Peter's Hospital. Rose and Blue Cloud were doing well. The doctor required the two of them to stay overnight in the hospital, but they would be scheduled for release tomorrow.

That night, back at the hotel was a wild and crazy time. Harry bought out the entire restaurant and bar area of the hotel, and every single, hotel guest was invited. In fact, I think Harry invited all of upstate New York. He also gave Jimmie Jack his "well-earned," one-hundred-dollar fee for locating the "lost" Rhino 500S. Harry was beside himself with excitement. He had made telephone calls to all the Redmond family, and Binky had called the Hobnobbers, Martha, the Sharps, and my parents. Even Bishop Von Houten called his wife at home and Rabbi Goldberg to spread the word.

All around the United States, the celebrations were underway. A Redmond celebration of this magnitude was able to shake the very ground of the Earth itself. Every two minutes, Harry was on the telephone with Rose checking on her and Blue Cloud's status. Rose finally had to tell him to stop calling so that she could go to sleep. We met more folks, Bishop Von Houten worked the crowd, and everyone had a great time. Officer Steinman brought his hockey buddies from the police force, and I had the pleasure of chatting with them. Sure enough, one or two of the policemen were diehard Flying Dutchman fans. I posed for pictures and signed hockey jerseys as well as some autographs.

It was quite a night of Redmond, Von Houten, and Henson fueled festivities.

The conference had some small events on the agenda for tomorrow, but in light of the birth of Blue Cloud, we made the decision to head back to New Jersey, once the doctor had released Rose and Blue Cloud from Saint Peter's Hospital. Binky had reminded Harry that he would need a baby's car seat for the Rhino 500S to transport Blue Cloud home, and he rushed out and bought the best Substantial Industries baby's car seat that money could buy. We were up early for the big day to pick up Rose and Blue Cloud from the hospital, and we snapped pictures, posed with the nurses and doctors, and had a grand exit from Saint Peter's Hospital. Only Harry could get a police escort out of the city of Albany by the police department. I do think the large donation that he made to purchase new bulletproof vests, the new ribbon on Officer Steinman's chest, and the money that Harry had promised to build a new recreation room at the local precinct house, had a little to do with it!

"Hello, Mr. Redmond."

"Hello, Howie."

"My sensors have detected Mr. Redmond, and bishop old boy, in the front seats. Twenty-seven, Bink-a-roo-ski and Mrs. Redmond are in the rear. Forgive me, but there is another slight detection that I cannot place and Mrs. Redmond could be an incorrect detection. Her weight is now about ten or so pounds less than her previous ride."

"No, Howie, you are correct about Mrs. Redmond. The new detection is Blue Cloud, she is our little baby."

"Oh, good a baby. No, Cocoa Two?"

"No, Howie. No, Cocoa Two."

"Is that as in Cocoa also, Mr. Redmond?"

"Click." Harry pushed the Howie power button to the "off" position.

"Twenty-seven, can you just tell me how to get to the New York State Thruway southbound?"

"Harry, make a left at the light here at the end of South Manning. Then all you have to do is follow that long line of Albany Police cars with their lights flashing. If I had to venture a wild guess, I do think they all know the way."

10

Not a Marble

Things were normal back home, well . . . then again, normal is always a precarious word to utilize in regard to describing our lives, but despite the circumstances, we all settled back into our daily routines.

I baptized Blue Cloud in a wonderful ceremony that the entire gang attended from far and wide, and every corner of the Harry M. Redmond Jr. Empire. Officer Robert Steinman attended, and he came along with members from the Albany, New York Police Department, who sent an entire color guard. The world famous, "Honest" Ralph Dennis and his family attended too.

It was a Redmond celebration of a magnitude that we have never seen before, and believe me when I say that this old world has seen a few of those events. I thought the party at the hotel on the night the baby had been born, was a glorious and amazing celebration. This shindig made the hotel party pale in comparison. It was 20 John Street on a hot summer Saturday night, all over again. I thought the party would never end.

For some strange reason, in which I could not quite understand, after the baptismal service concluded, I could not bring myself to pour the water that I baptized Blue Cloud with, out upon the base of a tree, or down a drain. I had a nagging, peculiar thought to save it. I sat in my chair in my office for a long time, pondering this enigma. I then decided, as I had for most of my life, to go with my gut instinct. Rather than pour it away, instead, I saved it, and poured it into a jug. I labeled it as, "water" and tucked it away in a cupboard in my office. Even for me, it seemed as though it was a strange thing to do.

It was now mid-October, and I returned home from work one night to find Binky on the telephone with Rose. I could tell by the conversation and concern on my wife's face that the subject was of some serious nature. I sat down at the kitchen table and listened. I had received a telephone call today from Harry while I was in the office, and he told me how ill little Blue Cloud was, and that she had been suffering a week or so with some type of stomach bug. I had a feeling that this call with Rose was serious, and that the subject was Blue Cloud's illness.

When Binky hung up the telephone, she turned to me and filled me in on the details, "That was, Rose. Blue Cloud has some type of virus or some type of other illness. She has been very sick for the last week or so. She cannot seem to keep any food down and her little belly is swollen. The pediatrician is quite concerned, and she wants her to go to a specialist for some more tests."

"Yes, Binky. I heard a little of the situation today. It does not sound so good. I spoke with Harry earlier, and he seemed very upset, but he thought it was just a virus. I can interpret the look on your face. You seem to think it is more than just a virus. I can tell. I know you. Why do you think her belly is swollen? Any research results? Have you checked into the symptoms?"

I knew my wife well enough that I could sense her intense concern. She sat down and nodded her head while she told me, "I have, Paul, and I am very upset and concerned with my preliminary results of what I have been able to read. The symptoms, the facts, and some family history background of Rose, leaves me very disturbed. I do think that we need to go with Rose and Harry when they bring Blue Cloud to the specialist. They have an appointment for tomorrow."

"Sure, sure, of course Binky, we will go. I will have Martha cancel my other appointments. Maybe your parents can watch the children."

Binky nodded in agreement as she continued, "I was over there today. Little Blue Cloud has lost weight, and she just cannot seem to keep any type of food down. The little baby is very sick, she is weak, lethargic, and has terrible diarrhea. Above all, as if that is not enough, the abdominal swelling is so troublesome." I did not know what to say, I bowed my head and said a quick prayer.

I stood up out of my chair, went over to the teakettle, turned, and asked Binky, "Do you want some tea?"

"Sure, Paul. Thank you."

"Where are the children?"

"They are fine. They are watching Dinky on the television in the living room."

Binky continued with her research results, I could tell that she wanted to convey some ideas to me and alleviate the thoughts in her head a bit by sharing them.

She continued, "I have been researching this all day now. The symptoms are very consistent with a childhood disease known as Wolman Disease. It is rare, and it is genetic. Rose told me today that she suspects a cousin in her family had a child with the same symptoms that she lost at six months or so. I am sure that Rose is not aware of the disease, only that her cousin lost a child many years ago. I have to say that I am very concerned because the pediatrician would not even venture a guess. I think the pediatrician suspects something because the blood work must have brought something to light. The doctor just does not want to guess. That is what makes me so upset. I hope and pray it is just a bad stomach virus, but I fear it is not."

The teakettle boiled, and I prepared us each a cup of tea. I brought the tea over to Binky and sat down next to her as I asked, "This Wolman disease, what is the treatment?"

Binky looked at me over her teacup. Immediately, I

spotted her eyes tear up.

She spoke in almost a whisper to me, "That is the problem, my dear Paul. There is none."

I felt my stomach turn and my head spin a little.

"I have had flawed research before, Paul."

"Dear Binky—only once my love. I will hope and pray that this is another one of those times."

It was a terrible night. I could not sleep a wink. I spent a good part of the night awake while wandering and reading. First, I read my Bible, then some papers that I had been starting and stopping for the last few weeks. A few months earlier, I had taken some advice that I received a long time ago from a gentleman who owned a bookstore in the old neighborhood. His store was there for many, many years, right on Belmont Avenue, a few blocks south of our family home. I had written a short novelette many years ago, about Christmas time with the Redmond family. My grandfather had given the story to the owner of the bookstore. He wrote me back a very nice letter, encouraging me to publish the story. I stopped by the store and thanked him, took his advice, and then tucked the story away for years, until a few weeks ago. In my spare time, I finally began to take his advice, and write down some of the many adventures of Harry and Paul, to begin to tell the world some of our extraordinary lives together. I had created random outlines, notes, and had not yet created any clear directions of where to begin. At this point, I was just compiling notes on our major adventures. After all, there were quite a few of them!

Tonight, was not the night for this project. My mind was swimming with not only adventures of the past, but I was being haunted by the present.

I simply could not concentrate. Apprehension consumed me and as the night went on, I felt a deep foreboding growing within me.

Creativity or sleep was not going to happen for me.

Most of the time, I sat in my chair, prayed, and thought. It was a long night of thinking, and it was tearing me apart.

I had called Harry, after Binky and I spoke, and told him that Binky and I would go with them to the doctor tomorrow. He was quiet, cold, and empty on the telephone, but I could tell that he appreciated the offer. He said that Blue Cloud was actually sleeping, as was Rose. The baby seemed better tonight; he said the symptoms were not as violent, but she still would not eat very much food. I encouraged him as best I could, but I still had a terrible, sinking feeling deep down, that Binky was as usual, correct in her research, and this was a very serious situation.

I put my vest on, wandered outside into the church parking lot. I stopped and stared at the new addition to the facilities. It had all gone so well, the big grand opening, the rededication of the church just a few short weeks ago. We were all so happy at the ceremony. Bishop Von Houten was in every picture. We made the local newspapers; the church was successful and overflowing. It was a place of joy, a place of great hope and peace. Yet tonight, my soul was so disturbed.

I looked up at the sky, and I sighed. There were no clouds in sight and the stars were brightly glowing at me. As I put my hands in my vest pockets, I looked over in the direction of the new addition to the spot where the giant, oak tree once hovered above us all.

Hello! What is this? I pulled from deep down in the vest pockets, four little acorns. I then remembered that these were the same acorns, in which I had gathered on the day when the arborist crew cut the red oak tree down. Funny, I thought that I had actually picked up five of them on that day. In my haste, I must have dropped one somewhere. I kept my hand on them for a long time and stared into the night sky.

Hope, dreams, and faith. That is all I had to offer. I had nothing concrete.

I was a fraud.

No, actually for some reason, I felt that I also had these four little acorns.

"Mr. Redmond, Mrs. Redmond, I am Doctor Berkhout."

"Pleased to meet you, Doctor Berkhout," Harry shook hands and greeted a tall doctor who had white hair, a kind face, and a determined look in his eyes. "Please meet our best friend, as well as our pastor. This is Pastor Paul Henson, and his wife, Binky Henson. There is nothing that you cannot say in front of them. Pastor Paul is our family pastor, but he and Binky, are also our best friends on the planet. They are our family."

Binky and I each greeted the doctor, who motioned for us to sit down on a couch in the room. Rose held onto Harry's hands tightly, and I held Binky's hands as we all sat down together.

Doctor Berkhout explained, "Look, I will be honest here, this is a difficult diagnosis, as well as a serious situation. I have run a multitude of tests on little, Blue Cloud. They are very specialized tests and due to the nature of them, they will take some time to research and compile. I also have been on the phone with some consultants from across the country about the symptoms. My concern is that she has a very rare, recessive, inborn error of metabolism."

Harry was annoyed as he waved his hands in the air, "C'mon, Doc, talk normal man, this is our daughter here! Please no medical, mumbo jumbo stuff!"

Doctor Berkhout looked away and then back at Harry, "It *could,* and I do stress at this point, the word could . . . be a rare genetic disorder that does not allow Blue Cloud to absorb nutrients from food. The tests focused upon the activity of a specific enzyme that is either absent or not active enough. In interviewing and compiling, past medical histories with Mrs. Redmond, and then with yourself, Mrs. Redmond indicated that there was a similar case with a very distant cousin on her mother's side. It is possible that a genetic factor has carried over here."

"What does that mean, Doc?"

"I need to obtain some more test results, Mr. Redmond. I cannot say yet. If it does prove out to be, Wolman disease, then I am afraid. . .." Doctor Berkhout drifted off, and he looked at me. Binky's eyes were already filling with tears, and I could feel her heart beating right through her hands.

How could this be really happening?

"Pastor Henson. Please, could we have a private moment? Please, excuse me. Please, Mr. Redmond, Mrs. Redmond, and Mrs. Henson, excuse us. I assure you all that we are doing everything we can for Blue Cloud."

Harry jumped up and his voice trembled, "Please, Doc. I will send her anywhere in the world, the best doctors, whatever it takes. Paul will tell you that money is no object here! Please, Doctor Berkhout!"

"I understand, Mr. Redmond. Please excuse us. Pastor Henson, please, just a moment alone. Please, pastor."

I stood up from the couch and looked back at Binky as she grabbed Harry's hands tightly. Rose's eyes were filled with tears, as were Harry's eyes, and they all began sobbing.

I followed Doctor Berkhout into his office and he closed the door. He motioned for me to sit down in front of his desk in a guest chair. I tugged at my white collar. It was stifling me, and I wanted to rip it off my neck. I sat down in the guest chair.

"Pastor Henson, if I might ask . . . what is your faith, sir, or your denomination?"

"Lutheran, Doc, I am a Lutheran pastor."

Doctor Berkhout leaned back in his chair and sighed.

"I knew that. The Lutheran clergy are always so caring. Look, Pastor Henson," Doctor Berkhout leaned in over his desk and stared at me, "I am ninety-five percent sure that Blue Cloud has Wolman disease. I just hope and pray that I am wrong. You seem as if you are a tough guy, Pastor

Henson, I can tell by your eyes. You are a fearless man, so I will give it to you straight."

I stopped the doctor in his tracks as I interrupted him, "I know. There is no cure. My wife suspected that was what illness the little baby has. She was, unfortunately, right on target."

"Your wife? Is she a medical practitioner?"

"No, she is into research sciences. She can research anything. I have only known her to be incorrect one time. How I wish and hope that she is incorrect a second time, doc."

"I see. Pastor Henson, your friends are going to need all of your support. I can see that they are both fragile individuals and they will need your strength and guidance here. There are some treatments we can do to offset the condition just a little, but most children do not survive much past the first year or so."

"I understand, Doc. It is just that Harry, I mean, Mr. Redmond, has had a difficult past with medical tragedies. He lost his first wife to cancer after they had only been married for a year or so. This might be a little too much for anyone to handle."

"I see. I do not envy you, Pastor Henson. I am Jewish, and I have seen what my rabbi goes through, and has to handle. You clergy are a special kind of people. The fact that the Redmonds are your friends makes this only tougher. Let's hope that five percent chance does come through. Please take them home, we can send Blue Cloud home too. She is comfortable now. I have given her some medicine to help with the food absorption. Here is a dose or two more to hold her over for a few days." The doctor slid a pill bottle across the desk to me. I put the bottle in my pocket, as he continued to explain, "The dosage instructions are on the label, and here is some paperwork to provide details on the medication. I promise that I will call the Redmond's home telephone as soon as I receive the test results. If you could be there when I call later today, I think that would be of some comfort."

"I will be there for them. I always have, and I always will be." I stood up and shook the doctor's hand, as I told him, "Thank you, Doctor Berkhout. Shalom and blessings upon you."

Doctor Berkhout smiled at me and he led me back out to the room where Rose, Harry, and Binky were waiting. A nurse had brought Blue Cloud out and Rose and Binky were checking her as Rose held her in her arms. They all looked up at me.

Harry stood up, "Well, Paul?"

"Look, the doctor requires the results of many tests. He does not want to jump to any conclusions here. He wants us to head back to your house, put Blue Cloud to sleep, and see what the test results are. He has given her some medication to make her more comfortable. I have some additional pills here for Blue Cloud. We just have to wait. It is only a matter of time now. That is all we have . . . time."

Harry nodded, and I put my arm around him and pulled him close. His usually strong body was limp, he was soft, and had very little energy. We all left together in stunned silence. I drove the Rhino 500S back to the house as Harry, Rose, and Blue Cloud sat in the back. Binky held my hand tightly while I drove, she refused to let go of me. The dried tears on her face and in her eyes were very painful for me, or for anyone to see. It was a quiet ride, a long ride, a ride full of apprehension and tenseness. The foreboding sense of fear was upon us all.

It was going to be an agonizing day and night, that was for sure.

We arrived back at the Redmond's house and spotted Linda and Ronzo's pickup truck in the driveway. They had keys to the house, and when we walked in, Linny and Ronzo greeted us, as did Cocoa Two. It was a solemn gathering, unlike most of the usual happy times that we always shared together. Harry sat with Rose as Binky, Linny, and Rose took turns holding and walking Blue Cloud. The baby seemed more comfortable than before the visit to the doctor, but the poor little girl still seemed to be in discomfort, and she cried a little. For some reason, despite the combined efforts of the three ladies, Blue Cloud just refused to go to sleep. Her little face turned up; her eyes followed all of us. She seemed alert, but she was still in some kind of state of unrest.

I sat in the kitchen around the old table, with Ronzo sitting across from me, and Cocoa Two sitting and watching my every move. It was just the three of us in the kitchen, so I decided to share with Ronnie how serious the illness could be.

Cocoa Two now moved to lie under the table at my feet, with his head resting on his paws. He would get up on occasion, go, and check on the situation in the other room, and then he would return. He knew that something was seriously wrong. I found it quite strange that Cocoa Two would focus his attention so strongly on me. It was as if the dog would not let me out of his sight. As if he felt that, I could help with this horrible situation.

"Tell me, Pastor Paul, why would God allow a little baby like Blue to get sick? Why not take an old dog like me? Why is there suffering for an innocent? I just do not get it, twenty-seven. I just do not understand. A hundred times over in Vietnam, I should have died, but for some unknown reason, I survived. Why did I survive, Paul? While, others never stood a chance. Poor guys, mowed down in blinding firefights, without even knowing what hit them. Now, I would die in place of that little baby. I really would. I just do not understand. I used to have such strong faith, Paul, but this makes it hard. It makes it really hard. I swear that I would trade places with Blue Cloud in a second."

Ronzo's eyes filled with tears and I reached over and

grabbed his hands as I told him, "So would I, Ronnie. I understand . . . my old friend. I do not have an answer for you. I just know that sometimes, we have to have faith in God's plan and purpose. That is all we have right now."

Harry walked in and sat down next to us. He had determination written all over his face. He folded his hands together and placed them on the table. I could tell by his actions that he now needed answers. Harry was not a patient man. I had known him way too long to think I could stall him for a little longer.

He looked like a wreck as he looked up at me and said, "Give it to me, Paul. I need to know."

"Harry, please, wait a bit longer for the tests, it is all still up in the air."

"No, tell me now, Paul. Tell me what the doctor told you!"

I knew he needed to know. I stood up, put my hands on his shoulders, and held him tightly in my hands as he put his head down on the table. Harry knew by my actions how serious it was at this time.

I told him, "Please keep in mind, there is a five percent chance, which remains that the doc is wrong, Harry. He thinks it could be, Wolman Disease. It is extremely serious, Harry. Most babies do not live more than a year or so."

I heard him start to sob. I felt his body heave and the pain begin as I continued to hold him by his shoulders. Ronnie stood up, came over, and put his hand on Harry's back. It was all we could do. It was all we knew how to do. This was a young man who had already felt so much pain, so much sorrow, and dealt with more than his share of tragedy.

Where was the justice from Heaven? What was God's plan? This cannot be part of it! It did not seem fair, and I had to admit, I felt anger inside of me. It was building just like all the fires that grew inside of me all of my life. I disliked admitting it, but it was anger building towards

God; and it was anger at my own profession, my own beliefs, for being so powerless, and so useless.

Here was Harry, once more dealing with something so serious, that it was tearing him apart before my eyes. It was past the point of sorrow. It was sheer agony to see him suffering like this.

Once more, as I have had to do much too often in the past, I mumbled, "Jesus wept." I told myself that surely, Jesus in his human form felt this same pain, when his own friend died. It was the only comfort that I had at this moment. Those two words from the Bible were perhaps, the greatest comfort of all, they held such power in their profoundly deep meaning. How profound that those two words out of all of the scripture could mean so much.

We sat in silence for a while as Harry moved between the kitchen and sitting with Rose in the living room.

No one said anything for hours.

The wait was agonizing.

The front doorbell rang, and I jumped up from the table. Ronzo, Cocoa Two, and I hustled our way towards the front door and we passed the ladies, Blue Cloud, and Harry in the living room. We motioned for them to stay put that we would check on whom it was. I opened the front door and there stood Dave Sharp.

"Dave! What a surprise, Dave. Please come in," I said as I led him into the house.

"Hello, Pastor Paul. Hey, Ronzo." Dave bent down and greeted Cocoa Two, and we walked into the grand foyer of the house.

"I am sorry, Pastor Paul, but I heard that Blue Cloud was very sick. I wanted to stop and wish her a speedy recovery. I do not want to intrude, but we have a present for the baby. I have been holding off on giving the gift, but Mrs. Sharp felt strongly that I should bring it over right now. Maybe it will cheer everyone up a bit."

Harry, Rose, Binky, and Linny appeared. Linny was

holding and rocking Blue Cloud, who was still restless and crying a bit.

Harry, even in his present despondent mood, lit up when he spotted Dave and rushed over to greet him, "Sharpie, come on in. Please, do come in!"

"Hey boss, hey, everyone. Mrs. Redmond, Mrs. Henson, Mrs. Boatmann. I am sorry, but I wanted to check on the baby and youse guys. I know it has been tough. I heard that Blue Cloud was not feeling very well. I do not want to bother anyone."

"Nonsense, Sharpie. You are family! There is no bother."

Rose came over and gave Dave a hug, "Please, Dave, you are always welcome here, you know that."

"Thank you, I actually have to get back to church to check on the boiler and the heat, it has been giving me fits all day. Once more, for some reason, Mrs. Sharp insisted that I bring this present over for Blue Cloud today. I have it in the truck. If Pastor Paul could give me a hand, then I will bring it in."

"Sure, Dave, let me grab my vest and I will go out with you. Binky gets mad at me if I go out without a coat these days."

Binky nodded to affirm that she was watching me carefully. I followed Dave out to the truck and he pulled down the tailgate to reveal a medium-sized item strapped down into the bed of the truck. Whatever the item was that was sitting in the bed of the pickup truck; I could see that moving pads and wraps completely covered it.

"It appears to be a bit heavy, Dave," I said as I tugged and poked at the piece in the back of the truck.

"Well, a little, but once I free it up, we can bring it in rather easily. I want to keep the pads on to protect it. It is a piece of furniture."

"Furniture, Dave?"

Dave nodded as he loosened up the straps and we each grabbed an end. We hauled it off the back of the truck and carried it into the house. It was heavy! Whatever it was, it sure was solid. We set it down in the foyer, at the base of the large staircase as everyone gathered around it. Dave worked to pull off the pads as Ronzo and I assisted him. Once the straps were free, Dave pulled and tugged at them to reveal the furniture underneath.

"I hope you like it. I made it myself in my workshop," Dave explained as he pulled the last cloth pad off and revealed that underneath was a baby crib. It was not just any crib, but it was a handcrafted wooden crib.

It was unbelievable!

The word beautiful could not even begin to describe the wonderful craftsmanship. It was solid oak, with an ornate headboard and footboard. It had hand-carved details, turned spindles for railings, and brass casters for rollers. It was not just a crib; it was a work of art!

"Dave, my goodness, it is fabulous! You made this? You made this for Blue Cloud?" The craftsmanship astounded Rose.

"Why yes, I did, Mrs. Redmond. I wanted to make her something special, so I made this crib in my workshop. I work with wood as a hobby, you know."

"A hobby? My goodness, this is better quality work than any craftsman could do," Harry said as he was in awe, as we all were, of the remarkable workmanship and skill that went into the crib. "Sharpie, you have to let us pay you for this! This is beyond belief."

"Oh, no boss, I could never take a dime for this! It is a gift from Mrs. Sharp and me. She helped me put the finish on it."

I walked over and stood next to Binky as we admired the crib. I ran my hands over the finish and studied the grain of the wood. It was really incredible.

Binky smiled as she looked at Dave and asked, "It is oak, is it not Dave?"

"Oh yes, Mrs. Henson. Solid, red oak along with solid

brass hardware."

"Sharpie! Solid oak and solid brass, that costs a fortune, please at least, let me pay you for the wood and materials," Harry was pleading with Dave.

Dave waved his hand in the air, "C'mon boss, you know me better than that. I learned how to work a deal from the greatest dealmaker of them all. You!"

Everyone laughed at that comment.

"I got all the wood for free. I still have more of it in my shop too. It is the wood from the big, oak tree that we cut down, when we built the new education building. You know the one that Mrs. Whipley made all the fuss over and Pastor Paul used to pour the water on! I worked a deal with James Peterson. Do you remember?"

I felt my hand jump as I pulled it off the wood and a cold shiver went down my spine.

Binky noticed the look on my face. She studied me for a moment, and she whispered to me, "Are you all right, Paul?"

"Sure, sure, Binky. Hey Dave, great work on the deal. I am so glad the tree still lives in your craftsmanship," I covered up my shock as best I could, but I knew that my wife had felt the tingle in my heart too. I was amazed that in front of me, I was staring at a reincarnation of the tree. We continued the discussion for a little while longer, and we all admired the fantastic gift of Dave's love and skills.

"I really have to be on my way. If Pastor Paul will help me, we can bring it up to the nursery now. The mattress is in that box over there."

I grabbed the end of the crib and we carried it together up the stairs. We placed the crib in the nursery room while Binky put the mattress in and dressed it with fresh linens. It was an awesome piece. We all thanked Dave, and he left with kisses for the ladies, handshakes from the men, a paw shake for Cocoa Two, and well wishes for Blue Cloud.

Dave's visit had provided a welcome diversion, and it

had broken the tense afternoon of waiting. We went back to our waiting game as we all sat, paced, and worried. It was brutal. Blue Cloud was still awake and restless. Nothing had changed there as everyone took turns holding her, rocking her, and comforting her.

I was sitting with Ronzo at the kitchen table when the telephone rang.

I nearly jumped out of my skin.

Harry rushed in and looked at me. He picked the telephone up on the second ring.

"Harry M. Redmond Jr. speaking," Harry said as his voice trembled and shook with trepidation.

We all gathered around him as he spoke on the telephone. My heart was pounding out of my chest while I stood next to Binky, who held her hand over her mouth. I could tell by the look on Harry's face, as to how the conversation was going, and what the results were. I had known him for so long; I knew the body language and the choking in his throat. He was being very brave.

"Yes, Doctor Berkhout. I understand. Yes, we can hope. I will follow your instructions, yes, I understand. Yes, Pastor Paul is here. Thank you and goodbye," Harry said as he slowly hung up the telephone.

I motioned Binky and Linny into action. I knew one of them needed to take Blue Cloud from Rose. Harry hung up the telephone, and stood there with tears running down his face, while Rose burst into tears of anguish.

It was a horrible moment, a moment of pure punishment, and heart wrenching castigation, as I watched Harry sink along the wall and collapse into a wall of tears. Oh Lord, have you forgotten us? That was the only thought that came into my mind as Binky and Linny comforted Rose. Ronzo and I picked Harry off the floor.

The next few minutes spun out of control, as it seemed as though all the tears of the entire human race were pelting down upon us. I had never felt any pain and anguish comparable to what we went through on that hillside when we buried Sky Blu, but this was surpassing it. The pain was tearing us into shreds; it was a torment of a new magnitude, and it was pure suffering.

I dragged Harry the best that I could to the living room while he and Rose embraced and held onto one another. Ronzo collapsed into Linny's arms, as Binky rocked Blue Cloud, while my wife held it together the best that she could. I looked deeply into my wife's eyes and mouthed to her to stay strong. She gave me a head nod and fought back the tears. I could see her mouthing The Lord's Prayer.

I was so proud of her.

Harry sat next to Rose, holding her hand with his one hand and covering his eyes with the other hand. He was hiding his face, working hard not to show the tears running down his face.

Harry suddenly stood up, and he walked over by me. The tears ran like a river out of him, while he struggled to speak to me, "Paul, do something, please do something, Paul. Help us, make it all go away, tell me that Blue Cloud can be saved, and tell me the doctors are wrong."

I put my hand on his arm, "Harry, please I know there is hope. It is in God's hands, Harry. We will pray. And, we will. . .." I was faltering, I did not know what to do, or say, and Harry detected the weakness. He knew me too well, and he knew that I had nothing to give.

"NO! NO! NO! PAUL, YOU HAVE TO DO SOMETHING! WHY DON'T YOU UNDERSTAND? THAT IS OUR DAUGHTER! A DOCTOR JUST TOLD ME THAT SHE IS GOING TO DIE!"

"Harry, Harry, I understand, but I am only a man, Harry. I am a man, just as you are. I can only do so much."

When I finished saying those words, Harry spun around angrily towards me, shaking off my grip on his arm. He grabbed me by the shoulders, shook me, and pushed me. Ronzo rushed in and Harry pushed him aside like a rag doll. His grief had overpowered his thinking. Harry was big and strong, but so was I, and I held my ground. Harry, as powerful as he was . . . could not overpower me, and I stood there and let his grief come out. The ladies screamed in horror, and Cocoa Two barked in fear.

"STOP SAYING THAT!" Harry screamed at me in anger. "I wish you would just stop saying that. You always solve problems, Paul! You never back down from anything, and you always stay strong and positive. That is what you do, and that is what we all count on! You are not just a man! You are the world famous, number twenty-seven. I know what you can do, Paul. I have seen it all of our lives together. All the different things, I have seen you do, on the rink and off . . . all the things we did together. I have never seen you back down from anything. I cannot imagine you backing down from this now! Harry M. Redmond Jr. and a lot of other people have always counted upon the long-haired kid who wore number twenty-seven. Now, when I need you more than I have ever needed you in my life, you are going to just stand here and tell me the same old story that you are just a man!"

Harry stood back and shook his head in disbelief.

"I wish you would realize what everyone else knows, Paul. You would have made it to the big time and would have been the greatest goalie of all time. Not one person whoever watched you play would disagree. Hall of fame, first ballot, hands down, the greatest! But no! God had a plan for you, Paul John Henson. He blew your knee up for a reason, so that you could do exactly what you are doing right now," Harry now shook me violently as he grabbed me and held me by my shoulders.

I was astonished, and I did not say a word.

Harry's words echoed inside of my mind and soul. My mind suddenly remembered an extraordinary night in Concord, New Hampshire, and a strange man who I met there in a pub while having dinner. His words to me on that cold November night came back clearly in my mind. He told a young man whose heart was set on being a professional goaltender in the big leagues, "That sometimes the direction you think you are going, is not where you will end up."

Suddenly, it hit me square in my mind. The cold, stark reality that I was not a pretender any longer, but I had chosen my path in life to be a leader of my family, friends, congregation, and an advocate of God's plan.

Harry's pain continued to manifest in his words to me, "Don't you see, Paul? Why can't you ever accept and understand what you are supposed to do now? It is what everyone always says about you that the hand of God steers you. You stand in front of us all the time, telling us to have faith, always believe! Well, wake up! It is time that you have faith, come to believe, and realize who you are! Just because Sky died and you could not make that save, does not mean anything. Sky was supposed to die, Paul, but I swear to you that Blue Cloud is not going to die. The eye of the tiger in my eyes will not help this time, Paul. It is out of my control! Only you can save her. I know you can do it, because you are the world famous, number twenty-seven, and I have faith in you, Paul. You never give up, ever. I cannot go through this twice in my life. I think that is something that only you, of all people, can understand. And my poor Rose, oh no, not poor Rose! Paul, what would it do to her? You love her as much as anyone else does. I cannot believe you would allow her to feel such pain for too long. You cannot just stand there, Paul, saying all the same, old, tired words. We need you to back it all up now!"

Harry was weeping violently now. He grasped onto my shoulders, and held on while he lowered his head. His voice lowered in volume as he struggled to speak, "Please Paul, get back in the net again, strap on the armor of God, put on your old goalie mask of hope, as Jesus wore a crown of thorns, and make this one last save, for me, for Rose, for Blue Cloud . . . for you! Please, twenty-seven. I feel you are our only hope." Harry sunk his head into my chest, and he clung desperately to my shirt as he sobbed his eyes out.

"I am so sorry, Paul. I am so sorry." His sorrow was so intense that he was lost in the misery. Rose came over, hugged him, and pulled him away. Ronzo came over and checked on me. I nodded that I was fine. Binky stood there with the tears rolling down her cheeks as she rocked poor, little Blue Cloud.

I was shocked, and I did not have a clue as to what to do. All my words seemed like rhetoric.

For certain, it seemed as if God had abandoned us all today.

Then again, had he? Perhaps not, and I had been too blind to see, or too deaf to hear?

I was supposed to be the leader, and I was powerless. I was a clueless dope, standing there without even a thought of what to do next. I was a bum, a worthless goalie who had just lost the biggest game of my career.

I looked up at all of my friends. I looked at my wife. Harry was right; they all counted on me to do something. That is what I was supposed to do, that is what they expected. I could not just stand here, and feed them meaningless words of hope and glory, unless I could back them up. Time had run out for that. All those fancy sermons, the glorious words; it was time to prove it all. It all came back to be not much different from when I was number twenty-seven, crouching low waiting for a shot in the net.

It was time to make a save.

It was time to win the most important game of all.

I simply said, "I will do what I can. God help me, I will do what I can."

I put my vest on to go outside to pick up my Bible from our jeep parked in the driveway. The plain and simple fact of the matter was that I still did not know what to do.

When I reached in my pocket for the keys to the jeep, I felt deep down in there . . . those four little acorns. I put my hand around them and held them. I felt a strange warmth come over me.

Despite the horror of the situation, my soul was suddenly still. The old, familiar flow returned to me once more. It felt so good, so comforting. Something very different filled me; I felt peace, calm, joy, and hope. I recalled in my mind, the Bible verse from the Book of Job. Yes, Paul, wake up! Of course! What were you thinking? I mouthed as I held the acorns in my hand, "The branches will never, ever cease."

I stopped in my tracks, spun around, and looked at Binky. Blue Cloud was really fussing now, as the medicine must have worn off a bit, and her discomfort had increased. I felt a strong flow come over me and my head was spinning, but suddenly, I knew what to do. I ran to the telephone on a table next to where Harry sat next to Rose with his head buried in his hands.

"Paul, I am so sorry, you know he did not mean those things he said, or to push you like he did," Rose looked at me as she reached out and put her hand on my arm.

"It is fine dear, Rose. It is fine. I understand. Harry is correct. I need to wake up and do something." I turned to walk away from her, and then I turned and returned to her side. I was inspired, and I needed to convey that to the baby's mother. I grabbed Rose tightly by her arm and knelt down next to her. I grabbed her and hugged her as tightly as I could and then kissed her cheek. I moved all my hair away and looked deeply into her anguish-filled eyes, as I told her confidently, "Sometimes, you just have to have faith, dear Rose."

She smiled with her eyes only, and I saw that despite all the horror and pain, her faith was strong.

"I have faith in God and in you, Paul. I always will,"

Rose said with tears running down her cheeks. "I sensed from the moment that Blue Cloud was born, that she was going to need you someday, Paul. God told me that fact right before she left my womb. I know now that I was correct."

I remembered that strange incident and the premonition from dear Rose in the birthing room. I now knew there was much more to this than anyone ever could realize. I thought as I studied her face; Lord, please be by my side and help me. This young lady is so glorious. I love her with all of my heart, and she is in such pain.

Lord, one last save, please, just grant me one more last save. I could not do it one time, when I needed to the most, but this time. . ..

I smiled and stood up. I went back to the telephone, picked it up, and I dialed the number for the church maintenance shop as I spoke in a whisper, "C'mon, Dave, answer the phone, will you. Dave answer, will you please answer?"

"Maintenance shop. Reunion Lutheran Church, Dave Sharp speaking."

"Dave!"

"Hey, Pastor Paul."

"Dave, listen, I need your help."

"Sure, what's up?" I could tell that Dave sensed my haste.

"Please, Dave, go into my office. In the left cupboard, next to the large wall painting, is a large, clear, glass jug. The jug is full of water. I need that jug of water, Dave. Please bring it to the Redmond's house as quickly as you can."

"A jug of water, Pastor Paul?"

"Yes, Dave, a plain jug of water. It is on the third shelf up from the bottom."

"I am on my way, Pastor Paul." I hung up the telephone. I walked quickly past Binky, stopped and kissed her on the cheek, and walked out the front door. Outside, I bowed in prayer.

"Lord, please; let me make this one special save. Let me have made a choice, let me have made a decision with your guidance. Let me have done something correctly at some time in my life to contribute here. Please, Lord, let me have interpreted your message correctly here. Amen." I picked up my Bible from the front seat of the old jeep and headed back inside.

Dave Sharp must have taken a jet plane, because he showed up at the door with the water jug in his hand, in no time flat.

"Here, Pastor Paul. I came as quickly as I could."

"Thank you, Dave, you did well. Thank you so much."

"Is everything going to be all right, Pastor Paul?"

I put my hand on his shoulder and squeezed it firmly as I told him, "It is going to be all right, Dave."

"I have to go, Pastor Paul. Please call me if I can help anymore," Dave Sharp said as he searched my eyes for a clue.

"Thank you, Dave. As usual, you have come through for us," I said, while shaking his hand and smiling at him.

He looked back at me and smiled too, as he told me, "I know it will be all right, Pastor Paul. It will be all right because you just told me that it would be." I took the water jug out of his hands. Dave turned, and he returned to his truck as I closed the door.

I must have broadcasted confidence, because no one asked me what my intentions were, everyone followed me without speaking a word. Looking back at the events of that day, it was faith . . . pure and simple faith, which carried us all. I carried the jug into the living room and poured some of the water into a small cup that we had taken from the kitchen. Reaching into my pocket, I took my old wooden cross on the cloth lanyard out, and placed it over my head, while asking Binky to hand Blue Cloud to

Rose and Harry.

"Please, Rose. Please, Harry, if you would each hold Blue Cloud together in your hands." I spoke the request in a low whisper while pouring some of the water from the cup into my right hand. I then rubbed the water over both of my hands, dipped two of my fingers into the water, and with those same fingers; I made the sign of the cross on Blue Cloud's forehead. I then said a simple blessing, "May the Lord Jesus bless you and keep you. May his countenance shine down upon you and give you peace and health. Bless again dear Lord, this holy water with which, we baptized Blue Cloud into your glorious kingdom. Amen."

"Let's take Blue Cloud upstairs to the crib. Ronzo, if you could please bring that jug of water." We all followed Rose as she carried Blue Cloud upstairs to the nursery. Poor Blue Cloud was really wailing now.

"Please, Rose, set her down in the crib and cover her with her blanket."

"But, Paul, she is crying so hard."

"I know, Rose. That is why she needs the crib."

I took the jug from Ronzo and poured just a little more water into my hand. While praying, and speaking in a whisper, the words to the verse from the Book of Job, I carefully sprinkled a few drips and splashes of water on the wood of the crib. I rubbed the rails and top section of the crib with the same hand while Rose set Blue Cloud down inside the crib and covered her. She fussed, screamed, and Rose went to pick her up, but I gently grabbed her arm to stop her. Rose looked at me and she eased back as I smiled at her. Blue Cloud whimpered a little, then she stuck her thumb in her mouth and she calmed.

In a second or two, she drifted off to sleep.

"Why . . . Paul, she is asleep," Rose turned to me and smiled.

"And, you should all do the same. I will take this chair here and watch her. Please, all of you. Listen to me, please, you need to go and rest. I will be on duty. Cocoa Two will stay with me. Ronzo, if you could relieve me during the night, it will work out well. We can all take shifts throughout the night. Please everyone, sleep and peace are what we need. We all have overnight bags packed, so we can stay here and help."

It seemed as though the entire gang willingly accepted my advice. I am sure that everyone must have been exhausted. No one wanted to eat. Everyone wanted to rest. Off to sleep they all headed, not one of them argued with me.

Harry came over; he clutched my arm and said, "Paul, I am so sorry. I just lost it, and you know how I feel about you."

"Harry, please just forget it, you were right. I need to help you and not just offer up more fantasy-filled, words of hope and glory. It is time for me to come up with the greatest of all of our famous Harry and Paul action plans."

I smiled at him and he forced a smile back.

I assured him once more with my eyes that I understood and said, "You're exhausted, Harry. Please go to sleep."

"I didn't mean to yell at you, Paul, but I am desperate."

"Harry, please, all the times guys wanted to stick a puck between my eyes! What do you think I am, like some old lady here or what? Please, I am standing in the net here. I need a defenseman, not some old crybaby. I am trying to concentrate on the game. Now, tap my pads with your stick, and go play defense in front of me will you. And please no screens, those pucks dead on in my mask, really hurt. All the things we have been through and all the things we have faced together. I will be there for you, my friend. My brother. I always have been and I always will be."

He laughed as best that he could, since he had

remembered a time so long ago, when I had told him the exact same advice. He hugged me and I felt his pain.

"Get some sleep, thirty-five. I have the crease covered. Cocoa Two will stay with me. Ronzo will relieve us and then you can take a shift. It is going to be all right, Harry."

He nodded his head, and he was gone.

Binky came over and hugged me, "Paul, are you, okay? You had a flow going on now. Didn't you?"

"Binky, I am fine, please get some sleep. I did have a flow, and you know that I am feeling good, really good."

Binky looked at me and then at the crib. She smiled and said, "Goodnight, my love. I know you now have marbles to stop, so I will leave you to them. I know now that God has given you a plan, and we all have faith in you. The dried tears on my cheeks tell of my pain, but they also tell of my love for you. . .." Her voice trailed off, and she was silent. Her emotions had captured her voice.

I kissed her, hugged her tightly, and she was off to bed.

Cocoa Two sat by my side, and I reached down and petted him. He looked up at me and smiled.

"Cocoa Two, it is going to be just fine." I took his head in my hands and I smiled at him. "You know, I knew a doggie just like you a long time ago. He had a friend named, Piggy, who he brought with him everywhere." Cocoa Two jumped up and put his paws on my lap. I warned him not to bark so as not to wake the baby.

He knew better.

"Cocoa was our companion, just as you are. I loved him with all my heart, and he loved me." Cocoa Two wagged his tail, and he whimpered softly at me, so I leaned over, and he gave me a big lick right on the kisser. I sat there hugging this dog in the stillness of the night.

Yes, it was going to be just fine.

"Cocoa Two, guard Blue Cloud, hold her in your heart, and watch her every move."

The dog jumped off my lap and sat right next to the crib,

watching and waiting. I sat there in the silence and I could hear Blue Cloud breathing softly. The shiny wood of the crib glowed at me, reflecting the little *Dinky the Orange Teddy Bear* nightlight in the electrical outlet in front of me. She was resting as peacefully as an angel would.

A little, tiny, baby angel.

I smiled, as I knew in my heart that the tree had returned. Somehow, for some reason, the tree had returned, and I think I now knew why. Perhaps Mrs. Whipley was just a crazy, old bird, who saw things in the air at night.

Then again, perhaps she was not so crazy after all.

Ronzo relieved me at about two in the morning. I took Cocoa Two outside so he could sniff around and do all the things that doggies do. Blue Cloud was still sleeping soundly. I told Cocoa Two that we were both off duty and that he should sleep with Harry and Rose and he was off. I climbed into bed with Binky and before I knew it, I was off into a dream world too.

Morning came, and I realized that I had overslept. Binky was not in bed next to me, so I jumped up and washed up in the bathroom. I dressed and then wandered out into the hallway and went to the nursery. Rose was sitting in the chair with Binky standing next to her. They both smiled at me and made a motion to go out into the hallway.

"How is she?"

Rose held my hands and said, "She is still sleeping, Paul. She has not slept this long in weeks and weeks. She seems so peaceful. It is wonderful."

"Good, well, maybe the medicine kicked in there and sleep always heals. Sometimes, it just takes a little rest, you know . . . to recharge."

Rose tilted her head towards me and placed her hand on my arm as she said, "Or, something like that, twenty-seven."

"Where is the rest of the gang?"

"They are all still sleeping. It has been exhausting for everyone. Harry and Ronzo each took shifts, then Linny, and now, Binky, and me. You would think sooner or later she will wake up and maybe, just maybe, she will eat." Rose's eyes had changed as she spoke. She had the eyes of faith, the eyes of belief, and the eyes of what only a mother would know.

"Did you call and check on the children, Binky?"

Binky gave me a rapid head nod, and she said, "All is well, Paul. They are all fine. Dear Father took Paul William to school and Heather Sarah is tearing the mansion up. Do you want me to prepare you some breakfast? None of us have eaten anything. It has been so difficult."

"No, thank you, Binky, but please you guys need to eat now. I will pick up something on the way into the church. I am glad to hear the kids are having fun. Putting the mansion back together will give your father something to do when he returns home. Say, I really need to go into the office for a bit. I have some appointments to take care of. Did Doctor Berkhout say when he needed to see Blue Cloud again?"

"Yes, he wants to start some experimental treatments tomorrow. He asked us to bring her in around nine in the morning."

"I am going to check this out today, Paul. I am on it," Binky was nodding rapidly as she spoke.

"Good, I knew you would be, Binky . . . one more of the million reasons that I love you so much."

Binky fluffed her hair and smiled at me while giving me one of those famous, seductive winks of her eye.

"I will be back soon."

I gave Rose a hug, I kissed Binky goodbye, and told them to call me if they needed me. I went out the door and passed Cocoa Two on the way out. I reached down, greeted him, said goodbye, and then told him, "Cocoa Two, please guard the house, the ladies, Ronzo, Harry, and Blue Cloud!

I will be back as soon as I can!" He sat down, barked twice at me, wagged his tail three times, and ran off. Amazing, it really was.

I drove back to church, and on my way, I passed row upon row of the fantastic colors of the autumn leaves in the trees. Glorious colors, displaying God's glory. I admired it all while I rode the roadways back to Reunion Lutheran Church. I was always amazed at people who poked fun at New Jersey and said how ugly, urban, and gritty it was. Once you venture off the highways, it was one of the most beautiful places on the whole planet.

It really was.

I pulled the old jeep into the church parking lot, which was also ablaze in the usual tapestry of color that comes around once a year. It was a clear, sunny, crisp fall day. Wonderful, simply wonderful. However, despite my efforts at admiring the beauty of this day, I had to admit that I was exhausted mentally and physically. My head hurt and my entire body ached. It was worse than the morning after a playoff game. I just had to suffer through a meeting or two, sign off on some invoices, and catch up on some sick calls.

Oh, no, more sick calls! Why were there so many sick people in this world?

I felt crushed in my spirit, devastated, and as if I had chosen a path of despair, and not made the correct choice in my course of action, to help my friends, my family, my own faith.

I walked in the backdoor of the office wing of the church and staggered my way up to Martha's desk.

"Morning, dear Martha."

"Oh, Pastor Paul, you look like a wreck. Have you slept?"

"Sure, well, a little."

"How is little, Blue Cloud? Dave told me. It is just awful. Those wonderful, Redmonds. I just want to burst into tears myself."

I placed my hand on her shoulders.

"She actually slept really well last night. The doc gave her some medicine, and it seemed to help. It is not good. Martha, we need a miracle here."

Martha at first did not say a word. She reached up and clasped my hands tightly. She stared at me with tears in the corners of her eyes, "Well, if anyone can drum one up, then it is you, Pastor Paul. I have faith in you."

"Thank you, Martha. Hey, any calls?"

"Not anything that I could not handle. Bishop Von Houten called, and I told him about Blue Cloud. He was so upset, that he could not speak, and said he needed to hang up and pray for her. I have never heard him so upset, Pastor Paul. I never knew that man to have compassion for anything or anyone, except for a set of golf clubs."

"He is not what he seems to be, Martha. He actually has more emotions, love, and compassion, than you could ever realize. He just puts up that big front to fool folks into thinking he is some old, grouchy, ogre. He is really very different."

Martha did not comment, but she went back to fiddling with some papers on her desk and handed me my messages.

"I know that I have some lingering paperwork here, I will sign the invoices for the month so you can send them to bookkeeping. I will make some calls, go to those two meetings, and then I think, I will head back over to the Redmond's house."

"I understand. I will only send in the most important calls, Pastor Paul. I will try not to bother you."

I went into my office and started to go to work. I needed to wipe this all out and get back out to Harry's house as soon as I could. The telephone intercom buzzed on my desk and I saw that it was Martha ringing me. Oh boy, what now?

"Yes, dear Martha."

"Pastor Paul, I hate to bother you, but Rabbi Goldberg is here to see you."

"Rabbi Goldberg? Wow, oh my, please send him in, please. Thank you, Martha." There was a gentle tap on the door to my office and it swung open.

"Thank you, Martha, thank you dear. You should have been Jewish. I would have married you. Paulie, Paulie, it is so good to see you!"

"Rabbi Goldberg, what a surprise. Please come on in!" I stood up and walked around my desk to meet him as the old rabbi shuffled over towards me.

He greeted me with a pat on the back, and then he warmly hugged me and kissed each of my cheeks.

"Shalom, Paulie. You are bigah than evah. What are you six feet twenty or something? Let me sit down, it is so far to walk here. If I was going to walk this far, I would be out on the golf course with Werner. You have added onto this church since I visited you last. It is wonderful. Not a synagogue, but it is wonderful, Paulie."

I smiled at Rabbi Goldberg's sense of humor, and I motioned to the chair in front of my desk. He was a slight man, a little bent over, but in very good shape. He was one of those guys that it was hard to tell how old he really was. He had very little hair, large brown eyes, a pointy nose, but a kind face. He smiled all the time, and he usually was as tan, if not even a little darker than Bishop Von Houten was, from chasing that little white ball around all summer. Rabbi Goldberg sat down in the chair and looked at me. He had carried a little bag in with him that he set down next to the chair.

He waved his hands in front of him while he spoke, "I am so sorry about just coming out here, without calling first, but I had to come as quickly as I could to visit your church here. I heard about the Redmond baby from Werner. He called me early today to cancel our game. He is such a mess! He loves that baby . . . let me tell you, Paulie. He will call you, but he is so broken up, it may take him a little while. You know, Werner! He is such a softie. I had to come out and talk with you in person. I did not just want to call. I thought we could pray together, Paulie. We can perform some morning prayers together."

"Thank you, Rabbi Goldberg, I really appreciate that. I would welcome the prayers. I need all the help that I can muster up. It is not very good, I am afraid."

"I heard, I heard, that is why I came to see you, Paulie. It is bad enough when it is a person in your congregation, but this, your best friends, yeeesh, my—it is so terrible. You are young, just starting out, but I tell you that you must not give up, my young friend. Never give up, ever, Paulie. HaShem is with you, I can tell. Father Mark, he knew too. He knew. He was such a man. Oh, what a great man he was!"

Rabbi Goldberg looked at me, and he then took some papers off my desk and fiddled with them.

"You are so much like him, Paulie. He was a mentor to you. You both love all religions and all people. It may say Lutheran on your church, but you are Jewish, Catholic, Methodist, Episcopal, all of them. You know strength, hope, peace, and joy. I think that is what makes you special, dear friend."

"Thank you, rabbi, but this one, it might be more than I can handle," I said as I looked at the rabbi, and saw his facial expression change.

Rabbi Goldberg's face grew suddenly angry. He jumped in his chair and pounded my desk with his fist. I nearly jumped out of my skin!

"It is never more than you can handle! HaShem is caring, and never gives you any more than you can handle, dear Paulie! Do you think this is the only time in your career that you will deal with a sick baby? Did you ever stop and think that this is what HaShem always wanted you to do with your life? This, instead of ending up in an emergency room after every hockey game, filled with stitches from that brutish game you used to play. To handle this very moment. To steer your friends in a time of such despair, to show them that faith, joy, hope, and trust exist. That is a little baby. Do you really think that little babies are supposed to become sick and die? It is so much more than just that, perhaps, it is to show you how great HaShem is, what gifts you have been given, and to never doubt your heart, Paulie. I just told you how I feel that you are so strong and that you know hope, joy, and peace. Now, wake up, Paulie, and know faith! Now, no more talk that you cannot handle this!"

Rabbi Goldberg sat back in his chair and waved his hand at me.

"Yeeshhh! I am so glad I came here today! You must trust in yourself, trust in your heart! Trust in your mind. I am sure that you have already received what you will need. We will pray together this morning that you have had the faith to believe enough that you have understood it. Look around here. You have done so much already. No one could ever doubt that the hands of Heaven and some of Earth have guided you!"

Rabbi Goldberg was intense now, more intense than any man in which I have ever encountered. He leaned in close and pointed his fingers at me as he instructed, "Never give up, and never doubt. Uncertainty is what the enemies of our spirit count upon. They bet upon us to be weak, to be soft, and to shrivel up in defeat! You stood fearless in the net as a goalie for years, now stand fearless for your faith, and for your friends! Think Paulie, they only have you now, they only have you, and your faith."

The old rabbi now relaxed and leaned back in the chair. He smiled widely at me and I had to say, his face glowed in his spirit.

I felt different. I felt renewed in my trust, in my own

spirit. Rabbi Goldberg was right, as was Harry yesterday, when he also told me to wake up and stand for our faith. They both had hit upon a nerve, and they each had touched my inner soul. I felt as if the steps I had taken yesterday had been correct. I was now confident, and the doubts in my abilities had completely left my mind. I was a pastor, a leader for God, and for faith. I needed to do my job and fulfill my calling.

"Rabbi Goldberg, have you ever seen a miracle?"

"Of course, Paulie! About ten times a year or so. Five times a year, my wife decides that we should have sex, and the other five times, I manage to beat Werner on the golf course. Let me tell you that those are both miracles!" Rabbi Goldberg was a kick. This man was a man of great wit, who loved all of his life, and recognized the gifts that God had given to us all.

He was a man of God.

After we finished laughing, he grew serious and asked, "You mean, as in a fire and brimstone, the skies then open up and angels float down, type miracle, Paulie?"

"Well, maybe not that dramatic rabbi, but perhaps something that you just could not really explain. Something that you had faith in that had to have come from HaShem."

Rabbi Goldberg sat back in his chair and put his hand over his mouth. He nodded his head as I could see his mind was flipping through memories of the past. He then leaned forward and looked at me as he started to speak, "In the big war, you know, that is where Werner and I became such friends. We were both chaplains together in the United States Army. We served as combat chaplains in the thick of it. Werner never speaks of it anymore. I think he has tried so hard to forget. We were in the medical wards, right on the front lines of the Allied Forces. Death was all around us every, single, day. Beyond description, Paulie, what man can do to fellow man. The blood, the gore, the death, it was not of this world. It wore you down because you can only pray so much. One day, a young Jewish soldier came in, a good boy, such a young boy. Ironically, I think he was from your home city of Paterson. Is there a large Jewish population on the eastside of the city?"

I nodded my head to indicate yes, there was.

"He was missing most of his guts. The middle of his body . . . torn away by some kind of explosion . . . it was terrible. He had been in the field for a long time, the rescue and medical teams could not reach him for a long time, and the doctors pushed him off in the corner of the ward to die. They pumped him full of morphine and just let him remain there. Werner and I . . . we both prayed over him. Werner said to me, Irving, I cannot take this any longer. This boy he will not die, we will not let him die. The two of us, we prayed for days, I prayed in Hebrew, and Werner prayed in German, English, and Dutch. We said every prayer we knew, and we made up some more. The soldier, he hung on and we went to the head surgeon who was a captain, and we asked him when he intended to operate on the boy. The doctor told us that he would not, as he was beyond hope, that he had to save others, who had a chance to live. Werner, who I never saw become violent, grabbed the doctor and threw him on a wall. He told him that he would operate and that he would save him, and that it was an order. Werner told him that if he had to, he should take the guts of Werner's own body, and put them in that Jewish boy from Paterson. Paulie, we were both chaplains, but we were full birds, so the doctor was far outranked. He operated and that good, Jewish boy he recovered. He fully recovered, and he was walking in a few days. He sent Werner and me a letter a few years after the war ended. He was married with a wife, and two little girls. Bernie Wurtzler was his name. I think, to my dying day, that I will always remember his name."

Rabbi Goldberg looked down at the floor and then back

towards me. He wiped the tears out of his eyes and continued with his story. His voice had grown softer now as the raw emotion overcame him.

"Yes, I think I always will, Paulie. I do not know, Paulie, how he recovered, except for the grace of a miracle. There were times with my very eyes that we saw him turn gray with the face of death, and the prayers brought him back. It was our mission, it was our purpose, and we would not allow him to die. We prayed for days without end over him, we did not eat or sleep. We fasted for him in sacrifice. It was like one of those, how do you say, like they do in Congress, those, filly, filly. . .."

"A filibuster."

"Yes, Paulie, you are a smart one, you are. Enough talk, it is time for prayers. We never pray enough, Paulie. Here, take, this yarmulke, all that hair, you need to cover it. I brought you a prayer shawl, so we can pray. I swear that I wish you were Jewish, Paulie. Yes, indeed, you are such a good boy."

Rabbi Goldberg reached in his bag and handed me the items, as he asked me, "How is your Hebrew, Paulie? I thought they taught you good Hebrew in school?"

"Lousy, rabbi, my Welsh is good though."

"Welsh smelsh, whoever heard of Welsh, Werner is right. You are so annoying. We will pray in Hebrew."

We prayed together for one hour straight and then we parted.

I think after Rabbi Goldberg left that I was partly Jewish.

I walked in the front door of the Redmond home. Cocoa Two immediately greeted me. He sat down, barked twice, and looked up at me. I reached down and greeted him.

"Good boy. I guess you have been on duty all this time. I am here now. I will help you. Where is everyone?"

Cocoa Two jumped up, wagged his tail, and barked once for me to follow him. I walked behind him as he hustled off towards the kitchen. He kept turning around to look at me; he seemed to want to make sure that I was on his trail. He seemed so anxious to show me something.

I walked into the kitchen, to, as Rabbi Goldberg would have said, "Such a scene!"

I could not believe my eyes.

I was astounded at the scene before my eyes.

Out of a lifetime of memories around the old kitchen table, this one was the best. There was not even a close second runner-up to this memory.

Blue Cloud was up on Harry's knee as he sat at the old kitchen table. She bounced along, laughing and smiling. Rose, Binky, Ronzo, and Linny stood around singing the *Dinky the Orange Teddy Bear* theme song as they clapped their hands.

"Hey there, twenty-seven! Don't just stand there like a doofus! After all these years of listening to this stupid song, I am sure you must have learned the words by now. You do know the words, don't you, Paul?" Harry looked at me and smiled.

I smiled, nodded my head, clapped my hands, and began to sing.

One of these days, I really needed to look up in the dictionary what the definition of a doofus was.

Binky came over. She put her arm through mine, and she tenderly kissed me. After our kiss, she signaled me to lean over and she gently whispered in my ear, "You are forever our hero. Another win, for the world-famous, number twenty-seven. Not a marble got by you, twenty-seven. Not even one marble." I looked around the room, then back at Blue Cloud, and I felt a little tingle ripple through my body.

"Hey Paulie, you want a Dingleberry beer or a Big Boulder?" Ronzo yelled at me as he held the door to the refrigerator open.

"Yeah, yeah, yeah, sure, sure, Ronzo. Thank you. Please let me have a Big Boulder. Those Dingleberries are way too sweet."

Harry later explained to me that Blue Cloud had awoken earlier that afternoon, after her long sleep in the new crib, and she had eaten everything in sight. She was ravished, and she was alert, happy, and laughing at everything. That night after playing all day, she slept soundly in her crib, just like a little, baby, angel.

The next morning, we took Blue Cloud back to Doctor Berkhout for her appointment. He was stunned at her improvement. The doctor checked her from head to toe, and he had no explanation for her miraculous recovery. He ran all sorts of tests, and they all came back normal.

She had even gained one pound in weight!

Doctor Berkhout cornered me as we were all leaving the office, and he shook my hand.

"Pastor Paul, I am very pleased and extremely happy, but I have to say that I am truly amazed at what has transpired with this extremely, unusual medical case. I really cannot say for certain what has happened here."

I looked at him and said, "Well, Doc, maybe the tests were wrong. You know, Doc, sometimes we make mistakes, even when we make every effort to prevent them. When it all boils down, we are just men doing our jobs the best that we can. Please do not feel bad, it may have been that Blue Cloud . . . just had a virus or some kind of nasty bug."

"No, no, no, those kinds of tests are triple-checked, Pastor Paul. I can assure you that there were no mistakes. You see, before I called Mr. Redmond with my final diagnosis, I consulted with four of the best-qualified and expert specialists on Wolman Disease that were available. These doctors are world-renowned within the entire medical community, for their expertise in the disease."

I grabbed him by the arm, smiled, and held him tightly, while telling him, "Then sometimes, Doctor Berkhout, when there is nothing else left, you just have to have faith."

11

The Return of the Tree

I was working in my office at Reunion Lutheran Church in early June 1996. Martha had stepped away from her desk for a few minutes, so she had directed all telephone calls to ring at my desk. I was deep into a sermon outline when the ringer on the telephone startled me. I picked it up on the second ring.

"Henson! That is, it! It is over! I cannot take any more of you, and your incessant, daily phone calls, endless inquiries to tap my vast knowledge, and the fact that you seem to be always right all the time."

Oh, joy. Bishop Von Houten was on the warpath.

"You really are the most annoying fellow that I have ever met!"

"Well, I am very sorry, Bishop Von Houten, but I have not spoken with you in about three weeks or so. If I have done something wrong, then. . .."

The bishop's voice on the telephone increased in volume, "You have not done anything, Henson, other than be your usual annoying self, but I am about to put you to work for once in your life. I am retiring, Henson. Packing it all in. After forty-seven years in the ministry, it is time for me to relax, kick back, and get out on the golf course every day. You know, enjoy life!"

"Oh my, well that is a shock, bishop. I am very happy for you, but I am sad at the same time. I will miss working with you. It has been quite a . . . experience, sir."

"Yeah, yeah, yeah, I know you cannot replace a leader

such as I have been, Henson. You will not have time to fret about it for too long, though. The new bishop is already here in New Jersey."

"I see. Bishop Von Houten, can I ask, would I know him?"

"I would hope so, Henson. It is you!"

I was not sure that I heard what he had said very clearly, and I paused for a moment or two.

"Excuse me, sir. But did you just say that the new bishop was me?"

"That is correct, Henson. I am promoting you to the position and title of, Bishop of the Northeast District as my replacement upon my retirement."

I did not know what to say. I stumbled into the conversation, "Sir, my goodness, I do not think I am qualified, there are many other pastors with a lot more experience than I have and they are. . .."

"Experience, Henson? Hah! Have you ever actually noticed the adventures of your weird and wacky world! Are you kidding me, Henson? Even drunk, I could not even make up the stuff that I have been a part of, and I have only known you for less than eight or so years! Your life experience makes up for ten normal human's lifetimes, Henson. Not to mention the weird, strange, and odd cast of characters that come along with you, wherever you go."

"Well, sir. That is very kind of you to say, but. . .."

"No, Henson, you are the best man for the job. I submitted your name to the executive board, most of whom had met you at the conference in Albany, and they elected and approved you in a unanimous vote. They were still all weepy-eyed over that sappy sermon you delivered up there last July. You and your friends, along with your wild, long stringy hair, beard, and weird demeanor, make you into some kind of folk hero or something, Henson. They have just elected me to another six-year term, and I suspect that you too can ride this job for consecutive terms.

The people will love you. For the life of me, I cannot understand the attachment, but I have to admit that, I will, well, I will miss you too, Henson. You have grown on me once I was able to get over that perpetual cloud of weirdness over your head all the time."

The telephone grew quiet for just a moment. It seemed as though Bishop Von Houten had covered the mouthpiece of the phone for just a second to clear his throat. When he returned, his voice crackled just a little. I could have been wrong, but it seemed as though he was choking up a little and his emotions were overcoming him for just a moment.

"Ahemmm, sorry, Henson. You will need to find a replacement pastor for Reunion, finish up your work there, and move down to the offices here in Newark. I will need your help to take down a few pictures, awards, certificates, and other memorabilia that I have on the walls here in my office."

"Yes sir, I will be glad to help. Should I borrow a truck from Harry to haul it to your house?"

"Yeah, yeah, yeah. That is a good idea. In retrospect, there is quite a bit of stuff in here. We have to have a big, fancy, installation service. You will need to wear a big, bishop's hat for the service. I hope it fits over all that hair. I imagine, after the service, that it will be another wild, Redmond party to suffer through again. Food, booze, beer, wine, Harry Burgers, Harry biscuits, singing and wild dancing. I know the drill."

"You are correct sir, you do know, Harry."

"Yeah, yeah, yeah, I guess you will need to find a home now, Henson, move out of that parsonage, and be the big boss. You will have a big salary now too. Henson, let me tell you no more loafing around the office or tinkering with wires and pipes! You also cannot spend all of your time on the golf course when you are serving as a bishop. You will be way too busy for fun and games! Moving out of Reunion and the parsonage, will be more weepy-eyed stuff.

It will be difficult when you tell the congregation there at Reunion that you will be moving on. For some odd reason, all these other bananas have attached to you too! Luckily, I do not have to deal with that emotional stuff any longer, Henson. I will be out on the golf course with Goldberg, every, single, day. He plans to pack it in soon too. We will be in Florida during the winter, far away from you and your strange and weird world. No more snow, ice, and cold. We plan to return to New Jersey only when it warms up."

"Bishop Von Houten, I do not know what to say, sir. I do not know how to thank you, and I will do my best, sir. I will make you proud of me."

There was more silence on the other end of the telephone, and I heard the bishop sniffle a little.

After a long pause, he began to speak once more, and his voice crackled with emotion, "There is no need to thank me, Henson. I know you will do a great job. I would not have picked you if I did not believe that you would. In fact, I should thank you, Henson. You taught this old dog an awful lot. You and that crazy, nutcase Redmond, and your wonderful wives and families. You taught me about trust, love, faith, and hope. You two pineapples taught me what it means to be friends and support each other through thick and thin. Most of all, Henson, you taught me to stay positive and have faith, no matter what the situation. For that alone, I thank you, Henson. I knew from the moment that I first met you that there was something about you. Knowing you and working with you, well, Henson. . .. I am not ashamed to say that . . . it has been one of the great joys of my life and career. I know I did not always tell you that or show you, Henson, but please know that I mean it with all of my heart and all of my soul. You are very special to me and special to many other people, Henson."

"Thank you, Bishop Von Houten. You are a great man, and I will always be grateful to you for giving this long-haired, hippie, whacko a chance, when no one else would. For that, I could never thank you enough."

"No, Paul, you are wrong. You earned the chance. I simply went with God's plan for you. You gave yourself a chance, because you never back down from anything, Paul. Despite doubts or the horrible situations that you need to deal with, you eventually always trust and follow your heart. That, Paul John Henson, is why God shines upon you, your friends, and your family. You told me on the day that you came into my office for an interview, that if I gave you a chance, then you would make the Lord, as well as this crusty, old bishop proud of you. You are truly a man of your word. You are like a son to me, Paul . . . the son . . . that my wife and I never had. I love you and I am proud of you. Prouder than any words could ever describe."

Bishop Von Houten could now barely speak as his voice now choked with raw emotion. He struggled to continue as he finally said, "I also know that the Lord loves you and is proud of you too, Paul."

"Click," the line went dead.

I hung up the telephone, smiled, and picked the phone back up to dial my home number.

Binky is not going to believe this one!

I told my wife the wonderful news, and she was thrilled. She always supported me, no matter what, and this case would be no exception. I did sense a touch of sadness when she realized that we would be moving not only out of Reunion but also out of the little parsonage that had been our home for so many years. The children may find it a little traumatic also, since it was the only home, they had known at this point in their young lives. I knew my wife would be jumping right away into the research to locate a new area to live in, one with good schools, and the neighborhoods that she wanted. The whole big, Binky picture.

"Please finish up early, twenty-seven. This is so exciting!

I need to call everyone now and broadcast the exciting news. It would be nice if you came home early. The children and I will make you a cake! Please, make sure that you finish up work and be home soon, dear Paul."

"I will, Binky, I love you."

"I love you too. I am so proud of you, Paul."

Sometimes, that is all you want to hear your wife or the lady that you love say to you. Even more than your wife telling you that she loves you, I think those words, "I am so proud of you" mean so much more.

Those simple words can inspire a man for a lifetime.

I walked out of my office and down the main hallway. Martha was still away from her desk, so I could not tell her the news.

I needed to tell everyone here the great news. Maybe Dave was still working in his shop. I turned and looked out the hallway window towards the maintenance shop, but his truck was already gone. Oh well, I will catch up to him soon enough.

I stood in the hallway and looked around. Oh my, I had an awful lot of memories here. Bishop Von Houten was correct; leaving here was going to be very tough.

In fact, it was going to be brutal.

I peeked into the sanctuary and looked up at the high, arcing ceiling. I could still see Harry up in that lift, welding the beams, and Ronzo and I working on the electrical panel. Who could ever forget that night at the fellowship hall when Rose and Harry reunited? I could not forget their wedding, and then over here, at this door looking out at the sunset, is where Binky told me that I was going to be a father for the first time. And how about the giving tree at Christmas time, over there, in the main lobby?

So much had happened.

So much had passed.

Oh boy, more ghosts, more memories of my life and of our adventures together.

Then, of course, there was the miracle tree. In my life, forevermore, there will always be the miracle tree.

I walked out towards the narthex and my eyes caught a large picture frame on the wall. A picture frame that contained small photographs of many of the church families, church leaders, elders, and so on, and so forth. Each photo had their name labeled beneath it. I had asked Harry a week or so ago to make some repairs on the pictures, because the glue had dried out from the original installation, and many of the photos had fallen to the bottom of the frame. Since Harry was a big blabbermouth and he knew everyone, he could easily place the photos back in the correct positions. I walked over and glanced at the picture to see how the repairs had come out.

Hello! What is this? I should have known better than to put Harry in charge of the project! Right at the top where the name tag read, "Pastor Paul John Henson," was a picture of Dinky the Orange Teddy Bear.

"Oh, Pastor Paul. I will miss you so much! I am very proud of you. To think, you are now a bishop! However, you know how it is when you lose someone . . . it is so terrifying. I was just saying to Mrs. Crankshammer that I bet we will never find another pastor like Pastor Paul, with all that hair and that beard! Do you think we will, Pastor Paul?"

"Well, Mrs. Whipley, perhaps. . .."

"I think you should put it on the job description, that long hair and a beard is required! That brings me to why I stopped by today. Pastor Paul, you see, it is my new neighbor across the street. I think he is a spy, or at least, he is a secret agent of some sort."

"What does that have to do with long hair and beards, Mrs. Whipley?"

"Well, Pastor Paul, my new neighbor has long hair like you do, and a beard, but his beard is very long. He has all these weird antennas up in his trees, and on his roof. He is always tossing wires up into the tops of the trees and bringing the ends of them into his house. I can see him through the window of the top bedroom of his house, sitting in front of these radios, talking strange gibberish into microphones, and beeping Morse code on his desk. I think he is a Russian spy!"

"Oh, Mrs. Whipley, it sounds as if he is just a ham radio operator, and that is his hobby. I think he is just a ham radio. . .."

"Oh no, Pastor Paul, it is much more than that! One day, he put this big dish antenna up on top of his garage and I watched him very carefully, as he. . .."

Oh brother, here we go with another afternoon of a meeting with Mrs. Whipley. I have to make sure that I forewarn the next pastor to serve here at Reunion of exactly what he is getting into! Between Mrs. Crankshammer, Mrs. Whipley, Johnson, and his merry band of the "old guard" contingent, it will take a special pastor to withstand the onslaught.

Or a pastor who is very hard of hearing.

After about two exhausting hours of Mrs. Whipley telling me all about her new neighbor, and me assuring her that the poor chap was just a ham radio operator, I finally managed to try to get back to work. I was not productive, as the memories of the times I had here at Reunion Lutheran Church and what led me here, was something that was going to stick with me for a while. It was only two days ago that Bishop Von Houten had told me of my new promotion. The news had spread like a wildfire throughout the church and the community. In all honesty, it was hard to get back to work. I found myself daydreaming about my life, and adventures with Harry as the afternoon waned, and I looked out the window of my office at the sunset.

The telephone rang on my desk and it startled me. I shook my head a number of times and came back to reality. I wondered how long I had been staring out that window at the sunset.

I picked up the receiver and before I could even finish saying my greeting, I heard Harry's voice ask, "What are you, Binky, and the kids, doing this weekend after church?"

"Well, I do not know, we had not really planned anything yet, why Harry?"

"Can you get away for the week with Rose, Blue Cloud, and me?"

"I don't know. I need to check. You know how it is, Harry, I need to check with Binky and plan out my work, see what is going on. . .."

"Oh please, you are the big chief guy now, are you kidding me!"

"Well, where are we going? Sometimes, Harry, I would just once like to know what you are planning in advance, just once in my lifetime, Harry."

"Oh, geez! Stop being such an old lady, will you, Paul! You of all people know that it is one adventure after another, so come along for the ride and see where it all takes us."

"Hey, Harry, about that picture in the narthex. . .. "

"Click." The line went dead. It seemed as though, as of late, I never really finished any sentences. Everyone tells me how wonderful my words and advice are, but I never really say anything, before I am hung up on or cut off. Oh well, maybe I should just smile a lot and not worry about it.

I reached for my pile of mail in my in-box and started to open it up. It was more of the usual advertisements for church products, insurance for clergy, a company that sells crosses that glow in the dark, and other junk.

Hello! Here is an actual envelope that just may contain some kind of actual correspondence! How unusual! It was addressed to, "Pastor Paul John Henson."

I took my opener, sliced it open, and pulled out a handwritten letter. I glanced at the letter and noticed how unusual the writing was. The writing was more like a scrawl; it was a bit difficult to read. Hmmm, unusual way of writing. The composer must be a southpaw, I thought as I leaned back in my chair and tried my best to read it:

"Dear Pastor Paul,

I hope this letter finds you well. Grace and peace to you. I would like first to congratulate you on your appointment to the office of Bishop of the Northeast District. I have never had the pleasure of meeting you in person, but your reputation precedes you, kind sir. I have heard many good things about you, and your fine work at promoting the Gospel, as well as the work that you did at Reunion Lutheran Church. I have no doubt that you will lead us all in further success and service to our Lord and Savior Jesus Christ. I look forward to meeting you in person at your installation services in the next week or so.

Enclosed, please find my resume, and a summary of my background, experience, and education. I would like to ask you to give your heartfelt consideration towards me, to fill the position of Senior Pastor of Reunion Lutheran Church. I would consider it an honor to follow in your very large footsteps.

You see, I have strong ties to Reunion Lutheran Church, as I have many faint, but fond memories of attending there. You may or may not recognize my name, but my father, Reverend Charles T. Braun, was actually the first pastor to serve at Reunion Lutheran Church, when they built the new campus on the location where it presently resides. I spent some time as a youth in that very same parsonage that is there now, and it would give me great joy to be able to return there with my young family.

It would also give me great joy to be able to serve where my father once served before me. I am currently serving a small church here in Essex County, and I am looking to lead a larger congregation in service to our Lord.

I look forward to speaking with you about the opening and I will pray for your kind consideration of my application and background.

In His Service,

Reverend Charles T. Braun Jr."

I reached in the top drawer of my desk, pulled out the journal of Pastor Braun Sr., and held an open page up to the letter written by his son. The writing was virtually identical. That same swirling, left-handed scrawl. I closed the journal up and placed it back onto the desk.

"Well, is that not amazing or what," I said aloud to myself. It was remarkable, but then again, maybe it was not so remarkable.

I think I just found the new pastor for Reunion Lutheran Church.

I wondered if a prerequisite for assuming this position for Reverend Charles T. Braun Junior should be a hearing test.

I looked up at the clock on the wall. It was time to quit early for once, so I packed up my case, closed off the light switch, and made my way out the door of my office. Martha had already left for the day. I think that she must have fled in terror during the visit from Mrs. Whipley. I went out the backdoor and walked across the parking lot of the church towards the parsonage. I was feeling just a little forlorn, as I wondered how many more times, I would make this quick journey from my office to the parsonage. As I walked up the side walkway to the door of our home, two excited, Henson children who were jumping up and down, met me.

"Dear Father, come quick, you have to see Mother's roses! Come and see them, she is over in the backyard by them now," Heather Sarah was waving her arms and yelling at me, while Paul William tugged at my arm and pulled me towards the rear of the house.

"All right, let's go! Wow, this is some greeting, I cannot imagine, what would have you two children tuned up like this," I said, as they pulled and tugged me along. As I came around the side of the parsonage and turned into the backyard, I spotted Binky, who was kneeling down along a bed of roses that we had planted a while back. She had picked out some special variety of rose bushes according to her research and ordered them via a mail order nursery. They had come shipped in a big box, and when we opened them, it did not seem very optimistic. The shrubs were shipped bare-root and in dormancy. I planted them according to Binky's very specific orders and researched details, while she followed my every move and barked out orders, to make sure that we planted them correctly. They had grown fairly nice, but they never bloomed.

They were just some nice-looking shrubs with some sporadic foliage. No blooms, but I never thought they looked that bad.

I know it frustrated my wife, with the fact that all she had were leaves, branches, and no blooms, so she and the children had dug into the rose bush research as of late.

Binky stood up when she spotted me, smiled a broad smile, and ran over to me, while she was speaking excitedly, "Oh, twenty-seven, come see this! You will not believe your eyes. Look at the fabulous blooms all over the roses!"

Binky then assisted the children as they dragged me over to the roses. They all pointed and smiled like big pumpkin heads. Sure enough, the roses were full of large, fantastic blooms, fragrant roses in reds, pinks, and wonderful yellows. They danced and twinkled at us as the wind gently blew the blooms on the ends of some more fragile stems. It was amazing, and it was tranquil, yet by the same token, it was a stunning display.

"Binky, my goodness, the blooms are quite remarkable. They are so beautiful. Congratulations. I know you have waited a very long time for them to bloom. Perhaps, I am wrong, but yesterday, I thought I was out here, and there was not a single bloom on those rose bushes. But, like I said, I could be wrong."

Binky was nodding her head in a rapid head nod agreeing with me. Paul William and then Heather Sarah stood next to their mother and nodded their heads in agreement. All three of them stood in a line, bobbing their heads up and down rapidly. The children had inherited the head-nodding gene from Binky. They were making me dizzy. I found my eyes following their heads, and my head was nodding along with them.

Finally, when it seemed as though they had all run out of bobbing power, Binky said, "No, you are very correct, dear Paul. There were not any blooms on the roses yesterday! That is what is so fantastic. You see, the children and I have been researching why the roses would not bloom, and one of the main causes of the bushes to not produce any rose blooms, was a loss of moisture in the soil."

"That is correct, dear Father! Heather, Sarah and I are researchers now, just like Mother is," Paul William proudly proclaimed to me while they then started another round of agreement head nodding.

This nodding round was shorter, and Binky continued, "There was a suggestion that we found in our research, to mulch the roots to keep the moisture down along the roots where it will be very beneficial. It is so dry here in this location that we thought it was a good idea to try. So early this morning, we all went downtown to the garden center and purchased a few bags of mulch. The children and I spread it out earlier today, and when we came out here just a few minutes ago, to play a little before dinner, we saw all these blooms!"

"That is incredible. You mean to tell me that they bloomed that quickly. I have never heard of such a thing. Have you?"

I was astounded at my wife's testimony. Oh boy, I asked a question. Here they all go again on an agreement nod.

"Never, and before the mulch application, the shrubs did not even have any rose buds. It is miraculous, Paul. It really is," Binky said as she came over and hugged me. She then gave me a kiss on the cheek as we all stood there admiring the roses. It was quite a spectacular sight for sure.

"It is such a shame that now that the roses have finally bloomed, we will be leaving the parsonage. But at least we know the secret now."

"Sure, sure, Binky, we will plant new roses for you and the children when we find a new house. We will make sure we find a house with a nice yard for your gardens."

"I want a big backyard, Father! And, I want a play set like Blue Cloud has in Uncle Harry and Auntie Rose's yard. Can we get one of those, dear Father?" Heather Sarah closed in for a stare as she asked the question. She had also inherited the stare gene from the Hobnobber side.

"Well, I do not know if. . .."

"Come along children, it is time to wash up for dinner now."

"Can we order pizza, dear Mother?" Paul William asked.

"Yeah, yeah, yeah! Yippee! Pizza time! Fritzie and I want pizza," Heather Sarah was tearing around a million miles per hour screaming for pizza.

I looked at Binky and said, "It is fine with me."

"Then, pizza it is. I will call Honest Ralph's Pizza Shop. He has opened a pizza shop downtown now and he will deliver."

The children tore off into the house as I walked over to the rose bushes. I bent down to check out an extra bag of mulch that Binky had not used. She had left the bag lying next to the rose bed on the grass. I turned it over, and I read the stamp on the bag's label. The only words printed on the bag were a simple and vague, generic "Bark Mulch" on the label.

"Say, Binky, where did you say you bought this mulch?"

Binky turned around just before she went to open the backdoor, "At the garden center downtown, Paul. The man there was so nice. He said that he only sold the best mulch. He told me that he obtains the bark and extra wood to produce the mulch from local trees, and then they grind that material up to make the mulch. I think he was quite correct. It is not only good quality, but it is like a miracle in a bag! I will be sure to call him in the morning and tell him how satisfied that I am with our purchase."

"Yeah, yeah, yeah. Be sure to do that and thank him. It is a good idea, Binky."

"Twenty-seven, you always enjoy a beer with your pizza. Would you like a Big Boulder or a Dingleberry?"

"A Big Boulder, dear Binky, those Dingleberries are way too sweet."

Binky nodded and called back, "Then come in, dear Paul, and wash up. I will pour you one in your special Substantial Industries beer mug that Ronzo gave you for Christmas. You can enjoy it while we wait for the pizza."

"Okay, Binky, one minute. I just want to admire your roses for a second here," I said as I heard the door close behind her as she went into the house.

Once Binky had disappeared into the house, I knelt down next to the rose bed, scooped up the mulch into my hands, and sniffed it deeply. It had the unmistakable smell of oak wood. I felt a cold chill run through my body, and the shock knocked me backwards, so that I was sitting on my backside on the grass.

My mind was spinning, and it went backwards in time.

I clearly heard Dave Sharp telling me on the day that the crew removed the oak tree, "They will use the entire tree, Pastor Paul, so you will be happy to know that none of it will go to waste. Quality lumber, wonderful, solid oak for some project somewhere. They will even grind up the oak bark and turn it into quality mulch. He works with the garden center here in town to supply them bark for the mulch. All of God's creation here will go to good use."

I smiled as I sat there and realized that the miracle tree had returned to our lives. It had returned to me, once more, in order to assure me that hope, faith, joy, trust, and miracles did in fact, exist in this tired, old world. It had returned to assure me, as well as Binky, Harry, Rose, Blue Cloud, our children, Mrs. Whipley, Bishop Von Houten, as well as all the others in our lives, that God was smiling upon us all.

God always had, ever since Harry and I had first met, and despite the trials and tribulations of our lives, God always will.

All I could think about in my mind repeatedly were the words to the Bible verses from Job 14:7. I mumbled as I picked myself off the grass, "The branches of it will never, ever cease."

The loud honking and the roar of the Rhino 500S horn startled me and my mind returned to reality. I realized that I must have dozed off on the bench, waiting for the gang to return. The sun was so warm; I guess it had made me sleepy. I heard the doors to the Rhino 500S slam, and the children tearing up the driveway. They found me there on the bench and jumped all over me.

Heather Sarah went into a long explanation, "We missed

you, dear Father! It took so long in the Foodworld! Mother met a lady from church who complained about her husband, and then we could not find the Big Bob's Fizzly Whizzly Sugar Crunch cereal. We tried to ask a man there, but Uncle Harry said that everyone who works there is blind in one eye and cannot see out of the other! What does that mean, dear Father?"

"Well, I think he meant that. . .."

"We are very sorry that it took us a little longer than we thought, twenty-seven. We met that nice young couple from church that you have been counseling. You know, Maria and Salvatore," Binky was speaking as she walked into the backyard carrying a few bags in her hands, followed by Rose, Paul William, and then Harry carrying Blue Cloud in his arms.

"Hello, Paul," Rose shouted out and smiled at me. I waved at Rose, but I felt as if I was still half-asleep.

Why was everyone so loud?

Binky was very loud and excited as she told me, "You would not believe what her husband did this time! You need to work with him, Paul! That Maria is so cute! She has recently dyed her hair purple. It looks so nice."

I nodded my head and asked, "Were they in the toilet tissue aisle?"

"As a matter of fact, they were. Then we ran into the nicest man in the female products aisle. He was shopping for supplies for his wife, and the poor man was extremely confused as to which products were which. He asked for our assistance. Rose and I assisted him as we explained very carefully the difference between the inside and the outside products. He was so cute, he was embarrassed, but he was so cute."

"That was nice of you, Binky. Did he. . .."

"We were very careful, you know, twenty-seven, we simply called them bullets versus shields, and he understood from there. Oh, well. Were you sleeping there on that bench? I can always tell by that look on your face when you have been napping."

"Well, perhaps. . .."

"You were napping! You need to get away and relax. You work way too much, dear Paul. This holiday is just what you need. You are not twenty years old anymore. Now, I will go finish packing and we will be right out. Then we can leave and begin our holiday." The children tore off, following Binky and Rose into the house.

Harry wandered over to the bench and sat down next to me with Blue Cloud on his lap. He sighed deeply and started bouncing Blue Cloud on his knee.

"How was Foodworld?"

"Those people are the biggest bunch of blind doofuses that I have ever seen. It is incredible, twenty-seven. That place is the pits. You can never find anything there, and then it takes you ten years to check out once you do. That Maria is cute though, she sure has it all together in the right places, if you know what I mean."

He whistled a little as Blue Cloud began to laugh.

"How many times did Rose punch you in the arm for gawking and making lewd comments?"

"Only five, or actually . . . it was six times. Oh geez, twenty-seven. Is Binky packing two of those giant suitcases that we will have to lug around?"

"No, Harry, the children are coming, so I think there will actually be four of them this time. Buckle up and bring youse muscles! Hey, where is Cocoa Two?"

"He is over at the Hobnobber's house. You know how they love dog-sitting him. Old man Hobnobber is teaching him legal language, so Cocoa Two is happy. Cocoa Two just might be the first dog ever to study for the bar exam. They love having him around."

I nodded my head and said, "I hope he does not teach him to get paper clips stuck in his ears."

Harry smiled, while his daughter squealed with glee as

she bounced happily on her father's knee. He looked at Blue Cloud and smiled at her. There really was no prouder Father on the face of the Earth than Harry M. Redmond, Jr. was.

Blue Cloud Rosalina Redmond was now about eleven months old or so. She had grown so quickly, and she had gorgeous dark hair and dark features, much the same as dear, lovely Rose has. It was indeed uncanny how much Mother and Daughter looked alike. Blue Cloud was just as beautiful as her mom was, that was for sure! She sure was a happy little girl now, but it sure had been a struggle to reach the point where we were right now. I reached over and grabbed her little hands and she laughed at me.

"Let her pull your hair, twenty-seven. She loves that! Blue, go ahead and pull Uncle Paul's hair! Pull it," Harry coached his daughter in the finer points of dealing with his longtime friend's long locks of hair.

I leaned over and Blue Cloud grabbed a hold of one of my long locks of hair and gave it a good pull. She had inherited her father's strength, that was for sure! I feigned that it made me fall down and Blue Cloud cried out with laughter, as I tumbled off the bench and rolled along the grass. All three of us laughed together, as I climbed back up on the bench, and sat back down next to Harry and Blue Cloud.

"Hey, look twenty-seven, Blue has a few, little choppers coming along in her mouth there. Harry was peering into Blue's mouth as she laughed.

"It looks as if in a few months, she will have more choppers than her old man does."

Harry looked at me and laughed, remembering his battle wounds from a hockey life that seemed as if it was a million years ago.

"Hey, where did Binky, Rose, and your son and daughter go? I thought they were just going to grab some things and we could be off."

"You never know, Harry. You never know. Hey, would you mind telling me where we are going? I never get to pick a place, or even know where we are going, Harry. Just once I would like to. . .."

"Ah, stop being such an old lady, twenty-seven! We never let you pick, because you always pick the boring, family, type places to visit. I cannot tell you yet, because the gang told me, I had to keep it a secret. I can tell you though that this is going to be the greatest adventure of all of ours put together!"

He slapped me on the back and almost knocked me off the bench.

"That is exactly what I was afraid of, Harry."

The backdoor swung open and Binky, Rose, and the children appeared.

"Yoo-hoo! All set now, guys! Here are the suitcases. You will need to put them in the back of the Rhino 500S. They are a little heavy. I may have over-packed them, dear Paul. I noticed how heavy they were when I carried them down from upstairs."

"We will handle it, dear Binky. Together, Harry and I can do anything. We always have and we always will."

It was April 18, 1997, and Pastor Charles T. Braun Jr. was sitting at his desk, in his office at Reunion Lutheran Church. He reached in the top drawer of the desk, in search of a paper clip, when he noticed a thin book tucked away in the back of the drawer that he had not previously noticed before. Pulling it out and opening it up, he was shocked as he recognized the distinctive handwriting of his father, Pastor Charles T. Braun Senior.

"Why . . . it is my father's daily journal," he shouted out as he sat back in the chair and thumbed through it.

He was thrilled, and a little choked up, as it brought

back so many memories. As he leafed through, page upon page, he stopped when he found a folded, single piece of paper inside of one of the pages.

He pulled the single paper out and set it aside.

He then read his father's entry on the journal's page: "January 13, 1960. The young acolyte on duty this Sunday, approached me after the service, and questioned me as to the fate of the water in the baptismal font. At first inclination, I went to instruct him to pour it down the sink in the communion kitchen, but for some reason, I stopped hard in my instructions, and thought about it. Rather than pour it down the drain or toss it out, I had the strange feeling that something more sacred should become of the blessed water. I led the young man outside, and I felt that the Holy Spirit was leading me the entire way. I looked around the property, and my eyes fell upon a smaller oak tree growing near the right side of the fellowship hall building, about twenty feet away from the southwest corner of the building. I recalled that this particular tree was part of the original, landscape construction project, and although the poor tree was still alive, it remained very small and feeble in appearance. I instructed the young acolyte to pour the holy water on the base of that tree. For some reason, the small tree seemed as though it was struggling to establish itself, and I felt compelled that the addition of some holy water would assist it in growing into a strong and powerful oak. Therefore, I began the routine of always pouring blessed or holy water upon that same tree."

Pastor Charles T. Braun Jr. then opened the paper that he found tucked in the page and had previously set aside. He read the first line on the paper, "Continued the tradition, 11 December 1994, Pastor Paul John Henson." Following the first line was another line that read, "Practice now discontinued due to construction of the new addition of the classrooms onto the fellowship hall. Original tree removed, 18 April 1995." It was signed, "Pastor Paul John Henson."

Pastor Braun Jr. looked up at the calendar. "Why isn't that strange . . . that is the same date as today is. The eighteenth of April."

Pastor Braun took out his pen and scrawled underneath the line that Pastor Henson had written, "Continued the tradition, 18 April 1997." He signed it, "Pastor Charles T. Braun Junior." He tucked the note back inside the same page of the journal and replaced the book in the top drawer of his desk.

He jumped up from his desk, walked out of his office and out the backdoor of the church. He made his way across the parking lot, walked around the fellowship hall, and went behind the new education wing.

Looking around, Pastor Braun Jr. carefully studied the ground, as well as the wooded areas in and around the exterior walls of the building. He did not immediately find what he wanted to see, therefore, he walked a little more through the thick underbrush, until his eyes settled upon a little oak tree. Pastor Braun Jr. was standing in the woods, about fifty feet or so away from the edge of the old fellowship hall, off to the left of the building. He bent down to see the little tree struggling to grow and make the way through the leaves and underbrush. The tree was young, fragile, and the trunk and leader of the tree was not much more in thickness than that of a pencil. Pastor Braun cleared some leaves and sticks away from around the base of the little tree and made a circle in the dirt around the base of the tree to catch some water.

He smiled and said aloud to himself and the little tree, "Now, you will have a chance little, oak tree. You look as though you have recently sprung to life, and have grown from a dropped acorn, from an older tree that once was here. This tree will do nicely."

That Sunday after the worship service, Pastor Charles T.

Braun Jr. led the acolyte who was assisting in the service on this Sunday, out the backdoor of the church, as the young man carried the stainless-steel basin from the baptismal font. The young acolyte complained the entire time as he followed the pastor across the church lot and into the woods to the little oak tree.

"Now, Thomas, pour the water from the baptismal font onto the root base of the little tree there."

Pastor Braun pointed to the little oak tree.

"That tree? This little tree is dead. This is stupid, Pastor Braun. All the kids in Sunday school say that you are a weirdo."

"Is that so, Thomas? Well, we will see now. Sometimes, you know, when there is nothing else left, you just have to have faith, young man."

The following Saturday, around two in the morning, Mrs. Whipley was sitting in her living room in her favorite old chair, listening to her Harvey Crooner records, when she thought she heard a noise and saw a light flash through the window.

"Oh my," she said as she jumped up. The old gal wobbled a bit, steadied herself, then made her way towards the window; she parted the curtain and peered out into the darkness.

Mrs. Whipley smiled widely as she looked out and she whispered, "Oh, this is so wonderful! I can't wait to call Bishop Henson and tell him the news!"

THE END

Epilogue

I stared at this green colored screen with a blinking whoosie winking back at me. On and off. The little green line blinked at me. It was very strange, as if it was an invitation for me to type.

The words of encouragement of my dear wife echoed in my head, "Embrace the new technology, twenty-seven. The nineteen seventies have now, long since passed. This new computer and word processor will make it so much easier for you to write your sermons, dissertations, Bible essays, and finally to begin work on your books."

I sat back in the chair at my desk in my office and placed my hands over the keyboard in front of me, and with two fingers slowly, "hunting and pecking" over the keys, I slowly tapped out, "The quick brown fox jumped over the lazy dog."

The little green whoosie was off to the races. It ran across the screen in a happy response to my typed commands, and off it went duplicating the words. Then it sat at the end of the sentence, blinking and winking at me. I stared in at the screen and sighed.

"Well, it does seem very fancy. Maybe, this is not so bad after all," I yelled out to Binky.

My wife faintly mumbled something back to me. She was working in the kitchen, and I am sure she could not quite hear what I was saying. I reached down into the top drawer of my desk and pulled out the now very worn and tattered manuscript that I had written so long ago. I spread the pages out on my desk, put it at a comfortable reading angle, placed my hands on the keyboard, and slowly typed the first sentences.

"My best buddy growing up was Harry M. Redmond

Junior. Even as a little kid and as a teenager, he was loud, bombastic, friendly, and outgoing. He had a mischievous side, but for the most part, he stayed out of trouble. He was a great friend to hang with; no one was more fun."

I sat back in my chair and laughed. Binky suddenly appeared behind me and placed her arms around my shoulders as she stared at what was glowing on the screen in front of us. Her long, flowing, blonde hair tumbled down over her and me as she leaned in. I placed my hands over hers as she read the screen aloud to both of us.

She smelled so good. My wife always smelled so good.

"Oh my, twenty-seven that is quite a way to start, I think you have summed it all up already."

She kissed my cheek and smiled at me.

"Do you think anyone will actually believe all of this stuff we did, and what happened to all of us, dear Binky?"

Binky stood up. Her face changed a bit as she pondered my question, and then she smiled.

"Of course, dear Paul. After all, it would take an awful eccentric and strange mind in order to make all of this up!"

I burst out into laughter. My wife of course was right, while I stated, "But then again, you never know, I could always just call it fiction."

Binky stood in front of me. She winked, and relaxed. Her face and posture suddenly changed to that alluring mode she could shift into so easily. I knew that look so well!

"Why don't you push the shift–f-twelve buttons on the keyboard, just as I showed you Paul, and save your work. Be sure to name the file. 'The Time Bomb in The Cupboard and Other Adventures of Harry and Paul,' if I remember it correctly. Please shutdown for the night. I have a much better way for us to pass this Saturday evening together . . . if you know what I mean. After all, even you, could never document a lifetime of Harry and Paul adventures in just one evening. It will take you many years, dear Paul, many,

many, years."

Binky stood, fluffed her hair, and posed seductively for me, emphasizing her alternative offer for this evening. I immediately jumped into action, saved the work, and shut the computer down. I watched the little green whoosie fade away . . . as it went to sleep until another day. I stood up and Binky took my hand while I shut the light out in my office and closed the door.

"What do you call that green winking and blinking whoosie?"

"A cursor, Paul. A cursor."

"Got it! I think. A cursor. You know, I think I am going to get used to all of this newfangled stuff. You are correct, dear Binky, the nineteen seventies and all those times are gone forever. It is time for me to move into the modern times and embrace them."

Binky turned and smiled at me, but she did not say a word. It seemed as though she knew a lot more than what she was willing to say. We climbed the stairs; I shut off the hallway lights and walked into our bedroom.

I thought to myself, how I just may eventually embrace the modern age, but I will never forget the memories of the old times.

Indeed not, my dear reader.

I can assure you that I will never, ever, forget.

ABOUT THE AUTHOR

If you ask Paul John Hausleben, he will tell you that he is not an author, he is just a storyteller. His mission is to continue to write and tell stories to warm your heart, make you laugh, and sometimes make you cry, just a little. Most of all, he deals in memories, and helps you to remember the good times of your own life, and the special people who touched you along the way. Paul was born and raised in Paterson, and then nearby Haledon, New Jersey, and began writing at an early age. He revisited a writing career later in his life, and he now is the author of a number of novels, compilations, short stories and audio and video works. Most of his work, touches upon nostalgic remembrances of simpler times, and tells the stories of heartfelt, humorous, and special human relationships. Other than writing, among many careers both paid and unpaid, he is a former semi-professional hockey goaltender, a music fan and music reviewer, an avid sports fan, photographer and amateur radio operator. He now resides in Somewhere, U.S.A., but his heart always remains along Belmont Avenue in good old Paterson, and Haledon, New Jersey.

Titles by the same author that you also may enjoy

The Time Bomb in The Cupboard and Other Adventures of Harry and Paul.

The Night Always Comes, Another story from the Adventures of Harry and Paul

Reunion, A sequel to the Night Always Comes and Another story from the Adventures of Harry and Paul

Heaven's Gain

The Adventures of Harry and Paul Series

The Autumn Collection

The Christmas Tree and Other Christmas Stories
Tales for a Christmas Evening

Ye Olde Book Shoppe
A Story for the Christmas Season

The Chronicles of Henson

And many others

Coming soon?

You may contact us via email at ctte27@gmail.com

www.ingramcontent.com/pod-product-compliance
Lightning Source LLC
LaVergne TN
LVHW020700110826
845149LV00012B/2064

9780988633650